RIPPLES
in TIME

RIPPLES *in* TIME

A Kendra Donovan Mystery

Julie McElwain

SESHAT BOOKS

RIPPLES IN TIME

First Seshat Books Edition

Copyright @ 2023 Julie McElwain

Interior design by Jessica Kleinman

Hardcover ISBN: 979-8-9873810-3-8
Paperback ISBN: 979-8-9873810-1-4
Ebook ISBN: 979-8-9873810-2-1

To James

RIPPLES *in* TIME

1

July 31, 1816

The night was unusually cold, the breeze carrying an autumnal bite one wouldn't expect in the summer months. Shandor and his people didn't track their lives like the *gadjo*, bound to timepieces and calendars, but they'd celebrated midsummer weeks ago, when the moon was the thinnest of scythes hanging in the evening sky. Another moon had come and gone without the fanfare of midsummer, and now the brilliant orb was nearly double its size, bright enough to illuminate Shandor's way as he glided on bare feet through a forest carpeted with icy nettles and hard earth.

Even though the *gadjo* were growing anxious about the unseasonably cool and wet weather, Shandor relished the crispness of the night. The air carried a whiff of wood and damp leaves, the scent of smoke that could be traced to his people's campfire, heavily laced with roasting meat from the wild boar that his father had felled earlier that afternoon. It made his mouth water and his stomach rumble.

It also reminded him why he'd been sent into the forest: to collect more wood to feed the fire.

He bent over to pluck a twisted branch, as thick as his arm, from the ground, then scooped up a handful of twigs. A rustling sound in the trees made him straighten and glance around warily. His knuckles went white as he tightened his grip on the branch, ready to wield it like a club. There was always a possibility that the boar on the spit had a mate still roaming the woods.

The girl came out of the inky shadows in a swirl of colorful skirts and tumbling curls.

"Kezia," he said in a huff of irritation, his tight grip on the branch relaxing. They'd played together as children, but he was now two and ten—three years older than Kezia, almost a man. She didn't seem to understand that he was no longer interested in childish games. Lately, she'd attached herself to him like a bramble that he couldn't shake free.

"What are you doing here?" he demanded. "Are you following me? Go away!"

She pouted. "I want to help."

"You're a *girl*."

"What does that matter? You're only gathering firewood." She leveled a scornful look at him. "I've carried water buckets heavier than those little sticks you're holding."

Shandor felt himself redden. "If I wanted a girl to help me, it wouldn't be a baby like *you*," he shot back. "I'd want Myri."

Myri was actually a year older than him. Her slender body had become more curvaceous and mysterious to him in the last twelve months, too, and every time he looked at her sun-warmed face and body he felt a strange quiver in his belly.

"*Myri*." Kezia's lip curled. "She's promised to Dawar."

"How do you know?"

"It's been an arrangement between their families since their births. Everybody knows."

He gave a jerky shrug. *He* hadn't known.

"Besides, Myri would never look at *you*. You are a boy, Shandor, next to Dawar."

That stung. "Begone, brat!" he shouted, and threw the twisted branch at her. She dodged the missile by gracefully leaping to the side, allowing it to crash to the ground behind her.

"Are you so simple that you will stay where you are not wanted?"

"Who wants to be around you, anyway, Shandor Black!" she yelled back. Her skirts flared as she abruptly turned and darted into the woods, the shadows swallowing her up again.

Though not before he'd seen the hurt in her dark eyes.

Guilt had angry teeth, nipping at him as he went about his task. He muttered an oath under his breath. Besides, it wasn't his fault. He hadn't asked her to follow him. She should have been back at the camp with the womenfolk, preparing the meal, not venturing out into the forest alone. She should have—

Relief rushed through him at the sound of twigs snapping underfoot, the shivery movement of shrubbery. It would be Kezia, no doubt returning to hurl another insult at him. It would be just like her. The brat was nothing if not stubborn.

Careful to keep the smile from his face, Shandor turned towards the noise.

It wasn't Kezia.

His eyes widened as a horse ambled out of the thicket, a rider slumped over its back like an ungainly sack of grain. A *gadjo*, Shandor saw, so foxed that he could barely keep his seat. Briefly, Shandor considered slipping into the woods before he was seen. But even as the thought flitted through his mind, he dismissed it as cowardly. He and his people had every right to be here. The powerful Duke of Aldridge owned these lands and had given them permission to camp there whenever they traveled through the area. This drunkard could even be a friend of the Duke's. If he was injured falling off his horse—even though it would be his own bloody fault—it might get around that the Romani had done nothing to help him.

That niggling worry prompted Shandor to drop the firewood he'd collected and sprint forward. Reaching out, he grasped the mare's bridle. The pretty chestnut's eyes rolled, and she made a skittish sidestepping move before he managed to bring her to a halt.

"Quiet, girl," he crooned softly in the language of his people, bringing his hand up to stroke her velvety muzzle. He frowned as his gaze slid over the white-crusted lather on the mare's coat. The horse wasn't huffing now, but she'd clearly been ridden hard at one point. Shandor's jaw tightened. One more strike against the *gadjo*. No Romani would punish a horse in such a manner.

The man groaned, stirring in his seat. Shandor's heart pumped hard against his ribcage when the *gadjo* suddenly lifted his head and locked glittery eyes on Shandor. The man's hand, encased in a black leather riding glove, whipped up to grasp Shandor's arm with surprising strength.

"*No… thief… no…*" he whispered hoarsely. "*Thief.*"

Shandor glared at the rider, furious but not surprised. How often had his people been called such insults by the *gadjo*? He started to jerk his arm out of the stranger's grasp, but the man's grip was already weakening. His arm eventually fell limply to his side as his eyes rolled up into his head and he swayed dangerously in the saddle. Muttering a curse, Shandor made a wild grab at the man's coat to keep him from toppling off his mare. He grimaced as his fingers curled around the wet wool. Had the drunken fool fallen into a lake or stream before mounting his horse?

Shandor set his teeth as he spent the next few seconds battling to keep the *gadjo* from tipping to the ground.

"*No… thief…*" the man moaned again, before collapsing against his saddle.

Relieved, Shandor released the greatcoat. His palm was sticky with moisture. He started to wipe it against his trousers, then froze when he caught sight of his palm in a beam of silvery moonlight. Shock jolted through him.

It was stained with blood.

2

Albert Rutherford, the seventh Duke of Aldridge, watched the woman pace the castle's battlements in the moonlight, the wind whipping her velvet cloak around her slender form. She made a striking picture. If he wasn't a man of science, Aldridge could almost imagine her a sorceress, casting spells on unsuspecting mortals.

He smiled slightly. Kendra Donovan wasn't magical, but she was a miracle. The American would argue with him on that score, he knew. Yet what else could one call a woman who'd come into their lives from two hundred years in the future?

Even though he'd made no sound, Kendra spun around to peer down at him. Her cloak's hood shadowed her face, but he caught the gleam in her intelligent onyx eyes.

"'Tis a bit cold for stargazing," he commented mildly.

She raised one dark eyebrow, flicking a look at the telescope he'd installed on the roof of Aldridge Castle. "Is it ever too chilly for stargazing?"

He laughed lightly. "For me, no." His interest in astronomy was well-known. "But I don't think you are up here to view the celestial bodies."

Moving to the bottom of the steps, he lifted his hand to assist her down. She didn't hesitate, placing her chilled fingers in his. *Progress*, he thought. Kendra Donovan was not someone who accepted help easily. Women of the future, he'd learned, had become fiercely independent creatures.

He studied her face. "What is troubling you, my dear?"

"Nothing."

She was lying, of course. In the last week, he'd noticed her distraction, the way she often stared into the distance, lost in her own thoughts.

He said carefully, "It occurs to me that we are approaching the anniversary of when you first arrived."

Kendra had landed on their doorstep by the power of what she called a wormhole or a vortex—basically a bridge connecting two disparate points in space and time. The concept was endlessly fascinating to Aldridge. As was Kendra's twenty-first century. Not that she'd given him anything more than small glimpses here and there. She feared that, by divulging too much, she would disrupt the natural course of events and change the future. Chaos theory, she called it. He understood the theory, even if he didn't accept it.

Still, he'd managed to glean a few details from her tales. He knew that his future counterparts would travel to the moon and send vehicles to Mars. How amazing, how bloody *marvelous*, must that be? He could feel his blood quicken at the thought of such advancements, which were now only fantasies spun by poets and writers of fiction. Someday, though, fiction and fantasy would become reality.

The world itself would also become much smaller, he knew. Instead of taking days, weeks, or months to travel great distances, it could be done in hours. *Hours.* And people would not even *need* to travel. They could communicate with each other via voice messages and written missives, sent from small devices that they held in their hands. They could *see* the person that they were speaking to, if they so desired. Who wouldn't desire such a thing? But Kendra had told him that many people preferred writing—*texting*—to speaking.

It was one of the many things about the future that baffled Aldridge. Considering his own mornings were fully occupied with correspondence—to family, friends, business acquaintances, and those who shared his interest in natural philosophy—he couldn't imagine *choosing* to write if he had the ability to talk to them as though they were standing in the same room.

The future was a marvel to him, but there was no denying that its people were a peculiar lot.

But now was not the time to ponder their peculiarities. He fixed his eyes on the American. "An anniversary such as this would leave anyone in a contemplative mood." He squeezed her hand gently. "Talk to me, my dear."

Kendra's gaze slipped away. "Next week there will be a full moon."

That surprised him. There was only one reason he could think of that she would be considering the phases of the moon…

"There is a full moon every month," he said cautiously.

"Yes, but like you said, it will be one year since I arrived."

He frowned. "You cannot recreate that evening, Kendra."

In fact, she had attempted to return to her own timeline just one month after she'd arrived, when the moon had returned to its full phase. But the phenomena that had transported her to his time had not materialized again. After Kendra's failure to return to her own time, Aldridge had concocted a story to explain the presence of the young, beautiful, unmarried woman in his household by presenting her to the world as his ward. He was aware that she found the notion that she needed a guardian to be ridiculous; it was one of many rules and restrictions of his timeline that chafed at her.

Aldridge waited a moment, but when Kendra remained silent, he went on, "You know as well as I do that the cycle of the full moon varies every year. Last year, when you arrived, it was August twentieth, but this year it will be on August eighth. I'd have to calculate the next time the moon will be full again on August twentieth—"

"It won't be for another forty-five years—1861." Her lips twisted as she swung her gaze back to his. "I've already calculated it."

Again, he was surprised. And, for the first time, Aldridge felt a thrill of alarm. He did not doubt her calculations—Kendra Donovan was an exceptionally intelligent woman—but he wondered about her motivation to do such calculations.

"I'll be seventy-one… No. Seventy-two. *God.*" She jerked her hand away from his, raising her palms to press against her face, looking appalled. "I'm a year older now, but I won't be born for another one hundred and seventy-three years. Do you know how *crazy* that is?"

Aldridge regarded her. They'd quietly celebrated Kendra's birthday a fortnight ago. Was that the cause of her recent contemplative mood? Ladies, in his experience, typically did not enjoy celebrating their advancement in age, especially after a certain number. But Kendra Donovan was not like most ladies.

"I realize that your circumstance is unusual," he finally said.

"Unusual?" She laughed without humor. "Unusual is seeing a long-eared jerboa."

"A *what?*"

"A long-eared jerboa. It's a rare rodent in Asia." She waved that away impatiently. "My circumstance isn't unusual, Your Grace; it's *impossible.*"

Aldridge had to force himself to put aside the idea of an unheard-of species of animal in Asia. "I thought you'd adjusted," he said slowly. He gave her a careful look. The next bit was delicate. "Mayhap there is something more on your mind?"

"Like what?"

He sighed. Kendra might accept assistance down the stairs, but she still wasn't one to easily confess her fears. "Are you having second thoughts about your betrothal to Alec?" he asked bluntly.

Alec—the Marquis of Sutcliffe—was his nephew and heir. And, as of a month ago, Kendra's fiancé. Aldridge had been pleased when they'd come to him with news of their engagement, even though, by custom, Alec should have approached him first to request Kendra's hand in marriage. Still, he'd become familiar with breaking customs when it came to the American. He suspected that Kendra and Alec had become… *intimate* in the last year. As her guardian, he could have demanded that his nephew marry her immediately. It was a matter of honor.

Except he suspected that Alec wasn't the one resistant to the idea of marriage.

The thought nearly made him smile. Kendra Donovan must have been a novel experience for his nephew, a prime catch since the day he was born. Their family's lineage and wealth had seen every matchmaking mama parading their daughters in front of Alec since he'd come of age, hoping to catch his eye and nudge him towards the parson's mousetrap. Yet at twenty- six… no, twenty-*seven*, Kendra Donovan had little interest in becoming a bride. She didn't even seem to care—or be aware—that she was entering the dangerous territory of potential spinsterhood that haunted every young lady in society.

He chose his next words with care. "I thought everything was settled between you and Alec. When he left for London yesterday, you both appeared to be in accord. Did you argue?"

"No." She released a troubled sigh, tipping her head back to look at the stars. "I don't know if I'd be doing Alec any favors by marrying him."

He studied her profile. Tension tightened her jaw, compressed the full lips into a thin line. "My dear girl, Alec loves you. I believe you love him." He hesitated. "Am I wrong?"

Her throat worked as she swallowed. She was silent for so long that he wondered if she would answer his question at all. Then she said softly, "You're not wrong. I do love him. More than I thought possible." She flicked him a sideways look.

"Well, then—"

"But that doesn't mean I belong here, or belong with him. He deserves someone who understands this world."

"My dear—"

"No one knows about the engagement. We can pretend it never happened." She turned to face Aldridge fully, her gaze direct and unflinching. "That's what your sister is hoping. It's why she asked us to keep quiet about it. She's hoping Alec will come to his senses or she can talk him out of making a disastrous mistake."

That was probably true—his sister was excessively proud of their family's heredity and found Kendra lacking in any number of ways. He settled on a half-truth. "Caro wants to announce your engagement publicly at the castle's annual ball, when the house party commences in a fortnight. It will be a feather in her cap. Now, my dear, what is this really about? You cannot be worried about my sister's disapproval. You are made of sterner stuff than that. I've never met anyone more courageous than you."

Kendra laughed, but it wasn't a sound of amusement. "I'm not so sure about that."

He touched her narrow shoulder. It always surprised him how small she was in stature. Almost delicate. Kendra was so fierce, so forceful, that it created the illusion that she was larger than she actually was. "What are you really afraid of, my dear?"

He watched her draw in a breath, and exhale slowly.

"Okay," she said, fixing her gaze again on the battlements and the stars pulsing beyond. "I'm afraid... I'm afraid that one day Alec will wake up and see me for who I really am. Someone who doesn't know how to run a household or do needlework. Or do any of the things that women here are supposed to know how to do."

Aldridge stared at her incredulously. *My God, she believes everything she's saying.* How could someone so intelligent be so utterly devoid in recognizing their own value? Good heavens, the woman had actually attended Princeton when she'd been only fourteen. He knew of that institution, of course; it had been built seventy years before America revolted against the British Crown. To think that Kendra had once been enrolled there—to think that one day *any* woman would be allowed to roam those hallowed halls alongside men—was simply astounding.

Aldridge did not adhere to the common sentiment that a woman's education should focus solely on language and the social graces—in short, topics that would make her more attractive in order to secure a husband. He did not agree with the scientific theory that a woman's mental acumen could never equal a man's, given the fact that the female brain was ten percent smaller than the male brain. His own late wife, Arabella, had been a mathematical wizard. Thankfully, her father had recognized her exceptional talent and hired the appropriate tutors to educate her. But Arabella would never have been able to study in a university, or any formal educational setting alongside men. It simply was not done.

"I don't belong here," Kendra said quietly, bringing her eyes back to his.

"Kendra—"

"It's not just that I don't know how to do any of the things that women here are supposed to do. It's… *me.*" She thumped a fist against her chest. "Don't you see? I don't *want* to do needlework. I don't want to spend my days painting watercolors or my evenings going to balls and social events. And I don't give a rat's ass about shopping."

Rat's ass? He was momentarily diverted by the colorful expression, but he was able to push the thought away. He put both hands on her shoulders to stop her from whirling away and frowned when he felt the tremors beneath her cloak. Maybe from cold, but he suspected it was caused by the enormous emotions she was clearly harboring.

"My dear, you do not see your value. Alec could have married any of the young debutantes who have perfected their needlework many times over. He has been introduced to legions of ladies who know how to conduct themselves properly. Alec doesn't want proper—he wants *you.*"

Kendra laughed.

Aldridge lifted one hand and tapped his index finger against her forehead. "You have an extraordinary brain. But you are thinking too much, my dear."

"It's hard not to." Her nostrils flared. She met his gaze, her eyes impossibly deep, impossibly dark. "I don't know if I can have children."

Shock jolted through him, convulsing the hand on her shoulder. He quickly removed it, staring at her.

She nodded grimly, keeping her gaze locked on his. "That changes things, doesn't it?"

He tried to school his features into impassivity, but by the glint in Kendra's eyes—really, she was far too intelligent—it was too late. But by God, it *did* change things. As a peer of the realm, primogeniture dictated that his title and the entailed portion of his estate be passed to the next male in the family line. His older brother would have inherited the dukedom, but when he died without heirs, the title and lands had passed to Aldridge. Twenty years ago, Aldridge's wife and daughter had perished at sea. While his daughter, Charlotte, would not have inherited, given that she was female, he and Arabella had been young enough to have other children. They had fully *intended* on having other children.

Pain knotted his stomach. Kendra wasn't the only person to have their life change in a brutal instant. After the deaths of his wife and only child, Aldridge had been young enough to remarry and set up a new nursery. God knows, his sisters had encouraged it. But the very idea had been repugnant to him. Arabella would always be the love of his life, and, as such, he'd been content to let everything pass to his younger brother, Edward, and, through him, to Alec, Edward's firstborn son.

It had never entered his head that Alec might not have a child of his own. If his nephew failed to conceive an heir, the title and estate would pass outside the immediate family line to a distant cousin Aldridge had met only once.

Once was enough—he'd thought the man a pompous ass.

He became aware that Kendra was watching him closely. His mouth felt uncomfortably dry. He swallowed. "How can you possibly know such a thing?"

"You know that I was injured on my last mission."

It wasn't a question, but he nodded. He knew that after she'd left Princeton, she'd worked for an organization called the Federal Bureau of Investigation, which was dedicated to capturing criminals and keeping America safe from all manner of threats. It was strange to think that women were allowed to be placed in such dangerous positions, but he had to admit that Kendra's expertise had come in handy over the last year.

Kendra continued softly, "The doctors told me that my injuries could reduce my chances of ever getting pregnant."

"Reduce—not remove the chance entirely."

"No, but still…"

Aldridge shook his head. The knot in his stomach relaxed. "You don't know for certain," he said, smiling slowly as he reached out to grasp her hand again. "My dear, you must have *faith*. You may be from the future, but you are not a soothsayer. You cannot see what's ahead for you in this regard. 'There are more things in heaven and earth, Horatio, than are dreamt in our philosophy.'"

She lifted her eyebrows, looking dubious. "Hamlet is killed in that play, if you remember."

Aldridge's smile widened. "It doesn't diminish the sentiment. Have you told Alec your fears?"

"I did, and he said the same as you—without the Shakespeare."

"Well, then." He squeezed her hand before letting it go. "Do not fret. Alec loves you. That will never change."

She frowned. "I hope so, because I can't change who I am."

"He would never wish that of you. Nor do I. You are remarkable just as you are." He was surprised to see the quick gleam of tears in her eyes before she turned away, clearly embarrassed by what he was certain Kendra viewed as weakness.

He was relieved when he heard footsteps approach. Glancing around, he saw Harding, his majordomo, materialize out of the shadows.

"Forgive the interruption, Your Grace," the butler intoned. A ray of moonlight revealed his solemn expression, his eyebrows pulled together in a faint crease. The expression was normal, but Harding took great pride in remaining unflappable, so the frown spoke volumes.

Aldridge asked, "What is happening?"

The butler cleared his throat. "There is a gypsy child at the kitchen door. Mrs. Danbury tried to run him off, but he insists on speaking to you, Your Grace. He says that there is a gentleman in their camp..."

Aldridge stiffened. "A gentleman. Is he causing trouble?" he demanded sharply. His family had a long tradition of allowing the Romani to camp on their lands. Like his father and his father's father, Aldridge had a policy that whenever they were here, they were under his protection. Unfortunately, that didn't stop the prejudice that was directed at them from every level of society. Nor did it stop those who would venture into their camp to create havoc.

"Ah, not exactly, sir." Harding hesitated. He flicked a brief, indecipherable glance at Kendra, before shifting his gaze back to Aldridge. "The boy says the gentleman in question has been most grievously wounded. His people are asking that you send someone to fetch him before he expires."

3

The Romani camp was located twenty-five minutes by wagon from Aldridge Castle, in a small clearing surrounded by alder, oak, apple, and hawthorn trees. More than a dozen lanterns glowed from nearby branches and the roofs of colorfully painted caravans, illuminating the faces of the men, women, and children moving about the area.

The gig that the Duke had procured for their journey hit a rock, and Kendra's heart shot into her throat as the vehicle dipped and swayed before coming to a halt on the edge of the encampment. *Damn these contraptions.* She knew that it would have been better to ride horseback here, but she had yet to learn that skill. As much as she hated these open-air vehicles, where every rock and rut threatened to eject her from her seat, it was better than riding on an enormous horse—*sidesaddle*, for Christ's sake. That seemed like a death wish.

It took her a few extra seconds to unpeel her hands from their white-knuckled grip on the leather seat. By the time she managed to do it, the boy, Shandor, had leapt nimbly down from his pony and darted forward to join his people. As the Duke secured the gig, Kendra scrambled off her perch, allowing her gaze to roam over the Romani gathered in the clearing. She'd had dinner, but her nose still twitched appreciatively at the scent of roasting meat that could be traced to the wild boar an old man was turning on a spit. At her look, the old man stopped the cranking motion and stared back at her. He wasn't alone in his steady regard. Kendra's neck prickled as the entire group stared at her with the same shuttered expression.

"Why do I feel like I'm entering the *Village of the Damned?*" she muttered.

The Duke cast her a startled look. "Pardon?"

"Old movie. Never mind." She'd explained the concept of movies to him.

Her gaze was drawn to a strikingly handsome man coming forward. He looked to be in his early forties, with a few silvery strands gleaming in his jet-black hair and eyes as dark as her own.

"Your Grace." The man's gaze shifted to look behind the Duke and Kendra, as two men arrived with a flatbed wagon to haul the injured man back to the castle. *A nineteenth-century ambulance,* Kendra thought wryly. Minus the professional EMTs—the two men were stable hands, and their expressions were stony as they eyed the encampment.

"Lensar." The Duke's greeting broke the strange spell that had fallen over the glen. The old man began turning the spit again, although his eyes remained on the newcomers. Younger children squirmed out of their mother's laps, skipping around and demanding attention.

The Duke gestured to Kendra. "This is my ward, Kendra Donovan. Miss Donovan, Lensar is the *voivode*—chieftain—for his people."

The man dipped his head courteously, acknowledging her presence, before returning his gaze to the Duke. "Thank you for coming, Your Grace. We do not seek trouble." Again, he glanced at the two sullen stable hands. They hadn't moved from their position.

"I know, my friend," the Duke said, "but sometimes trouble finds us. Where is the gentleman? What happened?"

"He is in here," said a new voice.

A woman emerged from a nearby red-and-yellow painted caravan. She was old, her white hair in stark contrast to her dark complexion. Her black eyes were fixed on the Duke with none of the obsequiousness that Kendra had come to expect. This woman, she sensed, would bow to no one, regardless of rank.

"Madam Patya." The Duke's face brightened, and he crossed over to her. "It has been too long."

"Several summers, at least." She held out both hands. More than a dozen gold bracelets circling her arms slid and jangled. More gold glinted in her ears and around her neck. "You look well."

The Duke clasped her hands in his. "As do you."

She gave a throaty chuckle. "You always were a charmer." Madam Patya glanced at Kendra, and Kendra felt the impact of her dark eyes. "This is the American who lives with you," the woman said. It was not a question.

"My ward," the Duke replied with a nod.

Madam Patya inspected Kendra in such a way that Kendra was certain that the old woman could see right through the ruse.

"Miss Donovan, this is Madam Patya. She is the *phuri dai* — the senior woman—of her clan," the Duke introduced, then glanced at the red-and-yellow caravan. "You have been caring for the gentleman?"

Madam Patya's eyes flashed with some unreadable emotion and her mouth drew taut. "I was. The gentleman died ten minutes ago."

Kendra and the Duke followed Madam Patya into the caravan. A dissonance of smells nearly knocked Kendra back on her heels. The coppery scent of blood was the most predominant, as thick as syrup in the small, enclosed space. That was mixed with the pungent odor of burning oil and melting wax, and then the more pleasant aromas of eucalyptus and lavender. Brass lamps revealed shelves and drawers along the curve of the caravan's walls, glowing like honey. A faded red, blue, and black woven rug covered the tiny floor space.

An elaborately carved narrow bed filled the back of the wagon. The gentleman was on the bed, sprawled on his stomach and stripped to the waist. A blood-flecked rag had been left scrunched on his back. Kendra's gaze traveled to the dead man's hands, which were encased in tight leather riding gloves. Odd, but understandable. Why bother removing the gloves to treat injuries that he'd sustained on his back? There was a tin washbasin on the floor beside the bed, the water in the bowl tainted dark pink.

"He never gained consciousness," Madam Patya said, moving to the bed, which took a total of four steps. The caravan's interior, with its rounded ceiling, was tight for one person; for three—not counting the dead man—it was claustrophobic. The cloying smell of blood didn't help.

"I had hoped to draw out the impurities," Madam Patya told them softly, lifting the cloth to reveal the mutilated flesh beneath. "But it was too late."

Kendra eyed the two black bullet holes piercing the flesh. They were deceptively small. "Did you hear the gunshots?"

"No." Madam Patya tossed the rag into the pink water with a splash, wiping her hands on her skirts. "Wherever this happened, I do not believe it was near our camp. Shandor found him when he was in the forest looking for firewood. He was already unconscious, but the mare he rode was lathered. Given his injuries, I'm surprised he kept his seat as long as he did."

"Shandor—the kid who came to get us? He didn't mention that he was the one who found the victim," Kendra said. "I'll need to talk to him."

Madam Patya frowned. "Why? He can be of no help. As I said, the gentleman was unconscious."

"I'd like him to tell me that."

"Kendra—Miss Donovan has a process in these matters," the Duke told the old woman. "You must trust her."

"I do not trust her. But I trust you, boy."

Kendra glanced at the Duke. On the fair side of fifty, with thinning blonde hair going gray, *boy* was not a description anyone would use for the aristocrat. It confirmed what Kendra had already suspected: that the Duke and Madam Patya went way back.

"I'll have my men transport him to the wagon," the Duke said as he crouched down to get a better look at the victim. Kendra heard his swift intake of breath. "Good God."

"You know him." Kendra had seen the recognition flare in the Duke's eyes. "Who is he?"

"Yes, I recognize him. I believe you may have been introduced to him, as well, at one of the balls we attended a few months ago."

Kendra gave the dead man a sharp glance. She'd been introduced to and danced with a number of gentlemen a few months ago. While she had an almost eidetic memory, those potential suitors were mostly a blur. She'd had a murder on her mind at the time.

You've got my full attention now, she thought, squatting down to examine the dead man's countenance.

Given his position, she could only view his profile, but she estimated him to be around her age, mid-twenties maybe. But that could be a trick of death, with slack muscles smoothing away facial lines and giving the deceased a more youthful appearance. His dark blonde curls had been cut into the fashionable Brutus style. Her gaze skimmed the breeches and boots he wore. Both well-made. She was starting to have an eye for such things.

"I don't remember him," she admitted softly.

"Reginald Lansing—the Earl of Craymore," the Duke identified. "He hasn't held the title very long. I was more acquainted with his father, Benedict, who was a few years behind me at Eton."

Kendra glanced around. "Where are the rest of his clothes?"

Madam Patya bent to retrieve a bundle from a cleverly hidden cubbyhole beneath the bed. Kendra quickly sifted through the items. Silky white cravat and shirt. Light gray waistcoat. Charcoal gray jacket. Tan wool greatcoat. All high quality and exquisitely cut. Nice, if you ignored the rust-colored blood splatter and fabric shredded by two bullet holes at the back.

Kendra checked the pockets. A small gold watch-fob was tucked into a tiny pocket in the waistcoat. In the deep pockets of the greatcoat, she found a purse, plump with coins; a square white linen handkerchief; and—more interesting—a small double-barreled gold-and-walnut flintlock pistol. Kendra was familiar with the weapon; she kept one exactly like it in her reticule.

"Where was he coming from, or going to?" she wondered out loud, weighing the pistol thoughtfully.

The Duke said, "Traveling alone at night, one tends to bring a weapon in case one is set upon by thieves. I wonder if that is what happened here?"

Kendra didn't reply. Instead, she looked at Madam Patya. "I'd like to speak to Shandor."

"He won't be able to tell you anything more."

"You don't know what I'm going to ask him."

The Duke put his hand on the old woman's arm. "Let Miss Donovan do what she must. I shall have my men carry the earl to the wagon."

"No. Lensar will do it," Madam Patya said with quiet authority. Her bracelets jingled as she motioned them to leave through the curtained door. Once outside, she addressed Lensar in their own language, then beckoned to the boy, Shandor, to come forward.

Kendra looked at the child. "Can you tell me what happened, Shandor? How did you find the man?"

Shandor glanced at Madam Patya, who gave a subtle nod. "I was gathering firewood. He came out of the trees. I thought he was in his cups." His gaze dipped briefly to his hand, which curled into a fist. "It was only when I took hold of his coat to stop him from falling off the mare that I realized he was wounded."

"What time was this?"

Shandor frowned. "No more than an hour ago."

"Nine-thirty, then? Half past nine?"

The boy shrugged and said nothing.

Kendra let it go. "Was he conscious at the time? Did he say anything to you?"

Shandor's gaze slipped to the side. "No."

Kendra kept her eyes on the boy. "Are you sure? You're not in trouble, Shandor. But it's important for me to know everything that happened when you found him."

"He called Shandor a thief," a small voice piped up.

Kendra glanced over at a girl who looked to be about eight or nine, with luxurious curls and bright, brown eyes. "How do you know?" she asked.

The girl flashed a defiant look at Shandor. "I was there."

"You were with Shandor when he found the man?"

"I was in the forest," she said evasively. "But I saw him. He looked like he was asleep, but he woke and grabbed Shandor's arm. I heard him call him a thief. He said, 'No, thief, no!' Then he swooned."

Kendra regarded the girl. "What's your name?"

"Kezia."

"Do you remember anything else, Kezia?"

"Nothing else." That was from Shandor, who glared at the girl as he spoke. "He said, 'Thief, no,' and then he passed out. I made sure he was secured in the saddle before leading his horse back here."

Lensar and another man emerged from Madam Patya's caravan. They'd wrapped a thin cotton blanket around Reginald Lansing. Kendra tracked them as they maneuvered the limp form—

rigor mortis wouldn't set in for another couple of hours, she estimated—across the glen to the waiting wagon. The Duke's men didn't budge from their position on the bench. They watched as Lensar and the other man went around and dumped the body on the wagon's flatbed.

She looked back to Shandor. "Did you notice what direction he was riding from?"

"He came out of the trees from the north."

"And you never heard gunshots before he rode out of the woods?"

Shandor shook his head.

"Kezia?"

"No."

"Where is his horse?" the Duke asked.

"I'll fetch it." A Romani man disappeared between two caravans. A moment later, he led out a pretty chestnut with a black mane.

The Duke frowned as he ran his hand across the mare's flank, still caked with soapy sweat. "The poor beast *has* been ridden hard. Lord Craymore obviously tried to outrun his killer."

"Maybe," Kendra said, her gaze drawn by the mare's tail twitching away several flies. "But you can't outrun a bullet."

Ten minutes later, Kendra was once again clutching the seat of the gig while the Duke steered the contraption slowly through the woods. Even with the light of the moon and a brass lamp, it was treacherous going, and several times Kendra's stomach flipped when they encountered an unexpected furrow. She sucked in a breath, and glanced at the Duke.

"Boy?" she murmured, and saw the Duke's white teeth flash in the darkness.

"My history with Madam Patya is a long one."

"I assumed as much. When did you meet?"

"You are trying to distract yourself," he said with a grin.

"Maybe a little. But I'm honestly curious."

"Very well. We met many years ago, when I was a child and I escaped my governess' watchful eye. I was determined, like most young boys, to dig up the earth's treasures."

"Gold."

"No—fossils. I was quite entranced with fossils when I was a boy."

"Of course, you were." Kendra had to smile.

"I was about nine when I read how John Somner discovered fossilized teeth and rather large bones on his land in Chartham about one hundred and fifty years ago. I confess, the idea of finding something similar was thrilling."

"Finding dinosaur bones is always thrilling, I imagine. Even for adults."

He shot her a careful look. "*Dinosaur* bones?"

Kendra realized her mistake. *Stupid, stupid, stupid.* Dinosaurs had been so commonly discussed in her childhood that she hadn't considered a time when people didn't know the word.

A memory surfaced: British paleontologist Richard Owens would be the one to coin the word in the mid-nineteenth century, after determining the fossilized bones he'd been studying belonged to a new species.

"There have been many disputes about what Mr. Somner found," the Duke went on. "Some insist that it was a rhinoceros. Others say it was a hippopotamus. But you say it's an animal called a dinosaur? Dino… saur. Greek. Derived from *deinos* and *sauros*." His face lit up with excitement. "Terrible lizard?"

She sighed. The aristocrat was too damned smart. "Yes. Now will you forget about it? Someone else is supposed to get credit for coming up with that name—not you."

He laughed. "Would civilization really fall apart if my name replaces this other man's in identifying a new species?"

"I don't know, but I don't want anything changed because of my slip."

"I don't believe a butterfly flapping its wings will cause a storm on the other side of the world. You worry too much, my dear."

The gig jerked and shuddered over the uneven ground, and Kendra let out a hiss as she clutched the edge of her seat. "There's a lot to worry about here," she muttered. Like: how many people were killed annually on these precarious vehicles? "Can you return to your original story? You were out fossil hunting…?"

He smiled. "Ah. Yes. I became hopelessly lost during my adventure. Madam Patya found me and brought me home. On the way, she regaled me with the most marvelous tales of the Romani. When I grew older, I made my way to their camp and spent many a summer in their company."

Kendra glanced around at the two men in the wagon following them. "Do you think the Romani will be harassed when news gets out about Lansing?"

"Lord Craymore," he corrected absently. "They shouldn't be, but people fear what they do not understand and the Romani have long been a scapegoat for society's ills."

"So, they'll leave?"

He said nothing for a moment. "Most likely. We don't know where the poor wretch was shot, but he died on my lands. There will be an inquest."

"Technically, he died in Madam Patya's caravan. She'll be asked to testify."

Inquests were strange affairs, where the corpse was put on display and a jury and coroner summoned. Anyone who had come into contact with the deceased was usually asked to testify, but not for the purpose of identifying the murderer. An inquest was only to determine whether a person died as the result of murder, suicide, manslaughter, an accident, or natural causes, also known as visitation by God.

The two bullet wounds in the earl's back would probably rule out anything but murder.

The Duke huffed out a sigh. "They'll be gone by morning. As Lensar said, they prefer to avoid trouble—and this is most definitely trouble." He gave her a sideways look. "There will be those who will blame them simply because they are here."

"If you ask them to stay, will they?"

"Why should I ask them to stay?"

"Because they're part of the investigation into Lansing's—Lord Craymore's murder."

"They know nothing. Why would it matter if they stay or go?"

"I don't like losing touch with possible witnesses until an investigation closes." It wasn't as though she could call them on the phone for additional questions if they left the area.

The Duke pressed his lips together as he considered the request. "Very well," he said slowly. "I shall send word asking them to stay—at least until after the inquest. But we must do what we can to prevent the Romani from being blamed for the earl's death. We need to find the fiend who shot Craymore."

He smiled at her. "Is this something that piques your interest, my dear? Something that you... ah, give a rat's ass about?"

Kendra laughed. "As a matter of fact, my interest is piqued, Your Grace."

"Good. And someday you will have to explain to me how the ass of a rat became part of your modern vernacular. I find that quite intriguing."

"I'll make a note."

4

They brought the Earl of Craymore to the icehouse. As she followed the Duke down the building's stone steps, worn from a century of use, Kendra was assailed by déjà vu. When she'd first arrived in the nineteenth century, they'd used these cold, dank chambers as a makeshift morgue.

Time was circular, after all, following repeating patterns, like the cycle of seasons.

She and the Duke lifted lanterns to light the way while the two men from the wagon carried Lansing's shrouded corpse behind them. Shadows slithered and slipped across the stone walls around them.

"I'd like to send for Dr. Munroe. And Mr. Kelly," she said. Sam Kelly was a Bow Street Runner—a nineteenth-century detective—and Dr. Ethan Munroe was essentially a medical examiner. She'd worked with them both several times during the last year.

The raw scent of blood hit them as soon as they entered the subterranean chamber. Unlike Madam Patya's wagon, the odor was entirely natural here, since the room was where wild game was cut and stored. At the moment, there were six carcasses—five pheasants and one deer—hanging from hooks in the corner, but Kendra knew that the stench itself was embedded in the walls and floor.

The Duke nodded, although his attention was on the two men swinging Lansing's body non-too-gently onto one of the work tables that was normally used to debone meat. "Mr. Kelly's services will come in handy, certainly. He can tell us if there have been any highwaymen active in the general vicinity. The road to London is near that area."

"You think this was a robbery?"

"It seems reasonable. He was traveling alone at night." He eyed her in the uncertain light. "You don't?"

"He still had a full purse on him. And a gun in his pocket that he didn't take out."

The Duke frowned as he considered that, until one of the stable hands cleared his throat, drawing their attention.

"Will that be all, sir?" the man asked, shoving the bundle of clothes on the table next to the dead man.

"Yes. You may go. Wait." The Duke held out his lantern. "You ought to take this to guide you. Those steps can be treacherous."

"Aye. Thank ye, sir." The man tossed the shrouded form another quick, nervous glance before snatching up the lantern. He and the other stable hand scurried out of the chamber, reducing the light in the room to the golden circle thrown by the lantern that Kendra held.

Kendra had to suppress a shiver. She was not a superstitious person—her parents, Dr. Carl Donovan and Dr. Eleanor Jahnke, were scientists and had trained her since birth to view the world through a logical lens—but the creepy atmosphere in this chamber had her longing for the bright lights and sterilized tiles of a modern morgue.

The Duke asked, "What do you hope Dr. Munroe will discover beyond what we already know—that the poor wretch was shot in the back?"

"We won't know until he conducts his postmortem," Kendra said, and shrugged. "It's procedure."

The Duke had a point. In her time, procedure meant possibly uncovering trace evidence, matching ballistics in a database. Here, the lack of forensic tools, testing and records made that doubtful. Still, you never knew.

"I'll send a messenger tomorrow at first light for Mr. Kelly and Dr. Munroe," said the Duke. "And word to Mr. Hilliard."

Roger Hilliard was the local constable for Aldridge Village and the surrounding area. He also owned the local haberdashery, since constable was an unpaid position.

"It's a mere formality, of course," the Duke assured Kendra when he caught her eye. He dropped his gaze to the dead man, sorrow lengthening his face. "Lord Craymore's family must be notified. I don't believe that he was married, but Caro would be better informed than I. Shall we?"

He took the lantern from her, and escorted her to the door. He paused briefly to glance over his shoulder at the cloth-wrapped body. "Remind me to tell Harding to put a note on this door. The last thing we need is for one of the milkmaids to faint and brain themselves when they come upon *that* in the morning."

Lady Atwood was in one of the castle's smaller drawing rooms, enjoying a cup of tea and reading a book in front of a crackling fire. She was a widow with grown children, but since her husband's death, she'd returned to her ancestral home to live for most of the year.

And to make my life miserable, Kendra reflected ruefully.

At their entrance, the countess' carefully plucked eyebrows rose, nearly touching the burnished gold satin turban that she often favored over the traditional lace caps donned by matrons of a certain age. The turban matched the evening gown she'd worn for dinner. A three- tiered pearl choker circled her throat. Lady Atwood did not do casual.

Carefully, she set her teacup on its saucer and placed a long silk ribbon to mark her page before closing the book with a snap. She laid the book next to her on the elegant burgundy-and- gray brocade tufted sofa.

"What has happened?" she demanded, casting a sharp look at her brother. "My maid said there is talk below stairs about gypsies finding an injured man in the forest?"

"What do you know of the Earl of Craymore?" the Duke asked, crossing the room to a rosewood cabinet that held decanters of spirits and glasses. Kendra settled into one of the chairs opposite Lady Atwood.

"I assume this is not a random question?" she said.

The Duke said nothing as he pulled out the decanter's stopper and splashed sherry into two small cut-crystal glasses.

Lady Atwood watched him bring the glass to Kendra. "I am not well acquainted with the family, but I know Benedict Lansing had some kind of fit last fall," she said finally. "I believe he lingered for some weeks before he eventually perished. The title passed to his son, Reginald."

"I recall that much. Anything else?"

"Well, there was the scandal, of course."

Kendra had been lifting her glass to her lips, but now paused to stare at the countess. "Scandal?"

"Yes." Deliberately, the countess picked up her teacup and took a slow sip before continuing. "The word is that the daughter— Lady Evelyn—suffered from terrible melancholy after her father's death. Her brother was forced to commit her to a private asylum."

"Good God," the Duke said, shocked. "I can only imagine how difficult that decision must have been for the family."

"There's no family. At least not immediate family. Lady Craymore passed away several years ago—when Lady Evelyn was still a child, I imagine. There are only the two siblings— Lady Evelyn and the new earl. He made the decision alone."

"Were they close in age?" the Duke asked, lowering himself into the chair next to Kendra.

"I believe Lord Craymore is in his late twenties. Lady Evelyn was presented last year, so that would make her eighteen or nineteen. There's probably a decade between them."

Kendra frowned. "Did she attempt suicide?"

"Not that I am aware," Lady Atwood said, her jaw going rigid. Kendra realized that suicide was probably considered a gauche subject to bring up in the drawing room—or any other room, for that matter. *Another mark against me, in Lady Atwood's eyes.*

Kendra couldn't let herself worry about it. "What did Lady Evelyn do to have her brother put her in a mental institution?"

"It was her behavior, of course." Lady Atwood flashed Kendra an irritated look. She added reluctantly, "There was gossip that Lord Craymore's action wasn't entirely altruistic."

"What do you mean?"

"When Lady Evelyn came out, she had plenty of suitors, even though she's a plain little thing." Lady Atwood shot her brother a significant look.

"Ah." The Duke took a swallow of sherry. "The Craymore fortune is substantial, I believe."

"Exactly." The countess' lips curved into a razor-sharp smile. "Unfortunately, the chit became quite infatuated with Basil Willoughby." She wrinkled her nose as though she'd gotten a whiff of an unpleasant odor. "The man is a scapegrace. Inherited a small fortune but went through it within a year. It was common knowledge that he's been on the hunt for an heiress. Most well-bred families have had the good sense to keep their daughters away from him, especially since he *is* devilishly handsome."

"But not Lady Evelyn's family," Kendra guessed.

"As I said, Lady Evelyn's mother died when she was still in the schoolroom, poor dear. And Lord Craymore—Benedict—was always an eccentric. You remember him, don't you, Bertie?"

"I told Kendra that we went to Eton together, although he was a few years younger. From what I remember, he was passionate about history, even when he was a lad in school. I believe his father was quite a collector of antiquities, and Benedict followed suit."

Lady Atwood didn't seem impressed. "He spent most of his time at his estate in Norfolk. Couldn't be bothered to come to Town for his only daughter's first season. Instead, he had a maiden aunt bring the chit out. Good heavens, the woman was eighty, if she was a day! Little wonder that Mr. Willoughby saw an opportunity with the girl and swooped in. Then Craymore had his fit and died. That, of course, should have put an end to the matter."

Kendra stared at her blankly. "What matter?

Lady Atwood shot her an exasperated look. "The courtship, of course! But Mr. Willoughby convinced the silly girl to run off with him. Can you imagine?"

"They eloped?"

"That was the rumor," Lady Atwood allowed. "Reginald managed to stop them before his sister was compromised, and hushed up the entire affair. Although such stories do have a tendency to spread, don't they?"

Kendra held up a finger. "Are you saying that Craymore was able to put his sister in an insane asylum because she tried to *elope*?"

"To protect her from a crass fortune hunter? Absolutely. Though it is not something one does lightly."

"But how could he do it at all?"

"I suspect he had no recourse. For heaven's sake, she should have been in mourning for her father. She shouldn't have allowed *any* gentleman to press their suit, much less go galivanting off to Gretna Green with a rogue like Mr. Willoughby!"

Lady Atwood looked as appalled as Kendra felt, but clearly for an entirely different reason.

"Does Lady Evelyn even have a mental disorder?" Kendra asked.

"I only met her a handful of times in the ballroom, but she did not strike me as a lunatic, if that's what you are asking," the countess admitted grudgingly. "Clearly, though, she is a headstrong creature. I'm certain Craymore, as head of the household, did what he thought was best to protect his sister."

Kendra could feel her lips part in astonishment. She knew that she and Lady Atwood rarely saw eye to eye on anything, but she was shocked that the countess wasn't horrified by Reginald Lansing placing his perfectly sane sister in a mental institution to stop her from marrying the wrong man. Her stomach knotted. *How will I ever fit into a world where something like this is accepted?*

"Now." Lady Atwood picked up her teacup and saucer again, and regarded them with her shrewd grayish-blue eyes. "What *is* this all about? I assume Reginald Lansing is the man who was injured at the gypsy encampment? Is he here? Do we need to send for the doctor?"

"It's a bit late for that." The Duke huffed out a troubled sigh. "He's in the icehouse. He was shot to death this evening."

"*What?*" Lady Atwood's nostrils flared as she inhaled sharply and the teacup rattled in her hand. She set it down hastily. "Why in heaven's name did you bring him to the icehouse? Why are you involved at all?" Before he could answer, she threw a hostile look in Kendra's direction. "This is *your* doing, isn't it?"

"Now, Caro—"

"No!" The countess thrust herself to her feet in an abrupt movement, and pointed an accusing finger at Kendra. "Ever since she came into our lives, we've had nothing but mayhem and murder!"

"That is not true. It is hardly Kendra's fault that the Earl of Craymore was shot tonight. The Romani found him and tried to save him, but it was already too late."

"Then send word to the constable and the earl's family!"

"It would seem that his family is in an insane asylum," Kendra pointed out drily. "Who is next in line for the earldom?"

Lady Atwood gave her a scathing look. "I don't know. Lord Craymore and Lady Evelyn were Benedict's only living children. I suppose the title and estate will pass to an uncle or cousin on the paternal side. And that is beside the point!"

Kendra's eyes widened when the countess actually stomped her foot in her agitation. Lady Atwood turned to her brother. "You do realize that in a fortnight we shall be hosting our annual house party to the Ton, Bertie. I shall not—*not*, I tell you!—allow my party to be ruined once again. Tongues are still wagging about the murderous misdeeds committed last year!"

Kendra's fingers tightened on her glass. "Would you rather we look the other way, pretend it didn't happen, and let a murderer go free?"

"I would *rather* you act like a proper miss and let the authorities handle these inquiries!" the older woman shot back. "You are aware that you are now affianced to my nephew? You will be a marchioness. And one day, you will be the Duchess of Aldridge. Have you no inkling what that means? You must learn how to behave!"

Thank God, Lady Atwood doesn't have the authority to commit me to an insane asylum.

Still, Kendra's chest tightened, a familiar sensation over the last two weeks. Not quite a panic attack. More garden-variety anxiety that cropped up whenever she contemplated marrying Alec. It wasn't marriage to Alec that unsettled her. It was everything that went with it—the title, the expectations… living in the nineteenth century forever. *As if I have a choice…*

Unless the vortex opened again with the next full moon.

That possibility had driven her up to the castle roof earlier that evening. She'd been doing a series of deep breathing exercises when the Duke had found her. She had spoken the absolute truth when she'd told him that she wouldn't be doing Alec any favors by marrying him.

"Enough!" The Duke stood up, too, his gaze on his sister. "I made the decision to bring Craymore to the icehouse. I shall be sending a message on the morrow for Dr. Munroe and Mr. Kelly. We will proceed from there."

The gray in Lady Atwood's eyes became more pronounced as she glared at her brother. "What are you saying, Bertie?"

"The Romani found Lord Craymore. He died in their camp. I plan on putting it out that I was with him when he died, but people are irrational. We must find the villain responsible for shooting the earl."

"To save the Romani?" Lady Atwood didn't look happy about it.

"And to bring a murderer to justice," said her brother. "I am in agreement with Kendra on this matter. We cannot look the other way."

5

"Is there really a lord in the ice'ouse?" Molly asked as she unbuttoned Kendra's evening dress and helped her into a billowy nightgown made out of fine lawn, delicately smocked around the square neckline and the ruffles at her wrists.

Kendra glanced over her shoulder at the maid. Molly was sixteen now, but still looked twelve with her fresh face, bright blue eyes, and light freckles scattered across her snub nose.

"Yes," she said, and moved to the mirrored vanity, rubbing her temples as she sat. She should have been used to Lady Atwood's acrimony by now. Hell, the woman acted like Kendra's sole purpose in life was to bring shame on the Aldridge good name.

"Do ye 'ave a 'eadache, miss? Should Oi fetch ye a tonic from the stillroom?"

"No." Kendra's lips twitched. "My headache went to her bed an hour ago." She began removing the pins from her hair. The throbbing eased a bit after releasing the heavy coil and braids.

Molly gave her a sideways glance as she carefully put away the evening gown, petticoat, chemise, stockings, and slippers in the enormous polished mahogany wardrobe on the other side of the shadowy bedchamber, lit only by candles and the fire blazing in the hearth.

"W'ot 'appened? Was 'e shot by an 'ighwayman? Or the gypsies?"

"Not the Romani. As to a highwayman…" Kendra frowned. "I don't know. That's why an investigation needs to be conducted."

"Oi reckon that ye'll be the one doin' the investigatin'?"

"Somebody has to."

"Why do ye think it might not 'ave been an 'ighwayman 'oo shot 'im?"

"I'm not saying that it wasn't, but he still had his purse, gold watch, and a handkerchief." Oddly, handkerchiefs were prized items for thieves in this era. Entire operations were devoted to stealing and reselling the tiny scraps of fabric.

"And," Kendra added, "he still had his gun in his pocket."

She found that the most troubling. Why hadn't he drawn his weapon? Unless he'd fled when he'd seen the other rider, not anticipating that his assailant would shoot him in the back.

Molly said nothing as she walked over to the vanity. She picked up the silver hairbrush and began to draw the bristles through Kendra's dark hair.

Kendra tipped back her head, closing her eyes. For a moment, she let herself enjoy the purely tactile sensation of having her hair brushed. She murmured, "Lady Atwood believes I'm bringing murder and mayhem into her world."

"Seems ter me like there was plenty o' murder and may'em in the world before ye came, miss. 'Er ladyship just don't like ter admit it. She likes ter view the world like it was a lady done up in 'er finery, all sparklin' in candlelight."

"Through rose-colored glasses."

"W'ot?"

Kendra opened her eyes and saw Molly's baffled expression in the mirror. "Never mind," she said. "That's very poetic, Molly."

"Oi reckon ye confound 'er ladyship. Most ladies would've taken ter their beds in a fit of vapors if they saw 'alf of w'ot ye 'ave."

"Most proper ladies, you mean."

"Aye."

Kendra gazed at the maid's reflection in the mirror. "I can't change who I am, even if that makes other people uncomfortable. Do you regret that you are my lady's maid, Molly? I'll never be"—*normal*—"conventional."

"Oi never thought Oi'd be a lady's maid, miss. At most, Oi 'oped ter be an upstairs maid. If ye not being… con-ven-tion-al"—she pronounced the unfamiliar word carefully—"means givin' someone like me a chance ter better meself, well, then Oi'm grateful, Oi am." Molly went quiet for a moment, then grinned suddenly at Kendra in the mirror. "We make a right pair, miss, cause Oi reckon Oi ain't a proper lady's maid either."

Kendra smiled. "That's a nice way to look at it."

Molly sobered. "But that's not ter say that Oi don't get scared for ye, miss," she said slowly. "There's pure evil in this world, and that's a fact."

"That is a fact."

"Oi figure that ye know w'ot ye're doin', even when ye're associatin' with the worst sort of villains. But Oi fear that one day ye ain't gonna see evil comin' and ye're gonna get 'urt." She paused. "More badly 'urt than ye already 'ave been. Oi know it ain't me place, miss, but promise me ye'll be careful. Oi don't want ye ter be the next one in the ice'ouse."

Kendra was still awake, watching the shadows dance from the reddish orange light from the fire in the hearth, when she heard the faint sound of the doorknob turning. A strange euphoria swept through her. She propped herself up on her elbows to get a better view of the intruder as he slipped through the door, wearing a silk black banyan. She could feel her mouth curve into a smile, because she suspected he was wearing *only* the robe.

She waited for him to ease the door shut. "You're lucky I don't have my pistol on me."

"Bloody hell." Alec spun around, his hand on his heart, to stare at her through the darkness. "You're awake. Why are you still awake? It's past two in the morning."

"Thanks. I can tell time." She shoved the blankets aside and swung her feet to the floor. "What are you doing back? Not that I'm complaining, but I thought you weren't supposed to return until tomorrow."

"Tomorrow is now."

"You know what I mean." She stood up and surprised herself by running towards him.

Surprised him, too. She caught the flash in his green eyes, the glimmer of white teeth as he started to grin, then she launched herself at him and laughed when he staggered back a bit. She wrapped her arms and legs around him like vines, even as his fingers dug into her hips to boost her up, anchoring her better against him.

"Well, this is a welcome—"

She kissed him. Lightly at first, but more deeply when he responded. Desire shot through her. They were both breathless when she broke off the kiss. "Disappointed?"

"Only a bloody simpleton would be disappointed with a welcome like this."

She giggled. The sound shocked her. She did *not* giggle. Alec always managed to bring out the oddest emotions in her.

Cradling his face with her palms, she lowered her forehead to his. "You look wonderful," she whispered, and kissed him again.

The world spun dizzyingly as he carried her across the room, and she gasped when they fell on the bed, limbs entangling.

Her gaze stayed locked on his. "I missed you."

"I love you."

God. Those three words coming from him still had the power to rock her like nothing else. Her fingers trembled slightly as she threaded them through his dark hair. She allowed her gaze to roam over his chiseled features before fixing on the sensuous mouth. "I hope so, because I think you're stuck with me."

"I guess you finished your business early," she murmured later, curled against him, feeling deliciously boneless.

"Not early enough. I should have been here hours ago. They couldn't locate the French buhrstone that the Duke had imported for the mill. After it was finally found, it took another three hours to transfer the rocks to a workshop for assembly." He toyed with a strand of her hair. "The stone ought to be delivered next week."

"Sounds like you had a busy day. I thought lords aren't supposed to be involved in something as lowly as trade?"

"I supervised the process—hardly trade. Though I confess that I prefer to be involved in my land and investments rather than have my man-of-affairs oversee it. I've seen too many of my peers find themselves in dun territory often due to lack of interest in their own affairs."

"Plus, you enjoy it."

"Plus, I enjoy it."

Kendra smiled. She'd watched both the Duke and Alec pour over their accounts, discussing possible investments and the latest technologies that might be beneficial to their estates. The Duke was currently exploring converting Aldridge Castle to gas lighting.

"I could have done without Lord Hilton insisting that we dine at his club before he signed the transfer of his Irish stud farm," Alec continued. "I suspect that he was hoping to get me foxed enough that he could drive up the price from what we agreed upon."

"Stupid man."

Alec chuckled. "More like desperate for capital. He recognized his mistake and accepted the original price. We toasted our good fortune with a fine bottle of burgundy that Hilton ordered—and I paid for. Unfortunately, I wasn't able to depart until well after midnight."

The image of Reginald Lansing's body flashed through her mind. "You should have stayed the night in London and returned in the morning."

"I had great incentive to return," he murmured with a smile, sliding a hand across her naked hip.

She lifted her head to look at him. "I'm serious, Alec. Traveling alone at night can be dangerous." Her throat tightened. "I don't know what I'd do if I lost you."

His smile faded as he regarded her closely. "What's this about?" His fingertips stroked her cheek, as light as butterfly wings. "I'm here, aren't I? Whole and unharmed."

"But you might not have been." Fear was like a beast that crouched in the darkest corners of her mind, waiting to rip her to shreds. It had begun to creep out of the shadows now. "You could have ended up like Reginald Lansing."

"Reginald Lansing..." Alec raised his eyebrows in bafflement. "The Earl of Craymore?"

"Yes. He was shot to death tonight."

"*What?*" He jackknifed into a sitting position, dislodging her. "How do you know?"

Kendra clutched the blanket to her chest as she scooted upright. "He was found on his horse near here—at the Romani campsite. Two bullets in his back. They sent word to the Duke. We brought him to the icehouse."

"The icehouse." Alec was silent for a long moment as he considered the implications. "What happened?" he finally asked. "Highwaymen?"

"That would appear to be the popular consensus."

He eyed her. "But it's one you don't share?"

"His purse was still on him."

Alec's brows drew together in a frown. "He could have gotten away before they took it off him."

"Possible. He also had a gun that he never took out of his pocket." She lifted a hand in anticipation of his next argument. "And, yes, I know that he could have escaped without engaging."

"You are investigating Lansing's death."

"I'm going to look into it, yes." She was silent for a moment. "This is who I am, Alec." Because she couldn't resist the temptation, she lifted her hand to stroke his jaw. Stubble scraped her fingertips. "Do you still want to marry me?"

"I am quite aware of who you are." He captured her hand and brought it to his lips, brushing a kiss so soft and gentle against her knuckles that it stole her breath. "You cannot frighten me off that easily."

Kendra decided not to press the point. Instead, she asked, "What do you know of Lord Craymore?"

"We were acquainted, but nothing more. I sat across the card table from him a handful of times, before he inherited the earldom. We exchanged pleasantries. He was… unremarkable, to be honest."

"The Duke said that I was introduced to him when we were in London a few months ago. We probably danced, and even I don't remember him. I suppose I must have thought him unremarkable as well. Although Lady Atwood said that he had his sister committed to a mental asylum when she tried to elope."

"Yes, I seem to recall that being mentioned in my club. And this is a conversation we need to have in the morning."

"As you said, it is morning."

"A *reasonable hour* in the morning, then." He dropped a kiss on top of her head, and rolled to his feet in one lithe movement. "We both need our rest."

Kendra admired the way the muscle flexed beneath his smooth skin when he bent to pick up his black silk robe and shrugged into it.

"Are you sure I'm not frightening you off?"

He smiled at her as he belted his robe. "We are betrothed, darling, not wed. And the thought of my aunt catching me in your bedchamber in the wee hours of the morning *does* frighten me."

"What's she going to do? Force us to marry? That's the last thing that Lady Atwood wants." She thought of her earlier conversation with the Duke. "She's still hoping you'll realize that you're making a terrible mistake and find someone more appropriate. More worthy to marry into your family."

"You are worthy."

"Yeah, right."

Alec returned to the bed, reaching out to grasp her shoulders. "I don't care what my aunt thinks. Nor should you." He studied her for a long moment. "I choose you, Miss Donovan. I choose you."

He lowered his mouth to hers. The kiss made her head swim. She clung to him, arching her body against his. Slowly, he pulled away, dropped a light kiss on her nose, then stood up.

Wow. Flopping against the pillows, Kendra watched him through veiled lashes as he went to the fireplace and tossed a log onto the burning embers, sending up sparks. She waited until he'd reached the door before saying softly, "I love you."

He grinned as he glanced back at her. "I'm counting on that." Then he was gone.

Kendra huffed out a breath, her gaze focusing on the overhead canopy again. Her own neediness worried her. A memory rose up, sharp and clear. She was fourteen and had just enrolled at Princeton. She'd argued with her father about wanting to explore subjects beyond her parents' pre-approved list. Hardly a rebellion, but it had been enough for her parents to walk away from her. More than a decade later, she could still recall the ice-cold terror curdling in her stomach, the sudden realization that she was absolutely alone in the world. She'd made a vow to never, ever again be reliant on another soul.

She'd kept that promise until now.

What am I doing? She was preparing to marry a man who was part of the fabric of this time. Her heart pounded. She licked her suddenly dry lips. There would be no going back.

Unless…

Again, she thought about the possibility that the wormhole would reopen during the next full moon. It was tantalizing. *Terrifying.* If the phenomenon returned, what then? She knew that there was no guarantee that if she went through, she'd end up in her own time. She could be catapulted even further into the past. Maybe to a time when she could be burned or hanged as a witch.

And she'd never see Alec again.

Kendra rolled onto her side and clasped a pillow to her chest. The fine Irish linen still carried Alec's scent, and she found herself pressing her nose against the softness, breathing deeply.

Love was a powerful force. She wondered if she would ever be entirely comfortable with it. She was more at ease with mankind's darker emotions—hate, jealousy, fury, and greed, all of which could explode into murder.

Which one of those sentiments, she wondered, was behind Reginald Lansing's death? Occam's razor: greed was the simplest explanation. Sometimes murder wasn't complicated; it was simply a series of unfortunate events, no matter the time period.

But the Earl of Craymore hadn't been defenseless. So, why hadn't he taken out his pistol?

That bothered her. Contradictions always bothered her.

Deliberately, she rolled to her other side, closing her eyes. In a couple of hours, they'd begin the investigation into Craymore's death. Maybe it was as simple as a robbery that had turned fatal. Or maybe it was more complicated.

Maybe someone had wanted the Earl of Craymore dead.

6

The next morning, Kendra walked into the morning room. Designed with large windows to take advantage of the early morning sunlight, the room was considered cozy, with a table that could seat a dozen people, as opposed to the castle's formal dining room, which could seat one hundred and twenty.

At the moment, the Duke was the only other occupant. He glanced up from cutting into one of the plump sausages on his plate.

"Good morning, my dear. I sent a messenger to London. He should be arriving there now, although it might take time to locate Mr. Kelly and Dr. Munroe. And they may be occupied and unable to come immediately."

"A summons from you is a pretty good incentive." She crossed to the buffet table, lifting the serving dishes' silver domes to inspect the scrambled eggs, sausages, mushrooms, and stewed tomatoes. "Hopefully, they'll be here by noon."

Fast, for this era.

"Alec returned home last night," the Duke commented casually, lifting his teacup to study her over its rim as she slid into the seat opposite him with her plate.

Don't blush, don't blush, don't blush. Christ, she was twenty-six… no, *twenty-seven* years old, and blushing like a teenager. Which was weird, because she'd never blushed when she was actually a teenager.

"Oh?" She concentrated on buttering her toast, but thought she detected a glint of amusement in the Duke's blue eyes.

"I suspect he didn't want to be away from his betrothed," he said slyly.

Kendra took a large bite of the toast to prevent herself from commenting.

The Duke sipped his tea. "By the by, I was thinking about Lord Craymore putting his sister in a madhouse."

Kendra swallowed. "Yeah. So was I. Lord Craymore locked up his sister in an insane asylum to prevent her from marrying someone he didn't like."

"A fortune hunter."

"It doesn't matter. He shouldn't have been able to do it at all."

"You are angry."

"You're damned right, I'm angry. And appalled. And…" Her breath hitched, and she had to take a moment. She was aware of the Duke regarding her carefully. She wasn't typically emotional. "Do you know that my greatest fear when I first found myself here was that I was having some sort of mental breakdown?"

"No, but I can understand the thought. As fascinating as I find your America, my dear, I cannot imagine how I would react if I suddenly found myself in it. I'd believe myself mad as well."

She blew out an unsteady breath. "There is something terrifying about not being able to trust your perception or judgement anymore. To not know what is real and what isn't."

"I'm sorry you were in that situation, even for a moment." He took another slow sip of tea. "How did you accept it?"

Kendra was quiet as she thought back to that time. "Everything was so damned *real*. I've never been particularly imaginative. How could my mind create this world? The taste, the texture… the *smells*. Although I suppose someone in a delusion might think everything is real, too."

Her mouth went dry. She picked up her coffee cup and drank.

"Maybe it was stubbornness or arrogance on my part," she finally said. "But I just couldn't accept that my mind had snapped like that."

The Duke smiled. "I knew you were different the moment you fell out of the stairwell. Then I found you in there the next day."

"And you invited me into your laboratory for tea." That had been her first day in the nineteenth century. And her first attempt to return to her own timeline.

"You called me a scientist and quoted William Wordsworth. It was clear that you were an exceptionally intelligent young lady—and you were hiding something." He chuckled. "Of course, I had no idea of the truth."

She shook her head. "You would have really thought I was crazy if I had told you the truth then." She took several bites of her eggs. "I worried that you would have me locked up. Could you do it?"

"I would never do such a thing."

"No, I mean could you do it legally—have me committed to an insane asylum?"

"Oh." He was silent as he considered the question. "Yes, I suppose. I am your legal guardian."

"You weren't at that time," she reminded him. "You thought I was a servant."

"That's true." He reached for the silver teapot, topping off his cup. "I imagine it would be simpler to dismiss a servant than have them committed. Why go through the bother?"

Kendra had to suppress a shiver. What would she have done if he had dismissed her during those early days? She'd been alone and penniless, and had discovered quickly how ill- equipped she'd been for this life. As a woman, she couldn't use the skills that made her so valuable in the twenty-first century. She'd been the youngest person ever to be recruited by the FBI, first in cyber-crime and later into its behavioral science division. But here… here, she couldn't even apply to be a Bow Street Runner.

Christ, fifteen-year-old tweenies had more marketable skills than she did. *What a difference a couple of centuries make.*

She asked, "As a legal guardian, what does it require to have someone committed?"

"It is not something that I ever looked into closely, but I believe one would need to obtain a certificate of lunacy."

"What does that entail?"

"Again, I am not an expert on this matter." He frowned, thinking. "I believe a diagnosis would need to be made by a mad doctor or a physician. Or apothecary. There's a fee involved."

"Sounds pretty easy to obtain, if you have the money."

He said nothing.

"Would I have any recourse to fight the certificate of lunacy?"

The Duke hesitated, choosing his words with care. "It might be difficult. As my ward, you are my responsibility. Just as Reginald Lansing became responsible for his sister's welfare after his father died."

Kendra set down her coffee cup, trying not to get angry again. "I'm responsible for myself."

"Of course, you are."

"Okay, now you're just placating me."

The Duke smiled at her. "Am I successful?"

She had to laugh. The door opened and she glanced over to see Alec strolling into the room. It had only been a few hours since he'd left her bed, but that didn't seem to matter. She could feel her breath quicken and that irresistible tug of attraction. He was looking ridiculously handsome this morning in a navy superfine coat over embroidered gray waistcoat, with buff-colored breeches tucked into hessian boots that gleamed from his valet's diligent polishing. Since she'd last seen him, he'd shaved and was freshly bathed, his dark hair damp and tumbling across his brow in a way that made Kendra's fingers itch with the desire to smooth it back.

"Good morning." The greeting covered both her and his uncle, but the crooked smile was directed only at her as he went over to the buffet.

"Good morning, nephew. I didn't expect you to return from London until later this afternoon."

"I saw no point in lingering after my business was concluded," he said, sitting down with his plate. He forked up the eggs, looking at them. "Continue with your conversation. I assume you are discussing Craymore's murder."

"You heard about that, did you? Yes, we were speaking about how Lord Craymore may have had his sister committed," said the Duke. "Do you recall the scandal?"

"Vaguely. I didn't pay much attention to the gossip because I was only slightly acquainted with the family." Alec took a bite of eggs, washed it down with coffee. "Craymore is—*was*—only a few years younger than I, and I don't know if I ever was introduced to his father. What does that scandal have to do with Lord Craymore being shot?"

"I don't know if it has anything to do with it, but it might be why he was on the road nearby."

Kendra looked at the Duke. "What do you mean?"

"That's what I was about to tell you. My valet, Wilson, reminded me that there is a private asylum near the village of Needlham, about twenty-odd miles northeast of here. Just across the border, into Essex."

"Shandor believes Craymore was coming from the north."

The Duke pursed his lips. "The Craymore country estate is in Norfolk. There would be no other reason for Lord Craymore to be in the area."

"Craymore has a townhouse in London," Alec murmured. "But I see your point. He had a destination in mind."

"There's only one way to find out." Kendra looked at them. "Is there a protocol for visiting an insane asylum?" God knew, there were protocols for everything in this era.

The Duke lifted his eyebrows. "I can send a rider to find out if Lady Evelyn is an inmate."

"How long would it take to get to Needlham?"

"Forty-five minutes, give or take."

"Mr. Kelly and Dr. Munroe won't be here until at least noon and I don't have anything better to do this morning." She looked between Alec and the Duke. "Do you?"

"Better than visiting a madhouse?" The Duke's lips quirked. "No, I don't suppose I do." He tossed his linen napkin on his empty plate and stood up. "I shall have the carriage brought around posthaste."

7

The village of Needlham was situated on the border between Kent and Essex. Eventually, the area would become part of greater London, its landscape dominated by concrete, glass-and-steel buildings, brick housing developments, and modern planned communities, though it was impossible to imagine that now, Kendra thought, as she let her gaze drift over the bucolic setting. A patchwork of fields and ancient woodlands surrounded the town. Sheep and cows grazed peacefully on hills in the distance. Needlham itself struck Kendra as oddly dour, with gray stone and heavy gothic architecture that had probably been built when the Normans invaded Great Britain in the eleventh century. Or maybe it just looked grim because of the pewter clouds that were now scuttling across the sky to cover the sun, leaving the day drearier than when she'd woken up that morning.

Since they didn't know the name or location of the private madhouse, they stopped at the first tavern they saw on the edge of the town. According to the shingle that hung outside the door, the pub was called the Red Pigeon. Despite its colorful name, the squat structure was gray, like the rest of the village. She waited with Alec and the Duke as Coachman Benjamin hopped off his perch and disappeared inside. He stomped outside a moment later, looking more disgruntled than usual.

"Mr. Enders says that 'e remembers names better when 'e's serving customers," he told them with an outraged huff. "Oi offered 'im a coin, but…" Benjamin shrugged, looking at the Duke. "Do ye want me ter drive on ter find someone more accommodatin'?"

Kendra had to smile. "It's not a bad way to drum up business."

"It's extortion, that's w'ot it is," Benjamin muttered.

"We might as well go inside," said the Duke. "I wouldn't mind a pint."

Kendra couldn't blame the tavern owner for wanting more customers. As they entered the low-ceilinged room, Kendra saw one lone patron parked in a chair at the end of the bar.

The man looked to be in the latter stages of life, but his eyes were bright with curiosity beneath white, wiry eyebrows. He slurped ale from a tarnished copper stein, tracking their progress to the scarred wood table in the center of the room.

The publican, Mr. Enders, was round of body and red of face. And now that he had customers, he smiled broadly as he bustled toward them to take the Duke's order.

"Now, are ye inquiring after Shay House, sir?" Mr. Enders asked as he served them ale in the same heavy copper tankards as the old man. He flicked a sideways glance at Kendra before his gaze returned to the Duke. "For a family member, perchance?"

Kendra didn't need to be a genius to understand his implication. She leveled a cool look at him. "*We* are inquiring because we're looking to see if a particular woman is a patient there."

"Meant no offense, ma'am." He threw up his hands in conciliatory gesture. "They only have female lunatics up there at Shay House, ye know."

"Shay House—that is the name of the asylum?" Alec asked, picking up his tankard.

"Aye. Used ter be a monastery afore King Henry ordered Cromwell ter sack 'em. Heard tell that the monks used ter take care of imbeciles back then, too. Then it became a private home for a nobleman. Was quite a showplace in me granddad's day. Leastwise, that's what he told me. But the gentry cove—he was a baron—had a fallin' out with the king and he and his family fled ter France." He scratched the back of his neck as he thought about it. "Dr. Shay bought it… oh, about fifteen years ago."

"More like twenty," the old man piped up from the bar, clearly eavesdropping.

Mr. Enders looked at him, and nodded. "Aye, well, ye'd know, Major. Shay House has been a madhouse ever since I came ter the village ter take over the pub from me granddad, nigh on ten years ago."

The Duke eyed the barkeep over his tankard. "And Dr. Shay still operates it?"

"Aye. He's a real physician, too. Not like one of those quackery doctors. Got hisself a practice in London Town, dealing with maladies for gentry morts. He opened Shay House for proper folk who were saddled with unmanageable females."

"Unmanageable females," Kendra repeated. "And what *exactly* is an unmanageable female?"

"Oh, ye know… females with improper thoughts. *Unbiddable*, I suppose ye'd say. I haven't seen Dr. Shay for several years now, but he used ter stop in for a pint now and then. Remember when he told me that he treated the wife of a wealthy squire. She took an unnatural interest in animal husbandry. Kept tellin' the squire how he should breed his cattle. Said there was a better way, 'cause she'd been studyin' up on it in books." He shook his head in disbelief. "Imagine that!"

"Yeah, imagine," Kendra said neutrally.

"Too much learnin' ain't good for females, ye know. And then there was another lady—the daughter of an earl," he continued, obviously warming to the subject. "He caught her smoking."

"Smoking. And that got her committed?"

Mr. Enders stared at Kendra. "Course it did! Everyone knows that the female mind is too feeble ter handle such an exotic substance as tobacco. The fairer sex are delicate creatures. I shouldn't have ter tell *you* that."

The old man at the bar gave a derisive snort. "I've known plenty o' members of the petticoat line that could flay a man alive with their tongue alone. Don't seem so delicate ter me."

"Yes, well." The Duke cleared his throat. "If you could give my coachman directions to Shay House, then we shall be on our way."

Mr. Enders looked briefly disappointed that they wouldn't be staying to order another round, but nodded. "Aye, Your Grace. I'll do that."

Kendra waited until the tavern owner disappeared outside before leaning forward to whisper, "So, smoking can drive a woman insane?"

The Duke opened his mouth, then wisely closed it. Alec picked up his tankard, and took his time draining it.

Kendra shook her head in disgust. Grabbing her reticule off the table, she rolled to her feet as Mr. Enders came back inside. He said, "I gave yer man directions, sir."

"Very good," the Duke replied, as he and Alec rose.

Kendra started for the door, but an impulse made her wheel back to the bar. She dug into her reticule, heavy with the muff pistol, to retrieve two shillings. Slapping the coins on the bar, she looked at Mr. Enders. "I want to buy the Major a drink." She glanced at the old man. "That's for saying women aren't delicate creatures."

Mr. Enders and the Major gaped at her. Satisfied, Kendra spun on her heel and walked out the door.

8

Shay House was located four miles south of the village. It was a rambling, three-story stone building on top of a hill, surrounded by dense forest and open fields. Maybe when it was a monastery, it had evoked a sense of peace and scholarly pursuits. Maybe when it was a nobleman's estate, it had blazed with a regal grandeur. But in its current incarnation as a mental hospital, Kendra thought it looked forbidding, its many windows cut into the stone reflecting the cold gray sky.

Of course, the negative vibes could be her imagination. What wasn't her imagination was the dilapidated condition of the estate. There was no denying that the roof was sagging in spots, several of its chimneys listed to the side, and the stone tower on the north end of the structure was crumbling.

"This is not what I was expecting," Alec murmured as he peered out the carriage window.

The two stone pillars and gatehouse marking the entrance to the property had fallen into disrepair. As the carriage turned down the long drive of crushed gravel, Kendra scanned the untidy grounds.

The Duke frowned. "I was under the impression from what Mr. Enders said that Dr. Shay operated a thriving business."

Coachman Benjamin steered the carriage past the main building's front steps and around the side of the asylum to where the stables were located. Like the former monastery, the structure looked like it had seen better days. The stable doors were open, revealing several stalls. Two were occupied, the tails of their present inhabitants swishing against the swarm of flies.

The carriage drew to a halt and Benjamin clambered down from his perch just as a short, stocky man in his forties emerged from the side of the stables. He had a firm hold of the leather leashes tethered to two enormous rottweilers, which trotted slightly ahead of him. The man wore a tattered tweed coat over a dirt-smeared smock shirt and wool breeches tucked into scuffed and muddied boots. Instead of a cravat, he'd tied a dark linen handkerchief around his throat. Beneath a coarse wool flat cap, his face was broad, his features blunt and oddly squashed-looking. Gray stubbled his jaw and streaked the greasy hair that was long enough to brush the collar of his coat.

"Nobody told me we were gettin' visitors," he groused as he and the dogs trotted toward the Duke's carriage.

Benjamin licked his lips nervously when both rottweilers began growling deep in their throats. "Aye, now, ye'd better have a hold on those beasts."

"Don't ye worry about me lads. 'Ooh are ye?" the stranger demanded, eyeing the ducal crest on the carriage.

Kendra pushed open the door of the carriage and hopped down before anyone could help her—or stop her, which Alec looked like he wanted to do. Instead, he muttered an oath and jumped down beside her, tensing as both dogs swung their heads to pin them with identical baleful glares. Kendra understood Benjamin's nervousness. She could feel her palms grow clammy at the canine scrutiny—and the knowledge that it would only take about three seconds flat for both dogs to be on them.

She forced herself to look at the man instead of the rottweilers. "We're here to see a patient. Lady Evelyn—the Earl of Craymore's sister. She's a friend of mine," she lied. "I was told that she was here."

The man squinted at her. "The Earl of Craymore, ye say? Aye, 'e was 'ere yesterday visitin' 'er. Dr. Shay didn't say nothin' about visitors. The doctor frowns on visits, 'e does. Says it agitates the ladies."

The Duke stepped down from the carriage. "I am certain Dr. Shay will see us."

"This 'ere is the Duke of Aldridge." Benjamin's chin jutted up with pride.

"Is that so?" The man hesitated, then slowly doffed his cap. "Well, Oi expect the doc would want ter meet with ye, Yer Grace, but 'e can't, seein' 'ow 'e ain't 'ere today. Sit, Freddie, Adolphus!" He snapped out the command. The dogs instantly obeyed, planting their butts on the ground. They stopped growling, but their gazes remained fixed on Kendra, Alec, and the Duke.

The Duke arched his eyebrows at the other man. "You named your hounds after the royal princes?"

The man grinned, revealing uneven, rotting teeth. "Aye, seemed right at the time."

"And what's your name?" Alec asked.

"Rowan Booker."

"What is your position here, Mr. Booker?"

"Ack, Oi'm a bit of everythin', since Dr. Shay let most of 'is staff go. Oi'm 'ead groom and groundskeeper. Oi 'ave a village lad 'oo works wit me, but the bloody whelp ain't showed up yet terday."

"Why did Dr. Shay let most of the staff go?" Kendra asked.

Booker's face twitched, then knotted into a sour expression. "Well, as ter that, Oi don't rightly know. Ain't none of me business, is it?"

Kendra didn't believe him, but didn't press the matter. She asked, "Where is Dr. Shay, if he's not here?"

"'E set off ter London early this mornin'."

"I would still like to see Lady Evelyn," Kendra said. "It would be a shame to come all this way and not see her."

Booker shrugged. "Ain't up ter me. Best ter go round ter the front door and use the knocker. Mr. McBride'll 'elp ye. Or that other one. McBride 'elps with the ladies, but 'e ain't a real doctor. Not like Dr. Shay is, leastwise. 'E's a sawbones. But afore that, 'e was an apothecary."

Kendra wondered at his tone as he said *that other one*, but moved on. "You said that Lord Craymore visited his sister yesterday. Do you know what time he arrived?"

"'E came around six, Oi think. Not like Oi pulled out me timepiece. Probably 'ad tea with 'er ladyship."

"When did he leave?"

He jerked his shoulders, his expression surly. "It 'ad ter 'ave been after eight, 'cause Oi drive the maids and Cook back ter the village then. They won't stay 'ere overnight." His lip curled. "Don't know w'ot they think will 'appen."

"The earl wasn't here when you returned?" Kendra persisted.

The man's eyes narrowed. "Nay. But Oi didn't come back until past eleven. Didn't expect 'im ter still be 'ere. W'ot's this about?" His gaze cut to Alec and the Duke.

Kendra asked, "Where did you go after you brought the women to the village?"

"Why's it any of yer concern?" He looked back at her. "Are ye a Jumper?"

Kendra didn't understand the reference, but Alec smiled. "We're not Methodists, nor are we against imbibing," he said. "I take it that you stopped at the Red Pigeon last evening?"

Booker pressed his lips together, but finally nodded. "Aye."

"When do you expect Dr. Shay to return?" asked Alec.

He scowled. "Oi dunno. It ain't me place ter ask. Oi gotta get back ter me work."

They gave the dogs a wide berth as they started towards the pebbled path that wound around bushes that needed a good trimming. As a groundskeeper, Mr. Booker left a lot to be desired, Kendra decided.

Alec used the large brass knocker, fashioned into the traditional lion's head, on the deep hunter green double doors. After several minutes of persistent knocking, the door finally swung inward. A young maid wearing a dark navy uniform, starched white apron, and mobcap peered out at them with a harried expression. "Can I help ye?"

"I'm Lord Sutcliffe. And this is the Duke of Aldridge and his ward, Miss Donovan," Alec said. "We're here to speak to Lady Evelyn."

The maid blinked. "Lady Evelyn?"

Kendra raised her eyebrows. "Is that a problem?"

"Nay, it's just—" She seemed to recollect herself, dropping into a quick curtsy. "Beggin' yer pardon, sirs, ma'am. Please come in. Dr. Shay ain't here, but I'll fetch Mr. McBride."

She opened the door wide, allowing them to step into the black-and-white-tiled entrance hall. The dark paneled walls and heavy gothic staircase made the space seem smaller than it actually was.

"I'm Meg," the maid told them as they followed her through the arched doorway on the left, which opened to a great room with a soaring cathedral ceiling and an intricately carved mahogany fireplace that held no fire to warm the cold room. The day's gray light streamed through the tall mullion-paned windows, revealing dust motes floating in the air, shabby furniture, and a few spots of grime on the wood floor that someone had failed to scrub away.

"If ye'll wait here..." She gave another nervous curtsy before crossing the room. Her shoes made clicking noises on the wood floor of the great room and the tile of the foyer, then dull thuds as she clambered up the staircase. Kendra moved to the doorway to watch the girl disappear from view.

Alec's mouth tightened as he glanced around. "I cannot fathom why Craymore would have left his sister in a place such as this. Surely, there are other establishments that are better maintained."

He probably had a point, but as far as Kendra was concerned, a madhouse was a madhouse.

"It does have a blighted atmosphere," the Duke admitted. "Obviously, Dr. Shay has had some sort of financial misfortune. Perhaps the earl saw it in better days."

Kendra shook her head as she tried to rub the chill away from her arms. It was cold in the room, but it was the madhouse itself that was responsible for her goosebumps. "He had her committed about six months ago. The neglect around here has been happening longer than that."

A clattering of footsteps signaled the maid's return. The man who accompanied her was tall and athletic, and much younger and more attractive than Kendra had been expecting. Early thirties, she estimated, with closely cropped light brown hair shot with gold. His face was narrow, and set in somber lines. His eyes were an unusual blue-violet. Still, it wasn't the color that one noticed as much as the sadness that seemed to lurk behind them.

"Good morning," he greeted them, his mouth curving into a polite smile that did nothing to erase the solemnity in his eyes.

This is a man who carries the weight of the world on his shoulders, Kendra thought. Maybe working in a madhouse did that to a person.

"Thank you, Meg," the man said, a clear dismissal, and he waited for the servant to leave before speaking again. "I am Mr. McBride. Meg tells me that you have come to visit Lady Evelyn. You must be the Duke of Aldridge..." His gaze fastened on the Duke, then flicked to Kendra. "And Miss Donovan."

Alec stepped forward. "And I am Sutcliffe—the Marquis of Sutcliffe."

"My lord." McBride gave a brief bow that encompassed everyone. When he rose, his expression was puzzled. "Pray tell, what is this about? Lady Evelyn does not normally have visitors."

"I thought her brother came to see her yesterday," Kendra said.

That seemed to surprise him. "Well, yes. But he is Lady Evelyn's family."

"And I'm her friend." She could tell that he didn't believe her, but this was the nineteenth century. He wouldn't call her a liar right to her face. At least not with the Duke and Alec standing right beside her. "Is there a reason we are not allowed to see her?"

"No, I suppose not," he said slowly. "Lady Evelyn is not a dangerous patient."

"What was she diagnosed with?" Kendra asked. She was curious what he would say. There was no doctor/patient confidentiality in this time, but even if there was, McBride wasn't even a psychiatrist.

"Lord Craymore was concerned that his sister was suffering from female hysteria."

Female hysteria, the catch-all phrase used for every ailment, real or not, since ancient physicians believed that the womb was actually a living creature and able to wander around a woman's body in the middle of the night, wreaking havoc.

"If you will follow me," McBride said, and gestured toward the staircase. "I shall take you to Lady Evelyn's room."

"We've been told that his lordship brought his sister here six months ago," she said as they started up the steps. "How often does he visit her?"

McBride's eyelashes flickered a bit at the question, but he answered readily enough, "He is a consistent visitor. He comes every month for one or two days. Lady Evelyn is fortunate. We have patients here who have no visitors."

"Where does he stay? Here?"

"No one stays here except the inmates, Dr. Shay, and certain staff members. Lord Craymore stays at an inn in the village."

"Does he come on the same day every month? Or does he vary the time of his visits?"

McBride frowned. "I never considered the matter before, but now that you mention it… yes, he has a fairly well-established routine. He visits Lady Evelyn on the last days of every month. I understand that the family has an estate in Norfolk, and he is settling his late father's affairs. He travels between there and his townhouse in London. We are near one of the main roads to London, so I suppose it's convenient for him to stop here on his travels."

"And he travels alone? On horseback?" Kendra asked.

"Yes. It's faster." McBride stopped, his hand resting on the banister as he turned to look at them. "Forgive me, but why are you inquiring about his lordship's visitation schedule and method of travel?"

Kendra ignored the question to pose her own. "How did he seem to you yesterday when he was here?"

"I don't understand. Why are you asking such a thing?"

"Lord Craymore was shot last night," she told him bluntly.

"*Shot?*" McBride's hand jerked, and he brought it up to press against his brow. "My God…… How is he?"

"Not very good. He's dead."

McBride inhaled sharply, dropping his hand. "But… You are here to inform Lady Evelyn that her brother is dead?"

Kendra suspected that he'd been about to ask something else.

"Yes," she said, responding to his question. "And to see if she has any idea how he might have ended up that way."

9

Emotions flickered across McBride's face, too quickly for Kendra to decipher. "How can Lady Evelyn tell you who shot her brother?" he asked as he resumed climbing the stairs. "She's been here. While she is allowed considerable freedom, she cannot leave the grounds."

"How would you know? I didn't see a wall keeping anyone in."

"I believe the monastery had a wall at one time. You can see portions of it in the undergrowth, but it fell away a long time ago. Not that it would matter. The grounds here are quite extensive. At least a square mile. Even if one of the ladies did attempt to escape, where would she go? To a neighboring farm? The village? Anyone who found her would only return the patient here."

Put like that, Kendra supposed a wall wasn't needed. She asked, "How many patients do you have staying here in Shay House?"

McBride didn't answer right away. "We have twelve ladies living here at present," he finally replied, as they reached the second-floor landing.

They stood in a wide hallway. Another flight of stairs continued to the third floor. Five skinny windows on one side of the corridor allowed light to stream in, giving a grayish tint to the faded mint-green walls. There were more than a dozen dark-paneled doors lined up opposite the windows. It could have been a hallway in any large residence, had the locks not been on the outside of the bedchamber doors.

At the moment, though, most of the locks were not being used. Some doors were slightly ajar. Others were thrown wide open. A soft, childlike voice drifted out of one of the rooms, singing offkey. The hairs on the back of Kendra's neck rose in response, and she had to suppress a shiver. *Creepy.*

The Duke said, "Twelve is not many inmates for a place this size."

McBride hesitated, seemingly engaged in an internal debate about how best to respond. Then he simply shook his head and walked to one of the open doors nearest them, rapping briefly on the doorframe. "Lady Evelyn? You have visitors."

Kendra didn't know what she had been expecting, but it wasn't what she saw when she crossed to the threshold to peer inside. Lady Evelyn's bedchamber was large with silk-papered walls, a pink canopied bed, and a velvet tufted settee. Gleaming Chippendale chairs surrounded a matching table. A Queen Anne writing desk with tapered legs and inlaid wood was positioned in the corner. There was nothing tattered or torn about this bedchamber. If Craymore had any misgivings about the rest of Shay House, maybe this room had eased his mind—or his conscience. The décor was a bit too girlish for Kendra's taste, but she recognized that the bedchamber could easily fit into a country manor.

A slender woman of medium height stood in front of large diamond-paned windows framed by pink brocade curtains. At their entrance, she turned to regard them.

Lady Atwood had described Reginald Lansing's sister as a plain little thing, and Kendra would have to agree. Lady Evelyn's hair was as pale as moonlight, her eyebrows and lashes so light that they appeared nonexistent. She was dressed in full mourning—from her father's death six months prior, Kendra realized. The unrelenting black was not flattering. In fact, Kendra thought she looked a bit like an albino rabbit, with sharp, narrow features that held a bitter expression out of place on one so young.

Then again, if Kendra had spent the last six months in a mental institution to prevent her from marrying someone that her brother disapproved of, she'd be bitter, too.

"Miss Donovan has come to see you—along with the Duke of Aldridge and Lord Sutcliffe," McBride said, his tone carefully neutral, as though waiting for Lady Evelyn to debunk Kendra's claim of friendship.

Lady Evelyn's almost colorless blue eyes fixed on Alec with unnerving intensity. "I know who you are! We have not been introduced, my lord, but I've seen you at balls in London—when I attended balls." Her laugh was a quick, harsh bark. She stepped forward, then sank into a formal curtsy that was incongruous, given the environment. "My lord, Your Grace."

"I apologize for the intrusion, my lady," the Duke said when she rose to her full height again.

Lady Evelyn's thin lips twisted into an ugly knot. "My social calendar is quite open, Your Grace."

There was an awkward pause.

Kendra said, "We need to talk to you about your brother."

The pale eyes shifted to regard Kendra with the same intensity that she'd bestowed upon Alec. "We have never been introduced either, but I've heard about you, Miss Donovan. The American who was instrumental in solving Lady Dover's murder. It was quite the talk of London, when I was there... Forgive me! I'm not used to entertaining guests. Please sit down." She motioned to the room at large, her hand trembling slightly. "I should call for tea. And cakes. Or would you like something stronger? Dr.

Shay frowns on spirits—for the inmates, that is. Dr. Shay has been known to imbibe."

"Lady Evelyn—" McBride began, his brow furrowing.

She rounded on him, her eyes flashing. "I've smelled it on him!"

"You are becoming overexcited, my lady. You must calm down."

Lady Evelyn's features quivered with something approaching hatred. But just as quickly, her expression smoothed out, and she pivoted away from McBride, smiling brightly at her guests. "Again, forgive me. Mr. McBride is always so considerate of my moods. Aren't you, Mr. McBride?"

"Perhaps we ought to wait for Dr. Shay to return before you are *introduced*"—he said that with only the tiniest bit of an inflection, but he slid a pointed look at Kendra—"formally to Miss Donovan."

"No! I so seldom have visitors." Lady Evelyn moved to the table. "We should sit. Please be seated."

"Thank you, Lady Evelyn." Kendra took up the woman on her invitation, following her to the table and sitting down. She kept her gaze on Lady Evelyn's face, which had become flushed—the only color in her otherwise colorless appearance.

She waited until Lady Evelyn, the Duke, and Alec joined her. McBride remained standing, his expression watchful.

"We ought to have tea, Mr. McBride," Lady Evelyn said again, her restless fingers plucking at her skirt. "'Tis the polite thing to do. They are my guests."

"That's all right," Kendra said calmly. "We don't need tea. We heard that your brother visited you yesterday."

"Yes. Reginald is a dutiful brother. He put me in here, but he visits me every month. Is that not dutiful?"

Kendra decided to treat that as a rhetorical question. She asked, "Can you tell me if your brother had any enemies? Or was having problems with anyone?"

Lady Evelyn's eyes narrowed. "And what is this about?"

There was no easy way to say it. "Your brother was shot last night, my lady," Kendra said. "He's dead. I'm very sorry."

Lady Evelyn jolted, her pale hand flying up to clutch at her throat. She blinked rapidly. "Reginald is dead?"

"Yes. I'm sorry."

"He was here last evening."

"He was shot after he left. Do you have any idea who might have wanted your brother dead?"

Instead of answering, Lady Evelyn jumped to her feet and rushed over to where McBride was standing. She grasped his arm, her thin fingers digging into the fabric of his coat jacket. "I shall be able to leave now, won't I? Reginald is the one who put me here, but he's dead now. You cannot hold me here!"

"Lady Evelyn…" McBride regarded her uneasily. "We must speak to Dr. Shay. He has traveled to London—"

"Basil is waiting for me!"

"You must stay calm—"

Lady Evelyn gave a sudden screech, and lunged for the door. Shocked, Kendra leapt to her feet, thinking that the woman's mind had snapped and she was trying to escape. But in the next instant, Lady Evelyn dragged a petite woman with tangled, bright red hair into the bedchamber.

"Sneak! Spy!" Lady Evelyn shrieked. "Thief! Wicked, *wicked* creature!"

The woman screamed and struggled to get away, but Lady Evelyn locked her fingers tight around the birdlike wrist, and began slapping her captive about the head with her free hand.

"Good heavens," gasped the Duke, and both he and Alec sprang to their feet.

McBride started forward to intervene, but Kendra got to the women first. She hissed out a curse when Lady Evelyn's hand whipped back, landing an unexpected blow against her cheek.

Gritting her teeth, Kendra pushed forward, dodging sharp elbows and fingernails and even more vicious slaps as she began disentangling the ladies. Lady Evelyn's chest heaved as Kendra shoved her back. The redhead cowered against the wall. She raised her arms to protect her face, sobbing hysterically.

"Stop it!" Kendra blocked Lady Evelyn from launching another attack.

McBride stepped forward to grasp Evelyn's flailing arms. "Calm yourself, Lady Evelyn!"

"She stole my bracelet!" Lady Evelyn thrashed against his hold, her pale eyes blazing at the cringing woman. "Bran-faced bitch! Light-fingered trollop! You know she is, Mr. McBride!"

"That's enough, Lady Evelyn!" McBride said sternly. "Will you be still?"

Lady Evelyn clenched her hands into fists. Her chest was rising and falling with quick breaths. But at last, she nodded. McBride waited a few more seconds, to assure himself that she would obey, then released her to go to the weeping woman, gently helping her to her feet.

Kendra caught a glimpse of the face through the tangles of long red hair. Not a woman—more of a teenage girl, though she could be as old as twenty. Perhaps the same age as Lady Evelyn. Cinnamon-colored freckles were scattered across a face now streaked with tears. Her body was boyishly thin in the plain beige gown that she wore.

"Come now, Miss Sybil." McBride patted her awkwardly on the back. "Hush. You're working yourself into a state."

"She's a sneak! A spy!" shouted Lady Evelyn.

Kendra positioned herself between Lady Evelyn and the girl named Sybil, prepared to forcibly subdue Lady Evelyn if she had to.

The commotion was drawing an audience. Several women wearing the same beige gowns as Sybil crowded the doorway. Two women had their hair hacked off in uneven tufts close to their scalps.

A burly young man pushed himself through the knot of women. "Do ye need help, Mr. McBride?"

Even though he was losing his hair, his scalp gleaming pink through chestnut brown strands, Kendra estimated the newcomer was only in his mid-twenties, with a broad, unlined face. He had the disconcerting look of a bullfrog, with bulging brown eyes spaced too far apart, a wide nose, and thick, fleshy lips. Several women recoiled. Kendra's own skin prickled as she watched him spread his feet, place his hands on his hips, and fix his gaze on Sybil. A small smile played about his mouth.

McBride eyed him with dislike. "Thank you, no, Mr. Crump. I have everything well in hand."

"W'ot's all this ruckus? Move aside! Move aside!" A large, middle-aged woman came barreling into the room, followed by another man. Meg also appeared, hovering anxiously in the doorway.

"Oh, dear," the older woman clucked as she spotted the weeping Sybil. She bustled forward to enfold the girl against her massive bosom. "What's got into ye, Miss Sybil? There, there, luv. Ye'll make yerself ill, ye will, if ye don't stop yer blubbering."

"She'll be blubbering all the way to the gallows!" Lady Evelyn snarled, which brought a fresh bout of wailing from Sybil. Lady Evelyn raised her voice to be heard over the sobs. "Your father won't be able to stop it this time, Sybil!" she taunted, and glanced at the circle of faces around her. "If her father wasn't a wealthy cit, she would have already faced the drop at Newgate for her filching ways. You know it as well as I do, Mrs. Maddox!"

Mrs. Maddox frowned at her. "Ye be quiet, Lady Evelyn. Miss Sybil don't mean ter take things. If she borrowed yer bracelet, I'll get it back for ye."

"*Borrowed*! The bitch is a bloody criminal!"

"Lady Evelyn, you must take hold of yourself," McBride said with quiet authority. "This behavior is unbecoming in a lady of your station. Mrs. Maddox, please take Miss Sybil back to her room for a lie down."

"Maybe we should bring 'er ter the treatment room?" Crump

suggested. "Dr. Shay is supposed ter return from London some-time this afternoon—"

"That will not be necessary, Mr. Crump," McBride said sharp-ly. "Miss Sybil only needs some quiet time." He looked at Mrs. Maddox, who nodded.

"Aye. Come along, Miss Sybil." Gathering the young woman against her, Mrs. Maddox hustled her toward the door. The four women who were peering into the room parted, allowing Mrs. Maddox to haul the distressed girl away.

"Shall I fix Miss Sybil and Lady Evelyn a soothing tonic?" That came from the handsome, slender man who'd arrived with Mrs. Maddox. He appeared to be of Indian descent, with jet-black hair, a warm brown complexion, and striking turquoise-blue eyes.

"Thank you, Mr. Lewis. I think all of the ladies ought to have tea," McBride agreed. "Mr. Crump shall assist you."

"Shouldn't I be bringin' the ladies back ter their rooms?" Crump protested.

"I can handle the ladies." McBride waited until the orderly, his expression sulky, grudgingly followed Mr. Lewis out the door. McBride then spread his hands toward the women loitering near the doorway. "Now, ladies, there is nothing here for you to see. Please go back to your rooms."

"She's evil—*Jezebel*," a painfully thin woman hissed. She was one of the patients with unevenly cropped hair. She pointed a fin-ger at Lady Evelyn. "She worships Baal and is free with her favors!"

McBride gave a put-upon sigh. "Miss Dora—"

"I've seen her in the woods cavorting with the devil!"

"Miss Dora, you will cease this talk at once," McBride said firmly. "Meg, take the ladies to their rooms."

"Shall I lock their doors?" Meg asked.

"I think that would be best. Now, ladies, go with Meg. Mr. Lewis is making his special tea for you."

"He's a pagan! I won't drink it!"

"Miss Dora, you know very well that Mr. Lewis's father was as British as you and I." He expelled an impatient breath, glancing at Meg. "Escort them to their rooms."

"Aye, Mr. McBride."

The women muttered amongst themselves, but were fairly docile as Meg herded them out the door. It was, Kendra realized, a madhouse version of a time-out.

Lady Evelyn put her hands on her hips and glared at McBride. "My brother is dead. You have no right to keep me here!"

"You cannot leave here without a relative signing for your release, Lady Evelyn." He was beginning to sound harried. "You know that."

"Basil will come for me. I will write to him now."

"He is not your husband, Lady Evelyn. He cannot help you."

She ignored him, hurrying to the Queen Anne desk. As they watched, she sat down, pulled out a piece of foolscap, and uncapped an ink bottle from the writing stand.

McBride grimaced as he turned to face them. "I apologize, but I must ask you to leave. As you can see, this is not a good time."

"Of course," the Duke agreed immediately. His blue eyes were troubled as he glanced at Lady Evelyn. She was already lost in her own world, scribbling furiously.

After they filed out into the hall, McBride paused to fish out a ring of keys from his pocket. They jingled as he sorted through them. Quietly, he pulled the door shut and locked it with the selected key.

"I thought you said that Lady Evelyn is not a dangerous patient," Alec commented.

On the far end of the hall, the maid, Meg, was in the process of locking the last door. The only sound in the corridor was their footsteps, the jingle of keys, and a high-pitched keening from inside one of the locked rooms. Miss Sybil, Kendra guessed.

"She's not dangerous exactly." McBride paused. "She has her good days and her bad days."

Kendra said, "She didn't appear to be upset about her brother's death."

McBride frowned. "She blames him for putting her in here. But I wouldn't put too much weight on her reaction. I believe that she will mourn his death when she has time to consider the matter."

"Has Basil Willoughby ever visited Lady Evelyn?" Kendra asked.

"Lord Craymore forbade it."

"Did Mr. Willoughby ever try to get around that restriction?"

McBride pursed his lips, and he was silent for a long moment before he said cautiously, "He has managed to get on the grounds whilst Lady Evelyn was outside walking."

I've seen her in the woods cavorting with the devil. Kendra wondered if Miss Dora had seen a lovers' tryst between Lady Evelyn and Willoughby. She asked aloud, "What happened?"

"Mr. Booker ran the man off with his hounds and Lady Evelyn was brought inside. But what does any of that have to do with Lord Craymore's death?"

"Lord Craymore had his sister committed to prevent her from marrying Mr. Willoughby," Kendra said reasonably. "He must have been upset."

"You think Mr. Willoughby shot his lordship in retaliation?"

"I don't think anything—yet."

McBride didn't seem to know what to say to that. They started walking again.

"Why would Lord Craymore permit his sister to continue to correspond with the man?" Alec wondered as they reached the stairs. "It's remarkably short-sighted of him."

Kendra noticed McBride's eyes dart away. "He didn't know, did he?" she prompted.

McBride sighed. "No. When Lady Evelyn arrived, she wanted to write to Mr. Willoughby, but Dr. Shay refused. She sank into a dreadful state of melancholy. She refused to eat, drink. Dr. Shay feared for her bodily health, as well as her state of mind. If she became ill, Lord Craymore would have blamed him."

"So you allowed her to write to him," Kendra murmured.

"Dr. Shay did. Her mood improved dramatically. We considered letting her write and simply not posting the letters, but Lady Evelyn is no fool for all her… eccentricity. She expected Mr. Willoughby to reply. Which he did." He paused again, spreading his fingers. "Again, it seemed a relatively harmless exercise."

"Did you read the letters?"

"They were locked."

Letterlocking, Kendra knew, involved folding paper and sealing it in such an intricate and ingenious way that it was impossible to open without the recipient knowing. Famous figures from Machiavelli to Mary Queen of Scots to Marie Antoinette had employed letterlocking in their correspondence.

"Dr. Shay felt it would not be worth upsetting Lady Evelyn by tampering with her letters," McBride added, and began to descend the stairs.

Two women were coming up the stairs. One was a young servant girl, the other a strikingly pretty young woman with deep auburn hair left to tumble in waves down her back. Kendra identified her as a patient by the loose beige dress that she wore.

The woman stopped as soon as she saw them, and tossed her head back in a defiant gesture. Her eyes, a greenish hazel that tilted upward at the corners like a cat's, studied each of them boldly before settling on Alec. Her full lips curved into a provocative smile.

"Well, well… no one told me that we had visitors. And such lovely visitors, too." She positioned herself in front of them to block their path. Her fingers toyed with the garnet-and- gold-filigree cross pendant dangling at her breast as she stared openly at Alec. "Won't you introduce us, Mr. McBride?"

"Mrs. Slater, you know very well that you should not initiate introductions. It's not done."

The woman laughed without humor. "If I did what I was told, I wouldn't be in this wonderful establishment, now would I?" She shifted her gaze to Kendra. "Have you brought us fresh blood, Mr. McBride?"

McBride's mouth tightened. "Please stand aside, Mrs. Slater."

"C'mon, Mrs. Slater. It's time fer yer tea," the maid said, her tone almost pleading.

"You can give my tea to Mrs. McBride—the poor lump," Mrs. Slater said, fixing her gaze on McBride. The gleam in her eyes was mocking. Malicious.

A shadow passed over McBride's face. Instead of responding, he brushed past the woman in a jerky movement. Mrs. Slater's laughter rang out harshly as they passed her.

"She's out in the garden, but what good does it do?" she called after McBride. "Does your wife even feel the breeze against her face? Smell the flowers?"

Kendra glanced back at the woman as they reached the bottom step. The maid was touching the woman's arm, trying to draw her away, but Mrs. Slater ignored her, shifting her gaze from McBride to meet Kendra's eyes. After a few seconds, Mrs. Slater broke eye contact, spinning around to follow the maid up the stairs.

"My wife had a seizure six years ago," McBride told them quietly, breaking the awkward silence that had fallen over the group. "She hasn't been well since then. I was fortunate to find Shay House. Dr. Shay allowed me to stay with Sarah, to care for her, along with my other duties."

Kendra was reminded of her initial impression of McBride, that he carried the weight of the world on his shoulders. *Now I know why.* "So you've worked at Shay House for six years?" she asked.

"A little over five. When Sarah... when she became ill, we were in Cornwall. I tried to care for her, but..." He sighed. "As I said, I am grateful to Shay House and to Dr. Shay."

"Was Shay House like this five years ago?" She gestured to the entrance hall and the door leading to the grand room with its shabby furniture. "A very large house with only twelve inmates?"

The lines on McBride's face deepened, making him look older than he was. "We have undergone a few changes," he admitted carefully.

"How many patients did you once have?" Kendra asked.

"Fifty, and more staff." He pressed his lips together and shook his head. "I would rather you speak to Dr. Shay."

"When will he be back from London?"

"I am not privy to the doctor's schedule. He has a practice in London as well. It depends on how busy he is there."

"How long was Lord Craymore here yesterday?"

McBride frowned at the change of topic. "He arrived at six. I believe he left some time after eight. I was tending to my wife at that time, and didn't see him leave."

"It was a quarter to nine." That came from Mr. Lewis, as he came into the hall carrying a large silver tray filled with delicate porcelain teacups. "Forgive me, Mr. McBride, but I couldn't help but overhear."

"Where is Mr. Crump?" McBride inquired, frowning as he looked past the other man. "I told him to assist you."

Mr. Lewis's jaw tightened and there was a glint of anger in his eyes before he dropped his gaze to the tray he carried. "Mr. Crump said that he had better things to occupy his time."

Kendra remembered what Rowan Booker had said earlier. *Mr. McBride will help you. Or that other one.* Lewis, with his obvious mixed ethnicity, would always be *that other one* to people like Booker and Crump.

Lewis lifted his gaze. "Why are you inquiring about when his lordship left last evening?"

"Lord Craymore is dead," McBride told him. "He was shot on the road last night after leaving here."

Lewis's eyes widened. The tray jerked slightly in his hands, rattling the teacups. "Little wonder why Lady Evelyn is in such a state." Lewis exchanged a veiled glance with McBride, then lifted the tray as though to remind them of the burden he carried. "Pardon me, but I must bring the ladies their tea before it grows cold. Good day."

They watched him as he climbed the stairs. Kendra turned back to McBride. "Can you tell us which inn Lord Craymore was staying at in the village?"

"There are only two—Needlham is not very large. But I believe his lordship always stays at the King's Arms." McBride regarded them. "May I ask why you have involved yourself in this affair? It is obvious that you are not acquainted with Lady Evelyn as you claimed."

"Shouldn't we all care when someone is murdered?" Kendra replied.

"The earl died on my lands," the Duke added. "I've already contacted a Bow Street Runner to help with the investigation."

McBride pressed his lips together and said nothing as he escorted them to the door. He ushered them through. Kendra noted, "You said that Lady Evelyn must stay here until she can be released by her next of kin. Do you know who that is?"

"No."

"So she stays here until you find them?"

McBride spread his hands, palms up. "She has no husband."

On that dour note, they returned to the stables, where Benjamin was rubbing down the horses and Rowan Booker and his rottweilers were, thankfully, nowhere to be seen.

"Shall I state the obvious?" Alec said after they'd climbed into the carriage and it started down the drive. "Mayhap Lord Craymore didn't put his sister into a madhouse to prevent her from marrying a fortune hunter. Mayhap he put her in Shay House because she really is mad."

"Maybe," Kendra conceded. There was no denying that Lady Evelyn had acted oddly, even erratically. Kendra glanced out the window, at the former monastery with its crumbling tower and tilting chimney stacks. "Or maybe six months in Shay House drove her insane."

10

The King's Arms was a three-story gray building on the high street, a stone's throw from the Red Pigeon. As the Duke opened the inn's sturdy door for Kendra and Alec, they were greeted with a furious shout: "I tell ye, he's not in his room!"

Kendra raised her eyebrows at Alec and the Duke, then looked at the man she assumed was the proprietor of the King's Arms. He reminded her of a dumpling—short and plump. His hair was the color of straw, cut in a fringe around a ruddy face that was now flushed a deep claret in annoyance.

The man standing before the proprietor could have been Methuselah's older brother. His face and body were whittled down to skeletal gauntness; his skin was like week-old crepe paper, stretched across his cheekbones and sagging everywhere else. The loose skin formed a turkey waddle beneath his pointy chin that fell over the frilly stock he wore around his neck. He had a beaked nose and rheumy eyes set deep into his skull.

When she'd first arrived in this century, Kendra had viewed every garment as old-fashioned. Now she recognized the differences, and knew that this gentleman was hopelessly out-of-date with his canary-yellow wool jacket and breeches, white wool knit stockings, and black buckled shoes. He even wore a short periwig with sausage curls rippling above his ears. It looked like a gray rat had curled up on top of his head and died. Despite his strange attire, the man was clearly not a pauper. Gold and jeweled rings circled several fingers, and his hands, bulging with veins and spotted with age, were clasped around a jeweled silver-tipped walking stick.

At their entrance, the innkeeper swiveled and forced a cheerful smile that didn't quite erase the irritation in his eyes. "Good morning! How can I help ye?"

"If you are playing me false, Mr. Bishop, I shall remember!" the old man threatened, shaking his walking stick at the innkeeper.

Mr. Bishop's flush deepened into a heart-attack-inducing puce. "I am not—" His voice rose an octave before it cracked. He sucked in a breath, clearly struggling to keep his composure. When he resumed, he moderated his tone. "I am not playing ye false, Mr. Griggs. Good day to ye, sir!"

The old man glared at him, then pivoted sharply on his two-inch heels. Ignoring his audience, he stalked past Kendra, Alec, and the Duke to the door, periwigged head held high. At the last minute, he spun around and said, "You shall send word immediately when he returns!"

He didn't wait for the innkeeper to reply before he yanked open the door and left.

The innkeeper muttered something under his breath before forcing another smile, his gaze going unerringly to the Duke. "I apologize that ye had to witness such a scene. The King's Arms is a respectable establishment, but some folks just don't listen. Me name is Mr. Bishop. Are ye looking for accommodations on your travels? We have several nice rooms available."

"Actually, we're here about Lord Craymore," Kendra said. "We know—"

The smile vanished instantly. "Devil take it—pardon," Mr. Bishop quickly apologized to her. "He's *not* here. That's what I've been tellin' Mr. Griggs for the last ten minutes. He has a room here, but I haven't seen the man since he left ter see his sister yesterday afternoon. She's up there at Shay House. I suppose he could've come back late and left early this mornin'. It ain't like I keep me peepers on me guests. But me wife knocked on his door earlier ter see if he wanted a tray like he usually does, and he ain't there now!"

Kendra blinked at the man. "The gentleman who just left was asking about Lord Craymore, too?"

"Aye. And that popinjay didn't believe me when I told him that I didn't know where his lordship was!" Mr. Bishop's face puckered in offense. "I told him—Oy! Where are ye goin'? Don't ye want rooms?" he called after them as they rushed to the door.

Outside, Kendra spotted the old man waiting near the public livery stables. "Mr. Griggs!" She picked up her skirts and sprinted over to him. "I need to speak to you."

His brows drew together as he gave her a regal once-over. "Who are you? I don't know you."

"I'm Kendra Donovan—"

"American, by the sound of it." His lip curled in disdain. "Uncouth country."

"Miss Donovan is my ward," the Duke said as he and Alec caught up with them. "I am the Duke of Aldridge. This is my nephew, the Marquis of Sutcliffe."

He was using what Kendra always thought of as his "duke voice"—icy and arrogant. It was clearly the right tactic. Mr. Griggs' faced changed like someone had flipped a switch.

"Oh, my word," the old man breathed. He put one arm behind his back and bowed deeply, like they were standing in a ballroom rather than a stable yard with the malodorous stench of dung hanging in the air.

"Your Grace, my lord. I am honored at the introduction. How may I assist you?"

Kendra asked, "Why were you looking for Lord Craymore?"

Mr. Griggs' faded eyes narrowed as he glanced at her. "We were supposed to meet last night, but he never arrived. I am aware that he is staying here." He pointed his walking stick at the King's Arms. "It is imperative that I speak with him."

"Why?"

His sparse eyebrows rose up into his periwig. He slid a side-long look at the Duke as though to gauge his reaction, no doubt thinking the question impertinent and hoping to see some agree-ment on the Duke's face. When none was forthcoming, he said stiffly, "We have private business to discuss."

"What sort of business?"

Mr. Griggs huffed out a breath, and turned to the Duke. "Your Grace, what is this about? Lord Craymore would not wish for me to discuss our private business with… with just anyone. Even with someone such as yourself."

Kendra said, "Lord Craymore is beyond caring. He's dead."

"*What?*"

"He was shot to death last night. Most likely on his way to see you." She didn't know if the latter statement was true—although the timing seemed likely—but she was curious to see the gentle-man's reaction. Still, she was surprised when he staggered back a step, his face seeming to elongate in horror, like a parody of Edvard Munch's *The Scream.*

"*No!* Oh, no, no, no!" Mr. Griggs gasped, shaking his head so violently that his periwig threatened to fly off. "This is dreadful! Absolutely dreadful! My God, the loss…"

"I'm sorry," she murmured. "I didn't realize that you and his lordship were so close."

He shot her a nasty look. "Don't be ridiculous. I'm not speaking of Lord Craymore. I'm speaking of the Anahita Pink."

She stared at him, then glanced at the Duke and Alec. But they appeared to be as mystified as she was. Turning back to the old man, she asked, "The what?"

"The Anahita Pink!" Mr. Griggs bounced in his buckled shoes in his agitation. "My God! *What happened to the Anahita Pink?*"

11

For the second time that day, Kendra found herself sitting around a table at the Red Pigeon with a smiling Mr. Enders serving them ale and the Major—still the only occupant in the pub—watching them from his perch at the end of the bar.

Kendra waited until Mr. Enders walked away to start the conversation. "Tell us about the Anahita Pink. What is it?" she asked, although she already had an idea. "And how is it connected to Lord Craymore?"

"This is devastating, simply devastating," Mr. Griggs muttered, scratching at his periwig. He glanced at the Duke and Alec. "With your impeccable lineage, you will understand what its loss will mean to England."

Alec lifted his tankard, eyeing the old man over its rim. "I confess, the name sounds vaguely familiar, but you shall have to refresh my memory."

"Have you heard of the Darya-ye Noor? The Koh-i-Noor?"

"Of course. They are renowned diamonds," Alec answered.

"Exactly so." Mr. Griggs beamed at Alec—not his best look, Kendra decided. He was missing a few teeth, and the ones he still had left were corn-yellow and crooked.

He continued, "The Koh-i-Noor means Mountain of Light. It is one of the largest diamonds in the world, reputed to be one hundred and ninety-one carats. Like many famous gemstones, it has belonged to kings and conquerors. Today it rests in the vaults of Ranjit Singh, who rules the Sikh Empire in the Punjab."

Not for long, Kendra knew. She'd actually viewed the Koh-i-Noor in person, when she'd visited the Tower of London as a tourist during an FBI training session with New Scotland Yard. The brilliant stone was—or, rather, would become—part of the British crown jewels after Queen Victoria inherited the British throne, when her armies took control of the Punjab region in India and Pakistan.

"The Darya-ye Noor is Sea or River of Light, and is reputed to be one hundred and eighty-five carats—maybe even one hundred and ninety-one, like the Koh-i-Noor," Mr. Griggs went on, in what was beginning to sound like a lecture. "Even if it is smaller than the Koh-i-Noor, it is more unique because of its unusual pink hue." He paused to let his gaze travel over them. "Pink diamonds are the rarest minerals on earth, which makes them the most prized, as well. The Darya-ye Noor is currently in the Shah of Iran's Qajar treasury."

And—despite some reports to the contrary—would remain as part of that country's treasury, Kendra remembered, the jewel resting securely in the Bank of Iran.

"Given the name, I assume that the Anahita Pink must be another pink diamond, like the Darya-ye Noor," Kendra guessed. "Unless whoever named it was colorblind."

Mr. Griggs scowled at her, apparently not amused by her attempt at levity. "It *is* pink. It was named after the Persian goddess Anahita. A water goddess. Legend has it that the diamond was mined on the banks of the Tungabhadra River, like the Darya-ye Noor. That is, of course, speculation. There is no record of its origin. What *is* recorded is its size—larger than the Koh-i- Noor—estimated at one hundred and ninety-eight carats."

He paused to scratch at his periwig again. Kendra couldn't help but wonder how often he cleaned the thing, or if it was infested with lice or some other bug. She was grateful that she was sitting opposite him.

Mr. Griggs said, "The Anahita Pink was once owned by Sayf al-Din Muhammad, the king of the Ghurid dynasty, but the gem passed into King Richard's hands during the Third Crusade. It is recorded that he sent the diamond home to England, where it became part of England's royal treasury. Of course, after King Richard's death, the crown was passed to his brother, John." He looked at the Duke expectantly.

"I am aware of this country's history," the Duke said slowly.

"I was certain you would be, sir, given your own impressive pedigree." Mr. Griggs leaned forward; his gaze locked on the Duke's. "Like the sword of Tristram, the Anahita Pink became part of King John's treasury."

"Yes, but…" The Duke's eyes widened. "Good God, man. You aren't suggesting… Are you speaking of—"

"*Yes!*" Mr. Griggs interrupted, excitement shining in his rheumy eyes. He thumped his fist on the table with enough force to rattle the tankards on its surface. "The Anahita Pink is part of the lost treasure!"

The Duke stared at the old man. "You are referring to the Wash?"

Alec said, "That's a legend."

"The Wash?" Kendra interjected, looking at the faces around the table. She was the only one who didn't seem to understand the reference. "What are you talking about?"

The Duke glanced at her. "'Tis a bay between Lincolnshire and Norfolk. When the tide is out, it is one the kingdom's most widely known mudflats. The tale goes that King John and his entourage were crossing the marsh on their way to Lincolnshire. However, the king became ill. He ordered the caravan to continue across the mudflats—known as the Wash—but he miscalculated the tide."

"The sea swept in and overwhelmed the king's caravan," Mr. Griggs interrupted. "One of the wagons was carrying England's treasury—including the crown jewels. It all vanished."

Alec shook his head. "'Tis English lore."

"No, not lore, sir," Mr. Griggs argued. "Do you know where the ancestral estate is for the Earls of Craymore?"

"Norfolk," Alec replied.

"On the border of Lincolnshire." Mr. Griggs' eyes glinted. He tapped the table with his index finger as though to emphasize his point. "In the Fens—the Wash."

Kendra processed the information with a frown. "Okay. What you're saying is that King John lost the royal treasure"—that actually rang a distant bell— "around this area known as the Wash. And the Anahita Pink was part of that treasure?"

"Yes."

It wasn't hard to connect the dots. "And Lord Craymore found the treasure?"

"Not the current Lord Craymore." Mr. Griggs frowned, perhaps remembering that the current Lord Craymore had recently become the *late* Lord Craymore. "His father, Benedict." He turned toward the Duke and Alec, all but dismissing Kendra. "Were you acquainted with the earl—the first earl?"

"Our acquaintance was limited," admitted the Duke. "We attended the same school, but I was several years older and we weren't friends. I spend a considerable amount of my time at my country estate, and I believe Benedict did the same. Our paths crossed a few times when we were both in London. He was a member of the Royal Society, as am I. But his interests lay in antiquities and history. I believe he was quite the collector."

Mr. Griggs nodded. "Oh, yes. He had a passion for such things, especially in relation to the history of this country, because of where his family's estate was located. His lordship once told me that he grew up steeped in its folklore and legends."

"Like King John's lost treasure," Alec remarked, picking up his tankard to take a swallow of ale.

"This is Reginald Lansing's father you're talking about?" Kendra asked.

Mr. Griggs gave her an irritated look. "Of course. Who else? Reginald had no interest in his heritage, no curiosity about this nation's great history. His father lamented about it to me. From my understanding, the lad spent most of his time in London until his father died."

"How did you become acquainted with the earl—Benedict?" the Duke inquired.

The old man's thin chest puffed out. "I am a historian and a gemologist as well as a collector of antiquities. I have written several books on the Roman hoards discovered throughout our kingdom. I wrote about the Backworth Hoard. Perhaps you have heard of it, Your Grace?"

"The gold and silver that was uncovered five years ago?"

"Four years ago, but yes. The earl sought me out after attending one of my lectures. He invited me to Pelsley Hall several years ago to evaluate his collection of Roman antiquities and Anglo-Saxon gold coins. I am no numismatic, but his collection was immense. And impressive."

"And he showed you the Anahita Pink?" Kendra asked.

"He did not have it then. As I said, he wanted someone to catalog his collection. Of course, I was interested, but…" The jewels in Mr. Griggs' rings winked in the tavern's dim light as he waved his hand. "From what he had collected, it would take years. Simply years. He had so much."

A picture was beginning to emerge for Kendra. Benedict Lansing sounded like a typical hoarder—except he was hoarding really good stuff. Kendra decided to cut to the chase. "Where does the Anahita Pink show up in this story?"

Mr. Grigg's mouth flattened and he shot her a look of dislike, clearly not appreciating her attempt to hurry him along. "The earl and I began to correspond. Every other month, I would travel to the estate and we would work together to catalog his collection. At the risk of sounding immodest, we became friends." He said that with another glow of pride. "But about a month before his collapse, his lordship wrote to me. He wanted me to travel to Norfolk to evaluate a gemstone that he'd come across. Obviously, he was well acquainted with the stories of King John's lost treasure, including the Anahita Pink. He believed the jewel was that one."

"Where did he find it?" the Duke wondered.

"That, I do not know. He only wrote that he'd recently made the discovery. But many people who live in that area, including his lordship, have been known to search for the lost treasure."

"He was a treasure hunter," Kendra interjected.

Mr. Griggs didn't seem to care for that description. "He was an antiquities enthusiast. He did not do it for the *monetary* reward." The old man spat that out like it was a dirty word. "He cared about England's *history*."

The Duke said, "That would be an extraordinary find, but I never heard of it."

"Well, no. His lordship was very specific in his directions. He swore me to secrecy, asked me not to discuss the possibility of his discovery with anyone. Quite understandable. He did not want to raise false hopes if the stone turned out not to be the Anahita Pink."

Alec's eyes narrowed. "If you determined that it *was* the Anahita Pink, what then? The jewel belongs to the crown."

"I assume he would have made arrangements to deliver the diamond to the royal household."

Kendra wondered if that was true. There was a type of person who coveted priceless treasures only for themselves, unscrupulous collectors who would never claim bragging rights to owning a Da Vinci or Degas. Instead, they derived a quiet, narcissistic pleasure at keeping works of art locked away in secrecy so that only they were able to view it, touch it, *own* it.

"But it became a moot point," Mr. Grigg's continued. "We were in the process of making arrangements for me to travel to Norfolk to inspect the stone when I learned of his illness. He died shortly thereafter."

Kendra looked at the antiquities collector. "So, you never had a chance to evaluate the diamond. You don't really know if it was the Anahita Pink or not."

Mr. Griggs' mouth turned petulant. "No, but his lordship wrote to me describing the stone in exquisite detail. He said that it was a true, vivid pink. Do you realize how rare that is? Most pink diamonds tend to be pale in color or muddied with other hues." Mr. Griggs bejeweled fingers glinted again as he picked up his tankard, and took a gulping swallow. "That description and its carats, along with the location of the earl's ancestral home, leads me to believe that there is an excellent chance that it is the diamond." He set down the tankard with a thunk. Foam coated the old man's upper lip. "Naturally, I sent a letter immediately to Reginald Lansing."

Kendra tried not to become distracted by the foam on his lip. "You told him that you had been corresponding with his father about the Anahita Pink?"

"Of course. Obviously, he was aware of his father's extensive collection and interest in antiquities and how I'd been visiting the estate to catalog his father's finds."

"But he didn't know about the Anahita Pink?"

"No. His father must not have shared the news with him. As I said, Reginald Lansing spent most of his time in London. Still, he knew of King John's lost treasure. He'd spent his childhood in the area, after all. We exchanged correspondence, and I even traveled to London to meet with him a few times while he was settling his father's affairs. He promised me that he would search for the diamond when he returned to Pelsley Hall. I confess that I had almost given up hope of hearing from his lordship. But then he wrote to me a few weeks ago."

The Duke leaned back in his chair. "He found the diamond."

"Yes. I offered to go immediately to Norfolk to examine the gemstone, just as I had planned to do for his father, but he said that would not be necessary. He would be in Needlham visiting his sister. Needlham is not far from Paddlewick."

Kendra eyed the collector. "Paddlewick?"

"I live outside of Paddlewick."

"Where's Paddlewick? How far is it?"

Alec said, "I believe it's a village on the road to London. About half an hour or so from here. North, northwest of Aldridge Village."

Craymore could have been riding in the direction of Paddlewick when he'd been intercepted. That would put him on course with the Duke's lands.

"If only he would have allowed me to come to Pelsley Hall as I'd proposed, the Anahita Pink would be safe." The loose skin under Mr. Griggs' neck trembled with emotion. "Was he waylaid by a highwayman?"

Kendra looked at him. "Why do you ask that?"

He lifted his hands. "What else could it be?"

She said evasively, "He still had his purse on him."

Mr. Griggs locked his gaze on Kendra. "But not the Anahita Pink?" He appeared to hold his breath.

"No."

He released his breath in a huff, his narrow shoulders slumping. "Then it has vanished again," he moaned. "This valuable piece of history. Priceless. *Gone.*"

"I'm sorry for your loss," Kendra murmured drily.

Mr. Griggs didn't seem to hear the sarcasm, and nodded. "'Tis dreadful. The Anahita Pink has graced the necks of empresses. To think that it may now be in some grubby blackguard's hands… It is not to be borne."

"What time were you supposed to meet his lordship?" Kendra asked.

"Our appointment was scheduled for half past nine."

"Why so late?"

"It is not so late, but I had business in Ashford that day. Meeting at my home in Paddlewick was convenient for both of us. Who would have thought something like this would happen? The road between Needlham and Paddlewick has always been safe."

"And yet the first thing you thought of was that Lord Craymore had been robbed by a highwayman," Kendra pointed out.

He gave her a baffled look. "The Anahita Pink is gone. What other explanation is there?"

"Who else knew of your meeting?"

"No one."

"You didn't tell anyone that you were meeting Lord Craymore that night to evaluate a diamond purported to be the Anahita Pink?"

"Certainly not! I observed the same code of secrecy with Reginald Lansing as I did with his lordship's father."

"What about Lord Craymore?" Kendra asked. "Do you know if he told anyone?"

Mr. Griggs frowned. "No. But why would he? At least not until after I inspected the stone." He shook his head, and reached for his walking stick. "There is nothing more I can say on the matter. I must beg your leave." He hoisted himself to his feet, and looked at the Duke. "I hope I have satisfied your questions, sir."

The Duke smiled slightly. "Miss Donovan is the one who asked most of the questions, but thank you, Mr. Griggs. I wish you good day."

Mr. Griggs gave an abbreviated bow. His heels clicked across the wooden floor. They remained silent as they watched the old man leave the tavern.

The Duke spoke up first. "It would seem as though Lord Craymore was killed by a highwayman after all. A priceless diamond is a powerful motive. You cannot discount that."

"It is, and I'm not discounting anything," said Kendra. "But highway robbery tends to be a random attack. It's a crime of opportunity. A highwayman wouldn't have been motivated because of the diamond. He wouldn't have *known* about the diamond. If we're dealing with a random thief, then he got very lucky."

She shook her head and added softly, "No one is that lucky."

12

They returned to the King's Arms. Even though Reginald Lansing wouldn't be needing the room again, Mr. Bishop was reluctant to let them search it without the proper authority. Alec took care of the innkeeper's qualms by offering him a gold guinea, and moments later, Mr. Bishop threw open the door to a small bedchamber furnished with a lumpy-looking bed; a nightstand that held a book, two stout candles and a teacup and saucer on its surface; a pine wardrobe; a small writing desk in front of stingy window; and a washstand behind a privacy screen.

"I can't believe his lordship is dead," Mr. Bishop said from the doorway, watching as they began to search the room. "He was a good guest. Came regular as clockwork ter see his sister up at Shay House."

"Same time every month?" Kendra asked, opening up the door to the wardrobe. A single chocolate brown superfine jacket dangled from a hook. Her gaze fell on a soft leather satchel.

She pulled the bag out and brought it over to the bed.

Mr. Bishop's nod confirmed what they already knew. "Aye. At the end of every month, and he usually stayed one or two nights."

"How long was he staying this time?" Kendra asked as she unbuckled the satchel and opened it.

"I expected him ter leave today. He came on Wednesday afternoon, then went up ter Shay House for his visit. He didn't mention stayin' an extra day, so I reckoned he would be leavin' today."

"You didn't think it odd that he didn't return last night?" Kendra sifted through the clothes in the satchel. Nightshirt, stockings, shirt, cravat, waistcoat. One of each. He was only planning to stay one night. No Anahita Pink.

Mr. Bishop huffed out an aggrieved breath. "It's like I told Mr. Griggs. I don't spy on me guests. I didn't know what he was doin' and it ain't any of me business. He paid for the chamber for last evenin'."

"I'm not criticizing." She put the clothes back in the satchel, and returned it to the wardrobe. She checked the pockets of the jacket hanging inside. Nothing. "What was his mood when you last saw him? Happy? Distracted? Upset?"

"I dunno. It's not as though he talked ter the likes of me."

Kendra decided not to point out to the innkeeper that he didn't need to talk to Craymore to assess his mood. She glanced at Alec, who was rummaging through the writing desk, and then the Duke, who was behind the privacy screen. "Find anything?"

"No."

"Aside from a chamber pot? No." The Duke stepped out as Kendra picked up the book on the nightstand.

Curious, she scanned the title. *Waverly*. By Anonymous. Except she knew that the author was Sir Walter Scott—before he'd been granted his title. She fanned through the pages, but there was no secret hidey-hole for a diamond within. It looked like Craymore had just been reading the novel.

She put the book back on the nightstand, and combed through the pillows, blankets and bed linens, slid her hands under the mattress, and looked beneath the bed. There was nothing but a thick layer of fuzzy gray dust and mouse droppings. Nineteenth-century hostelries didn't exactly have high standards of cleanliness. Then again, twenty-first century hotels didn't always look so good either under a blacklight.

"What are ye lookin' for?" Mr. Bishop asked curiously.

"Has anybody been in here besides Lord Craymore?" she asked as she rose to her feet.

"Nay. Me wife opened the door after she knocked, just ter make sure his lordship was all right. When she saw he wasn't still abed, she came downstairs and told me. Then Mr. Griggs showed up ter inquire after his lordship..." The innkeeper gave a rolling shrug. "Course, I didn't know that his lordship had already cocked up his toes. How could I know that, eh?"

"No reason for you to," Kendra agreed easily, and moved toward the door. "Thank you for your help, Mr. Bishop."

"What should I do with his things?" Mr. Bishop wondered as they went back downstairs.

"We'll be informing the earl's family about his death," Alec said. "We'll let them know that he has a few personal items here."

They left the innkeeper and returned to the carriage.

"Lord Craymore obviously had the gemstone on him when he visited his sister at Shay House," the Duke said once they were barreling down the road again. "It would take at least half an hour to travel to Paddlewick. There would not have been enough time for him to return to the inn to retrieve the diamond if he wanted to make his appointment with Mr. Griggs at half past nine."

"If the diamond is as valuable as Mr. Griggs says it is, Craymore wouldn't want to leave it in his room. Safer in his pocket. At least that's what he probably thought."

"A fatal error," murmured Alec.

The Duke looked at Kendra. "I know you do not think that the two incidents are connected, but whoever shot the earl *must* have the diamond."

"I didn't say the two incidents aren't connected. I said that this wasn't a random robbery. Our unsub knew Craymore had the diamond on him."

"Who could have known such a thing? Other than Mr. Griggs," said Alec. "And I don't see Mr. Griggs lying in wait for Craymore on a cold, dark country lane, do you?"

Kendra had to laugh at the image. "No."

The Duke rubbed his chin thoughtfully. "Mr. Griggs could have hired someone to steal the diamond."

Kendra considered that for a moment, but shook her head. "I have two problems with that possibility," she admitted. "One, it would be stupid for him to come to the inn demanding to see Lord Craymore today. It would be in his best interest to keep their connection quiet, not advertise it like he did with Mr. Bishop."

"Or Mr. Griggs was being clever, pretending not to know that Lord Craymore was dead," said Alec.

"Possible," Kendra acknowledged. "But there's reason number two: I can't imagine Mr. Grigg's trusting anyone to steal the diamond. He'd expect a double-cross."

Alec inclined his head. "You make a good point."

"I have a few other points. Lord Craymore left Shay House at around quarter to nine to ride to Paddlewick. Let's say you're Lord Craymore. It's dark. Another rider approaches. You've got a priceless diamond in your pocket. What do you do?"

Alec answered first. "I'd be on guard—even without such a valuable gemstone in my possession. And if I had a weapon, I would have had it in my hand and at the ready by the time the other rider caught up to me."

"Exactly," she said, nodding. "But we know that Craymore left his weapon in his pocket. And he had his purse on him. Now, let's say the rider caught him unawares, tried to rob him. Wouldn't you throw out your purse first before you hand over a far more valuable diamond? But Craymore apparently hands over the Anahita Pink and *then* tries to escape?"

The Duke frowned. "Not everyone is as quick-thinking in volatile situations as you are, my dear."

"This is about instinct, not calculation. Craymore's instinct would have been to protect the diamond. His instinct would have been to go for his gun to protect himself."

"As you said, this was not a random attack. The thief somehow knew about the diamond, and demanded it," Alec said.

"Maybe, but I think there's more to it than that."

The Duke eyed Kendra curiously. "Like what?"

"I don't know yet. But something isn't adding up."

13

Dr. Ethan Munroe was in the middle of stitching up the Y-incision in Reginald Lansing's chest when Kendra, the Duke, and Alec walked into the icehouse chamber an hour later. The light from the lanterns glinted off the heavy hook needle that Munroe was using and bounced off the golden circular spectacles that he'd pinched on his hawk-like nose, concealing his intelligent gray eyes as he looked up at them from his gruesome task.

Munroe was a big man in his early fifties with striking black eyebrows that contrasted sharply with his thick silvery hair, which he wore in a ponytail. The hairstyle was unorthodox, much like Munroe himself. He'd once trained as a doctor, a profession held in high esteem by the Polite World. But he'd abandoned that to become a surgeon, which was not so well-regarded. Then he'd really stunned and horrified society when he became a doctor for the dead, opening his own anatomist school in London's Covent Garden. *That* profession didn't even have a rung on the medical ladder.

"Excellent timing, as I've just finished the postmortem," he greeted them with a smile, before switching his attention to finish up the final stitches.

"Thank you for coming so quickly," Kendra said.

"Not at all. I had to rearrange a few of my duties, but I am always pleased to be part of these investigations."

Kendra watched him push the needle through the cadaver's flesh. It reminded her, in a strange, macabre way, of how the ladies of the Ton did their needlework. Of course, Munroe made no attempt to keep his stitches nice and even. She asked, "Where is Mr. Kelly? He didn't come with you?"

"He did, indeed. But Mr. Kelly thought his time would be better served making inquiries about highwaymen operating in the area." Munroe glanced at her as he removed the heavy needle and tied off the thick black thread. "He said that you mentioned in your note that Lord Craymore"—his gaze dipped briefly to the corpse on the table—"may have been a victim of a highway robbery." He flashed her a grin. "I also don't think that Mr. Kelly enjoys attending postmortems."

Kendra let her gaze drift over Reginald Lansing. Munroe had draped a linen cloth over Lansing's pelvis in anticipation of her attendance. While the doctor may have accepted her presence during an autopsy, Kendra knew that he still tried to preserve her maidenly modesty by covering the cadaver's genitals.

"It might be a little strange if he did," she commented.

Munroe laughed. "You have a point, Miss Donovan."

"What can you tell us?"

"Unfortunately, not a lot more than you probably already know. His lordship was shot by two forty-caliber balls from what was most likely a double-barreled flintlock pistol." He went to a tin washbasin on the shelf, and, using his index finger and thumb as a vice, picked up a misshapen lead fragment to show them. When he tossed it back into the basin, it gave a sharp metallic clang and rolled a bit before settling into silence.

"I can tell you that the victim was not shot at point-blank range. I've inspected his lordship's clothing." Munroe wiped his bloody hands on the leather apron he wore, and shifted to the bundle of clothes nearby.

Kendra tried not to wince. She wasn't a germophobe, but the lack of latex gloves in this era did freak her out a bit. It was why there was a bottle of whisky on the shelf next to the water bucket. At her recommendation, Dr. Munroe had begun to rinse his hands with whisky after he finished his autopsies to neutralize what they believed were microscopic "insects." It was a far cry from the medical grade antiseptics of her time, but it was better than nothing.

Munroe shook out Craymore's greatcoat. "There doesn't appear to be any gunpowder residue. At least to the naked eye."

The Duke looked at him. "But under a microscope?"

Dr. Munroe smiled. "It might be a different story. With your permission, Your Grace, I would like to use one of your microscopes in your laboratory to inspect the coat, in order to give you a more conclusive answer."

"You are always welcome to use my laboratory, Dr. Munroe."

"Thank you, sir." Munroe's gaze returned to Kendra. "I've measured the holes against the wounds. If you notice, the tears in the fabric are slightly elongated, which indicate that the victim was leaning forward when he was shot."

"The victim was on horseback," Kendra said. "Could the shooter have been on a ground when he discharged his weapon?"

"No," Munroe shook his head. "The angle would have been much steeper."

Alec looked at Kendra. "Perhaps Craymore bent forward to urge his horse into a gallop to escape his assailant."

"The evidence supports that hypothesis, yes." Munroe shoved the greatcoat back on the shelf and returned to the body. "Now, if you notice, there are no exit wounds on the front torso. What we have instead are posterior entrance wounds, which are deceptive in appearance. My lord, if you would help me reposition the body?"

After twelve hours, the cadaver was in full rigor mortis, so it wasn't difficult to flip Craymore onto his stomach. The real trick was to turn him over while keeping the linen wrapped around his loins. Kendra had to stop herself from rolling her eyes.

Once the body was in position, Munroe pointed to the two bullet holes burrowed into Craymore's upper back. "As you can see, we're dealing with fairly small wounds."

The wounds were a little larger than raisins, the flesh around both injuries puckered and black. Like the gashes in the great-coat, the injuries were more oval than round.

"But they did considerable damage upon penetration, striking bone and organs," Munroe pointed out. "Internal bleeding was extensive. One of the balls nicked his aorta. The injury was min-iscule, really. If the bullet had ripped a hole in the aorta, his lord-ship would have been dead within seconds. But as it was only a tiny tear, his lordship did not succumb to the injury immediately."

The Duke lifted his gaze from the dead man to look at Munroe. "He had no chance? No one could have saved him?"

Kendra knew he was thinking about Madam Patya.

"In my medical opinion? No. I've heard how his lordship rode his horse into a gypsy encampment. I don't know how long he'd been riding, but every moment he was in the saddle, every move-ment he made, put a terrible strain on the aorta, ripping open the gash a little more. Even without that mortal injury, I think he would have succumbed to fever and died. I found bits of fibers from his clothing in his wounds. In my experience, that would have become infected."

Munroe sighed and shook his head. "Lord Craymore's death may not have been instantaneous, but from the moment he was shot, I believe it was inevitable."

14

Harding escorted Sam Kelly into the study five minutes after the Duke and Munroe made use of the hidden passageway to go up to the Duke's laboratory to inspect Craymore's greatcoat under the microscope. The Bow Street Runner was a short, muscular man with a mop of reddish-brown curls, graying sideburns, and features that had an upward tilt, which gave him an almost elfin appearance. A very scruffy elf at the moment, Kendra decided, taking in his dusty coat and boots, and the stubble along his jaw. His eyes were his most distinctive feature, so light brown that they appeared gold. Kendra had witnessed those eyes glimmer with good humor or go as flat and hard as any cop she'd dealt with in the twenty-first century.

His eyes twinkled now as he greeted Kendra and Alec, and brightened even more when Alec poured the Bow Street Runner a glass of the Duke's finest whisky. "Thank you, m'lord," he said, smiling appreciatively as he took the glass. "Me throat is parched from quizzing every tavern owner, innkeeper, blacksmith, stable hand, and local constable from here ter the border of London Town."

Kendra leaned a hip against the Duke's desk as she regarded him. "Did you learn anything?"

"Aye. I learned that folks complain a lot." He grinned at her. "They were quick ter give me their grievances about illegal poachers in the woods or how they'd been wronged by a neighbor. But no one has heard about any highway robberies in the vicinity. In fact, they said it's been peaceable in these parts more'n a decade. No rumors or reports of any hightoby operating near their villages."

"Including Needlham?"

"Aye, and every hamlet between."

"And you believed them?" Kendra asked.

"Why would they lie? Aye, lass, I did. Sometimes you have tavern owners and stable hands that work with the criminal element as lookouts. They would have reason ter lie, for certain. But everyone I spoke ter told me the same tale. It ain't likely that everyone, far and wide, would be keepin' the secret. Besides, someone who was relieved of their purse would have complained about it, and Bow Street would have heard."

Kendra nodded. "I agree with you, Mr. Kelly. And that fits with the theory that we're not dealing with a random robbery. Lord Craymore was targeted specifically."

"Someone knew he'd be on that road at that specific time," Sam guessed shrewdly.

"Yes, but it's more than knowing a wealthy lord is in the vicinity," she said.

"It would seem that Lord Craymore was traveling last evening with a very valuable gemstone—a rare pink diamond with a possibly unusual provenance," said Alec. "The Anahita Pink."

While Alec told the Bow Street Runner about the diamond, Kendra organized the retrieval of the slate board from the castle's schoolroom. She'd used the board for the first time almost a year ago. At that time, she hadn't realized that a slate board couldn't be wiped down with a dry eraser like a chalkboard; it needed a wet cloth. Now the process was as familiar to her as the jagged piece of slate that she held in her hand.

A year ago, she'd had no points of reference in this timeline other than what she'd read in history books. Automatically, she lifted her hand to touch the pendant that she wore beneath her dress. A few months ago, the Duke had had an arrowhead from ancient America (or maybe not so ancient, for this time period) fashioned into a pendant. He'd given it to her as a way of reminding her that something could be taken out of its original time and purpose and still fit in somewhere new. It had been a lovely gesture, even if Kendra felt the Duke was being a little too optimistic about her ability to fit in.

Maybe she would never fit in completely or comfortably, but she was forming relationships and building memories that were anchoring her to this era. *I'm no longer the outsider I was a year ago.*

"God's teeth." Sam let out a low whistle, breaking into Kendra's reverie. He glanced at her. "Do you think it's true—that the bauble was part of Bad King John's lost treasure?"

Kendra heard the wonder in the Bow Street Runner's voice. "It doesn't matter whether it's true or not. It only matters that someone *thought* it to be true."

"Maybe this Mr. Griggs is behind the theft. *He* knew Lord Craymore was comin' ter meet him with the diamond," Sam pointed out.

"We considered the possibility, but if you met Mr. Griggs, you'd understand why we ruled him out," said Kendra.

"It's difficult to envision the man playing highwayman," Alec agreed with a slight smile.

Sam looked skeptical. "A sparkler like that might encourage a few folks ter play highwayman. People get a fever."

Kendra regarded the Bow Street Runner. "Like gold fever?"

"Gold and jewels bring out the worst in men."

"I can't argue with that." Avarice ran deep in humanity. In Kendra's experience, greed ranked as the top motive for most homicides, followed closely by jealousy. Many times, those two sentiments overlapped. "But Lord Craymore was bringing the Anahita Pink to Mr. Griggs so he could verify its authenticity. If I were Mr. Griggs, I'd tell the earl that I needed more time to determine that and then switch it with a paste copy. Craymore wasn't a collector like his father. He probably wouldn't know the difference."

Sam grinned at her. "You have a devious mind, lass. I'm grateful you're on the right side of the law." He took a thoughtful sip of whisky, then said, "Of course, Mr. Griggs would've been takin' a considerable chance. His lordship could have refused ter leave the diamond with him. Most folks would've been leery over letting something that valuable out of their sight. Probably why the earl's father wanted Mr. Griggs ter travel ter him when he first found the sparkler.

"Mr. Griggs could've been cunning enough ter have a copy on hand, ready ter switch when the moment came," added the Bow Street Runner. "He had enough time ter do that after the first earl told him about it."

Kendra shook her head. "Mr. Griggs never saw the Anahita Pink. He couldn't have replicated the diamond with any degree of accuracy."

"There's another possibility," Alec said. He walked to the side table that held silver coffee pots and teapots. He glanced at her as he poured himself a cup of coffee. "We've already discounted the possibility that Mr. Griggs would have hired someone, but it's reasonable to assume that he employs staff. Maybe he mentioned the diamond to one of them."

Sam raised his eyebrows at Alec. "You think one of his servants took it upon themselves ter steal the bauble, killing his lordship during the robbery?"

Kendra jiggled the piece of slate in her hand. "Mr. Griggs barely talked to me. I don't think he's the kind of man who confides in his servants. He would consider them beneath him."

The hidden panel swung open, and the Duke and Dr. Munroe emerged from the stairwell.

"Mr. Kelly," the Duke greeted, his gaze going to the Bow Street Runner. "'Tis good to see you again."

"Your Grace." Sam offered an abbreviated bow in the nobleman's direction. "You have once again come across an interesting case. *Very* interesting."

The Duke smiled. "I was just apprising Dr. Munroe of the Anahita Pink and its historical implication. Of course, we are relying on the word of one man—a man who didn't even see the diamond for himself."

Sam nodded. "Aye. But as Miss Donovan pointed out, someone only needed ter believe that the diamond is the one lost by King John. Folks have killed for a lot less. And as I was tellin' Miss Donovan and his lordship, sparklers are enough of a motivator."

"Without the historical significance, you mean." The Duke went to the sideboard, and splashed cream into a porcelain cup, followed by tea. "That is certainly true. Dr. Munroe, would you fancy a cup of tea? Or something stronger?"

"Tea would be fine. Thank you, sir."

"Black, two sugars?"

Munroe smiled. "Your memory serves you well, sir."

Kendra looked at the doctor. "Did you find anything under the microscope?"

"Minor contamination." Munroe hesitated. "There are many variables, so you understand that I can only offer an estimate?"

"I understand."

He nodded. "All right, then. Based on my findings, I would say that the assailant was approximately five feet away from his lordship when he fired the pistol. Any more than that, we would not have found residue. However, the fact that the contamination was minimal suggests that we are dealing with a certain amount of distance. I'm not sure how that helps you."

"Details are always important, doctor. They help build a picture."

The Duke looked at her as he handed a teacup to Munroe. "And what picture is emerging for you, my dear?"

Kendra had to smile. "Unfortunately, one that is full of holes. But we do have some facts.

"Timeline." She swiveled to the slate board, and began writing. "We know that Lord Craymore left Shay House around quarter to nine. Shandor found—"

"Shay House?" Dr. Munroe interrupted, his tone sharp. "Forgive me, Miss Donovan," he said when she swung around to look at him. "Are you referring to the private asylum operated by Dr. Theodore Shay?"

"Yes. You know it." She saw the recognition in his eyes. "Lord Craymore committed his sister there six months ago. What do you know about the place and Dr. Shay?"

Munroe's dark brows pulled together in a frown as he sat down. He took a slow sip of his tea in such a way that told Kendra he needed time to formulate his answer.

"I don't know much, really," he admitted finally, lowering his cup to its matching saucer. "Dr. Shay has a London practice specializing in maladies suffered by ladies in the upper classes and wives of wealthy merchants. I know he also owns a private madhouse on the outskirts of London."

"We know that much," Kendra said, studying the doctor's face. "When we were at Shay House, it was obvious that something had happened. We were told that they once had fifty inmates, but now they only have twelve. There was a grandeur about the place, but it's now falling apart."

Munroe remained silent.

"Do you know why?" Kendra pressed.

"I seem to recall some sort of scandal involving Shay House several years ago. In truth, I do not know the details, other than I had heard many families removed their daughters from the asylum, and even Dr. Shay's London practice has suffered. He lost clientele, except for older matrons who have been with him since he first put out his shingle."

The Duke asked, "What was the scandal about? Did one of his patients die on his watch?"

"I am not certain. It might be nothing more than a family member becoming disgruntled in how their loved one was progressing with her treatment. Or they may have been upset by how they themselves were treated. In my opinion, when people are dissatisfied, they tend to make their dissatisfaction known."

And this is before Yelp and Twitter, Kendra thought as she moved to pour herself another cup of coffee.

"I have heard talk that Dr. Shay has been doing his best to court the Beau Monde," said Munroe. "If the late Lord Craymore placed his sister in Dr. Shay's facility, then he must be having some success in the matter."

A vision of Lady Evelyn's luxurious bedchamber rose up in Kendra's mind. Was that what had convinced Craymore to have his sister committed to Shay House? She imagined there were far worse conditions in other asylums, where women were locked in cells rather than bedchambers, and slept on cots rather than soft beds. Shay House might be shabby, but there were much grimmer mental institutions out there. Especially in this era.

"I am only slightly acquainted with Dr. Shay." Munroe was frowning into his teacup. "We have attended the same functions. We are both doctors, although I am now less acceptable than Dr. Shay by society..." He smiled wryly as he lifted his gaze to meet Kendra's eyes. "However, despite my chosen profession, I am still allowed into a few clubs and drawing rooms run by intellectuals and science-minded circles."

"Dr. Shay was not at the asylum when we were there, so we didn't meet the man," said the Duke. "Give us your impression of him. Can you tell us of his character?"

Munroe was silent for a long moment, then said, "If I may be permitted to speak frankly, sir?"

"I would hope you will always speak freely in our presence, Dr. Munroe."

"Thank you, sir." Munroe blew out a breath. "If you must know, I found him to be a bit of a tuft hunter."

Kendra choked on the swallow of coffee she'd just taken. "A *what*?"

"Forgive me, Miss Donovan, I sometimes forget that you are an American and are not as familiar with our slang." Munroe smiled at Kendra. "I found Dr. Shay to be a sycophant, courting wealthy aristocrats and cits. He had no interest in pauper lunatics."

"I see." *Another way to say ass-kisser.*

"Mind you, it's not unusual among physicians in London to seek patronage among its wealthier citizens, but in my limited dealings with the man, I found him to be particularly pompous regarding his approach."

Kendra set down her coffee cup. "In other words, he's not as interested in helping those with mental illness as he is in the money he can make off of their psychological problems."

"Precisely. I'm certain he addresses his patients' complaints by dutifully filling their prescriptions of laudanum and tonic water." Munroe's lips twisted in derision. "And Shay House is for families burdened by females of a nervous disposition."

Kendra's mouth tightened. "Don't you mean females with an *independent* disposition? It seems to me that doctors have a lot of latitude in diagnosing women in"—*this century*, she nearly said—"this country."

"I confess that I am not an expert on the emotional maladies suffered by females, but I agree with you, Miss Donovan. There are ladies who need treatment, certainly, but I was not impressed with Dr. Shay in the few discussions that I had with him. He was condescending and…" Munroe paused, seeming to search for the right word. "Unenlightened," he finally said. "I found his opinions about the female sex and treatment methods to be rigid."

Kendra suddenly remembered Crump wanting to take Miss Sybil to the "treatment room," and McBride overruling him. Even the name had an ominous ring to it, she thought.

"However, this is not my area of expertise. I deal with the dead," Munroe went on with a shrug. But his gray eyes remained troubled. "I believe that Dr. Shay follows commonly accepted practices. He is not introducing anything new or unusual to the profession. Perhaps I simply did not like the man."

"I do not doubt your assessment, Dr. Munroe." The Duke offered the man a smile before looking at Kendra. "But what can Dr. Shay or his asylum possibly have to do with Craymore's murder? Whatever scandal happened there years ago cannot possibly have anything to do with the theft of the diamond."

Kendra shook her head. "We don't know what connects or doesn't at this point." She picked up the piece of slate and wandered back to the board with her coffee. She often thought that the investigative process was like panning for gold—long hours of tediously sifting through mountains of dirt before you found something of value.

"Here's what we do know: Craymore left Shay House about a quarter-to-nine to meet with Mr. Griggs at his home near Paddlewick. Their appointment was for nine-thirty. Instead, Shandor found Craymore on his horse near Aldridge Village around that time." She began writing the timeline. "He must have been intercepted by the killer not long after leaving Shay House. The killer got close enough to leave gunpowder residue on the earl's greatcoat."

Kendra stepped back to study the slate board, trying to imagine the scene. "He was shot in the back." The nape of her neck prickled. "This was not a random attack," she whispered, staring at the slate board.

"You made that point," Alec commented. "And we are in agreement. The villain must have known that Lord Craymore had the Anahita Pink on his person last night."

"That should narrow down the field," said Sam.

"This was not a random attack," Kendra repeated firmly. "Lord Craymore knew his killer. That's why he allowed the other rider to approach without taking his pistol out of his pocket, without making any move to protect himself. He didn't feel threatened."

"What if he didn't recognize the other rider, but rather than engage in an ugly confrontation, he tried to escape?" Munroe offered. "The ruffian gave chase and shot him in the back when he was close enough. That fits with the physical evidence, too."

"Yes—except Craymore *did* escape," Kendra replied. "So, where's the diamond? He should still have had it in his pocket, along with his purse and weapon."

Everyone was silent for a beat.

Sam cleared his throat. "I know he was found by a gypsy—"

"The boy did not steal the diamond, nor did any of the Romani," the Duke said sharply.

No one said anything.

The Duke huffed out a breath and said, "Forgive me, Mr. Kelly. I am well aware that the Romani have a certain reputation, but I know this particular clan. They would not have done such a thing. In fact, they did everything they could to save Lord Craymore's life."

Kendra hesitated. "One thing doesn't necessarily have to do with the other," she said, meeting the Duke's eyes. They were more gray than blue, which was a sign of temper. She rarely encountered it with the Duke; she was more used to seeing that steely look in his sister's eyes.

"I tell you I know these people, and they are not thieves."

"The boy, Shandor, said that Craymore briefly regained consciousness and accused him of being a thief," Alec said.

"'No, thief, no,'" Kendra murmured, remembering the words. She moved to the slate board to write them down. "The girl—Kezia—also confirmed that Craymore called Shandor a thief." She tapped the piece of slate against her chin, trying to imagine the scene. "He's out of his head from loss of blood, but the first thing he speaks of is theft. And the diamond *is* missing."

"That suggests that the ruffian managed to relieve Lord Craymore of the diamond before shooting him," said the Duke. "He hands over the diamond and then spurs his horse to a gallop. Unfortunately, he doesn't get far before the villain shoots him in the back."

"Even though he's wounded, Craymore keeps his seat and manages to escape into the woods," Alec added. "The thief has the diamond, so he doesn't bother going after the earl."

"Or he does, but Craymore's mare is faster and he is able to lose the villain in the forest," the Duke put in. "Either scenario works."

Sam scratched the side of his nose, his gaze on the slate board. "Aye, but how'd the fiend know that his lordship would be on the road at that specific time, with the sparkler? There had ter have been a spy involved. Someone in Mr. Grigg's household or Lord Craymore's."

The Duke shook his head. "I don't think it was anyone in Craymore's household. They'd known about its existence since his father came across the gem. They had every opportunity to steal it before last evening. The best time would have been right after Benedict had his seizure, before Reginald returned home."

Kendra frowned. The prickling sensation was growing stronger. She was missing something obvious. *Something, something…*

"Based on what Mr. Griggs said, there are more treasures to steal at the family estate than the diamond," Alec pointed out. "The thief wouldn't need to resort to murder."

"Aye, but their neck gets stretched either way—being found out as a thief or a murderer," said Sam. His gold eyes narrowed. "The fiend would have been cleverer to wait for the earl to return to London. Footpads and cutthroats are thick in town. It was sloppy of him ter try ter make it look like highway robbery, especially in a peaceable stretch of road."

Kendra stared at the Bow Street Runner. She knew what was bothering her now. "It was sloppy," she said slowly. "Lord Craymore was riding away from Shay House but he recognized the other rider. That's why he allowed him to get closer."

The Duke eyed her. "You've already made a compelling argument for that, my dear."

"Yes, but don't you see?" She turned to face him. "He *recognized* his assailant—the unsub never tried to conceal his identity. If the thief was only after the diamond, why let himself be recognized?"

There was a long silence as everyone considered the killer's motives.

"We might not be dealing with a thief who became a killer," Kendra said quietly. "We might be dealing with a killer who became a thief."

15

"Well, that changes things," the Duke said. "Why would anyone want Reginald Lansing dead?"

"*Cui bono?*" Alec murmured. "Who benefits from the poor wretch's death?"

"I can think of one person." Kendra said. "Lady Evelyn."

Sam frowned. "Ain't she locked in the madhouse?"

"Yes, and she cannot leave until a relative has her released," Alec said. "So, she does not really benefit. Her brother's death does not automatically mean her freedom."

"Shay House has lax security. No walls around the grounds, and the patients seem to have a lot of freedom to roam around." Kendra held up her hand to prevent the protests she saw on their faces. "I'm not saying that she actually shot her brother herself. She'd have to gain access to a pistol and a horse. She'd have to sneak out and then back into the asylum. Things are lax at Shay House, but not *that* lax."

She didn't see Lady Evelyn carrying out such a mission. That would require a cool head and careful planning. Lady Evelyn was too… erratic.

The Bow Street Runner gave her an uncertain look. "Well, then…"

"But she does have access to pen and paper. She could have written to Basil Willoughby. He could be her accomplice." It was an old story—star-crossed lovers conspiring to murder someone that they thought was keeping them apart.

The Duke stared at her. "You think Lady Evelyn told Mr. Willoughby to kill her brother?"

"At the moment, I'm not thinking anything specifically. I'm just throwing out possibilities. And Mr. Willoughby is definitely a possibility. He even visited Shay House a few times—unofficially." *I've seen her in the woods cavorting with the devil.* "Their relationship clearly isn't over. She's in a position to know about the diamond. Maybe she even knew her brother would be bringing it to Mr. Griggs that night." Kendra paused. "We need to find out where Willoughby was last night."

"I'll find him," Sam offered. "He's not a peer, so it'll be easy enough for me ter quiz him."

Kendra nodded. She still found it strange that law enforcement couldn't interview the aristocracy during a murder investigation. Or, at least, they couldn't without trouble.

Alec lifted a finger. "There's one other person who benefits from Lord Craymore's death—the new Earl of Craymore."

Since Lady Atwood didn't know who was next in line to inherit the earldom, there was one other person Kendra knew could supply that information easily—Lady St. James. Several months ago, the Duke's sister had introduced her to the matron. Not only was she a very good friend of Lady Atwood's, but she was one of the most notorious gossips in London. In other words, the perfect source.

Kendra could ask Lady Atwood to send a messenger to London for the information, but she preferred talking face-to-face. In her experience, unexpected information could be uncovered during such interviews. Unfortunately, traveling to London was a logistical nightmare. Correction: traveling as a single, upper-class lady in the early nineteenth century was a logistical nightmare. Ironically, it would have been easier if she had been a member of the lower classes. Then she'd be able to jump on a public coach without anyone looking at her sideways.

As it was, it took the rest of the day to hammer out the details. The Duke couldn't go because he was scheduled to meet with Constable Hilliard about Lord Craymore's inquest. Given the victim's decomposing state, he didn't want to postpone that too long. Lady Atwood was in the middle of organizing her upcoming house party, which prevented her from accompanying them. *Thank God.* Kendra had to bite her tongue to stop herself from telling the countess that she hadn't been invited anyway. Then she had to bite it again when Lady Atwood expressed disapproval that Alec would be traveling with her—even though she would be bringing Molly along as her de facto chaperone.

Of course, the main problem was the journey would most likely require an overnight stay.

Even though Kendra could make use of the Duke's Grosvenor Square residence, which was currently manned by a skeleton staff, Lady Atwood was concerned where Alec would stay. He had his own home in Berkeley Square, but his aunt seemed to fear that he would be sneaking over to the Duke's house.

Jesus Christ. Kendra was twenty-seven years old. *What is wrong with these people?*

Alec finally eased his aunt's mind by promising to spend the night at his club—where plenty of people would see him.

The planning was enough to give Kendra a headache. Or maybe that came from all the eye-rolling that she'd been doing. She was half afraid that Lady Atwood would change her mind and join them at the last minute.

Kendra only relaxed when she, Alec, and Molly were in the carriage the next morning, lumbering down the drive. With four horses and clear blue skies, they made excellent time—a little less than four hours. Even after a year here, Kendra was fascinated to see the vibrant green hills give way to city buildings and the ever-persistent yellowish haze hanging over London. Here, beggars huddled in doorways, ignored by the streams of working-class pedestrians and costermongers. Raggedy children darted along the pavement and across streets congested with lone riders, wagons hauling barrels and coal, public stages, private carriages, and hackneys. Kendra also continued to be amazed by the livestock—cows, sheep, goats, chickens, and pigs, as well as countless stray dogs and cats—moving along London's main thoroughfares.

Like any major metropolis in the twenty-first century, there was a vast gulf between the rich and poor sections of the city. The poor areas were marked by crumbling tenements; rotting trash, flowing with mud and sewage; and a stench so strong that Kendra found herself breathing through her mouth, with her gloved hand held to her nose. They all breathed easier when they reached the city's more fashionable enclaves, oases of green parks, leafy trees, and scrubbed buildings. Local residents and merchants hired an army of street urchins to continually sweep the muck off the cobblestones. Unlike the poor neighborhoods, where the citizens stared out at the world with hungry, desperate eyes and hollowed faces, the residents of the wealthier districts walked around in fashionable gowns and exquisitely tailored coats. Even their servants were freshly scrubbed, their uniforms laundered and starched.

Lady St. James lived in one of those wealthier neighborhoods where no one had to hold their nose to walk down the street. While the smoke churning out of the city's one million coal and wood fires did not discriminate between neighborhoods, here was the fragrance of honeysuckle, lilac, and roses from outdoor gardens and small parks around the countess' fashionable, three-story limestone townhouse.

Benjamin parked the carriage along the curb and leapt off his high seat to come around and open the door. Instead of getting out, Alec handed over his card. The general rule of thumb for morning calls was that they were never actually done in the morning. Just one of the many things that made absolutely no sense to Kendra.

The coachman took Alec's card to the door to give to Lady St. James' butler, who would then find out whether the countess would be "at home" to them. The higher a guest's position in society, the more likely a person would receive them. Sucking up wasn't unique to this era, but the Beau Monde had codified it into their rituals in ways that never failed to astound and amuse Kendra.

The entire process took less than five minutes, and Kendra wasn't surprised when Lady St. James agreed to receive them. Even if Alec's title hadn't outranked the countess', Kendra suspected the matron's curiosity would have made it impossible for her to refuse seeing them.

Molly was sent off to the kitchens to wait out their visit while the butler showed Kendra and Alec into the same fussy drawing room that Kendra had been in once before. Egyptian, Roman, Chinese, and Indian influences were all represented. It wasn't so much a melting pot as a cultural clash.

"Good afternoon, my lord, Miss Donovan. This is an unexpected pleasure," Lady St. James greeted them with a smile and a flutter of her feathered fan. She used the fan to indicate the chairs surrounding a small round table draped with a chintz linen tablecloth. "Please, sit down. I've sent for tea and cakes."

Lady St. James was a plump matron with a particular fondness for frilly things. Today, she wore a long lace cap—trimmed with a satin ruffle and decorated with several tiny satin bows—over her graying brown curls. Her gown was a pink-and-white striped cotton muslin with a stiff ivory organza chemisette gathered around her throat. It reminded Kendra of something Queen Elizabeth I would have worn. There were more bows at the cuffs of her puffy sleeves and three tiers of ruffles decorating the hem of her skirt. Kendra thought that the outfit made the countess look like a gooey French pastry.

"My good friend, Lady Atwood, did not come with you?" Lady St. James inquired as she sat down in one of the chairs and fluffed out her skirt.

The question was obviously rhetorical, but Alec shook his head. "My aunt remained at Aldridge Castle. She is busy with preparations for her annual house party. She sends her affection and is looking forward to your visit in a few weeks."

"I am excited to attend the house party." Lady St. James cocked her head to the side as she regarded them with shrewd eyes. "There is a rumor that an announcement is to be made. Is that true, my lord?"

Alec smiled. "I would not dare steal my aunt's thunder. You shall find out when you attend."

The matron laughed, leaning across the small table to rap his knuckles lightly with the feathered fan. "Wise of you, dear boy. Now..." She slid her gaze toward Kendra. "Is this a social call, or something else?"

Kendra didn't see any point in playing coy. "We're hoping you will be able to provide us with some information. Do you know who is next in line to be the Earl of Craymore?"

Lady St. James' face changed, her soft features sharpening like a bloodhound catching scent of its prey. "*Next* in line? Dear heaven, has something happened to the *current* Earl of Craymore?"

Alec replied, "Unfortunately, Lord Craymore was shot the other night. He's dead."

"Dear heavens," breathed Lady St. James, and she unfurled her fan. "Pray tell, what happened?"

Before Kendra or Alec could answer, a young maid came into the room, carrying a silver tea tray. "I shall pour," Lady St. James announced, flicking her fan at the servant to send her away. She looked at her guests. "How do you take your tea?"

Once everyone had teacups in their hands, the matron settled back in her chair. "Now, then. How on earth did Lord Craymore get shot? It couldn't have been a duel; I would have heard. Even though such things are frowned upon, that sort of news would have been around town by the time everyone broke their fast." She picked up her teacup. "It could not have been in London. I would have heard about that, too."

Kendra contemplated her. "No, it happened outside of London."

Lady St. James made a tutting noise. "How dreadful. I'm beginning to believe that poor family must be cursed. Reginald Lansing inherited the title not very long ago, after his father had an apoplectic fit and died. Then there was that nasty bit of business with his sister, Lady Evelyn. And now you say Lord Craymore has been shot to death."

Kendra feigned ignorance. "Lady Evelyn?"

"Yes, Lord Craymore's sister. He was forced to commit her to a private asylum earlier this year."

Kendra kept her tone neutral as she asked, "Why? Is she insane?"

Lady St. James reached for a lemon tart. "Well, I always thought she was an odd creature." She took a bite of the tart, chewed thoughtfully, and swallowed. "Plain as pudding. Not that it hurt her prospects," she said, unwittingly echoing Lady Atwood's assessment. "Or, I should say, it didn't hurt her prospects with suitors who were punting on the River Tick. No one plump in the pockets looked twice at the chit. But it wasn't only Lady Evelyn's lack of looks and charm, you understand. I'm certain Lord Craymore—Benedict, that is—would also have given anyone pause. Marriage is serious business—one has to consider the family one is marrying into."

Kendra wondered if Lady St. James was sending a warning to Alec.

"The Craymore title is an ancient one," Alec said carefully. "I would think anyone would desire an association with the family."

"It's not the title, it was Benedict. The man was mad about moldy old relics and English history. I am as much an admirer of our great country as anyone, but I would never talk somebody's ear off about it! Did you never meet the man, Sutcliffe?"

"I can't say that I ever did, no."

"You were fortunate then. He did not travel to London very often, and when he did it was usually for intellectual pursuits. When his wife Mary was still alive, she managed to persuade him to attend a few social events. I was cornered by him on a few occasions. I nearly expired from boredom!"

Lady St. James leaned forward and said in a conspiratorial tone, "It wasn't only his lack of conversation, you realize. It was well-known that he had collected bits and pieces of antiques from all over the kingdom, filling up Pelsley Hall. Mary once told me that she feared one day she would simply disappear into one of the many piles of stuff that he'd collected, or be crushed to death when they toppled on her. The poor creature! Who could live like that, I ask you?"

Kendra tried not to look around at the overdone drawing room with its fussy bits and pieces.

Lady St. James went on, "I'm telling you, he was a very *odd* creature. Lady Evelyn obviously took after him rather than her mother, more's the pity."

"When did Lady Craymore pass away?" Kendra asked.

"Oh, several years ago. Consumption, poor dear. Maybe it was a blessing that she passed before Lady Evelyn had her season. She would have been positively humiliated to watch her daughter make such a cake out of herself, especially with a wretch like Basil Willoughby. Bad ton," she sniffed. "Do you know that they even attempted to elope to Gretna Green?"

Kendra said, "Maybe they were in love."

Lady St. James stared at her. "What does that have to do with anything, pray tell? Her father was in the grave less than a month. It is simply not done!" Amusement replaced the outrage. "I didn't take you to be a romantic, Miss Donovan."

Kendra didn't reply. She wasn't here to be an advocate for Lady Evelyn's love life. In fact, she suspected that Basil Willoughby was the fortune hunter that everyone purported him to be, and Lady Evelyn had been gullible enough—or desperate enough—to fall for his claims of undying love.

The matron continued, "Thankfully, the earl—Reginald, that is—managed to catch them before any damage was done. Then he sent his sister away."

She made it sound as though Reginald Lansing had sent his sister away to some exotic retreat, not a lunatic asylum.

"One would hope that would be the end of the affair, but I am not so certain," Lady St. James confided. She looked at them expectantly.

Kendra asked dutifully, "What do you mean?"

The glint in Lady St. James' eyes turned sly. "Mr. Willoughby hasn't pursued any other heiress in the last six months. I suspect he believes that his prospects with Lady Evelyn are still in play." She paused, then admitted grudgingly, "Of course, it could simply mean that he's been thwarted in sinking his hooks into anyone else. Still, I think I would have heard about such a thing. And I have not. The Polite World closed their doors to the rascal after news spread of his shocking behavior with Lady Evelyn. The Ton tolerates a lot from our young bucks, but an attempt to seduce our innocent, gently-bred daughters is *not* one of them."

"What about common folk?" Kendra asked before she could stop herself.

"Pardon?"

"Would the Beau Monde condemn young bucks who were seducing the innocent daughters of common folk?"

The countess's eyebrows shot up. Then she laughed. "Miss Donovan, you are really quite amusing."

Kendra didn't know what was so funny about it, but didn't pursue that line of questioning; she was getting off-topic. "So, you think that Mr. Willoughby might be waiting for Lady Evelyn?" she asked instead, thinking, *And sneaking onto the grounds of Shay House to keep Lady Evelyn's interest engaged.*

Lady St. James shrugged, reaching for another tart. "Fortune hunters tend to move on fairly quickly to the next susceptible creature. But, as I said, there's been no talk of Mr. Willoughby pursuing another lady." She looked thoughtful as she nibbled daintily at the cake. "Pity Reginald didn't insist on a commission of lunacy, and instead obtained a certificate. A mistake, I think."

Kendra recalled the Duke mentioning this certificate. She asked, "What's the difference?"

"A commission of lunacy would have allowed him to strip Lady Evelyn of her fortune. 'Tis a more cumbersome process, I grant you, but perhaps worthwhile in this case. Lady Evelyn currently retains her fortune. Mr. Willoughby is aware of this."

Alec said mildly, "A commission of lunacy would also have brought a certain notoriety. I doubt that Craymore would have wanted that for his sister."

"That is true. Still, her fortune keeps the rogue interested."

Kendra watched the woman dust crumbs off her fingers. "Do you think Mr. Willoughby could have killed Lord Craymore to continue his pursuit of Lady Evelyn?"

Lady St. James let out a theatrical gasp, her eyes widening. "Gracious, that is a scandalous thing to say, Miss Donovan!"

Kendra sipped her tea, and waited.

"I am scarcely acquainted with Mr. Willoughby, you understand," the countess finally said. "He certainly was not in *my* social circle."

"You do yourself an injustice, my lady," Alec spoke up, and shot the matron a crooked smile. "You have a remarkably keen eye. Whether or not you were acquainted with the man, I suspect you read his character accurately."

Lady St. James beamed at him, pleased with the compliment. "Thank you, sir. Still, it is shocking to think that an acquaintance—even one as remote as Mr. Willoughby—could resort to murder. I suppose it might depend on how many creditors are knocking at the scapegrace's door. The fear of debtor's prison or the workhouse has pushed some to do the unthinkable."

"An excellent point, my lady." Alec lifted his teacup in a mock salute at her brilliance. "Desperation can certainly push a man to extremes."

Lady St. James held her smile for a moment, then allowed it to collapse into a frown. "Mr. Willoughby may be desperate and a rogue, but murdering Reginald Lansing makes no sense. Lady Evelyn will remain in the madhouse until she receives permission to be released."

"The new Earl of Craymore will be able to release her," Kendra said. "Who stands to inherit?"

The countess pursed her lips in thought. "Reginald wasn't married and has no heir. And his only sibling is—*was*—Lady Evelyn. The title and fortune will naturally pass to the eldest male on his father's side. I seem to recall that Benedict Lansing had two brothers, both dead, one without issue. The other went into the clergy and had five children… Oh, dear." Her hand went to her throat, a horrified expression on her face. "Oh, my goodness."

Kendra frowned. "What's wrong?"

"The Craymore title and entailed fortune will go to Jonah Lansing."

Alec's eyes were on the matron. "Jonah Lansing. Why does that name sound familiar?"

Lady St. James collected herself, compressing her lips into a thin, disapproving line. "I dare say, you have read about him in the broadsheets, my lord. He is a known associate of Henry Hunt." She said the name in dire tones, as if speaking of one of the four horsemen of the apocalypse.

"Ah, yes." Alec nodded, and glanced at Kendra. "Henry Hunt is a great champion of worker's rights and democracy in general."

"Oh, the horror," Kendra muttered.

Lady St. James shot her a reproving look. "England is not America, Miss Donovan. Our system works."

Sure, for you, Kendra wanted to say, but kept quiet.

The matron said, "Mr. Lansing is a subversive. Like Mr. Hunt, he has denounced both the Whigs and the Tories and advocates a new form of government."

"I don't believe Mr. Hunt advocates insurrection, but rather reform," Alec countered.

Lady St. James' sniffed. "I disagree. And for all his advocacy of the hoi polloi, I don't see Mr. Hunt giving up his lands or his wealth—both of which are reputed to be quite extensive—to the common man."

Kendra asked, "What about Jonah Lansing? Does he have lands and wealth?"

"Good heavens, no," she laughed. "I told you, his father was a younger son and went into the clergy. Mr. Lansing operates a printing press here in London, churning out seditious propaganda for the likes of Mr. Hunt and other likeminded radicals."

"You are remarkably well-informed," Alec murmured.

She gave him a sharp look, sensing criticism. "I make it a point of being well-informed on everything, my lord. And I read the papers, too. *The Morning Chronicle* has quoted Mr. Lansing speaking out against the Corn Laws, and has addressed his political ambitions. He wishes to run for the House of Commons. He is quite… oh, dear heaven." Her mouth parted in shock as she looked at Alec.

Kendra frowned in confusion.

"If Jonah Lansing is the new Earl of Craymore, he will become a peer of the realm," Alec told Kendra. "He can no longer be elected to the House of Commons, but he will be able to sit in the House of the Lords."

Lady St. James' nostrils flared. "The man is already a radical. Can you imagine what he will be able to do with the Craymore fortune behind him?"

16

"You do know that Lady St. James is ordering her carriage to be brought around right now so she can make calls all around town," Alec murmured with a sideways glance at Kendra as they walked toward their own waiting carriage. Molly scurried behind them. At their approach, Benjamin unfolded the steps and held open the door.

"Reginald Lansing's death will be on everyone's tongue by nightfall," Alec continued, climbing in.

"Not just his death," Kendra replied. "She seemed genuinely horrified that Jonah Lansing will be the new Earl of Craymore."

"She has a point—I'm not referring to her obvious dismay that a firebrand like Mr. Lansing will become a peer," he added when Kendra raised her eyebrows at him. "I'm speaking of Mr. Lansing being able to further his cause with the Craymore fortune behind him."

Kendra shrugged. "Would that really be so bad?"

Alec gave her a crooked smile. "You're quite the firebrand yourself, Miss Donovan. Well, let's go tell Mr. Lansing about his good fortune."

"Yeah. Unless he already knows."

Kendra always found it fascinating how easy it was to track down people in a city the size of London, inhabited by more than a million souls, without the Internet or, in the olden days of her own era, a telephone book. In these *very* old days, all one needed was a name and the person's profession. To find a proprietor of a printing shop like Jonah Lansing's, you only had to stop by any printing shop. Everyone knew where their competitors were located. Often, they were clustered together like pearls on a necklace.

Those in the printing trade gravitated to Paternoster Row, an ancient cobblestone lane that cut a narrow, winding path between Greyfriars and Blackfriars road. Booksellers sold their products in stalls set up outside their establishments, in the shadow cast by St. Paul's familiar dome. Kendra was surprised at how crowded the street was with traffic and pedestrians.

Jonah Lansing's shop was called Polaris, situated in a narrow building crammed between other narrow buildings, distinguished by a bow window and a door painted a bold crimson.

Alec and Kendra sprinted across the street to avoid an oncoming milk wagon, and pushed open the door to the shop. Warm air rushed over them, along with the strong scent of wood pulp and warm paper, plus hot oil and carbonized soot from the ink. Cubbyholes and shelves lined the walls, overflowing with paper and packed with ink pots and bits and pieces of metal. Most of the space was taken up with an old-fashioned wood and iron printing press. A boy of about nine was cranking the wooden spindle of the press, while a tall man with thinning fair hair and wearing gold-wired spectacles and an ink-splattered apron, pounded two inkballs that resembled oversized mallets against the letterpress' chase.

Another man was in the corner, sifting through a drawer to pick out metallic letters. He glanced over his shoulder when Kendra and Alec came through the door.

"May I help you?" he asked, wiping his ink-stained fingers on his apron as he walked toward them.

"Jonah Lansing?" Alec inquired.

Something that might have been wariness flashed across his face, but the man nodded. Jonah Lansing looked to be about the same age as his dead cousin, with narrow features, light brown hair, and intelligent brown eyes with faint crow's feet, as though he viewed the world through a perpetually narrowed, suspicious gaze.

Kendra introduced herself and Alec. "We are here about your cousin, the Earl of Craymore," she said, watching Jonah closely. There was a faint flicker of his lashes at the mention of his cousin's name, but nothing else.

"My cousin and I are not close."

Although she couldn't explain it, Kendra's first thought was, *This is a man with secrets. And a man who knows how to guard those secrets well.* She asked, "When was the last time you saw him?"

He said nothing for a long moment, simply staring at her as though debating what to say. Finally, he shrugged and said, "I haven't seen my cousin in years. As I said, we aren't close. My family has always been the poor relation to that branch of the family, if you must know." He lifted his hand to indicate the shop in an almost wry gesture. "As you can see with your own eyes. Now, why is that any concern of yours, Miss Donovan… my lord?" He slid a glance at Alec to include him in the inquiry as well.

Kendra kept her eyes on Jonah, but she was aware of the other occupants in the room. She heard the *squeak-squeak-squeak* as the boy turned the spindle, and the dull, rhythmic thumping as the man whacked the goose-skinned mallets soaked in ink against the steel chase. But the steady pounding ceased for just a fraction of a second, like there had been a tiny glitch, before continuing. *Interesting.*

She asked, "How about your other cousin, Lady Evelyn?"

"We're not close, either, if that's what you are asking. Especially since she's in a madhouse."

"You're close enough to know that she's been committed to Shay House."

He snorted. "I expect most of London knows that. It isn't a secret, even if the so-called Polite World likes to pretend that it is." His tone turned sour, and he gave Alec another sidelong look. "The Beau Monde is very good at pretense, isn't it, sir?"

Alec smiled slightly. "It sounds like you do not like the Beau Monde very much."

"I don't like pretense. I don't like it when hardworking folks lose their livelihood and are forced into the workhouse, or are deported or hanged for stealing a potato. My God, do you know how many soldiers have returned from our endless wars to starve or beg in the streets?" His brown eyes blazed and a faint flush rose in his cheeks. "And the Prince Regent spends taxpayer money on such frivolous undertakings as the Royal Pavilion. It's little wonder people want to rise up against our so-called betters."

"Careful," Alec warned with a quelling look. "You are coming perilously close to sedition, Mr. Lansing."

"Somebody needs to speak out." But he moderated his tone slightly. "Speak the truth."

"Is that what you are doing here?" Kendra gestured to the old-fashioned printing press. The other man had stopped his thumping, and now was setting aside the inkballs so he could help the boy remove the damp paper from the machine. She couldn't make out the words, but it looked like a regular flyer for this era: black and white, of course; densely printed; no illustrations. This was a time when attention spans lasted more than ten minutes.

She shifted her eyes back to the radical. "You're speaking the truth?"

"My printing shop is called Polaris for a reason, Miss Donovan. 'Tis the pole star that is used to guide people on their journey. By your accent, you're an American. I would think you of all people would understand what I'm doing."

She didn't want to get caught up in a political discussion or philosophical debate, so she ignored the comment. "Where were you on Wednesday night? Between eight and ten?" she asked.

He turned and walked back to the workbench. "Why?" he asked without turning around.

"Humor me."

He began sifting through the metal letters again. Then he pivoted back to regard her. "I dislike being questioned for no reason. However, I shall tell you. I was here. Alone," he added when she glanced at the boy and man. "Now what is this about?"

Alec asked, "When do you close your shop?"

Irritation thinned Jonah Lansing's mouth, but he replied, "Six. We try to be prudent in using candles and oil lamps. Candles, especially, are expensive for working folk, given the burdensome tax on them."

"And yet you chose to stay here burning candles on Wednesday night?" Kendra said.

"There are a few nights when it's unavoidable," he told her, jaw tight. "I had an order to finish."

"Alone."

"Yes. Now please tell me what this is about or leave. As you can see, we are busy."

Kendra said bluntly, "Lord Craymore was shot Wednesday night. He's dead."

Jonah's face went slack with shock and he staggered back a step. "My God." He ran a hand over his hair, shaking his head. "What happened?"

Kendra wondered if she'd just witnessed a fine bit of theatrics. "We don't know. That's why we're investigating."

"He's at Aldridge Castle for the time being," Alec told him. "There will be an inquest, of course. I assume you will want to know when that will be?"

Jonah blinked. "Of course."

"Afterwards, you will need to make arrangements for his burial. As next in line, it is your duty."

Jonah said nothing.

Kendra asked, "Do you know anyone who might want to kill your cousin? Someone he may have upset or someone who was upset with him? Maybe someone he had an altercation with recently?"

"What? No. No, of course not."

Kendra waited, but he didn't add anything more. Like, *I told you I haven't seen him in years.* Apparently, he'd forgotten his earlier denial. She asked, "Do you know of any reason Lord Craymore may have been killed?"

"You just asked me that. I told you no!"

"No, I asked if you know anyone who might want to kill him. Now I'm asking if there was any reason to kill him?" *Like the Anahita Pink.*

"No. No, I don't."

Kendra studied him carefully. "I guess life is going to become a little awkward for you." She gestured to the printing press. "You've spent a lot of your time attacking the aristocracy. But you are the new Earl of Craymore. You are now part of the very class that you say you despise." She waited a beat, then smiled. "Good day… my lord."

"He seemed genuinely shocked by his cousin's death," Alec said, once they were settled in the carriage across the street.

"Hmm."

"You don't think he was shocked by Craymore's murder?"

"I don't know. He struck me as a pretty contained man, but his reaction was … expressive. And I'm pretty sure that he lied about seeing Lord Craymore recently. When I asked if he knew of anyone that his cousin might have argued with recently, he said—and I quote—'No, of course not.' That's pretty definite for somebody who hasn't seen someone in years."

"He was in shock. He could have simply misspoken."

"Maybe. His alibi still sucks, though. Supposedly working late, all alone, when he just admitted that he usually closes the shop at night to save money on candles."

"Why didn't you ask him about the Anahita Pink?"

"There didn't seem to be any point. If he already lied about seeing his cousin, he would've lied about the Anahita Pink. I'd like Mr. Kelly to have his men canvas the area, see if anyone else was working late on Wednesday. Maybe they remember seeing Mr. Lansing in his shop—or they might remember the opposite. I'd like to dig up a little more information before we interview him again."

Kendra's gaze was on the door of Jonah's shop. They'd left a few minutes ago and she'd asked Benjamin to pull the carriage a little farther down the street, far enough away so as to not attract the attention of anyone leaving the shop but close enough to keep Polaris under observation.

A moment later, the door to the printing shop opened, and Jonah Lansing emerged. He'd discarded his apron, replacing it with a greatcoat. He paused a moment, adjusting his tricorn hat on his head, then strode purposefully down the street, disappearing quickly into the crowds.

Kendra glanced at Alec. "Where would you go if you just received news that you were the new Earl of Craymore?"

Alec smiled. "To find a solicitor, if I didn't already have one. Do you want to follow him?"

"No. I'd rather use this time to talk to his employees." She opened the door. "Let's see what they say when the boss isn't around."

As they reentered, the man was locking letters on the chase. His mouth parted slightly at their entrance and Kendra heard the swift intake of breath.

"Mr. Lansing has left—" he tried.

"I know," Kendra said quickly. "We came to see you. I'm sorry, I didn't catch your name?"

He didn't look like he wanted to give it to her, but politeness forced him to say, "Mr. Stevens. I cannot help you."

"How do you know? I haven't asked any questions yet."

He sighed and simply shook his head.

Kendra turned to the boy, who was watching the exchange with bright-eyed interest. "What's your name?"

The kid's eyes rounded. "Me?"

"Yes."

"Niles, miss. Niles Birch."

"Well, Mr. Birch, could you do me a favor? I saw a sweet shop down the street." She fished out a few coins from her reticule. "Could you run there and get some treats for me?"

The boy glanced uncertainly at Mr. Stevens. The man hesitated, then gave a slight nod. Niles snatched the coins from her palm. "W'ot do ye want, miss?"

"Whatever you think looks good." She waited until the kid bolted out of the shop, then shifted her gaze back to Mr. Stevens. "Now that we're alone, you can speak freely. When you left on Wednesday night, was Mr. Lansing here finishing an order?"

Mr. Stevens nervously moistened his lips. "He was still here when we left."

"But you aren't aware of any orders that needed to be finished?"

"I wasn't aware—that doesn't mean there weren't any."

Kendra let that go. "What do you know about Mr. Lansing's relationship with his cousin?"

"Why do you think I know anything? I am Mr. Lansing's printing apprentice. We are not friends. He does not confide in me."

Kendra kept her gaze level on his. "Mr. Stevens, it would be in your best interest to tell me the truth."

"I'd dislike having to involve Bow Street in this, but that can be arranged," Alec added in a hard voice.

Mr. Stevens' paled. "But… but I haven't done anything!"

"Then tell us about Mr. Lansing and Lord Craymore," Kendra urged. "You know something. Tell us before the boy returns."

Mr. Stevens' eyes flicked to the door, then back at them. The internal war he was waging was reflected on his face: loyalty to his employer against fear of Bow Street. Fear won out.

"He—Mr. Lansing—wasn't being entirely truthful when he told you that he hadn't seen Lord Craymore in years," he finally said quietly. "Last week, Lord Craymore came into the shop to speak to Mr. Lansing."

Kendra exchanged a glance with Alec before asking, "What did they talk about?"

"I don't know. I truly don't! Lord Craymore was upset when he arrived, and told Mr. Lansing that he'd received his note. But Mr. Lansing took his lordship into his office to speak more privately." He indicated a door on the other side of the room, and chewed on his lower lip.

"You heard them, didn't you?" Kendra pressed.

"Their voices were muffled mostly. But they began to argue. I heard Mr. Lansing mention the Prince Regent's name—well, he said Prinny. And he mentioned a Lady Evelyn. He said that name quite clearly. Lord Craymore shouted that his sister was not well, and Mr. Lansing had best leave her alone."

"How did Mr. Lansing respond?"

Stevens frowned. "He… he called his lordship a dandy."

"A dandy?" Alec raised an eyebrow, surprised. "I've never heard that Reginald Lansing was part of the fashionable exquisites. If anything, he was a Corinthian—a member of the horse set," he added for Kendra's benefit.

Stevens said, "Mr. Lansing called his lordship a pink. Pinks and tulips are dandies."

"Pink?" Kendra exchanged another quick look with Alec. "You're certain he said that word—*pink*?"

Stevens' frown deepened. "Yes. I recall that specifically, because it was so unexpected that Mr. Lansing would resort to that type of insult. It seemed rather… petty. Not like him at all."

"Did you hear anything else?"

"Well, I also heard the word radical. That was from his lordship. It wouldn't be the first time Mr. Lansing was called such a thing, though." His eyes darted back and forth between Alec and Kendra, his expression worried. "I'm telling you everything. You won't involve Bow Street, will you?"

"I don't think that will be necessary." Kendra smiled at the apprentice. "Thank you, Mr. Stevens. I appreciate your help." She turned to leave.

"Niles will be returning shortly," the apprentice called out as Alec opened the door. "What about your sweets, miss? And your change?"

"Keep them—my treat."

As they stepped out onto the street, Alec said in a low voice, "Reginald Lansing did not have a reputation for being a popinjay."

"I think we know what 'pink' was referring to," Kendra replied, her gaze on a costermonger pushing his cart down the pavement, shouting that his salted eels were only six pence. "Our brains are designed to fill in missing pieces and gaps all the time. It's why we can still read sentences when there are missing letters or they're all jumbled up. Unfortunately, it also makes our memories faulty, because we unknowingly make up things to fill the holes. If Mr.

Stevens heard Lansing say the word *pink*, his brain would have associated it with its most common reference."

"It would seem that the new Earl of Craymore will fit quite comfortably into the society that he says he loathes," Alec remarked, as they dodged a hackney to cross the street. "Jonah Lansing appears to be quite good at pretense, too."

17

I t took Sam most of the day, but he finally found Basil Willoughby at one of Piccadilly's silver hells, where the play wasn't too deep and there was plenty of ale—served by buxom wenches who were not averse to other forms of entertainment, if they were rewarded with an extra shilling. Unlike the city's more exclusive gentleman's clubs, here the clientele was a mixture of classes. Nobles bored with their private establishments and excited to mingle with a rougher crowd. Tradesmen who found themselves plump in their pockets, and keen on sitting next to a lord with whom they normally would never have had the chance of associating.

And then there were the men who were not so easily defined. A few who looked like Johnny raws, fresh from the country and ripe for the plucking, and others who looked like they might be the ones who'd do the plucking. Sam kept his eye on the more nefarious types as he wound his way through the room. Smoke as thick as fog rolling off the Thames hung over crowded green baize tables that offered games of cards and dice. Basil Willoughby was one of the players throwing dice in the ancient game of hazard.

Sam sidled up to the table just as the throng clapped and cheered. Willoughby had just won. Sam cut his gaze to Willoughby himself. He was an extraordinarily handsome man with tousled golden curls. Sam thought he resembled the baby angels painted on the ceilings of churches.

Willoughby celebrated his win by turning to a pretty lass standing next to him. She held a drink in one hand, a lit cheroot in the other. Willoughby snatched the glass and tossed back its contents in one swallow, then looped his arm around the wench's waist and yanked her to him for a deep, carnal kiss.

"You bring me luck, sweet," he murmured with a wicked smile as he lifted his head.

The girl giggled. Sam couldn't tell whether it was feigned or genuine. Most soiled doves could be on stage, with their superior acting abilities.

"Mr. Willoughby?" Sam took a step toward the rogue.

Willoughby plucked the cheroot from the wench's fingers and took a drag as he glanced at Sam. His eyes, a vivid blue like a summer sky, flicked over Sam, dismissing him as a nonentity, and he blew out a thin stream of silvery smoke, his hand continuing to rove intimately over the lass's hills and valleys. Sam had to resist the temptation to pull out the gold-tipped baton that identified him as a Bow Street Runner. While he wouldn't mind shoving it under Willoughby's long nose, he didn't necessarily want to draw attention from anyone else in the hell. Men from Bow Street, unless they were gambling, would not be welcome here.

"Sam Kelly," he introduced himself. "If I may have a word? Privately."

"What's this about?"

"Lady Evelyn."

Willoughby stared at him for a moment. Then his hand fell away from the wench. "Very well," he said. Under the sharp and none too happy eyes of the hazard operator, he collected his winnings, stuffing them in his pockets before he spun around and walked past Sam.

Sam set his teeth as he followed the blackguard through the gaming room into another chamber that had been set up for refreshments (and other pleasures). Only a few candelabras lit the room, leaving many of the paneled booths draped in shadows. Dark, but not dark enough to conceal the couples inside writhing and groping.

Sam ignored them, and the sounds that they were making, as he followed Willoughby to an empty booth. The man slid onto a hard, wooden bench. After a moment's hesitation, Sam followed suit. Across the table, the tip of Willoughby's cheroot glowed orange-red, like a demon eye peering at Sam in the gloom.

"What about Lady Evelyn?" Willoughby asked, cocking his head to the side as he blew out another stream of smoke.

"When did you last see her?"

"At a soiree. Lady Linley's, I believe. Or mayhap it was Lady Margarite." He shrugged lazily. "It was more than six months ago. I scarcely remember."

Sam gave the other man a long, appraising look. "What if I told you there are witnesses who saw you with Lady Evelyn on the grounds of Shay House?"

Willoughby smiled slowly, unrepentant. "Then I must confess that they are correct. You must forgive me for attempting to protect the lady's honor."

The man was quick, Sam would give him that.

A serving wench sidled up to their table. "Do ye want anythin' ter drink?"

"A hot whisky," Sam told her, and waited for Willoughby to add his order and the maid to leave. "Mayhap you ought ter have thought of the lady's honor when you tried ter run off with her.

Gossip says that her brother stopped you. Must've peeved you ter have your plans interrupted."

"You really shouldn't listen to gossip, Mr. Kelly," Willoughby drawled, leaning forward to stub out his cheroot on the table, and toss the remains on the floor.

"Are you saying it ain't true?"

"Why are you inquiring? Who are you, Mr. Kelly?"

"Bow Street."

Willoughby arched his brows. "When did the romantic lives of ladies become the business of Bow Street?"

Sam said nothing.

"Tender emotions make fools of us all," Willoughby went on with a shrug. "Lady Evelyn and I were caught up in the moment."

Sam smiled sourly. "Caught up in the moment all the way to Gretna Green?"

He laughed. "Obviously we didn't make it to Gretna Green."

Sam scowled, not liking the sensation that the bastard was playing with him. "Where were you Wednesday evening?" he demanded abruptly.

"Again, I have to wonder what business it is for Bow Street where I was on Wednesday?"

"Wednesday evening—after eight p.m. It would be helpful."

Willoughby's eyes narrowed, but he lifted a shoulder in a shrug. "I was doing what I am doing now. Gaming."

"Where? With who?"

"Nowhere in particular. With no one in particular." Willoughby paused when the barmaid returned with their drinks.

Sam fished out a few coins. After the maid was gone, he picked up his glass and said, "I was wrong. That ain't helpful, Mr. Willoughby."

Willoughby laughed.

"His lordship was shot and killed on Wednesday evenin'," Sam stated, and watched the other man's face change.

"Are you joking?"

"Why would I joke about something like that?" Sam took a swallow of his hot whisky, keeping his eyes fixed on the other man. "Lady Evelyn didn't write ter tell you?"

"No. Or if she did, I have not received her letter yet," Willoughby said slowly, lowering his eyes. "Wednesday evening, you say?"

Sam couldn't quite decipher Willoughby's expression, but the conversation felt cagey. "Aye. That's why it would be helpful if you had an alibi."

Willoughby's eyes snapped up to lock on Sam. "Are you suggesting that I killed the man? That's absurd! I told you that I was here in London!"

Sam cocked his head as he regarded the rake. "How do you know Lord Craymore wasn't killed here in London?"

Willoughby froze and seemed genuinely at a loss for words.

"You could have easily slipped out of one of these gaming hells ter kill him with nobody being the wiser," Sam said softly.

"I am no longer amused by your insinuations, Mr. Kelly." Willoughby jerked forward, his chin jutting up in an aggressive manner. "I am a gentleman—not some rum cove, the likes of which are more in line with the company you keep, Mr. Kelly. You would do well to remember that and mind your tongue!"

"You have a temper, Mr. Willoughby," Sam observed mildly.

"I don't have to listen to this."

"Have you heard of the Anahita Pink?" Sam asked before the other man could fling himself from the booth.

"What?" Willoughby looked startled. "No."

Sam didn't believe him. "Are you certain you've never heard of it?" He stared hard at the rogue. "Lady Evelyn never mentioned it ter you?"

"No. Why? Does it have to do with Craymore's murder?"

Sam sipped his whisky in reply.

Willoughby's mouth thinned. "I'm finished with your games, Mr. Kelly. You'll catch cold with that if you think I killed Craymore. Do I need to point out that his death would serve no purpose? The lady in question is locked up in Shay House and shall remain there until a relative has her released."

"Aye, but it seems ter me that if Lord Craymore was out of the way, maybe Lady Evelyn's next of kin might be more sympathetic ter her plight." Sam paused deliberately, then added, "Maybe a gambler would play those odds."

Willoughby shoved himself to his feet. "This grows tiresome. I shall not sit here and allow you to imply that I am a murderer."

"I wonder what Lady Evelyn would think about your activities here?"

Surprisingly, Willoughby laughed. "Ladies understand that a gentleman requires… variety. It is in our nature. Not that Lady Evelyn would believe it if anyone attempted to slander my character. She is quite enamored with me."

"You say that Lady Evelyn never mentioned the Anahita Pink ter you," Sam said, changing tracks, "and yet you never once asked me what *it* was. Aren't you curious?"

Willoughby hesitated, then shrugged. "I can hazard a guess. I'm not a flat. It sounds like the French Blue."

"You know your diamonds."

"I know all manner of things—except who killed Lord Craymore." Willoughby shot him a taunting smile. "You will have to find that out all on your own. I wish you luck."

Cheeky bastard, Sam thought, aware that the other man hadn't specified what kind of luck—good or bad—that he was wishing for him. He picked up his whisky glass and watched the man walk out of the room.

Taking a slow sip, Sam replayed the conversation in his head. He didn't know if Willoughby was a murderer, but he knew he was a liar.

18

By the time, Benjamin steered the carriage into London's busy Mayfair district, ominous gray clouds had scuttled in from the north, resulting in an early twilight and a sudden downpour. Well-dressed pedestrians cried out and sprinted for cover in the many elegant limestone retail shops that lined the street. Street sweepers huddled with their brooms under trees or ran for livery stables.

"It's just as well that we aren't returning to Aldridge Castle tonight," Alec murmured as the rain pinged needle-sharp against the carriage roof and cobblestone streets. "We would no doubt be stranded at some country inn. This is better."

Kendra remembered the dust and mouse droppings under Lord Craymore's bed at the King's Arms in Needlham, and silently agreed with Alec. The Duke's London residence might only be staffed by a few servants, but they'd been hired and trained by Harding and Mrs. Danbury. No one had higher standards.

Twenty minutes later, they arrived at Number 29 Grosvenor Square, and she discovered that her faith in the butler and the housekeeper hadn't been misplaced. The Duke had sent a messenger to alert the staff that they'd be coming. As a result, rooms had been opened, dust cloths removed, and even the furniture polished. The scent of lemon, beeswax, and linseed oil wafted through the air, along with the tantalizing smell of roast beef coming from the kitchens. With darkness falling even earlier because of the storm, wall sconces and candles had been lit and fires crackled in the hearths of the main drawing room and dining room.

"We've put fresh linens on the beds," said a maid, who introduced herself as Ellen. She followed Kendra and Alec into the drawing room, where Kendra gravitated to the fireplace, holding out her gloved hands to absorb the heat from the leaping flames.

"I shan't be staying overnight," Alec told the maid when he caught her speculative glance. "I'll be staying at my club."

For some reason, Ellen blushed. "Very good, sir. If I may take your coats?" She stepped forward and waited for Alec and Kendra to remove their coats, hats, and gloves. "Do you have a trunk, miss?"

Molly held up one of the leather bags she was carrying. "Oi'll bring it ter Miss Donovan's bedchamber meself," she said with a proprietorial air.

As Molly trotted off with the bag, Ellen looked at Alec. "We've put on the tea kettle. Shall I bring in a tray, sir? 'Tis miserable outside, and you may wish for something to warm you up."

"We do, but I am thinking something stronger—a hot buttered rum." Alec raised an eyebrow at Kendra. "Miss Donovan, is that acceptable to you?"

Kendra listened to the rain thrumming against the windowpane. A hot buttered rum and relaxing by the fire sounded perfect. "Yes, thanks."

Ellen nodded and smiled. "I shall bring it in immediately. Mrs. Burkes has a joint of beef in the oven. We weren't given a menu. If you wish for something else—"

"No, that will be fine," Alec said.

The moment was disrupted by a pounding on the front door. They all moved to the drawing room's doorway just as one of the liveried footmen sprinted across the entrance hall's pink-and-gray marble floor. When he caught their eyes on him, he slowed to a more dignified walk, opening the front door to find a young boy standing on the steps, soaked to the skin.

The footman frowned repressively. "W'ot are you doin' knocking at the front door, boy? Go around ter the servant's entrance at the back!"

"Got a message for t-the gov'ner that l-lives 'ere." The child's teeth chattered from wet and cold.

"The gov—er, His Grace is not in residence."

The boy wiped his running nose with the back of his hand. "A-are ye c-certain? The doc thought 'e'd be 'ere."

"I would know—"

"Wait." Kendra strode forward. "Do you mean Dr. Munroe?"

"A-aye. That's t-the one."

Alec joined her at the door, holding out his hand. "I'll take the note."

The boy dug out a wet scrap of paper from his pocket and Alec scanned the message.

"Dr. Munroe is at the Maiden Queen. He says he has information on Dr. Shay," he told Kendra, then fished out a coin from his pocket, handing it to the boy. He glanced at the footman. "Take him to the kitchens. Get the boy some linens to dry himself and a plate of hot food."

The footman's mouth parted in shock. So did the child's. "Are ye certain, my lord?"

"Quite certain. And have the carriage brought around." Alec glanced at Kendra. "It looks like we'll be having our evening meal elsewhere."

The Maiden Queen was ablaze with warm, buttery light from the many wall sconces and lamps, and a cheery fire burning in the hearth of a smoke-streaked redbrick fireplace. The tavern was bustling. Serving maids scurried about the room, delivering trays of food and drink and cleaning up after departing customers. The patrons were mostly men, although there were a few older matrons, most likely married to their dinner companions. Most had probably come in to get out of the rain rather than sample the food, but had stayed for both.

The rain hadn't let up, pounding on the roof and mullioned-paned windows like thundering hooves. The windows were cloudy with steam from the heat rising inside the pub. The scent of roasting meats, garlic, and onions made Kendra's mouth water as they crossed the room.

She was also aware that more than one gentleman in the Maiden Queen turned to track their progress. Besides the maids working there, she and Molly were the youngest females in the tavern. No doubt the reason for their intense scrutiny, but it still made the back of Kendra's neck itch.

Munroe had secured a corner table, near the fire. He wasn't alone—Sam sat in one of the stout chairs, as well. They both pushed themselves to their feet as Alec helped Kendra off with her pelisse, draping it over an empty chair.

"I wasn't certain you would come. I was hoping the rain would have stopped by now," the doctor confessed as they sat down.

"We've only just ordered." He signaled one of the serving maids over. "I would recommend the boiled fowl with oyster sauce. It is a specialty here and quite excellent."

Alec took the doctor up on his recommendation, and requested a bottle of burgundy wine to accompany it. Molly settled for pigeon pie, while Kendra ordered a beef-steak.

"Mr. Kelly, I didn't know that you'd be here," Kendra said. She set down her reticule, and then took off her damp bonnet and tugged off her gloves. "Did you locate Basil Willoughby?"

"Aye, lass. The man's a babe o' grace, ter be sure."

Kendra lifted her eyebrows. "And that means...?"

Sam grinned. "He looks like one of those baby angels you see flying on ceilings of churches. But if he ever sets foot in a church, folks better be prepared for a few lightnin' bolts."

Kendra laughed. "You obviously didn't like the man."

"I certainly understand now why Lord Craymore feared for his sister. I managed ter locate Mr. Willoughby in one of the silver hells, playing hazard." He paused when the drinks arrived, continuing after a beat, "He was being free with his favors with one of the bits o' muslin who worked there. Said Lady Evelyn would understand, 'cause gentlemen need 'variety.'"

"Somehow I don't think Lady Evelyn would agree," Kendra murmured, watching Alec pour her a glass of wine. "Maybe Lord Craymore actually saved Willoughby by having his sister committed."

Munroe gave her a quizzical look. "How so, Miss Donovan?"

The image of Lady Evelyn viciously slapping Miss Sybil came to mind, but all she said was, "Just a feeling. Lady Evelyn is not a meek or forgiving woman. What exactly is a silver hell?"

"A gaming establishment where the wagers aren't too steep," Alec told her, handing her the glass of wine.

Sam told them, "Willoughby first said that he ain't heard from Lady Evelyn since her brother put her in Shay House."

"He's lying, if Mr. McBride is to be believed—and I have no reason to doubt his credibility," Kendra said.

"Aye. When I mentioned that he'd been seen at Shay House, he changed his story, smooth as you please. Said that he'd lied ter protect Lady Evelyn's honor. Like he knows anything about honor." Sam gave a snort. "And that's not all. He said that he didn't kill the earl because he was in London, gaming."

Kendra looked at the Bow Street Runner. "In London? He said that?"

Sam nodded. "He pretended that he didn't know anythin' about his lordship's death. So how did he know Lord Craymore hadn't cocked up his toes in London? When I quizzed him about it, he got angry, said he's a gentleman and I would catch cold at questioning one of me betters."

Alec sipped his wine. "So, he didn't explain himself?"

"Nay. But he did make a point of saying that he wouldn't benefit from Lord Craymore's death, as Lady Evelyn is in a madhouse and not free ter marry."

"He's correct about that," Alec acknowledged.

"Aye. But he would benefit if he stole the Anahita Pink, wouldn't he?" Sam's gold eyes glinted in the tavern's mottled light. "I asked him about it, and he claimed not ter know what it was. He never asked me what it was neither, but when I challenged him, he said the name spoke for itself and he assumed it was like the French Blue."

The French Blue, Kendra knew, would one day become more widely known as the Hope Diamond.

"'Tis a reasonable assumption, I suppose," Alec commented.

The serving maid approached, balancing a large tray with one hand and unloading the cloth-covered plates and cutlery with the other. Kendra removed the linen square which had the dual purpose of keeping the meal warm and being used as a napkin during the meal.

"But you don't believe him?" Kendra guessed, once the maid departed.

Sam frowned. "He ain't the truthful sort. Whether he's lying about all this… I don't know. But I'm not inclined ter believe the rogue. He didn't have an alibi, other than ter say he was gaming in London. No specific place. No witnesses." He paused to stab a boiled potato with his fork. "I think it might be worth me while ter see if anyone in Needlham may have seen someone matching Mr. Willoughby's description around the area on Wednesday evenin'."

"Good idea." Kendra cut into her steak. "Jonah Lansing's alibi is also weak. He said that he was in his printing shop working—alone—on Wednesday evening. We need to find out if anyone else on Paternoster Row will verify his account—or not."

Sam raised his eyebrows. "Jonah Lansing. He's next in line for the earldom?"

"I've heard of him," Munroe said slowly. "I believe he's a radical, printing pamphlets in the same vein as William Cobbett's, railing against government tyranny."

"Didn't Cobbett go ter prison for printing subversive leaflets?" Sam asked.

"Yes," Alec replied. "Mr. Lansing owns a printing shop here in London and is a radical, but he has not been sent to prison to my knowledge." He sliced into his fowl, releasing a puff of steam. "He has political ambitions like Cobbett, though. House of Commons. That, of course, is impossible now."

The Bow Street Runner let out a low whistle. "It'll be interestin' ter see what he does in the House of Lords." He picked up his whisky, eyeing Kendra over its rim. "You think he killed his cousin ter better himself?"

"I think anyone can kill with the right motivation. A mother protecting her child. A man defending himself. A person fueling their ambition…"

"For a priceless diamond," Alec added softly.

"Did Mr. Lansing know about the sparkler?" Sam asked.

"He claims that he wasn't close to his cousin, but his apprentice told us that Lord Craymore was in the shop last week and he and Lansing argued," Kendra said. "The timing is interesting. Why lie?"

"They may have seen each other, but the argument seems to suggest that they weren't close," Munroe pointed out.

Kendra shook her head. "Lansing also said that he hadn't seen his cousin in years. Plus, one of the words that his apprentice overhead in their conversation was *pink*. I think it's likely that the diamond came up during their argument."

Each member of the group focused on eating their meal as they pondered that information. Wind and rain rattled the windowpanes, adding background noise to the low murmur of conversation and sharp clink of cutlery around them. Kendra wondered if anyone else in the tavern was having a conversation about murder and ancient jewels.

Sam eventually broke the silence. "How do you think Jonah Lansing found out about the sparkler? If he and his lordship weren't close?"

Kendra said, "Good question. I'm not sure. Benedict Lansing actually discovered the gem. Maybe he mentioned it to his nephew."

Alec frowned, taking a long sip of his wine. "The Anahita Pink is valuable, but so is the Craymore fortune," he finally said. "If Jonah Lansing was motivated by greed, why not kill his cousin months ago, when he first came into the title?"

"Maybe he realized that he would become a suspect," Kendra said. "He obviously benefits from his cousin's death."

"He could have killed his cousin—or hired someone to do it—before Benedict Lansing died," Alec argued. "Unless his uncle married and got another heir, Jonah Lansing was always next in line."

Kendra considered that. "Maybe we're dealing with a recent trigger then. We need to find out more about Jonah Lansing.

Who he is, what he's capable of..." She tapped the side of her wine glass as an idea came to her. "I think I know who could help us with that." She glanced at Sam and added, "Someone who has a curious mind, who is well-informed in politics."

Sam frowned. "Who?"

"Phineas Muldoon."

She wasn't surprised when Sam's puzzled frown turned into a scowl. Phineas Muldoon was a reporter for *The Morning Chronicle*, and he had a cantankerous relationship with the Bow Street Runner. In a way, their relationship was remarkably similar to the uneasy line that existed between law enforcement and the press in the twenty-first century. Except in the last month or so, she'd begun to suspect that something else was going on besides professional disagreements. Sam was a dedicated cop—even if the word *cop* wasn't in this era's lexicon—but he was also a product of this time, comfortable in his own way with society's status quo. Muldoon, on the other hand, tended to push boundaries. Maybe that was why Kendra liked him.

She said mildly, "He covers Parliament; he knows all the players. If anyone knows about Jonah Lansing's character, it would be Mr. Muldoon."

"Aye. I can't argue with you there, lass, but he won't leave it at that. Mark me words, he'll want ter stick his long nose into this whole business."

"We can bring him in—with the same deal as before. Whatever we say is off the record."

Sam looked like he wanted to argue, but retreated behind his whisky instead.

"There's another angle to pursue as well," Kendra said, but hesitated, because she knew her next suggestion would be even more poorly received than talking to Muldoon. "The Anahita Pink was stolen. Whoever now has it will need to fence it. They won't be able to go to any legitimate jeweler or pawn broker."

Sam nodded. "Aye, if the fiend has made inquiries here in London, there's bound ter be whispers in the flash houses and rookeries. I'll send some of me lads ter make inquiries."

Kendra twisted her glass of wine, feeling more nervous than she cared to admit. "That would be good, but I think there's a quicker way to get answers." She moistened her suddenly dry lips. "Bear might know."

Bear—aka Guy Ackerman—was one of London's most notorious crime lords. Once, he and Kendra had both threatened bodily harm to each other, but their association—if you could even call it that—had shifted into something else. The closest thing that Kendra could compare it to was the relationships she'd previously developed with criminal informants.

"The man is dangerous!" Alec exclaimed.

Kendra met his eyes. "Yes, to those who pose a threat. I don't."

"You cannot know what's in the bloody criminal's mind."

Sam cleared his throat, looking uncomfortable. "Ah, lass, unless you have something specific ter say ter the ruffian, I can speak ter him."

She could feel irritation heating her blood. Who were these men to tell her who she could and could not speak to? She wanted to argue with the Bow Street Runner—but she could also acknowledge that Sam was right. She didn't need to be the one who talked to Bear. But she hated, *absolutely hated*, giving in to what sounded a lot like an order.

Kendra drew in a breath, counted to ten, then let it out. "Thank you, Mr. Kelly," she finally said, then shifted her gaze to Dr. Munroe. "What did you learn about Shay House?"

Munroe took a moment to sip his drink, but Kendra saw the troubled light in his gray eyes.

"This is a very sensitive matter, you understand," he said carefully, setting down his glass. "I would not want to contribute to the gossip, for all parties concerned."

Kendra raised her eyebrows. "This is a murder investigation, Dr. Munroe. We're hardly going to gossip about whatever you found."

"I realize that, and I meant no insult. However… you will understand once I explain," he said. "Four years ago, the father of a young lady removed her from Shay House. He accused Dr. Shay of being a charlatan, of mistreatment, and threatened to take him to court. That threat never materialized, with good reason. You see, another rumor surfaced." He paused again, choosing his next words with care. "There were whispers that the young lady was with child."

There was a shocked silence.

"Gor," Molly whispered, wide-eyed.

Kendra felt a chill. "Are you saying that Dr. Shay molested a patient?"

"No. Not Dr. Shay," Munroe said. "An attendant. Of course, Dr. Shay dismissed the man without references, but the damage had already been done."

"What about formal charges?" But Kendra had been in this time period long enough to know what the answer would be.

"No family would want it to become known that their daughter's virtue had been compromised."

Sam asked, "How'd they prevent it with the babe?"

"The girl was married off quickly. Her husband claimed the child as his own."

"Why would he be cuckhold like that?"

Alec seemed to understand. "Who is the father of the young lady?"

Munroe hesitated, then said, "Mr. Pierce Osmond."

"The financier?"

"Yes. He is also active in the spice trade. I believe his new son-in-law is in the spice trade as well." Munroe spread his hands. "With the marriage, all parties are satisfied."

Kendra's fingers clenched around her wineglass. *It's so easy for them to gloss it over.* What about the girl? First, her family committed her to Shay House, then, after being sexually assaulted, she was forced into a marriage to cover up the rape. Where was *her* voice in any of this?

"So, the attendant is allowed to go on and molest other women?" she said, unable to keep the emotion from her voice. "Where's the justice in that?"

Munroe shook his head. "The attendant claimed he was innocent, but he later killed himself. Most likely from guilt. So mayhap there was some justice."

"What can this old scandal have ter do with Lord Craymore's murder?" Sam broke in. "Miss Osmond's misfortune happened long before Lord Craymore put his sister in the madhouse."

He was right. The only commonality between the two incidents was Shay House. But two deaths that were connected to one place left Kendra with a hum of disquiet.

"Mr. Osmond was vocal in his displeasure with Shay House, without being specific," Munroe shared. "Whether or not people guessed the truth, they began to remove their female relatives from the place. I've been told that Dr. Shay has been quite desperate to redeem his and the facility's reputation ever since. It's not just his loss of status, you understand. There is the money involved."

"Considering the derelict state of Shay House, it doesn't appear as though he's been successful at redemption," Alec observed.

"I'm not so certain about that, my lord," said Munroe. "From what I heard, Dr. Shay increased his standing with the Polite World considerably when Lord Craymore chose his institution for his sister. He's the first peer of the realm to do so since the scandal."

"Havin' his lordship shot dead after leavin' Shay House ain't gonna be good for business," Sam put in sardonically. He took a moment to finish his whisky, then set the glass down with a thunk. "But I reckon, if Dr. Shay managed ter get his hands on the Anahita Pink, he wouldn't have ter worry about his creditors for long."

19

Later that evening, Kendra stood in front of her bedchamber's window in Grosvenor Square, gazing out into the rainy night. She was dressed in her filmy nightdress, giving her a ghostly reflection in the windowpanes. Behind her, the room flickered warmly from the brace of candles and the fire in the hearth. The park across the street was pitch black. Grosvenor Square was one of the few enclaves in London that eschewed the new gas lighting craze, preferring the meager light given out by the oil lamps that each household was, by law, required to have on their front steps.

She turned when the door opened and watched Alec slip into the room.

"Were you waiting for me?" He smiled at her, tossing his wet beaver hat and gloves on a nearby chair.

"It would seem so." She crossed the room to him, helping him take off his greatcoat.

He sat down to remove his boots, eyeing her as she shook the moisture from the greatcoat before draping it over the same chair that he'd thrown his hat and gloves. "Hopefully, you weren't thinking about me—you are frowning."

"We need to talk." She almost smiled at the wariness that flashed across his face. Apparently, *we need to talk* had the same ominous ring here as it did in her time.

"About?" Alec asked.

"Bear."

He said nothing as he shrugged out of his tailcoat.

"If I want to talk to the man, I will talk to him. This isn't a social engagement, Alec. This is a murder investigation."

He jerked at the knot in his cravat, irritation in the gesture. "God forbid I dislike the idea of my fiancée consorting with a bloody criminal."

"Why? Because it would embarrass you?"

"Don't be a fool. Have you forgotten what he threatened to do to you?"

Kendra sighed. "We've already had this argument. You know that I've been alone with him several times, and he hasn't harmed me. In fact, he even tried to rescue me a couple of months ago."

"And that's supposed to make me feel better? The villain is too interested in you!"

Kendra decided to ignore that, mostly because there was a tiny bit of truth in the statement. She moved forward, brushing his hands aside to undo the buttons of his shirt. She locked her eyes on his. "Alec, you need to trust me. Trust me to handle myself. This isn't going to work otherwise."

A muscle jumped in his jaw. "You cannot ask me not to worry about you."

She glided her hands past his open shirt to rest against chest. She could feel his heartbeat against her palm. "I don't need a protector. I need a partner. I can take care of myself."

"I seem to recall you objecting to me riding alone the other night. Need I point out that I can take care of myself, too?"

"That's…" *Different,* she wanted to say, but couldn't.

He raised his hands to gently cradle her face, smiling slightly. "I love you. Love means wishing no harm will come to you. And worrying about you. Worrying about *each other.*"

"Worrying is one thing. Issuing orders is another."

"Hmm." He brushed a stray tendril of hair off her forehead. "Such as you ordering me not to ride alone at night."

She was torn between annoyance and laughter. Laughter won. "Okay. Point taken." Some of her amusement faded as she shook her head, her gaze on his. "This isn't going to be easy, is it?"

"Easy never produces anything worthwhile. Maybe we should think about our relationship like the Anahita Pink. Intense pressure created something rare and valuable. And durable." He drew her to him, brushing a kiss against her brow. "But I shall try not to be so heavy-handed when issuing orders in the future."

She arched an eyebrow at him. "That implies that you will continue to issue orders."

"When it comes to your welfare? Absolutely."

"Alec—"

"And I am quite certain you shall put me in my place. We will argue. My mother died when I was a child, but I remember that she and my father had passionate quarrels. I also know that they loved each other with equal passion."

Kendra saw Alec's eyes darken, and knew he was thinking about the time that had come after that life—when his mother had died and his father remarried. Unlike Alec's Italian mother, Emily Telford was a proper English lady. She'd disliked her stepson, a dislike that had only grown after Alec's father died and the title and most of the wealth passed to Alec. Emily had wasted no time in shipping her stepson off to boarding school, no doubt hoping Alec would have a nasty accident, so her son would inherit. Instead, she'd died, and a year ago, Alec's half-brother had also been killed.

"You were lucky to have your parents, to be part of that family even for a short time," she murmured. "My parents never argued. They had disagreements, which they addressed in the most dispassionate, logical terms. Their relationship wasn't about love—it was a scientific alliance." And she had been its experiment.

"My father's second marriage was more of an alliance, as many marriages can be in the Ton. I am fortunate to know that there is a difference." Alec smiled softly. "I found that difference with you. I love you, Kendra Donovan."

Kendra felt her heart swell in her chest, and let out an unsteady breath. "You don't play fair, my lord. You're a sweet talker." She raised herself up on her toes and kissed him. "Now let's try for a little less talking."

He smirked at her. "It would seem that you are quite adept at issuing orders too…"

"What are you thinking?" Alec's voice was a low murmur in the darkness behind her. "I can hear you thinking."

Kendra laughed, rolling over so she could see his face. The firelight had been reduced to a few glowing embers in the hearth, leaving the canopied bed cocooned in darkness. "I don't believe in telepathy."

"Good. It sounds dreadful. What exactly is telepathy?"

"Reading someone's mind."

"Ah. I can't read your mind, but I know you. I suspect you're thinking about Craymore's murder."

"I keep thinking about what you said to Lady St. James. Desperation can push a man to extremes."

"I was referring to Willoughby."

"I know. But he's not the only desperate man that we're dealing with."

"Is it desperation? Or is it greed?"

She was quiet for a moment. "Sometimes," she said softly, "there's not a lot of difference between the two."

20

Instead of crawling into his warm bed at his lodgings on Russell Street, Sam Kelly found himself walking into a coffeehouse on Drury Lane. Somewhere nearby, the bells of a clock tower struck one. The rain had softened to a thin, miserable drizzle, as the fog thickened to the consistency of wet wool. Sam was cold and damp and feeling out of sorts after traversing London's streets looking for Phineas—Finn—Muldoon, who was currently installed at one of the coffeehouse's scarred wood tables, reading a newspaper.

"You ain't an easy lad ter find," he groused, walking up to the reporter. He removed his tricorn hat, smacking it against his knee to remove the beads of moisture that glistened on the crown.

"Well, now, if I had an inkling that Bow Street was looking for me, I'd have made sure every street urchin in the city knew my whereabouts," Muldoon murmured pleasantly, glancing up. At thirty years old, he had a mop of bright reddish-gold hair, a prominent chin, and cerulean blue eyes that seemed to view the world with a blend of cynicism, mocking humor, and razor-sharp intelligence. "Because me fondest desire is to make your life easier, Mr. Kelly."

Sam snorted and plopped down on the seat opposite the Irishman.

"Do join me," Muldoon drawled, folding the newspaper and setting it aside.

Sam lifted a brow as his gaze fell on the newspaper. "The *Times?*"

The reporter shrugged, picking up his coffee mug. "I like to see what the competition is writing about." He took a sip, grimaced at the obviously cold brew, and shot up two fingers to attract the serving wench's attention. "What's this about? Me sainted mother didn't raise any fools, so here I'm thinking you've got more on your mind than my reading material for this fine evening—or, I should say, early morning."

The maid shuffled over and refilled Muldoon's cup. She looked at Sam. "Are ye wantin' anythin', sir?"

"Might as well have a cup. He's buying." Sam jabbed a thumb in Muldoon's direction.

Muldoon leaned back against his seat, regarding the Bow Street Runner. "You obviously think my wages are more ample than they are." Still, he dug in his breast pocket for a coin, and handed it over.

"What do you know about Jonah Lansing?" Sam asked after the maid scurried off. "Lansing?" Muldoon's eyes narrowed. "Why?"

"'Cause I'm askin', that's why."

"And, of course, I live to serve you. I need a wee bit more than that."

God's teeth. Sam had known the Irishman wouldn't simply give him information without first needing to pry. Hadn't he warned Miss Donovan? The scribbler was bloody annoying.

Muldoon wiggled his eyebrows when Sam remained silent. "Why is Bow Street interested in Jonah Lansing? Did he set fire to Carlton House?"

"Would he? Is he that much of a radical?"

Muldoon laughed. "I was joking."

The maid returned to deposit a steaming mug for Sam, and then Muldoon continued, "Jonah is passionate about reform. He uses his printing shop to dispense his propaganda, and he's spoken at a few organized protests and rallies. He walks a thin line, but so far, he *has* managed to walk it. I wager he'll be in the House of Commons before too long."

"You'll lose."

Muldoon's face changed, sharpening with interest. "So, something has happened."

Sam gave himself a moment to think by sipping his coffee. "What I tell you stays between us. I don't want you ter be blabbing it all over London Town or writing about it in *The Morning Chronicle*."

Muldoon wrapped his hands around his coffee mug, leaning forward. "What's happened?"

"First, I want your word."

"Devil take it. You sound like…" Muldoon' lips parted, his eyes widening. "You sound exactly like Kendra Donovan. Jonah Lansing was murdered, then?"

"Why do you say that?"

"Because anytime Miss Donovan is involved, somebody has cocked up their toes. And it isn't a visitation by God." The blue in his eyes seemed to crystalize. "That's it, isn't it? Somebody killed Jonah Lansing."

"Calm down, lad. You're leaping ahead of yourself." Sam huffed out a breath. "I want your word."

Muldoon eyed him for a moment before nodding. "Fine. You've got me word. Now what is it? What's happened?"

"Jonah ain't the one who's dead. It's his cousin. Reginald Lansing—the Earl of Craymore."

As soon as he said it, he could see the wheels begin to turn in the other man's head.

"Cousin, you say? Did the Earl have any brothers, uncles?"

"They were first cousins, on the father's side. Jonah Lansing is next in line."

"Sweet Jesus, Mary, and Joseph. Lansing is now a peer of the realm." Muldoon started to laugh. "That's going to be meddlesome for some of the lords." He sobered as he looked at Sam. "You cannot expect me to ignore this. The news will be all over town by tomorrow."

"It's not his lordship's murder or Jonah Lansing's inheritance that you need ter keep under your hat. It's the *investigation* into Lord Craymore's murder. And for God's sakes, keep your lips sealed about Miss Donovan's involvement in this. You don't do the lady any favors by writin' about her."

"I only wrote about her once—and I didn't even mention her by name. Other broadsheets haven't been as circumspect. But you know as well as I that she's already gained a reputation in London Town. Gossip tends to flow with or without the help of the papers." He shrugged. "I don't see her becoming a pariah in town, banished from the Ton's fancy balls."

Sam knew that the American wouldn't mind being banished from society's never-ending soirees, but all he said was, "You know that the only reason she continues ter be accepted is because of her connection ter the Duke of Aldridge. Folks ain't likely ter give her the cut for fear of getting on the wrong side of His Grace."

Muldoon pursed his lips thoughtfully. "I'm not so certain about that. I get the sense that the Beau Monde is quite fascinated by Miss Donovan. She's like one of those exotic pets some of the ladies have recently begun to acquire."

"Oh, the lass would love ter be thought in such a light."

Muldoon laughed. "I would never tell her such a thing. She's a fearsome creature." He lifted his coffee cup and took a swallow. "Now, cut line," he said as he set down his cup with a thud, his blue eyes narrowing. "What do you want from me?"

"You may hear talk that Lord Craymore was shot to death by a highwayman, but we think it was somebody who knew him. Or, at least, somebody he recognized."

"Jonah Lansing."

"He is one suspect. You know him. Could he have done it?"

Muldoon turned the coffee cup around in his hands. "I don't know the man personally, mind you, but what I do know of him… he always struck me as a man of conviction. He wouldn't be so covetous of his cousin's title that he would commit cold-blooded murder."

"Maybe not the title, but what about his cousin's fortune?"

"Well, I doubt he's as flush in his purse as his cousin is—was—but… no, I don't see him committing murder for that reason either."

Sam raised his eyebrows. "That's a curious way ter say it, lad. You see him committin' murder for some other reason?"

Muldoon lifted a shoulder in a half-shrug. "I told you, he's passionate about his causes. And he's been known to have a temper. If Lansing and his lordship got into an argument, he might have killed him in a moment of rage. What does Miss Donovan think? She has a unique way of looking at murder."

"The earl was shot in the back while traveling alone at night between Needlham and Paddlewick. He was found by gypsies that were camped on the Duke's land nearby."

"Shot in the back?" Muldoon echoed. "I don't see Lansing doing something so cowardly. If his lordship was riding at night, why don't you think it was a knight of the road who killed him? It's the most logical explanation."

"Aye, but not common where the earl was shot. By all accounts, there haven't been any robberies on that stretch of road for many years. We think it was somebody he knew."

"You? Or Miss Donovan?"

Sam wanted to take exception to the remark, but he had to confess that the Irishman had a point. "As you said, the lass has got an uncommon way of lookin' at murder. And, as I said, there's been no reports of highwaymen in those parts for years, so I'm inclined ter agree with her." He picked up his mug for a sip. "It's strange that his lordship had a pistol on his person that he didn't bother taking out ter defend himself."

"Ah. That's why you think the earl knew his killer. When exactly did this happen? It can't have been long ago, otherwise I wouldn't need you to deliver the news."

"The other evening. Lansing told Lord Sutcliffe and Miss Donovan that he was working alone in his print shop when his cousin was shot. Tomorrow, I'll be having me men quiz nearby shop owners, see if they remember it the same way."

"Miss Donovan is in London, then? Is Lady Rebecca with her?" Muldoon asked with studied casualness, even as his cheeks suddenly surged with color.

Sam bit back an oath. He'd hoped that the foolish affection that the scribbler had developed for the Duke's goddaughter, Lady Rebecca Blackburn, had worked itself out of the lad's system. No good would ever come of it, for either of them. They belonged to different worlds. *And it's none of my business.*

"Nay," Sam said, and was careful to keep his tone neutral. "Miss Donovan and Lord Sutcliffe only came ter London ter find out who was next in line for the earldom."

"I see." Muldoon lifted his gaze from his coffee mug to look at Sam. "Well, for what it's worth, I have a difficult time imagining Jonah Lansing murdering his cousin in cold blood like you describe. Hot blood, yes. In a fight, with tempers flaring; maybe even a duel. Cold blood, no. Lansing has—*had*—his eye on the House of Commons. His rhetoric has been resonating with folks, and he's been making some good points in his pamphlets. I think he would have won a seat if and when he chose to run. Why jeopardize that?"

"For a seat in the House of Lords rather than the House of Commons?"

"I told you, he wasn't covetous of the title. He isn't impressed with his betters."

Sam shrugged. "Fine. Then there's the blunt."

"I told you—"

"Aye, he's not a greedy bastard like the rest of the world. But I reckon his causes need money."

That seemed to shut up Muldoon. At least for the moment.

"All revolutions need money," Muldoon admitted softly. "But to go about it in such a way, by murdering his cousin?" The reporter shook his head. "Connections are even more important than money, you know. And Jonah Lansing has been building those with the pamphlets he produces and the men that he's been associating. In the last year or two, he's allied himself with Henry Hunt, who is a powerful speaker and well-liked by commoners."

Muldoon pinned Sam suddenly with his vivid gaze. "There's something you're not telling me, Mr. Kelly. I realize that Mr. Lansing may be a suspect because he benefits from his cousin's death, and that's why you're looking at him. But there's something else. Something more."

Sam wanted to curse the Irishman's perceptiveness, but decided it was a waste of breath. "Lansing was overheard arguing with his lordship last week. They may have been quarrelin' over a diamond."

"A diamond?" Muldoon's eyebrows flew up in surprise.

"A very specific diamond." Sam stared hard at the younger man. "This next bit is what you need ter keep quiet about, do you hear?"

"I already gave you my word."

Sam leaned forward. "Lord Craymore's father may have found a diamond," he said, his voice low. "Have you ever heard of the Anahita Pink?"

"Can't say that I have."

"It's a rare pink diamond that's supposed ter be part of bad King John's treasure."

Muldoon's nostrils flared as he inhaled sharply. "Bloody hell. Are you saying that the Earl of Craymore found the lost treasure?"

"For Christ's sake, keep your voice down," Sam whispered furiously, glancing around. The few individuals scattered around the coffee shop didn't seem to be paying them any mind, but the last thing he needed was for this to get out. As he'd told Kendra, tales of treasure caused a man's palms to sweat. "It ain't the whole treasure, just the diamond."

"The Anahita Pink," Muldoon repeated, but dutifully lowered his voice. "That's what the cousins were heard arguing about?"

"Possibly. Seems ter me, a priceless bauble would even tempt an admirable man like your Jonah Lansing inter committing the most unpardonable sin."

"You're saying the earl had the diamond on him the night he was killed—"

"And it's gone."

"Ah. And you think that's why Lansing killed him?"

Sam sipped his coffee and waited.

"Jonah Lansing wouldn't be tempted by the money he'd get from selling the gem," Muldoon said slowly, his eyebrows drawing together in a reflective frown. "But the history… the history of such a diamond might be another matter."

"What do you mean?"

"If it's really from King John's treasure, then it's more than a diamond—it's a symbol, Mr. Kelly. And symbols are powerful tools for kings, prime ministers—"

"Radicals?"

Muldoon smiled. "Reformers."

Sam raised a skeptical brow at the scribbler.

"Think about it, Mr. Kelly. There's a reason why symbols are so bloody important." The younger man leaned across the table, chin jutting forward. "The Romans used to carry the eagle standard into battle. Why? Because it was a symbol that would terrify the peasants, remind them of the power that Rome held over the lands they'd conquered. The Roman soldiers viewed the Aquila with an almost religious fervor. Rulers love their flags, crests, and crowns. It gives them *influence*. And influence *is* power."

"What kind of influence would the Anahita Pink give Jonah Lansing?"

"A piece of England's history, something to hold up to the common folk to remind them of how reckless our rulers have been to lose such a priceless object. To tell them that the diamond belongs to the citizens—the *people*, not the monarchy that continues to fail us." He shrugged. "I don't know. You'd have to ask him."

Sam shook his head. "Seems like a bloody stupid reason ter murder someone. You really think he'd kill his cousin just ter possess such a symbol?"

Muldoon was quiet for a long moment. "I don't know. It's not about reason or logic, Mr. Kelly. It's about emotions and passion. It's about *believing* in something, an idea that is represented by that symbol. Even Napoleon wanted a crown—not for the gold it was made of, but for what it symbolized to the French people. He eschewed France's royal family, but he still wanted the crown. Such things *mean* something to the populace."

"Hmm." Sam drained the remaining coffee and shoved himself to his feet. "'Tis something ter consider, I suppose."

"When is the inquest?"

"I'm not certain. The body's at Aldridge Castle. The inquest will be held in the village." Sam put on his hat, and glanced down at the reporter. "You'll be looking into Jonah Lansing's activities, won't you? And send word if you learn anything?"

"I'll do more than send word, Mr. Kelly." The reporter's grin was cocky. "I'll find you."

21

The rain tapered off sometime during the early morning hours, leaving the city soggy beneath gray skies. Mist pearled along the pavement as Kendra, Alec, and Molly climbed into the carriage and swirled around the ankles of milkmaids and street sweepers—the only other people who seemed to be about. The ladies and lords of the Beau Monde wouldn't be up for hours yet. Normally, Kendra regarded their habit of lounging in bed until noon to be annoyingly self- indulgent, but now she was grateful, because it allowed her to enjoy the rare, oddly hushed quality to the city, with the only sounds being the rhythmic clip-clop of horses' hooves, the rumble of carriage and wagon wheels over cobblestone, and the splash from puddles left by the rain.

"Do you like London?"

Kendra turned her gaze away from the window to find Alec studying her with an intensity that made her realize that this was not a random or casual question. And because she realized it, she found herself answering with more caution than the question warranted. "I suppose I'm getting used to it."

He smiled slightly. "Let me be more direct. Would you like to live here?"

Kendra frowned. "You mean, instead of Aldridge Castle?"

He gave her a strange look. "I mean after we are wed. Naturally, we shall visit Aldridge Castle, but it will not be our home. You didn't think we would be living in my uncle's pockets indefinitely, did you?"

Kendra's throat felt oddly tight. She was acutely conscious that they had an audience, with Molly pretending not to listen, her gaze glued to the window.

She admitted, "I guess I never thought about it."

She'd been so focused on her fears—disappointing Alec, not measuring up, having him eventually abandon her like her parents had—that she hadn't given any thought to the logistics of the actual marriage. In the last year, Alec had traveled occasionally to London and to Alcott Park, his country estate in Northamptonshire, but, by in large, he'd been living at Aldridge Castle.

Her stomach knotted as she considered the future—not the twenty-first century, but her future in the nineteenth century. One day, Aldridge Castle would be Alec's home. But it wasn't his home *now*. And after the wedding, Aldridge Castle would no longer be *her* home.

If someone had told her a year ago that she'd view Aldridge Castle as her home, she'd have laughed in their face. But there was a familiarity in the ancient fortress that came not only from living there for the past twelve months, but also from her life before. The castle was her touchstone; the one thing that connected her to her own timeline. It was where the vortex or wormhole or whatever it was had opened up.

It's where it could open up again.

But she wasn't waiting for that to happen. Was she?

Alec leaned forward, touched her knee. "Breathe, Miss Donovan. You look quite stunned."

She expelled the breath that she'd been holding. She licked her lips, meeting Alec's eyes. "What are you thinking?" she asked.

Alec contemplated her. "I suppose I was thinking that we should spend some time at Alcott Park after the wedding. Maybe a fortnight, if that's acceptable to you. Then I'd like to take you to Venice."

"Venice?"

"I want to introduce you to my family there."

Kendra's head was beginning to spin. She knew that Alec's late mother, Alexandria, had been an Italian countess, who'd met and married his father when he was on his Grand Tour. She also knew that Alec had used his maternal connections in Italy when he'd operated as a spy against Napoleon during the war.

Except Venice was not part of Italy now. In fact, Italy wasn't even Italy; it was a cluster of fragmented city-states, and Venice was technically considered part of Austria. Christ.

"Family?" she said faintly.

Amusement brightened the gold flecks in Alec's green eyes. "I am not close to my Venetian relatives, but I do have two aunts, an uncle, and several cousins. I've written to them about you—us. They've issued an invitation. Would you like to travel to meet them?"

"I…" *God.* "Sure."

"And when we return… I think you would be more comfortable living in London."

Panic tickled the back of her throat. "I guess you've given this some thought."

"And you haven't." He sighed, and shook his head. "Do you realize that I have yet to take you to the theater, or drive through the park?"

Probably because she'd always had been involved in a murder investigation whenever she'd been in London, Kendra realized.

She didn't reply as she considered the future that Alec was painting. London—even a London without Big Ben, which wouldn't be built for another twenty-eight years—would be more familiar to her than living in the wilds of Northamptonshire. At least she knew Sam and Dr. Munroe. There was even the possibility that she could continue to assist the Bow Street Runner. There was always crime, especially in a city.

The thought nearly made her smile. "Living in London has a lot of appeal."

Alec studied her. "Why do I feel as though I ought to keep smelling salts on hand?"

Now she did smile, her spirits lightening. "I seem to recall you promising me that if we married, you would accept us having an unconventional life."

"Did I?"

She stared at him, disbelieving, but then he laughed. Capturing her hand, he brought it to his lips to brush a soft kiss across her knuckles. "Well, a promise is a promise, Miss Donovan."

It made sense to stop at Shay House, as it was on their way back to Aldridge Castle. By the time they arrived at the madhouse, the morning's gray clouds had broken apart to reveal blue skies and sunshine. It didn't make a difference: Shay House remained a forbidding pile of stone. Molly, who hadn't seen the asylum before, shuddered visibly.

"It's grim, ain't it?" the maid murmured.

"My thoughts exactly," Kendra said, as the carriage made the loop around Shay House and rumbled to a stop in the stable yard. Like the previous day, Rowan Booker emerged from the building, accompanied by the black-and-tan rottweilers. He jerked their leashes in warning when they bared their teeth and growled. A gangly teenage boy peered out from one of the stable's stalls, pitchfork in hand.

"Ye're back," Booker muttered darkly, watching them climb down from the carriage.

"Is Dr. Shay here?" Kendra asked.

"Aye. 'E came back last evein', like Oi told ye 'e would. Don't know if 'e'll see ye, though." His mouth twisted into a malicious grin. "'Eard that 'e's dealin' with one of the ladies. She caused a ruckus last evenin'."

Kendra regarded the caretaker coldly. "Your compassion touches my heart, Mr. Booker." She didn't wait for his response, swinging around and hurrying up the pebbled path. Alec easily caught up to her, while Molly followed. Kendra paused when they reached the door, looking back at the maid.

"Molly, maybe you can go down and get a cup of tea in the kitchens. See if you can find out any gossip." Servants always saw more, heard more than those who lived above stairs realized. Or wanted to admit. And they tended to be more talkative with a fellow servant than the ward or nephew of a duke.

"W'ot gossip are ye lookin' for, miss?"

Kendra shrugged. "Anything."

Alec lifted the knocker to rap it against the panel. It took a few minutes, but the same maid from the day before—Meg— opened the door.

"Good morning, Meg," Kendra said. "May we come in?"

"Oh." She looked startled, but recovered quickly, bobbing a curtsy. "Aye. Mr. McBride is out in the gardens with his wife. I'll fetch him."

"We came to speak to Dr. Shay."

Meg lifted her eyes to the ceiling in an automatic and telling gesture. "I don't know if he's available. He's in the treatment room."

"Where is Lady Evelyn?"

"She's in her room—"

"We need to speak to her, as well." Kendra knew she was being

high-handed, but she started for the staircase. "We'll show our-
selves up to her room. Unless, she's locked in?" She paused, hand
on the banister, glancing back at the maid.

"Nay. Her door is open, but—"

"Please show Molly to the kitchens, Meg. I think she needs a
cup of tea."

"Aye, Oi'm awfully parched," Molly dutifully remarked.

Meg bit her lip uncertainly, staring at Kendra and Alec as
they began to climb the stairs. Alec grinned at Kendra. "You shall
make a wonderful marchioness, sweetheart."

Kendra rolled her eyes. "You're delusional, which is pretty
ironic given where we are—"

She broke off at a muffled scream from upstairs. She threw
Alec a startled look, then yanked up her skirts and dashed up the
stairs unencumbered. Alec raced after her.

Her heart was pounding when they reached the second-floor
landing. She slipped a hand inside her reticule, closing over the
muff pistol.

"Oh, miss! Milord!" Meg panted, running after them. "Ye
don't understand."

Another shriek made Kendra look upward again. She didn't
hesitate, sprinting towards the next staircase. Alec joined her.

"Ye can't go up there!" Meg yelled. "'Tis the treatment room.
Dr. Shay is in the middle of his treatment!"

Kendra didn't bother responding, pounding up the staircase.
It deposited them in the middle of a large landing. Across from
them was a pair of double doors. Two corridors branched off on
either side. A scream, followed by a string of curses, came from
behind the double doors.

"Milord! Miss! *Please…*" Meg huffed as she rounded the top of
the stairs. "Wait!"

Alec reached the double doors first, turning the knob and
shoving them open with such force that they banged against the
walls. Kendra barreled across the threshold into a spacious room.

It had probably once been a ballroom. Ivory walls, gilt crown moldings, and large Palladian windows still adorned the space. Leftovers from the room's elegant past—and completely incongruent with its present.

Shelves lined one wall, filled with rows of amber-tinted glass bottles and jars. The dirt moved in a few of the jars. Wriggling black worms, Kendra thought, but no—*leeches*. In the middle of the room was a strange contraption: a metal box bolted in the middle of a steel pole that ran floor to ceiling. A crank jutted out at the top of the pole. The box was big enough to hold a person, and the leather restraints fixed inside the container indicated that holding a person was indeed its purpose.

Then Kendra's gaze locked on the real spectacle—the one that stole her breath in horror.

A woman, wet and naked, was blindfolded and strapped to a chair. The woman screamed and unleashed furious obscenities as the orderly Crump poured a bucket of cold water over her head. Another man was standing in front of her, holding a hose attached to a barrel. He pumped a pedal with his foot to get the water going, squirting water into the woman's cloth covered face.

This man—Dr. Shay, presumably—was older, somewhere in his sixties, with closely cropped gray hair and a face that in any other circumstances might be described as avuncular. Somehow that made his presence in this room, as a participant to the torture, even more obscene.

"*Bloody hell,*" Alec expelled in a shocked breath.

That broke the spell that rooted Kendra to the spot. Fury rushed through her, roaring in her ears. She was almost dizzy with it.

The older man spun around to gape at them.

"Who the devil are you?" he demanded, outrage flashing across his face. "You have no business being in here! Get out!"

"You son of a bitch!" Kendra stared at the man. "Get away from her!"

"*Kendra*," Alec said sharply, reaching for the pistol that she hadn't realized she'd taken out of the reticule. For one dark moment, she resisted, her heart pounding. Her skin prickled like a million hot needles were scoring her flesh. She held her breath, then let it out slowly. Just as slowly, she relaxed her fingers and released the weapon. Alec slipped the gun into his pocket.

Dr. Shay's eyes followed the movement of the pistol, aghast. As soon as it was safely out of sight, he lifted his gaze to Alec. "What is the meaning of this, sir? This is a private room. Mr. Crump, show these intruders out!"

Crump set down the wood pail and began swaggering toward them. Kendra rolled on the balls of her feet, flexing her hands. Adrenaline sang in her bloodstream, clearing her mind, energizing her. Here was a much-needed target for her rage.

"I don't think so." Alec stepped in front of her. Whatever Crump saw in Alec's face stopped him cold. The orderly glanced at Dr. Shay for direction. Annoyed, Kendra moved around Alec so they were standing shoulder-to-shoulder.

"Who are you, sir?" Dr. Shay glared at Alec. "You and this… this creature"—he flicked a disdainful look at Kendra—"are interfering with a medical treatment. I order you to leave!"

"I am the Marquis of Sutcliffe." Alec said with icy formality. "And this 'creature' is the Duke of Aldridge's ward, Miss Donovan. And my betrothed."

Wariness flickered across the doctor's face. "You were here yesterday with the duke."

"For Christ's sake—the woman's freezing to death while you make your introductions."

Furious, Kendra pushed past Dr. Shay. The woman had fallen silent but was shivering violently. Her wet hair was plastered to her head and the blindfold hid most of her face, but Kendra recognized the garnet cross dangling between her breasts. Mrs. Slater.

Kendra was shaking almost as much as Mrs. Slater as she tore off the blindfold and tossed it to the floor.

"Now, see here—"

"Get her some damn clothes!" Kendra didn't bother looking at Dr. Shay. She concentrated on unbuckling Mrs. Slater's restraints. The water had swelled the leather, making the process difficult. Mrs. Slater began to sob.

"It's all right; it's over," she reassured the distraught woman. She glanced up to meet Mrs. Slater's eyes. Shock stabbed through her again when she realized that Mrs. Slater wasn't sobbing. She was laughing.

"Stop this!" Dr. Shay darted forward to grasp Kendra's hands, yanking them away from the leather straps. "You do not understand. We are not hurting her. We are balancing Mrs. Slater's humors!"

Kendra stared at the older man, at a loss for words.

"Last evening, Mrs. Slater became emotionally unstable when her husband visited her," he went on. "This is the required treatment."

Mrs. Slater stopped laughing. Her cat-like eyes blazed with hatred. "B-because I refused to s-submit to his l-lechery!" she shouted through chattering teeth.

Dr. Shay frowned at her. "Mr. Slater is your husband. There can be no lechery between a man and his wife. It is your duty to behave like a proper wife and submit!"

"He is not t-the husband I-I wanted. M-my father forced him on me. F-forced me to marry the bastard. He's an o-old m-man!"

"Oh, for God's sake." Kendra removed her pelisse and covered the naked woman. She glared at Dr. Shay. "Get her out of this chair. Get her some clothes!"

Dr. Shay's chest rose in his indignation. "Young lady, I am the doctor at this facility. You have no right to issue orders." He turned to Alec. "Sir, if you could please escort Miss Donovan out of the room. Gently bred females are too delicate to understand these treatments."

Kendra's hands curled into tight fists. Red mist shimmered across her vision. If this were the twenty-first century, she'd be slapping handcuffs on Dr. Shay and Crump.

Alec laid a hand on her shoulder. Kendra wasn't certain if it was meant to comfort or restrain her.

"Miss Donovan's concern regarding this treatment is justified, I'd say." Alec's upper-class accent was so sharp, it could have cut through stone. "This is barbaric."

Dr. Shay stiffened, his nostril's flaring in insult. "This is the approved treatment for such maladies, my lord." He paused, appearing to wrestle with himself. When he spoke again, he'd moderated his tone. "I am, however, aware how shocking this might appear to someone unused to such procedures to treat madness."

"*This* is madness." Kendra's hand shot out to point at Mrs. Slater. Her chest still felt tight, her stomach jittery. *Breathe in; breathe out.*

Dr. Shay turned to offer her an indulgent smile. "As I said, I understand your dismay, Miss Donovan. You need a restorative." He spotted Meg, who was hovering in the threshold next to a wide-eyed Molly. He snapped his fingers. "You there, girl! Escort his lordship and—"

"I'm not leaving here until you release Mrs. Slater," said Kendra. "*Now.*"

"My lord." Dr. Shay appealed to Alec. "Perhaps you ought to take Miss Donovan to the gardens? A walk might calm her mind."

"We will go to the gardens," she said, pushing the words through her tight throat. "And Mrs. Slater will join us in ten minutes."

"'Tis cold outside," Dr. Shay said. "You will need this." The doctor whipped the pelisse off Mrs. Slater, leaving her cold and naked again.

Bastard.

"Mrs. Slater appears to need it more than I do," Kendra replied. "She can bring it to me when she joins me outside. Ten minutes, Dr. Shay—no more."

22

Kendra needed air. She needed to kick something. She needed for the vortex to open up again to take her out of this backwards century.

She strode toward the stairs; she forced herself to walk, not to run.

"Kendra," Alec murmured, catching up with her as she started descending the staircase.

"I need a moment."

She realized that her legs were shaking and she was having a hard time breathing. She focused on filling her lungs with air, then letting it out. She glanced in the direction of Lady Evelyn's room as they hit the second floor.

"Lady Evelyn is probably out in the gardens now," Meg said, intercepting Kendra's look.

"Are you aware what is done in the treatment room?" The question exploded out of her as she looked at the servant.

Meg licked her lips nervously. "Aye. Everyone knows what's done. But only Mr. Crump assists Dr. Shay with the treatments."

"I'll bet he does." She started down the second flight of stairs. "Does every woman here get treatments?"

"Nay. Mrs. Slater is more…" Meg paused as though searching for the right word. "Rebellious, I suppose ye'd say. Dr. Shay uses the bathing chair with her ter restore her humors and make sure she behaves more proper-like."

"What about that other contraption? The one with the metal box?"

"That's where a patient is spun around ter help her come ter her senses."

Yes, of course, Kendra thought irritably. *Perfectly reasonable.*

"Sometimes Dr. Shay bleeds Miss Sybil when she's caught nicking things," Meg continued. "And he cups Miss Dora ter draw out her noxious humors. Miss Dora is the one who usually gets spun about when her wits have fled and she fancies herself Joan of Arc, fighting the devil."

"Has Lady Evelyn been given any treatments?" She managed to keep her tone civil and not sneer over the last word.

"Oh, she's been put in the strait-waistcoat when her passions have become inflamed," Meg admitted. "And she's spent time in solitary confinement. But nothing too harsh."

"Can family members request what kind of treatment is given?" Kendra asked, wondering if Lady Evelyn's more mild treatment was a request by her late brother, or if Dr. Shay was just more careful with a member of the aristocracy.

"I don't know."

On the ground floor, they followed Meg down a long hallway which opened up into what appeared to be a combination library and music room. The walls were lined with bookshelves.

Several tables and chairs occupied the space, arranged around sofas and settees. On one side of the room were a pianoforte and a harp. There was only one person in the room, a thin, middle-aged woman sitting in a wingback chair in front of the empty fireplace. A patient, obviously, identified by her shorn head and plain brown gown. She was embroidering, but watched them out of the corner of her eye. As the group moved into the room, she hunched her shoulders, curving into herself as though she could become invisible.

"Good day, Mrs. Tilly," Meg called out cheerfully. "The poor dear ain't been right in the head since she lost her daughter ter smallpox," she told Kendra and Alec, not bothering to lower her voice as she crossed to the French doors that led out into the gardens. "She doesn't speak to us, but sometimes we hear her talkin' ter her dead daughter."

"Good 'eavens," Molly whispered, eyes rounding. "'Ow terrifyin'."

"It might be more terrifying if they heard her daughter talking back," Kendra remarked, earning wide-eyed looks from both maids and a soft chuckle from Alec.

Kendra paused just outside the French doors, letting her gaze travel over the gardens. They were better maintained than the gardens at the front of the asylum. Pale pea gravel paths wound around flowers, trees, and shrubbery. Several white-painted wrought iron tables and chairs were arranged around the lawn. In the distance, a large S-shaped lake shimmered grayish-blue, and beyond that, a heavily wooded area that stretched over the hills into the horizon. Mrs. Maddox and a young maid were ushering seven of the sanitarium's inmates along the footpath. Both Mrs. Maddox and the maid wore bonnets and wool coats; their charges were bareheaded and instead of coats, they were wrapped in plain wool shawls.

Kendra recognized Sybil and Dora in the group. Lady Evelyn was missing. McBride was at a table fifteen yards away, kneeling next to a woman wrapped in a heavy shawl who sat in an old-fashioned wicker wheelchair. She wore a bonnet, but beneath the brim, Kendra could see her face was slack. McBride lifted a teacup and carefully pressed the rim against the woman's lips.

They moved slightly in response, like a baby's innate sucking. Mc-Bride tilted the cup. Liquid trickled down her chin. He brought up a linen napkin to gently dab at his wife's face.

"I'll leave ye here, miss, milord," Meg said, and glanced at Molly. "I'll bring ye ter the kitchens for that cup of tea."

"Aye. Oi could use a restorative," Molly muttered, and gave Kendra a sidelong look before following Meg back through the French doors.

"Are you all right?"

Kendra turned to meet Alec's eyes. His mouth quirked in a faint smile. "For an instant, I thought you were going to shoot Dr. Shay," he went on.

"For an instant, I considered it." She shifted her gaze back to the women walking along the paths. Mrs. Maddox reminded her of a mother duck with her ducklings.

She said softly, "One of the first investigations that I was involved in as a field agent was a sex trafficking case." She kept her gaze on Mrs. Maddox and her charges. "We followed a lead to a house. An average-looking house, really, in an average-looking neighborhood. There was nothing sinister about it. It was all so damn normal."

Her stomach knotted at the memory. "But there was nothing average or normal about what we found in the basement of that house. At least thirty half-naked, half-starved girls— *children*—in shackles. There were a few cots, but most slept on the concrete floor. And the buckets were overflowing with…" She shook her head. "It smelled like piss and shit and body odor. Most of those kids had been there for one hundred and ninety days—more than half a year. They'd been raped, drugged, and beaten into submission, until they accepted their fate. Then they were handed over to prostitution rings."

Alec touched her arm. "I'm sorry."

"Why? I wasn't the one being tortured."

"But it hurt you. Still hurts you."

Kendra had nothing to say to that.

"You freed them. You saved them."

"We freed them. I'm not sure if we saved them. Or at least not all of them." She glanced at Alec now. "It was ugly and awful, but we had the law on our side. What we saw in that basement was illegal. But what I just saw in the *treatment* room... that's perfectly legal here, isn't it?"

It was Alec's turn to remain silent.

"How can I live here when this sort of thing is accepted? Tolerated?"

What choice do I have? Unless the vortex opened with the full moon next week...

"There are movements to reform asylums, you know," Alec said slowly. "Many Quakers have become fierce advocates for different methods of treating the mentally ill."

"But it's not only the mentally ill who are here. This is for women who don't know their place. The fact that women can be put in a place like this because she was caught smoking, or reading too much, or—God forbid—expressing an opinion that contradicted her husband's..." Kendra pinched the bridge of her nose in frustration and shook her head. "And there's nothing I can do about it, because it's not against the damn law."

"You can lend your voice to organizations that are speaking out against this sort of thing."

"It won't change anything." She hesitated, then huffed out a breath. "And if it does, then *I* am the one changing it, and that, in turn, could change history."

"Kendra, this is your life. You cannot live in its shadows."

She wanted to remind him that this *wasn't* her life, that she was a woman out of her own time.

McBride had seen them, and rose to his feet. He walked towards them. "Miss Donovan, my lord. Good day." He gave an abbreviated bow.

"Mr. McBride," Kendra nodded, automatically glancing behind him at the woman in the wheelchair. Mrs. McBride was staring vacantly into the distance.

"My wife," McBride identified unnecessarily, a spasm of pain crossing his face. "I didn't realize you would be returning today. I believe Dr. Shay is in the treatment room."

"Yes, we know," Kendra said brusquely. "We were there. Have you taken women into the treatment room?"

He gave her a sharp look. "No," he said cautiously. "Dr. Shay is the only one authorized to use the room. I have found bringing the ladies into my office and allowing them to speak of their worries can be effective."

"But you know what's happening there?" Despite her best efforts, she couldn't stop the anger from rising in her voice. "And you condone it?"

McBride glanced at his wife, then raised his hand to indicate the garden path. "Shall we walk?"

Kendra and Alec fell into step beside McBride. Instead of following the footpath, though, he stepped onto the grass, leading them down a slight slope toward the lake and trees, away from the rest of the garden's occupants. They walked for a few moments in silence. Kendra was aware of her skirt swishing against the blades of grass, the stirring of branches and leaves in the breeze, the faint drone of insects, the lush smell of vegetation and sunshine around her.

"I told you that my wife had a seizure six years ago," McBride finally said, each word weighed down in sorrow. "During the birth of our son. He was our fifth child. And the fifth we were forced to bury."

Kendra said, "I'm sorry."

McBride acknowledged her sympathy with a brief nod, then continued, "Cecilia—Mrs. McBride—has always had delicate health, but I wonder if she would have come out of her current state if the child had survived." He released a troubled breath.

"The loss of another child was simply too great, and I watched the light vanish from her eyes.

"Cecilia can still function," McBride went on after a moment. "She can eat and swallow. She is alive, but she is not living. I had hoped she would begin to heal here."

"Why Shay House?" Kendra wondered.

"I told you. Dr. Shay was the only proprietor who allowed me to stay with Cecilia, to care for her," he replied. "I am not a wealthy man, Miss Donovan. I once apprenticed as an apothecary, but I put that aside when I joined the fight against Bonaparte. I became a surgeon on the battlefields and that's what I did in Cornwall." His mouth curved into a brittle, bitter smile. "Yet I did not have the skills to save my wife."

Kendra was reminded of her first impression of McBride, that he was a man suffering.

Now she understood the sadness shadowing his eyes.

"I do not have the resources to care for my wife on my own," he added quietly as they stopped near the lake. "Thankfully, I have skills that are useful here. However, I am learning that healing the mind is more difficult than healing the body."

"Maybe the mind would heal faster without such things as the treatment room," Kendra couldn't stop herself from saying.

McBride gave her a careful look. "I believe Dr. Shay was planning on using hydrotherapy on Mrs. Slater this morning. It is not an uncommon treatment, you know. In fact, it is used in most lunatic asylums. Dr. Patrick Blair wrote in several medical journals that he found the treatment very effective in curbing behavioral problems plaguing women."

"Women? Not men?"

He hesitated. "I believe the treatment is used on men as well, but Dr. Blair only referred to the success he had when treating women."

"Of course, he did."

McBride spread out his hands in a conciliatory gesture. "Personally, I favor less punitive methods. I have been hearing good reviews on Brislington House set up by Dr. Edward Long Fox. He's a Quaker and has a more enlightened view of mentally ill patients. The Quakers' interest in good works appears to be genuine. I have been speaking to Dr. Shay about implementing some of Dr. Fox's practices, and he has allowed me the freedom to incorporate my own ideas with a few of the patients. He has given Mr. Lewis the same freedom. So, you see, Dr. Shay is not such a terrible fellow, Miss Donovan."

"He allowed one of his patients to be raped by an attendant a few years ago," she said bluntly, and watched McBride's nostrils flare as he drew in a swift breath, his pupils dilating in shock. Maybe it was a verbal sucker punch, but she refused to feel guilty, even when she saw his hand tremble as he ran it over his hair.

"That is an ugly accusation," he finally said. "There was no rape."

"Only a female patient who ended up pregnant." Kendra gestured to the former monastery. "She was an inmate in an asylum, Mr. McBride. Could she really give consent?"

He was silent for such a long time that Kendra didn't think that he'd answer. Then he shook his head. "That is ancient history, Miss Donovan. Dr. Shay dismissed the attendant who committed the indiscretion. Why are you bringing this up now?"

Indiscretion. Such a bland word to describe what had happened. "I'm bringing it up now because Shay House is still dealing with the aftermath. Dr. Shay has been trying to rebuild his reputation ever since. That takes money."

McBride frowned. "Yes. That is why Dr. Shay often is in London."

"Raising funds? Trying to convince wealthy families with… with unmanageable females to consider Shay House?"

"I suppose."

"Maybe he found a shortcut. Have you heard of the Anahita Pink?" Kendra asked abruptly.

McBride's eyes widened in surprise. "I have, actually. Lady Evelyn has spoken of it." He lifted a shoulder. "I confess that I thought it was a figment of her imagination. It wasn't?"

"No." Kendra covered her own surprise. She hadn't expected that. "When did she mention it?"

"I can't recall exactly. A month ago, perhaps. I thought it was a convenient delusion."

Alec raised his eyebrows. "Convenient?"

"She tried to use it as a bribe to help her escape." A small smile flickered around McBride's mouth, but disappeared as quickly as it had come. "You've witnessed Lady Evelyn's mercurial behavior. How could anyone take her story of a rare pink diamond seriously? Especially when she said that it was part of the treasure that King John had lost. It all sounded quite…"

"Mad?" Kendra finished for him. "I suppose it does."

McBride's gaze darted between Kendra and Alec. Whatever he saw in their faces made his eyes widen. "My God," he breathed. "Is it true?"

"We're not sure; the diamond seems to have vanished," Kendra said. "Lord Craymore was bringing it to someone to evaluate the night he was killed." She changed tracks. "How often did Lady Evelyn ask you to help her escape?"

McBride frowned, saying nothing for a moment. Then he shrugged. "Several times. Obviously, I refused."

He glanced toward Shay House, his face changing subtly. Kendra followed his gaze to find Dr. Shay emerging with Mrs. Slater.

"I must return to my wife," McBride said, already turning to go. "If you have any further questions, I suggest you speak with Dr. Shay."

Alec, staring thoughtfully after McBride's departing figure, said quietly, "It appears as though the Anahita Pink might not have been the secret that we believed."

"It would appear not."

23

"My lord, Miss Donovan… again, I must apologize for what you witnessed in the treatment room," Dr. Shay said as they met him on the pebbled path. His hand was locked around Mrs. Slater's arm. His smile was firmly in place. He extended the arm that had Kendra's pelisse draped over it. "Here, Miss Donovan. I hope you haven't been cold."

"Not as cold as Mrs. Slater."

The woman was dressed in the familiar beige gown and had the same shawl wrapped around her shoulders as the rest of the inmates.

"How are you doing, Mrs. Slater?" Kendra asked.

"She is perfectly fine," Dr. Shay answered. "I comprehend that the corrective methods used for mental illness are shocking to those unfamiliar with our procedures—especially young ladies with delicate sensibilities, such as yourself, Miss Donovan."

Kendra had to work to keep her composure. "I think you underestimate the sensibilities of women, doctor."

"Hydrotherapy is a proven treatment to—"

"Drive out demons?" Kendra suggested sarcastically.

"Don't be absurd." He gave her a repressive frown. "If you will come with me to my office, I shall endeavor to explain the methods that are employed in all reputable asylums. I assure you that Shay House follows the practices endorsed by the medical community."

The same medical community that advocated bloodletting and doling out teaspoons of opium and heroin on a regular basis.

Alec put his hand on Kendra's arm. "Perhaps you can explain your methods to me, Dr. Shay, while Miss Donovan speaks privately with Mrs. Slater? Let us go to your office."

"But—"

"Miss Donovan shall join us shortly," he added firmly, cutting off the doctor's protests.

"Very well, my lord," Dr. Shay conceded grudgingly. He looked at Kendra. "I must caution you, Miss Donovan, that you shouldn't believe anything Mrs. Slater may tell you. She is deceptive. It is part of her instability."

Kendra kept her eyes on Dr. Shay. "I find most people to be deceptive, doctor."

That seemed to flummox the man. Frowning, he allowed Alec to usher him down the path toward the asylum. Kendra watched their retreating figures, smiling when Dr. Shay cast an uncertain glance over his shoulder at her and Mrs. Slater before he and Alec disappeared through the French doors.

She turned to Mrs. Slater, who was studying her with a strange expression on her pretty face.

"Do you want to walk?"

Mrs. Slater shrugged indifferently.

Aware that they had an audience—Crump was watching them with narrowed eyes, and Mrs. Maddox and several of the inmates were giving them sidelong glances—Kendra began to walk the same route that she and Alec had with McBride. Clutching her shawl around her, Mrs. Slater fell into step beside her.

"What's your name?" Kendra asked. "Your first name?"

Suspicion flared in Mrs. Slater's cat-like hazel eyes. "Why?"

Kendra was quiet for a moment as she analyzed her own feelings. "Maybe I'm tired of women being invisible here," she said finally, letting her gaze travel to the wooded area as they came to a stop next to the lake. A bright fleck of color caught her attention. A goldfinch hopping in one of the trees. "You are an individual, and shouldn't only be known through your husband's identity."

Mrs. Slater laughed, but the sound was as brittle as glass. "Good heavens. I am astonished that you are not locked up in Shay House with the rest of us, Miss Donovan. Those are radical thoughts."

Kendra tore her gaze away from the goldfinch to look at Mrs. Slater. "I got lucky," she said with complete truthfulness.

It was Mrs. Slater's turn to look away, her delicate jaw tightening. The silence between them seemed to hum. Finally, Mrs. Slater brought her gaze back to Kendra. "My name is Lillian."

"And I'm Kendra."

Lillian's lips twisted sardonically. "I would be punished if Dr. Shay heard me be so familiar."

Kendra's stomach tightened as a vision of Lillian Slater, wet, naked and blindfolded, in the treatment room flashed through her mind. "Okay," she conceded. "We can use our first names with each other when we won't be overheard."

Lillian stared at Kendra with distrust. "What do you want from me, Miss Donovan? Are you some religious do-gooder, trying to save my soul from eternal damnation?"

So much for gratitude, Kendra thought wryly. She hadn't expected to form a sisterly bond with the other woman, but she was surprised by her unrelenting antagonism.

"I'm no religious zealot," she said. "I just think what was done to you was"—*horrifying, barbaric, criminal*— "excessive."

Lillian averted her face, her gaze on the lake, watching small waves lap against the rocky shore.

Kendra waited. When Lillian seemed in no hurry to engage in conversation, she asked, "How long have you been at Shay House, Lillian?"

Something flickered over Lillian's face. "Since Mr. Slater's own corrective measures failed. And he caught me in bed with another man." Now she turned to look at Kendra, her lips curved in a provocative smile. There was a challenging glimmer in her lovely eyes. "Does that shock you, Miss Donovan? To know that I enjoy sexual relations—just not with my husband?"

"Your husband caught you having an affair and had you committed?"

Lillian frowned. She drew her shawl more closely around her shoulders. "I was seventeen when Mr. Slater asked my father for my hand in marriage," she said quietly. "My father gave his consent. I had no say in the matter." Her expression was unreadable as she said flatly, "I submitted to Mr. Slater for a full year before I sought my pleasure outside the marital bed. That is how it's done in the Beau Monde, is it not?" She threw Kendra a defiant look. "It is acceptable, as long as you are discreet."

From what Kendra had heard, that was a fairly accurate description of many unions in the Polite World.

"I will concede that a wife ought to first bear her husband a son or two before being allowed her indiscretions," Lillian continued in the same neutral tone. "My husband is wealthy but he is not gentry nor a member of the aristocracy. There is no title to pass on, no estate to consider. Even if there were, Mr. Slater already has children from his two wives before me."

"*Two* wives?"

"*That* is what shocks you, Miss Donovan?" Lillian gave Kendra a strange look, shaking her head. "Mr. Slater is nearly seventy. He's buried two wives, and has nine children. His youngest daughter is two years older than I am."

Kendra asked, "And no one took your side when your husband put you in Shay House?"

"Oh, that is rich!" Lillian laughed bitterly. "He is my *husband*, Miss Donovan. You are correct when you say that women are invisible. My husband threatened to put me in a madhouse when I disobeyed him and he fulfilled that threat. He visits occasionally, demanding his husbandly rights. And when I protest, I am brought to the treatment room the next morning to purge me of my unnatural temperament." Her throat worked as she swallowed. "My willfulness."

Kendra thought she saw the sheen of tears in Lillian's eyes, but when the woman glanced at her, her eyes were dry. And hard.

"How long have you been here?" Kendra asked again.

"Mr. Slater brought me here when I turned nineteen. I am now six and twenty."

"What about your parents? Your family?"

"My father is the reason I am saddled with my husband in the first place. My mother is ashamed—ashamed that I have not been a good wife to Mr. Slater. My brothers and sisters... what can they do? Why does this even matter to you?"

"It should matter to everyone," Kendra replied. "It's a travesty what's being done here."

Lillian's lips parted in astonishment. "You are a peculiar creature, Miss Donovan," she said at last. "There are countless other madhouses with similar treatment rooms. Shay House isn't as terrible as some. Speak to Dora. She nearly died when London mad doctors bled her. At least Dr. Shay uses leeches instead of knives."

Kendra could only shake her head in amazement. "I heard about the patient who was sexually assaulted by an attendant."

"Assaulted? Is that what you heard?"

"Yes." She regarded Lillian closely. "Why? Isn't it true?"

"Some things are not always what they may seem."

Kendra frowned. "What do you mean?"

Lillian appeared not to hear her. Her attention was focused on the hillside. Kendra spotted Mr. Lewis and Mr. McBride standing together. They were in a conversation, but both men's eyes were on her and Lillian. They were too far away to read the expressions on their faces.

Kendra shifted her gaze back to Lillian. "What do you know?"

Lillian cocked an eyebrow at Kendra. "You are not here about what happened years ago."

"No, I suppose not," Kendra had to agree. "Especially since the attendant who committed the assault killed himself."

That seemed to startle Lillian. "Mr. Dodd killed himself?"

Kendra wondered at the emotion flaring in the other woman's eyes. "You didn't know?"

Lillian lowered her lashes, veiling their expression. "Dr. Shay ordered him to leave, and that was the end of it."

Kendra sensed something more. "What aren't you telling me?"

Lillian gave her a sideways look. "You're not here to inquire about that incident. You are here because Lord Craymore was shot."

She was right, but Kendra didn't like the feeling that there might be something about that long-ago scandal that remained hidden from view. She hated loose threads. But she pushed the scandal aside for the moment to focus on the present crime. "Did you see Lord Craymore when he came to visit his sister the other day?"

"Of course. He attended our musical recital." Her lips twisted. "That is Mr. Lewis' contribution to Shay House. Recitals, just like ladies have in well-established households. He likes to say, 'Music has charms to soothe the savage breast,'" she quoted. "I think it's from the bible. Ironic."

"It's from a book by William Congreve," Kendra corrected absently. She eyed the woman. "Why is that ironic?"

"Because most Englishmen regard Mr. Lewis as a savage."

Kendra frowned. "Why?"

"You cannot be that much of a simpleton, Miss Donovan. Or is it because you are an American? Even the lowliest guttersnipe views himself as better than a foreigner—as long as he is a full-blooded Englishman. Mr. Lewis's father may have been English, but it only matters that his mother was Indian."

Kendra remembered again Booker's sneering words. *That other one.*

"They met in the Kingdom of Mysore," Lillian said softly. Her gaze strayed to the lake. "Mr. Lewis's father worked as a clerk for the British East India Company. Mr. Lewis said that his father saw his mother washing clothes in the river, and fell in love at first sight. A quixotic story, if you believe in such things."

"You don't?"

Lillian's lips twisted. "Given my situation? No," she said flatly.

Kendra didn't blame Lillian for her cynicism. But she was a little puzzled as to why Mr. Lewis would have shared such a personal story with her.

Lillian seemed to guess what she was thinking. "You think it is odd that he should speak of such matters to me? We do converse, you know."

"Mysore… I'm not familiar with that name."

Lillian shrugged. "'Tis the name he used."

Something niggled at the back of Kendra's mind. Something she should be considering. When nothing came to her, she forced herself to let it go, circling back to Craymore. "The earl stayed for the musical recital?"

"He did. Until Mrs. Allard had one of her episodes." For the first time, Lillian smiled with genuine amusement. "She mistook Lord Craymore for one of Napoleon's agents. It was quite entertaining, especially when Dora, Sybil, and Lady Evelyn joined in. There was plenty of wailing and flailing." She chuckled. "Lord Craymore was quite shocked."

"I can imagine," Kendra said drily.

"Dr. Shay ordered Mr. Crump to escort Mrs. Allard to a solitary room after she threatened Sybil with the fireplace poker, and the daft creature flung herself at the earl. Then Lady Evelyn began screaming that he'd put her in hell, and she would kill him."

Kendra glanced at her sharply. "She said that? That she would kill him?"

"Yes. The poor man actually looked stricken. Like he was concerned."

"Maybe he was concerned."

"Obviously, he was more concerned about keeping his sister away from her suitor."

"What do you know about the man?"

Lillian smiled slyly at Kendra. "I know quite a bit. I know that Lord Craymore was not successful in keeping them apart. I know that Mr. Willoughby and Lady Evelyn had a few rendezvous on the grounds. I know he was here earlier that day."

"Willoughby was here on the day Lord Craymore visited his sister?"

"Yes. And when Lord Craymore found out about it—and about the other times Mr. Willoughby had been here on the grounds— he flew into a rage." Lillian's catlike eyes glinted with malice. "You really ought to ask Dr. Shay about that. They had quite a row when the earl threatened to take his sister away."

24

Sam Kelly stared at the black-painted door with something approaching trepidation. The tavern's name was Ye Olde Beelzebub—appropriate, he thought, considering it was one of the most notorious flash houses in London Town. It was not the kind of establishment that would welcome a Bow Street Runner such as himself.

He could feel the comforting weight of the four-inch Sheffield blade he'd tucked inside his boot, and the double-barrel flintlock pistol inside the pocket of his greatcoat. But neither weapon would protect him for long against the vicious cutthroats on the other side of that black door.

Which was why he'd sent a street urchin inside with his message.

Of course, he didn't know if staying outside was much safer, not in this section of London. The back of his neck itched as he noticed the pinched expressions of the folks walking past him. Hostility burned in their eyes, like they knew he was from Bow Street.

He kept his back to the wall, and carefully dipped his hand into his pocket, feeling marginally better when his fingers closed over the polished wood stock of his weapon. The action was instinctive, and made him think about Lord Craymore riding alone that night. Kendra Donovan was right. The earl would have reached for his weapon, just as Sam was doing now, if another rider had approached. He most certainly would have brought the barking iron out to protect his person, his purse, and the valuable bauble that he had on him.

Unless he'd recognized the other rider. Recognized him and felt no threat.

Sam straightened when the door swung open, and the boy re-appeared. Looming behind the child was an enormous man, so tall that he had to duck his head in order to clear the doorway.

Sam fished out a shilling and tossed it at the urchin. Grin-ning, the boy caught the coin midair and darted down the street, disappearing into the crowds shifting around them. Sam barely noticed; his gaze was fixed on Bear.

The crime lord smirked at him. "Afraid ter come inside, are ye?"

Bear's gold earring winked in the sunshine and his bald head gleamed. The scar puckering the flesh near his left eye wriggled like a fat pink worm. Sam wondered fleetingly how he'd gotten it. He couldn't imagine anyone having the temerity to attack the giant.

Sam said coolly, "Let's just say, self-preservation is a keen in-terest of mine."

Bear laughed, a big, booming sound that drew the eyes of pe-destrians. And because Sam wasn't the only one who had a keen interest in self-preservation, he noticed how quickly they averted their gazes from the crime lord.

"Seein' how this ain't likely a social call, what do ye want?" Bear asked, folding his arms across his massive chest as he sur-veyed Sam with flat brown eyes.

Sam had no interest in drawing out the conversation with the criminal, so got right to the point. "Have you heard about anyone wantin' ter sell a valuable sparkler?"

Bear raised his eyebrows. "If I have, why should I tell ye?"

"It may be connected ter the murder of a nobleman."

"Lord Craymore." Bear laughed again when Sam stared at him. "Ye think I don't know w'ot's happenin' with me betters? Heard tell someone put a hole in him the other night. It wasn't a highwayman."

Sam nodded. He wasn't going to argue with the man. "We already determined that it most likely was someone his lordship knew."

"We?" A glint came into the predatory eyes. "The American wench is involved in this, ain't she?"

"Why would you say that?"

Bear grinned. "'Cause ye are as thick as thieves. And I heard tell that the gentry cove was found by a duke."

"Miss Donovan may be involved," Sam admitted reluctantly, feeling no need to correct Bear's recounting of events. "It would be helpful if you send word ter Bow Street if you hear about a diamond—an uncommon pink diamond—being shopped around."

"Now why would I be helpful ter Bow Street?"

"Damned if I know," Sam muttered, shaking his head. "Miss Donovan seemed ter think that you would let us know if you heard about someone tryin' ter sell the sparkler."

"Ye're not interested in the bauble. Ye want ter know who the thief is."

Sam thought about how the Crown might be interested in the bauble if it really was from King John's treasure. But he wasn't about to argue with the crime lord on that point either. He said, "Aye. The thief is a murderer."

Bear rubbed his jaw. "I ain't heard nothin' yet. But when I do, I'll give ye a name."

Sam hesitated. "And the diamond?"

Bear shrugged and grinned. "It's probably in France by now. I won't be able ter help ye with that."

Sam grunted, understanding. If Bear found the diamond, he wasn't handing it over. But he'd hand over Lord Craymore's killer. Sam had to be satisfied with that.

"Is that all?" Bear asked.

"What do you know of Basil Willoughby?"

"Why?"

"Just curious."

Bear snorted. "Not bloody likely. Willoughby's proof that good stock don't make ye a gentleman. He's a wily one. Heard tell that he was hanging out for an heiress."

"Aye, Lord Craymore's sister."

"Ah. Ye think the bastard killed his lordship ter have the chit?"

"Do you think he could've done that?"

Bear gave a shrug. "Don't see why not. But what about the sparkler? Sounds like it's worth more than the wench. If he stole that, I doubt he'd allow himself ter be caught in the parson's mousetrap."

Sam scowled. "There's the rub. Send word if you hear anything about the bauble."

"Ter ye or ter Miss Donovan?"

Sam narrowed his eyes. "Ter me."

Bear grinned at him. "Do ye think there's more like her in America?"

The question threw Sam for a moment. "I don't know," he said after a beat. "Maybe you ought ter sail over there ter find out." With that parting shot, Sam pivoted on his heel, leaving London's most vicious crime lord laughing behind him.

25

"She's lying."

Kendra studied Dr. Shay's flushed face. Five minutes ago, she'd joined Alec in the doctor's office. Like Lady Evelyn's bedchamber, the room was well-maintained, with heavy oak cabinets and shelves. Dr. Shay sat behind a massive gothic desk that looked like it might have been used at one time by the abbot when Shay House was still a monastery. She wondered if that man had been as pompous as the mad doctor before her.

Although right now, Dr. Shay looked less pompous and more pissed.

It made Kendra want to smile. She indulged in arching her eyebrows at him instead. "Lord Craymore didn't threaten to take his sister out of here?"

"No, of course not."

She waited a beat. "This is something easily verified," she pointed out, and Dr.

Shay's expression shifted slightly, his eyes darting to the side.

He cleared his throat. "What I am saying is that Mrs. Slater is prone to exaggeration. There was some… excitement during the music recital. Several ladies became quite hysterical, including Lady Evelyn. Naturally, Lord Craymore was distressed to witness such melodrama. These incidents can be unnerving."

"I think he was more unnerved to find out that Mr. Willoughby had been on the grounds," she challenged. "After all, the whole point of the earl having his sister committed was to keep her away from the man."

Dr. Shay didn't deny it. "That incident was an anomaly," he said stiffly.

"Really? Because I've heard that there was more than one incident. I can understand why you and Lord Craymore argued on Wednesday evening."

He huffed out a breath. "We did not quarrel. I brought Lord Craymore to my office to discuss the matter, much as Lord Sutcliffe and I were discussing the methods asylums employ when it comes to corrective measures." He looked at Alec. "We were not quarreling, were we, my lord?"

"No, you were giving me a rather lengthy defense of your methods," Alec drawled.

Dr. Shay's mouth puckered. "These are not *my* methods. These are methods that have been used to treat lunatics for decades."

"Maybe it's time for a change," Kendra snapped, her temper quickening.

He planted his elbows on his desk, steepling his fingers together as he eyed her. "Miss Donovan, I am aware that what you saw in the treatment room was disturbing for one untrained in the science of medicine, but you have to trust us to know to know what is best for our patients." After a beat, he smiled. "I already told you, these treatments are used by facilities everywhere, including Bethlem Royal Hospital. I'm certain you would not accuse that prestigious institution of wrongdoing."

The doctor's reasonable tone set Kendra's teeth on edge. She wanted to argue the point, but the practices of madhouses, no matter how despicable she thought them, was not why she was here. She circled back to the earlier topic. "You don't deny that Mr. Willoughby was here on the day that Lord Craymore was shot?"

"As I said, it was an anomaly. Mr. Booker chased off the scoundrel. No harm done."

"I doubt that Lord Craymore felt the same way."

"Yes, well... he was upset. Naturally." Dr. Shay dipped his head to concede the point. "However, he and I discussed his concerns, like gentlemen. We certainly did not quarrel."

"Lord Craymore didn't tell you that he was removing his sister from the premises?"

"Good heavens, no. We discussed the situation rationally. He told me about Mr. Willoughby's character. A blackguard, to be sure. I promised him that no such breach would happen again, and Mr. Booker would be more diligent about patrolling the grounds."

"And he accepted that?"

"Of course. Why would he not?" He smiled at her, showing too many teeth. "I would not put too much stock in what Mrs. Slater says if I were you, Miss Donovan. The woman has demonstrated an unnatural proclivity for causing trouble. Now..." He flattened the palms of his hands on his desk and made to push himself up. "I hope I have put your worries to rest."

"After you and his lordship finished your discussion, what happened then?"

Dr. Shay paused, sinking back down in the chair again. "What do you mean? His lordship left."

"And what did you do? After his lordship left?"

"I'm not certain I understand the question."

"Did you leave Shay House?"

"No. Why would I? It was evening."

"What did you do for the rest of the evening?"

"I was here." His brow crinkled in puzzlement as he gestured to his office. "Working."

"Can anyone verify that?"

Dr. Shay stared at her, eyes narrowing. "Why would I need somebody to prove that I was in my office? Are you implying that I am under suspicion?"

"It would be helpful to eliminate you entirely from all suspicion."

He turned to look at Alec. "My lord?"

Alec shrugged. "It's a simple question."

Dr. Shay's face tightened. "I was here alone," he snapped. "No one disturbed me, but everyone knew I was in my office."

"Door open or closed?"

He swung his gaze back to Kendra. "Closed. I had no reason to kill Lord Craymore. That is what you are suggesting with these questions, is it not?" He drummed his fingers on the desk, an irritated staccato, as he regarded her. "Miss Donovan, I am concerned that you are displaying a certain paranoia."

"I find Miss Donovan's questions to be perfectly reasonable," Alec said before Kendra could respond.

Dr. Shay's lips thinned at the rebuke, but he simply replied, "As I said, I have no reason to kill the earl."

"Have you ever heard of the Anahita Pink?" Kendra asked.

He hesitated for a fraction of a second. "The what?"

"The Anahita Pink. Lady Evelyn never mentioned it?"

He shook his head. "What is it?"

"A valuable heirloom that Lord Craymore may have had on him the night he died."

"Well, then, it would appear Lord Craymore was robbed after all. Perhaps you ought to be considering a highwayman." He rose, gesturing to the door. "Now, if there is nothing further, I shall have someone escort you to your carriage."

"We came here to speak to Lady Evelyn," Kendra said, pushing herself to her feet.

Dr. Shay fished out his pocket watch, and made a show of studying the time. "Very well. The ladies ought to be having tea in the library. No doubt Lady Evelyn shall be there." He slipped the watch back into his vest pocket and headed for the door. "If you'll follow me."

The ladies were grouped around tables in the library, drinking tea and playing cards. It resembled any other social gathering that Kendra had been to in this era, except for the shorn heads of a couple of the inmates and the identical beige dresses.

And the watchful eyes of Crump and Mrs. Maddox, who stood like sentinels guarding the door.

Mrs. Tilly had moved to another chair, shoulders still hunched in an effort to dissociate herself from everyone else in the room. She looked fragile, like she'd shatter into a million pieces if someone spoke harshly to her. Lillian Slater was standing near the French doors, staring outside. There was something in her expression that made Kendra follow her line of sight, and she spotted McBride sitting next to his wife outside on the verandah. He held a small book in one hand, and was reading to Mrs. McBride. His other hand was clasped around his wife's, his fingers laced through her pale, limp ones. Despite Mrs. McBride's unresponsiveness, there was tender intimacy in the scene that made Kendra feel like an intruder for observing it.

She shifted her eyes away as she and Alec followed Dr. Shay to where Lady Evelyn was sitting at a table, holding a cup of tea. Like Mrs. Tilly, she was sitting alone, also seemingly disassociating herself from the other occupants of the library. Unlike Mrs. Tilly, there was nothing fragile about Lady Evelyn. Her pale face was set in smug, contemptuous lines as she regarded those around her. It occurred to Kendra that Lady Evelyn was the only peeress in the asylum. Her elevated status was likely responsible for the gleam of arrogance in her pale eyes.

"Lady Evelyn." Dr. Shay stopped in front of the aristocrat. "Lord Sutcliffe and Miss Donovan wish to speak with you. However, if you prefer your solitude, I shall not force you into conversation."

Lady Evelyn dismissed the doctor simply by looking at Kendra and Alec. "Have you found out who killed my brother?" she demanded abruptly.

"We're still looking into it," Kendra said. "Can we walk in the gardens, my lady?"

Lady Evelyn surveyed her for a long moment. "Very well." She stood up, pausing to pick up the black shawl that matched her mourning dress, draping it about her narrow shoulders.

Smiling at Alec in an almost coquettish manner that was inappropriate given the circumstances, she held out her hand. "My lord?"

Alec adroitly offered his arm. "My lady."

Dr. Shay started to follow them, but Lady Evelyn rebuffed him with an icy glare. "I insist on privacy with my guests, doctor."

"I'm not certain that is wise, my lady. I do not want you overset."

"We shall treat Lady Evelyn with the utmost care," Alec assured him.

Dr. Shay seemed to recognize he could not argue with a marquis, and lifted a hand in concession. "Very well, my lord. But I strongly advise you not to say anything that might further fray Lady Evelyn's nerves."

Kendra could feel Dr. Shay's eyes on them as they wove their way around the tables to the French doors. There, they were forced to step aside so that McBride could wheel his wife across the threshold. He offered them a sad smile. For some reason, Kendra found herself glancing at Lillian Stater, who still stood a few yards away. Her gaze was fixed on McBride and his wife, but when she caught Kendra's eyes on her, she looked away quickly.

"Pray, tell me, sir, what is happening in London?" Lady Evelyn asked once they were walking outside. "Is there any delicious gossip?"

Alec exchanged a look with Kendra over Lady Evelyn's head. His expression was unreadable, but she knew that he found Lady Evelyn disturbing. She was treating the stroll like a social event, clinging to Alec's arm and smiling up at him as he guided her along the footpath.

The pea pebbles crunched beneath the soles of their shoes. The breeze feathered the leaves of nearby bushes and trees. Kendra followed close behind them, ignored by Lady Evelyn. *This must be how Molly feels in her role as chaperone.*

"I have been mostly at my uncle's country estate," Alec said carefully, neatly sidestepping the question.

"Oh." Lady Evelyn pursed her lips. "Surely, you must have heard something, though? Is Prinny being as wicked as always?"

"I don't know if the prince can be any other way."

Lady Evelyn laughed. "That is true. And what of Princess Charlotte? Basil told me that she and her new husband have returned to London."

Seeing an opportunity, Kendra quickened her pace to draw level with Lady Evelyn. "Did Mr. Willoughby tell you that when he was here on Wednesday?"

"Possibly. He is my fiancé. He has every right to visit me." Hostility brightened Lady Evelyn's pale eyes as she glanced back at Shay House. "They're trying to keep us apart. Everyone wants me to be unhappy."

Deliberately, Kendra adopted a soothing tone. *I'm on your side.* "I'm sorry. It's not fair that you are being kept apart."

Lady Evelyn drew in a quick breath, shooting Kendra a look. "No, it's not. It's wrong to keep two people apart who love each other."

Kendra nodded. "I agree."

"Basil pledged his love for me and told me that I needed to

be strong." Lady Evelyn lifted her chin, the gesture defiant, as though expecting Kendra to contradict her. "He vowed to get me out of here."

"How does he plan to do that?"

"Basil was confident that he could persuade Reginald to accept our betrothal." Lady Evelyn huffed out a breath. "But now Reginald is dead."

"Was he hoping to speak to your brother about it on Wednesday?"

Lady Evelyn frowned, her eyes narrowing. "Why are you inquiring about Basil?"

"I'm certain Mr. Willoughby wanted to persuade your brother that his intentions were honorable," Alec put in smoothly. "It was fortuitous that they were both visiting you on the same day."

The suspicion vanished from Lady Evelyn's face, and she smiled at Alec. "Yes, Basil is becoming impatient. He tried to call upon Reginald in London, but my brother refused to see him." Lady Evelyn's mood changed again, her thin lips knotting. "My brother was really being quite monstrous. He said he cared about my happiness, but that was a lie."

"Mayhap your brother was being overprotective, as brothers can be," Alec offered diplomatically.

Lady Evelyn stared into the distance, and said nothing.

Kendra waited a moment, then tried a different approach. "How about after your brother left Shay House? Did you know where he was going?"

Lady Evelyn gave her a sideways look. "Why are you quizzing me about this?"

Kendra studied the woman's pale face and wondered at her evasiveness. "We're trying to understand why your brother was on that road." Not exactly the truth, but she hoped it would lower the woman's guard. When Lady Evelyn remained stubbornly silent, she asked, "Do you know Mr. Griggs?"

Lady Evelyn looked like a skittish animal sensing a trap.

"We've been told that Mr. Griggs is something of an expert on antiquities," Alec murmured.

They'd been told that by Mr. Griggs himself, but they had no reason to doubt the old man.

Lady Evelyn's expression cleared. "Oh, he is. Papa invited him often to Pelsley Hall." She blew out a breath. "It was quite vexing, if you must know. We rarely had visitors, so it was *most* unfair that Mr. Griggs was the one visitor that we had regularly. Papa and Mr. Griggs would spend hours talking about some dusty relic that Papa had purchased or that one of his tenants had found in the field."

Kendra hadn't considered that Lady Evelyn actually was acquainted with Mr. Griggs, but of course, it made sense. She'd been presented in society only the year before. Prior to that, she would have been living in Norfolk, when her father had first asked Mr. Griggs to inspect his antiquities. Lady Evelyn would've been a teenager, even if the concept was foreign to this era.

For the first time since meeting Lady Evelyn, Kendra actually felt sorry for her. She'd been stuck in the countryside with a father completely absorbed by his interest in antiquities, with Mr. Griggs as their only guest. Was it any wonder that the girl had been desperate during her first season in London?

And like any predator, Willoughby had recognized Lady Evelyn's vulnerability. Kendra had seen the same pattern in her own timeline, especially when she'd worked in the FBI's cybercrime division. The Internet was flooded with predators targeting vulnerable teens. A particular favorite were young girls who lacked a father figure, who were desperate to be loved.

Human nature never really changes.

Kendra asked, "What do you know about the Anahita Pink?"

Lady Evelyn gave an irritable shrug. "Papa found it in the fields, and wanted Mr. Griggs to inspect it." She paused. "But then Papa died."

Kendra waited for Lady Evelyn to continue. When she didn't, she prodded, "Your brother came across the diamond then?"

"Yes. When he was settling Papa's affairs." She frowned. "I think Mr. Griggs wrote to him about it. Reginald was excited when he came across it. He sounded just like Papa."

"Did your brother show you the diamond when he was last here?"

"Yes. He was taking it to Mr. Griggs to inspect. I'd seen it before. Papa showed it to me," she said in a strangely flat tone. "Papa said that it was once part of King John's treasure. He was prodigiously fond of history."

It occurred to Kendra that a rare pink diamond might not hold the same allure for Lady Evelyn. In a way, the gem had been a rival for her father's affection, just as his hoard had been.

Kendra asked, "Did you mention the diamond to Mr. Willoughby?"

Lady Evelyn let go of Alec's arm, turning to face them both. "Basil is my fiancé. I told him many things. I don't want to talk to you about him. He had nothing to do with Reginald's death, and I refuse to help you implicate him."

Lady Evelyn might be batshit crazy, Kendra thought, but she wasn't stupid. She asked, "Did you write to your cousin, to ask for his help?"

The change of topic seemed to throw Lady Evelyn. "Jonah?"

"Yes.

A sudden gust of wind rattled the tree branches, sent swells across the lake, and ripped delicate petals from their moorings on a nearby rosebush, scattering them across the blades of grass. Kendra thought they looked like blood splatter.

"He is my cousin." Lady Evelyn's jaw tightened. "I am allowed to write to him."

"I didn't say otherwise," Kendra said calmly. "Are you two close?"

"I do not wish to speak to you about this anymore." Lady Evelyn spun around, and started walking up the sloping hillside.

Kendra shot Alec a look, then went after the woman, matching her stride. Alec fell back, now the third wheel.

"Did you write to your cousin about the Anahita Pink?" Kendra asked again, her gaze on Lady Evelyn's tense face.

Lady Evelyn shot her a sidelong look before glancing away. "Why would I?"

"Incentive."

"Incentive? How absurd!" She laughed, but it sounded shrill. "I don't know what you are implying, Miss Donovan, and I no longer care. I am done with these ceaseless questions!" She stopped walking suddenly, spinning to glare at Kendra. "I thought you agreed with me. I thought you wanted to help *me*!"

"I am trying to help you, Lady Evelyn. I'm trying to find out who killed your brother. I would think that is something you want as well."

Sudden tears welled in Lady Evelyn's eyes. "I loved Reginald… he was my brother. But he abandoned me," she whispered brokenly. "He chose his path. Now I must choose mine."

Kendra studied the woman's plain face, pinched with bitterness. "We know that you offered Mr. McBride the Anahita Pink if he helped you escape. Did you offer it to your cousin?"

"What does it matter if I wrote to him? Jonah has a right to know!"

"Did he respond?"

"I am done with this conversation!" Lady Evelyn snapped, and started forward again, the small pea pebbles spitting out from her heels as she strode furiously down the footpath.

Kendra and Alec watched the departing figure in silence. "The lady doth protest too much," Kendra said softly.

"You think she's lying."

"I think she's afraid."

Alec raised his eyebrows. "Afraid? What is she afraid of?"

"She tried to use the Anahita Pink as incentive to get her out of Shay House. Maybe she's afraid that she unintentionally got her brother killed."

Unless it wasn't unintentional.

The thought whispered across Kendra's mind twenty minutes later when they were once again in the carriage, barreling down the drive. Maybe Lady Evelyn had known exactly what she was doing when she told Basil Willoughby and Jonah Lansing about the Anahita Pink. She certainly had known what she was doing when she tried to tempt McBride with the diamond. The difference was the outcome. With McBride, she'd hoped to gain her freedom. But with Lansing and Willoughby, what had been her intention? To strike out at the man who'd put her in Shay House?

Lady Evelyn was unpredictable and emotional, but Kendra sensed a sly cunning in the woman as well. Could she have deliberately painted a figurative bull's eye on her brother's back, hoping someone would take aim?

"Did you learn anything in the kitchens, Molly?" Kendra asked.

"Just that everyone is blue-devilled 'cause of w'ot 'appened ter 'is lordship. Mrs. Strong—she's the cook—says that it's even worse than the first scandal. Thinks that this time it'll be the end of Shay 'Ouse.

"Mrs. Strong lives down the road a bit with 'er 'usband," Molly added. "It ain't like she wanted ter work at á mad'ouse, but there ain't a lot of positions for cooks layin' thick on the ground around Needl'am."

"Did you ask her about the first scandal?"

Molly nodded. "Aye. Thought ye'd want me ter. Mrs. Strong said it was a terrible thing ter 'appen. She couldn't believe that Mr. Dodd took advantage of Miss Osmond, but then 'e went and blew 'is brains out. No innocent would commit such an 'orrible sin, she said, so 'e must 'ave done the deed. Could 'ave knocked 'er over with a feather, she said, 'cause she thought 'e was such a nice lad. But Oi told 'er, Oi did, that if there's one thing Oi've learned about being yer maid, it's that ye can never really know about folks."

"No, you can't," Kendra agreed easily enough, but felt a twinge of guilt for being responsible for Molly's more jaundiced view of humanity.

The carriage swayed and slowed as Benjamin steered it onto the main road. Kendra's gaze strayed back to Shay House. Murder and mayhem—that was what Lady Atwood had accused her of bringing into their lives. But both had existed here long before Kendra.

26

Kendra planned to update the slate board with the new information and spend time running through the possibilities and probabilities of why someone had felt the need to put two bullets into Lord Craymore's back. Something was niggling at the back of her mind, something that she should be considering…

But she knew that she'd be putting aside those plans when Benjamin drove into the Aldridge Castle's stable yard, and she saw the carriage with its distinctive crest near one of the outbuildings. Several stable hands were in the processes of unharnessing the team of horses. As the carriage rolled to a stop, a rider galloped into the yard.

"Finally, you have returned!" the horsewoman declared, expertly bringing her mare to a fidgety standstill. She watched them alight from the carriage. "I have been waiting most anxiously."

"Becca," Alec said with affection, grinning at Lady Rebecca Blackburn. "What brings you to Aldridge Castle? I didn't think that we would see you until the house party."

Rebecca guided her horse to a nearby mounting block. Despite the pockmarks that pitted her face from having contracted a nearly fatal bout of smallpox when she was six years old, Rebecca looked fetching in a velvet riding habit that matched her cornflower blue eyes. Her auburn hair was swept into an elaborately braided coiffure, which was set off by the straw hat decorated with a blue bow and two jaunty, silver-dyed ostrich plumes.

"It's because of the house party that we're here," she said, throwing her reins to Dylan, the lead stable boy. "Papa has business in Town, and Mama thought we ought to accompany him to visit our London modiste. We're in desperate need of new gowns for Lady Atwood's ball. Aldridge Castle is far more pleasant to stay than a public inn. Besides, you know how much Papa loves peering through Duke's telescope whenever he has a chance. Given the sun today, it should be an excellent night to stargaze."

She lifted her leg over the saddle's pommel, gathering her long skirt with one gloved hand while extending the other for Alec's assistance to climb down the three stone steps of the mounting block. Once on the ground, she rushed over to Kendra, giving her an enthusiastic hug. "'Tis good to see you again, Kendra!"

The warmth of that gesture always took Kendra by surprise, but she no longer hesitated in returning the embrace. She smiled. "You, too, Rebecca."

"Duke told us about Lord Craymore," Rebecca said. She regarded Kendra with shrewd eyes. "He said that you are of the mind that it was not a random act, but someone deliberately killed him."

"It looks that way."

"Do you have any suspects?" Rebecca asked, then laughed. "Do you realize that is a question I never asked before I met you?"

Kendra wasn't sure how to take that. It reminded her too much of Lady Atwood's accusation and Molly's increased cynicism.

Maybe Rebecca sensed her ambivalence, because she chuckled again and linked her arm companionably through Kendra's, nudging her towards the castle. "Life is never dull around you, Kendra—thank heavens. Let me change out of my riding habit. Then I want you to tell me everything."

Kendra fully intended to tell Rebecca everything—in the privacy of the study. However, Lady Atwood insisted on holding a more formal lunch with the arrival of Lord and Lady Blackburn.

Unless it was the occasional nuncheons during the Beau Monde's country house parties, the midday meal tended to be an informal affair of cold cuts, cakes, and fruits, served mostly to ladies to stave off hunger pangs until the grander, multiple course evening dinner. That day's nuncheon might have been formal, but the fare was simple: tiny triangle sandwiches filled with shaved meat. Eaten with a knife and fork. Of course, Kendra was the only one who thought that weird. She supposed they'd think it just as weird if she picked up the sandwich and ate it with her bare hands. Who was to say which way was right?

There were also platters filled with traditional cold cuts, accompanied by relishes, sauces, and jellies, and bowls of sliced pineapple and oranges that had been grown in the castle's orangery.

"The inquest is set for Monday morning," the Duke informed everyone as he cut into his sandwich.

A pained expression crossed his sister's face. "Really, Bertie. Must you speak of that at the dinner table? We have guests."

Lady Blackburn smiled at the countess. "Do not concern yourself about our sensibilities, Carolyn. Maybe I am being frightfully vulgar, but I confess that I am curious."

Lady Blackburn had the look of her daughter, with the same glorious auburn hair and intelligent eyes, though hers were a warm caramel rather than cornflower blue. She turned to regard Kendra. "Duke says that you believe the earl's murder was personal in nature, even though he was carrying a valuable diamond at the time."

Kendra glanced at the Duke.

He shrugged. "I told Neville and Jane about the Anahita Pink."

"I cannot believe that Craymore—Benedict, that is—came across such a valuable find and said nothing," Lord Blackburn said, spooning a dollop of horseradish sauce for his roast beef. He was a handsome man, his chestnut hair threaded with silver and with the same cornflower blue eyes that he'd passed on to his daughter. Those eyes were now filled with wonder. "My God. Think of it, Bertie! King John's lost treasure. 'Tis something every English schoolboy has dreamed about finding."

"He didn't find the entire treasure," Alec replied, sipping his ale. "Only the diamond."

"Still, that alone is worth a king's ransom," Lord Blackburn said. "In fact, it belongs to the king. Craymore should not have kept it a secret."

"In all fairness, we don't know what Benedict would have done," the Duke pointed out. "He had yet to have it authenticated when he had his fit and died. And now the gem has vanished, so it's impossible to say that it really is the Anahita Pink."

Lord Blackburn sighed. "I wish I had seen it. Pink diamonds are excessively rare, you know. I was fortunate enough to purchase a very small one when Jane and I traveled to India several years ago, and even then, its hue was not a true pink, but rather a brownish-orange."

"The value of a diamond is not its color, but the sentiment in which it is given." Lady Blackburn smiled at her husband. "We had the gem set as the center stone in my pearl necklace. It is a lovely reminder of our travels."

"You went to India with your husband?" Kendra didn't know why she was surprised. A year ago, Rebecca had attended Lady Atwood's house party alone because her parents had been traveling to Lord Blackburn's sugar plantations in Barbados.

Lord Blackburn chuckled. "My wife is no Penelope. She is not one to stay behind, waiting patiently for my return."

"I adore travel," Lady Blackburn agreed. She shifted her gaze to include the rest of the table. "My husband has extensive interests in the spice trade, and rather than rely on reports sent to him by his stewards, he prefers to personally review his investments. And I prefer to go with him. We used to bring Rebecca along on our adventures when she was a child, but my poor darling becomes dreadfully ill at sea."

Rebecca grimaced. "Mama stayed behind with me for several voyages until I convinced her that I was quite capable of looking after myself."

"Or staying in a sizeable manor house with dozens of servants to look after you," Alec teased lightly.

"Beast," she replied with a laugh. "I might remind you that if it wasn't for my seasickness, I would not have been here at last year's house party, and become such fast friends with Miss Donovan."

Kendra smiled automatically, but she couldn't help but think how tiny, random decisions could so easily change the course of one's life. *What if, what if, what if...*

Last year, Rebecca had elevated Kendra's status from that of servant to Rebecca's companion, to assist her in her hunt for a serial killer. Their friendship had been forged under the intense pressure that accompanies murder investigations, much like comrades during war. Rebecca's presence last year at the house party had been integral to her own survival.

Kendra reached for her glass, taking a slow sip of boiled water. She was always so focused on her own actions—how they could twist up this timeline and change the future—that she never took into account how the actions of those around her may have af-fected *her*. Without Rebecca's intervention that fateful day almost a year ago, Kendra might not be alive now.

Was the course of a life so fragile that one small incident—turning left instead of turning right—could change it forever? Or were the steps already predetermined? Fate or faith? This was the discussion that she and the Duke often had. And like those times, Kendra felt uneasy and out of her depth.

"And what of you, Miss Donovan?"

Kendra blinked as she returned to the present. Her cheeks tingled with heat when she realized everyone was staring at her. "I'm sorry. What?"

Lady Blackburn smiled. "I asked whether you were seasick on your voyage from America?"

A memory surfaced of being plunged into an icy current and spun around, the sensation of being shredded into nothingness and knit back together. She had to suppress a shudder. "It wasn't a pleasant experience," she admitted with utter truthfulness.

The Duke lifted his glass of ale, eyeing her over the rim. "We are grateful that she made the voyage."

"And you have never considered returning to your homeland, Miss Donovan?" Lady Blackburn asked.

"I've considered it," Kendra murmured, and her throat tightened unexpectantly as she thought how the full moon would rise in the night sky in less than a week. *What if, what if, what if…*

She looked across the table and met Alec's eyes. His expression was grim, as though he knew exactly what was going through her head.

"Well, I, for one, am grateful that you've resigned yourself to your fate here in England," Lady Blackburn smiled, and lifted her glass in a mock toast. "We English are not an easy lot to live with. I commend you on your fortitude, my dear girl."

Kendra forced herself to return the woman's smile. Awkwardly, she cut her sandwich and took a bite. After a moment of chewing and swallowing, she asked, "Tell me, when you traveled to India, did you ever hear about the Kingdom of Mysore?"

"Mysore?" Lady Blackburn lifted her eyebrows. "Yes, of course. 'Tis in the southern part of India. A fascinating place with delightful people. Although, I fear, there are tensions between that princely state and England."

Lord Blackburn said, "It's where I purchased the diamond that I spoke of."

"Is that where the Tungabhadra River is located?" Kendra asked.

"Yes," Lord Blackburn replied.

Rebecca gave her a shrewd glance. "What are you thinking, Kendra? These are not random questions."

Kendra shrugged. "I was told that Mr. Lewis—one of the attendants at Shay House—was born in the Kingdom of Mysore. His father worked for the British East India Company, and met Mr. Lewis' mother while she was washing clothes in a river."

"There are many rivers in the kingdom, but the Tungabhadra River is the most notable." Lady Blackburn frowned. "Though what does it matter where this attendant's parents met?"

"The lore around the Anahita Pink is that it was discovered on or near the Tungabhadra River in India, like the Darya-ye Noor," said Kendra. "It's an odd coincidence."

The Duke looked at her. "I am aware that you do not care for coincidences, my dear, but what can it have to do with Lord Craymore's murder?"

"Lady Evelyn told Mr. McBride at Shay House about the Anahita Pink. There's no reason to think that she didn't also tell Mr. Lewis. He probably knew the diamond's history and lore. As Lady Blackburn said, the value of a diamond is sometimes as much about sentiment as it is about size and color."

"The value of the stone would be incentive enough to bring out a man's darker nature," the Duke argued.

"Yes, but it meant something more to you when you heard it might have been part of King John's treasure."

"Well, of course!" Lord Blackburn stared at her. "'Tis part of England's history."

"It was part of India's history before King Richard managed to get his hands on it," Kendra pointed out. "Some might even say that it rightfully belongs there."

"You can't be suggesting that Mr. Lewis would kill a man to return a diamond to its homeland," Alec remarked drily. "Greed is far more likely."

"Why would this Mr. Lewis even be motivated on behalf of India?" Lord Blackburn shook his head. "If his father works for the East British India Company, then he's an Englishman. His loyalty would be to England."

That other one. Booker's words came back to her. And Mrs. Slate's observation that Lewis was considered a savage because of his mixed race. More importantly, did *he* consider himself an Englishman?

"I don't know Mr. Lewis's story. I didn't have the opportunity to speak to him." *And that needs to be rectified,* Kendra decided.

Rebecca said, "Mr. Lewis's parents may have met in the Kingdom of Mysore, on the banks of the Tungabhadra River, but that doesn't mean he spent his childhood there. He may have no affiliation or affinity to the place. They most likely moved around, especially considering his father's work."

"Maybe, but he mentioned the place where his parents met. That suggests an affiliation, even an affection."

Alec leaned forward to pick up an orange from the fruit platter. "If I was going to place a wager on who killed Craymore, I'd put my blunt on Willoughby."

"Basil Willoughby?" Rebecca paused in taking a bite of her sandwich.

There was something in her voice that made Alec look at her sharply. "I wasn't aware you were acquainted with the man."

"We were introduced during my first season, and he pressed his suit."

"Good God. I had no idea." The Duke looked at his friend. "You never mentioned that the scapegrace was pursuing Rebecca."

Lord Blackburn waved a hand. "I never mentioned it because nothing came of it. Willoughby hadn't stepped beyond the pale at that point, but we were well aware of his reputation as a fortune hunter at the time. If Rebecca hadn't had the good sense to cut him off, her mother and I would have stepped in. However, I raised my daughter to have more than fluff between her ears." He smiled at Rebecca. "She saw through him immediately."

"You may be giving me too much credit, Papa. The first season is a vulnerable time for many young ladies. It can be…unpleasant. Mr. Willoughby recognizes this, and preys on one's weaknesses."

Kendra studied her friend. Willoughby would have seen the pockmarks marring Rebecca's face and assumed they signaled weakness. He would never have seen beyond the disfigurement to the keen intelligence in her eyes, the dignified set of her shoulders, the proud tilt of her chin.

"Mr. Willoughby is quite handsome, and I may have found my head turned briefly by his flirtatious manner," Rebecca admitted. "But he made a mistake."

Curious, Kendra asked, "What did he do?"

"He mocked Mary Wollstonecraft's *A Vindication of the Rights of Woman*."

Kendra laughed. Rebecca was passionate about women's rights. She said, "He's an idiot."

"No, he's not. But he is arrogant." Rebecca smiled slightly, but the merriment faded quickly. "I am aware that he charmed Lady Evelyn last season."

Lady Atwood made a hiss of disapproval. "Scandalous behavior, both of them."

"But it was Lady Evelyn who paid the price," Kendra said, and shrugged when everyone looked at her. "Lord Craymore put her in Shay House because of it." She picked up her glass and looked at Rebecca. "You know Willoughby. Would you wager that he shot the earl and stole the Anahita Pink?"

Rebecca took her time in answering. "Mr. Willoughby would steal a valuable gem—if he was certain that he would never be caught. He's a coward at heart. And lazy. It's why he always chooses heiresses that he believes are disadvantaged in some way and ripe for the picking." Her lips twisted. "Yet as despicable as I find the scoundrel, I don't think he would commit murder."

"Lord Craymore was shot in the back. That's pretty cowardly."

Rebecca frowned. "True. But if he managed to snatch this diamond, I think he would have fled for the continent. You said that he's still in London?"

"Yes, but it won't be that easy to sell a diamond like the Anahita Pink," Kendra said. "He would have to make arrangements, and that will take time. Mr. Kelly is going to ask Bear if he's heard any rumors about a possible sale."

"Bear?" Lady Blackburn's eyebrows rose, shocked. "Isn't that the ruffian who attacked you last year?"

"He's in the best position to hear about a stolen diamond," Kendra pointed out.

Lady Atwood cleared her throat. "I think we have had enough talk of murder and criminals at the table. Let us discuss another, more appropriate topic, shall we? Sutcliffe, why don't you tell us about the Irish stud farm you recently purchased from Lord Hilton. Or the mill in the village that is being repaired."

Alec smiled crookedly. "I don't think my acquisition of Lord Hilton's stud farm or the French buhrstone for the Aldridge Village mill will make for exciting conversation, aunt."

"We have had enough exciting conversation," she snapped. "I wish for normalcy."

27

They put aside talk of Lord Craymore's murder until later that afternoon, when Kendra, Alec, and Rebecca finally escaped to the study. Pots of tea and coffee were ordered, and it wasn't long before Rebecca considered the slate board as she sipped her tea.

"Are we certain that the child—Shandor—didn't steal the diamond when he found Lord Craymore?" she wondered. "Obviously, it was Craymore's first thought when he regained consciousness. He must have had a reason."

Kendra's gaze traveled to the last words Craymore spoke. *No, thief, no!* "There was another witness, a girl, who backs up Shandor's story. Craymore had lost a lot of blood by the time Shandor found him. I'm surprised he regained consciousness at all. When he did, I think he was simply replaying his encounter with his attacker. *That's* who he was calling a thief—not Shandor."

"I suppose that's logical. 'Tis a shame that Craymore wasted his last breath, not identifying his attacker."

"He was obviously delirious," Alec said.

Rebecca's gaze shifted to the next section: Shay House. Below, Kendra had listed the men who worked at the asylum.

"What was it like?" she asked, swinging around to look at Kendra and Alec. "The madhouse?"

"Criminal," Kendra said. A fresh wave of outrage rose up inside her.

"I don't think we need to get into specifics," Alec cautioned.

Rebecca's eyes flashed. "I do not need you to coddle me, Sutcliffe!"

Kendra shot Alec a pointed look. "Sutcliffe and I have talked about his overly protective tendencies."

Alec smiled. "I forget that I am surrounded by independent-minded females."

"Dr. Shay was treating one of the patients when we arrived," Kendra told Rebecca. "She was tied, naked and blindfolded, to a chair while Dr. Shay and an attendant poured water on her to force her into submission." Despite her best efforts, her voice trembled with anger. "It's not therapy—it's torture."

"Dear heaven," Rebecca gasped.

"It was shocking to witness," Alec agreed, his eyes on Kendra. "But you cannot fault Dr. Shay for using what is the norm in madhouses. This is not your America, Kendra."

"You don't need to tell me that; I know."

"It sounds like America treats their mentally ill far better than we British," Rebecca observed. "We ought to follow the colonies' example."

Kendra looked away from Rebecca's approving smile. She felt like a fraud. Nineteenth-century America was no more enlightened than England when it came to its mental institutions. She was grateful that Rebecca suffered from seasickness. Otherwise she might sail to America and discover that Kendra had lied to her about where she'd come from... *when* she'd come from. Throughout the past year, there had been several times when she'd tried to tell Rebecca the truth. But the words always had stuck in her throat. She'd never had a friend—a *best* friend—before, and she didn't want Rebecca to look at her differently.

"What's this notation about Miss Osmond's scandal?" Rebecca asked, pointing to the slate board.

"She was a patient at Shay House when she was molested by one of the attendants."

Alec shook his head. "I don't even know why you included that information. It happened four years ago. What happened then cannot have anything to do with Lord Craymore's death."

"No, but it started Shay House's decline. Would it be possible to interview her?"

Alec frowned. "I can't imagine Pierce Osmond talking to you about his daughter's molestation. Nor would her husband allow such a thing."

"Are you speaking of Pierce Osmond, the banker?" Rebecca asked in an odd voice. "His daughter was molested?"

Kendra looked at her. "You know him?"

"Not him. *Her.* Mrs. Christina Devaney is the eldest daughter of Mr. Osmond. If this happened four years ago, it must be her. There is a younger daughter, but she's still in the schoolroom."

"How are you acquainted with her, Becca?" Alec asked. "She doesn't exactly run in your social circles."

"I met Mrs. Devaney at Mrs. Shubert's literary salon. I cannot say that we are friends. She is not talkative; more prone to listen rather than participate in the discussion. When she does speak, however, she makes excellent points. She always struck me as painfully shy."

"That probably got her locked up in the first place," Kendra muttered darkly.

"Kendra may be soon joining the Religious Society of Friends to reform madhouses," Alec told Rebecca.

"As it happens, I find the Quaker attempts at reform quite admirable, Sutcliffe." Rebecca shot Alec a quelling look. "Did you know that they were among the first to petition for the abolition of slavery? And they have been the staunchest proponents of the rights of women. If they weren't so... strict in their practices, I might consider joining them as well."

Alec's green eyes glinted with amusement. "You are not interested in giving up your spirits or fripperies, Becca?"

Rebecca smiled reluctantly. "I confess that I enjoy a bit of color in my evening gowns. It's difficult to be a paragon." Her smile vanished. "Dear heavens, I had no notion that Mrs. Devaney had been molested, much less a patient in a madhouse. Then again, 'tis not something one would advertise. I'm surprised that Mrs. Devaney told her family what happened to her. Even a strong character would find that difficult to admit."

Kendra said slowly, "I don't think she volunteered the information."

Rebecca frowned, puzzled. "Did someone inform her family what was happening to her?"

"We were told there were consequences."

"Consequences? What... oh!" Rebecca's blue eyes widened in sudden comprehension. The teacup rattled in the saucer. She set it down on a nearby table. "Oh, dear heaven." She walked to the window, her expression pensive as she stared out. "She has two children," she murmured, almost to herself. "The oldest is a girl. Nearly four." She swung back to look at Kendra. "You are saying that the child is a by-blow from this... this attendant?"

"It appears so, yes."

Alec said, "Her father quickly arranged a marriage. Mr. Devaney has obviously accepted the child as his own, if you are aware of the girl's existence."

Rebecca rubbed her arms as though chilled. "What happened to the attendant? Mayhap the relationship was consensual, but Mr. Osmond would not accept the attendant's low-born status? The family is not part of the aristocracy, but Mr. Osmond is wealthy and has high expectations."

Some things are not always what they may seem, Lilian had said. Was this supposed "relationship" what she'd been hinting at? Kendra tended to think that the power dynamic between a patient and an attendant made true consent questionable, if not impossible. Still, there was no getting around the fact that the results of their relationship had been tragic.

"Regardless of what happened to Mrs. Devaney, I have to agree with Sutcliffe," Rebecca said, snapping Kendra out of her contemplation. "It happened years ago. What could you possibly gain by interviewing Mrs. Devaney? Lord Craymore's killer was after the Anahita Pink."

Kendra said, "Mrs. Devaney knows everyone at Shay House. She might be able to give me some perspective." She turned to look at the names she'd written on the slate board. "Like which man on this list is capable of murder."

"We already established that the Anahita Pink would be a terrible temptation for most men," Alec commented.

Kendra couldn't argue with that. But something was bugging her. *What am I missing?*

She sighed. "The killer will have to sell it eventually. Until then, we continue the investigation the old-fashioned way." *Here, the* really *old-fashioned way.* "Interviews. Apply pressure. It's not easy to maintain a lie. Cracks form. Inconsistencies develop. Apply enough pressure, lies begin to fall apart."

Dr. Shay. Mr. McBride. Mr. Lewis. Even Crump. Then, Jonah Lansing and Basil Willoughby. "Someone is lying," she continued. "Hopefully, Mr. Kelly will have news about Lansing and Willoughby. Tomorrow, we need to return to Shay House."

Rebecca shook her head. "Tomorrow is the Sabbath. That's why we are staying until Monday morning."

Kendra knew the rule—unnecessary travel was frowned upon on Sundays. It was considered bad form. She thought back to her own time. Even then, unless they were up against a deadline—a kidnapping, a child missing—everyone was entitled to a day off.

She'd just never taken it. While her colleagues spent time with their families, she worked the case. She recalled invitations to Sunday backyard barbecues that she'd always declined. Eventually, the invitations had dried up.

"Everyone deserves a day to relax," Alec said, as though reading her mind. He smiled as he met her eyes. "I think my aunt mentioned a game of charades."

Kendra stared at him. "You call *that* relaxing?"

Rebecca laughed. "I relish charades. And dancing. I might be able to persuade Mama to play the pianoforte so we can dance."

Kendra couldn't stop herself from glancing at the slate board.

Alec noticed. "Nothing is going to happen tomorrow, Kendra," he said, and took her hand. "You might even enjoy yourself."

But the next morning, a messenger arrived, delivering a note from Sam Kelly informing them that a body had been found in the lake at Shay House.

28

Sam trotted up to Kendra, Alec and Rebecca as they stepped through the French doors into the back gardens of Shay House. "Well, I have ter say, this is an interestin' turn," he announced, then gave a quick bow in Rebecca's direction. "Lady Rebecca. I didn't expect ter see you."

"My parents and I were at Aldridge Castle when your message arrived. I offered to act as Miss Donovan's chaperone in place of her maid."

Kendra looked at Sam. "Your note was a little short on details, Mr. Kelly. What happened?"

"Aye, well, at the time, I didn't know anythin'. I had one of me lads staying in Needlham. Wanted him ter keep his peepers on Shay House and the men there, and do a bit of sniffin' around the village."

Kendra nodded. "Good thinking. Did he report anything interesting?"

"Aye, a dead body." He grinned at her. "He was in the tavern this mornin', breaking his fast when the groundskeeper—Mr. Booker—came in, lookin' for the constable. He sent a rider immediately ter me, and I sent a message ter you. Figured you'd want ter know."

"You figured right." Kendra spied nine men and a teenager gathered around the lip of the lake. Five men stood to one side—Dr. Shay, McBride, Crump, Lewis, and Booker. Booker was accompanied, as usual, by his two rottweilers. A few feet away were three other men. Standing between both groups was the lanky teen that she'd seen in the stables the other day.

"C'mon," Sam said.

They followed the Bow Street Runner down the grassy slope. Kendra eyed the strangers, pegging the large, middle-aged man with curly salt-and-pepper sideburns as the local constable. A lean, young man stood next to him. Two other men were shivering violently in wet clothes. Locals, Kendra suspected, who'd drawn the short straw and had to fish the body out of the lake.

Her view of the body was blocked by the men, but then everyone shifted as they turned to look at Sam, and she got her first view of the dead man. His hair was unnaturally darkened by the lake water, and plastered to his skull. His eyes were open, now glazed in death. His visage was strikingly handsome, even in its present state. She didn't need Sam to tell her the man's identity or hear Rebecca's gasp of recognition.

Basil Willoughby.

She didn't realize that she'd whispered his name until Sam nodded grimly. "Aye, lass. Looks like someone brained the rogue."

"That's ridiculous!" Dr. Shay glared at Sam before looking at Kendra. "What are you doing here again? You have no business at Shay House!"

"You've got a dead man on your property, and you're worried about my presence? I think you have your priorities mixed up, Dr. Shay."

"The poor wretch slipped and obviously hit his head on a rock. He had the misfortune of being near the lake."

"Aye," Rowan Booker spoke up. "Found 'im floatin' like a bloody carp in the middle of the pond."

"Mr. Booker is the one who gave hue and cry," Sam told them.

"Me and me lads," Booker added. The dogs' ears twitched and they shifted on their haunches, as though aware that they were being talked about. "We were takin' our turn around the grounds, as we do every mornin', when Oi saw 'im floatin' in the pond. Gave me a bloody start, it did. Went straight up ter the 'ouse ter tell Dr. Shay."

Kendra raised her eyebrows. "You didn't think to pull him out?"

"Why would Oi? Could see that 'e was dead, w'ot with 'is face in the water."

"He was facedown in the water?"

"Oi jest said that, didn't Oi?"

"Clearly, it was a terrible accident," insisted Dr. Shay.

"Aye. Quite terrible," echoed the man with curly sideburns. He clasped his hands behind his back, rocking back on his heels with a self-important air.

"This here is Mr. Gulliver, the local constable," Sam introduced. "Lord Sutcliffe, Lady Rebecca, and Miss Donovan."

"I sent for Mr. Gulliver immediately. I didn't expect Bow Street to come." Dr. Shay pressed his lips together in a tight seam of disapproval, his eyes narrowing as he looked at Sam and the lean young man.

The latter grinned and doffed his hat. "I'm Mr. Durst—Bow Street."

Mr. Gulliver bowed. "Good morning, sir, milady—eh, what's she doing?"

His eyebrows shot up as Kendra pushed past him to squat down for a closer look at Willoughby. Kendra ignored the constable, and began patting down the body. "Any weapons on him?"

"If he had a weapon, it's in the water," Sam said.

"Okay. Let's turn him over."

Alec and Sam joined her to roll the body. The injury wasn't immediately apparent. Willoughby had thick hair and the water from the pond had washed away any telltale blood.

Grateful that she was wearing kid gloves, Kendra began to methodically separate strands of hair to peer at his scalp, finally revealing three odd lacerations on the back of his head. The skin was split open, the skull crushed on the left parietal bone.

Kendra met Sam's flat cop-gaze. He wasn't kidding when he said that someone had brained him.

"Oi think the bloke fell inter the lake last evenin'," said Rowan Booker.

Kendra glanced at the groundskeeper. "Why do you say that?"

"'Cause Freddie and Adolphus caught the scent of somethin' and began barkin' somethin' fierce. Oi gave 'em their 'eads, and they brought me 'ere. The moon was shinin' like a lamp, but Oi didn't think ter look in the pond. Why would Oi, eh? Oi thought the lads 'ad caught the scent of a skunk or some other night vermin. After a bit 'o walkin' around, Oi got Freddie and Adolphus settled down, and we went back ter me room over the stables."

"What time was this?" Kendra asked.

"Near midnight, Oi'd say. Oi was ready ter turn in when the lads began actin' up."

"The fool had no business sneaking onto the grounds," muttered Dr. Shay. "It isn't our fault that he tripped and died."

Kendra studied the doctor's flushed face. Who was he trying to convince—them or himself? "He didn't trip," she said finally. "Mr. Kelly is right. Someone hit him from behind. And based on those injuries, it wasn't a rock. I'd like Dr. Munroe to confirm it."

Sam nodded. "I sent a note for him as well."

"Confirm what?" Dr. Shay demanded, his voice rising as his gaze swung between Kendra and Sam. "What are you implying?"

"I'm not implying anything—I'm saying it outright." Kendra pushed herself to her feet, and let her eyes travel around the circle of faces. McBride and Lewis both looked uneasy. *If they examined the wound, they know,* she thought. "Willoughby didn't fall. He didn't hit his head on a rock and slip into the lake. This injury was caused by something long and cylindrical. And heavy."

Sam nodded. "The barrel of a barking iron, I'd say. The poor sod was pistol whipped."

Mr. Gulliver inhaled sharply. "You're saying this man was murdered?"

"Aye. Mr. Willoughby was most definitely murdered."

"The only question is how he actually died." Kendra let her gaze fall to the prone figure. "Did the blows kill him? Or was he only stunned when the killer threw him in the lake, and he drowned?"

"He should never have been on the grounds in the first place," Dr. Shay snapped. "It would have been within our rights to shoot him for trespassing."

"That may be, but he wasn't shot," Sam countered. "This wasn't self-defense."

Kendra's gaze was drawn to a familiar figure walking down the grassy knoll. Dr. Munroe had one hand clamped tightly on the brim of his curly beaver hat to prevent it from being blown off when a sudden gust of wind swept the hillside. His other hand was fisted around the wooden handle of the black leather medical bag that he carried.

"Dr. Munroe, good mornin'." Sam stepped forward, and repeated his introduction.

"We are acquainted," Dr. Shay said stiffly. "You've come a long way for little reason, doctor. Mr. McBride here is a sawbones. He learned the trade while fighting Boney. He can conduct the post-mortem, I'm certain."

Everyone looked at McBride, who pressed his lips together and said nothing. His expression was grim. Perhaps caught between his boss wanting Willoughby's death declared an accident—and the truth.

"Nothing better than the battlefield to sharpen one's skills," Munroe agreed smoothly.

"Dr. Munroe made the journey. He'll do the postmortem," Sam said in a flat, hard voice.

"Now, see here!" Dr. Shay thrust out his chin as he swiveled around to confront Sam. "Bow Street has no authority here! You can't come here issuing orders."

"What about Mr. Dockery?" the constable interjected, clearly wanting to diffuse the tension that had suddenly sprung up.

McBride jumped at the suggestion, no doubt seeing it as a way to extract himself from the uncomfortable situation. "Whenever a postmortem needs to be done, he usually does it."

Rebecca looked at McBride. "Mr. Dockery is the local surgeon?"

Mr. Gulliver answered. "Nay. The village butcher. He won't have a problem with the blood."

Kendra stared at the constable. "I thought you said Mr. Dockery has done autopsies before?"

"Aye. Not that we've had much call for it. When folks stick their spoon in the wall around here, it's usually a visitation by God—not mischief. But every once in a while, there's been questions. Mr. Dockery conducts the postmortem and testifies at the inquest."

It wasn't all that long ago—a hundred years or so—when barbers in England were allowed to act as surgeons, amputating limbs and giving enemas in between picking lice off customer's heads while offering haircuts and shaves. In Europe, the red-and-white pole outside barber shops supposedly could be traced back to their connection with surgery—red representing blood and white for bandages. The father of modern surgery, sixteenth-century Frenchman Ambrose Paré, had gotten his start as a barber-surgeon.

That didn't make this any less strange. *A butcher.* Jesus Christ.

"If Mr. Dockery has no objections, I could use his assistance," Munroe said diplomatically.

Mr. Gulliver waved that concern away. "Ack, Mr. Dockery will be right pleased to have a London doctor such as yourself using his shop to conduct the postmortem."

"Dr. Munroe gave up his practice in order to open an anatomy school." Dr. Shay shot Munroe a veiled glance, his lip curling with spite. "Tongues are still wagging about it in London."

"Right now, an anatomist is exactly what we need," Kendra said coolly.

"Me and young Bruce 'ere will fetch the wagon ter transport 'im," Rowan Booker offered, snapping his fingers, and the kid—apparently named Bruce—snapped to attention. Kendra wasn't entirely sure who the command was directed at—the kid or the dogs. Regardless, they all jogged after the groundskeeper.

Lewis cleared his throat. "If you'll excuse me, I shall attend to the ladies. They've been confined to the house, but that alone may overset them. Many do not like their routine changed."

Kendra saw her opportunity and moved toward him. "If you don't mind, I'll walk with you, Mr. Lewis."

Something flickered in his eyes, then was gone. He inclined his head. "Certainly, Miss Donovan."

"I didn't have the chance to talk to you yesterday," she said as they started up the hill.

"What do you wish to talk to me about?"

Instead of answering, she asked, "Does Lady Evelyn know that Mr. Willoughby is dead?"

He expelled a heavy sigh. "No. We've been keeping the ladies isolated from this ugliness. They realize somebody was found in the lake. They don't know who." He hesitated. "Or how. Lady Evelyn will not react well to Mr. Willoughby's death. She has developed a tendre for the man, despite his unscrupulous reputation. I can only hope that her cousin will comfort her."

"Her cousin?" Kendra was surprised. "Do you mean Jonah Lansing?"

"Yes—the new Earl of Craymore. He came to visit Lady Evelyn yesterday."

"Yesterday." She stopped, which, out of politeness, forced Lewis to stop as well. The wind tugged at her skirts and ruffled Lewis' dark hair. Unlike most of the men, he hadn't put on a hat. "What time was he here?" she asked.

Lewis frowned. "Early afternoon. Half past one."

"When did he leave?"

Lewis regarded her steadily. "He was here only a few hours. He was gone by three, I think." He paused. "Long before midnight, if Mr. Booker is to be believed that was the time his beasts brought him outside."

"Do you have reason to doubt Mr. Booker?"

"Not about that."

That other one. There was no love lost between the two men. Kendra decided not to point out the obvious—that Lansing could have returned later to meet Willoughby on the grounds and kill him. That was something to ponder. But not now. She asked, "Why was he here?"

Lewis shrugged. "I assume he wanted to speak to Lady Evelyn about his new position in the family."

"But you don't know?"

His mouth twisted in a wry smile. "Lady Evelyn would hardly confide in someone such as myself, Miss Donovan. I can only tell you that she was much less agitated after her cousin left than when her brother last visited."

"I heard that Lady Evelyn made a scene in the middle of the music recital. Music failed to soothe the savage breast that time."

He shot her a startled look.

"Lillian Slater told me that it was your idea to incorporate music into Shay House," Kendra explained.

"I suggested it, but I cannot claim it as my idea," he said modestly. "I read that it was being used as a treatment in other madhouses. More enlightened madhouses."

Kendra studied the attractive face and intelligent turquoise eyes. "How did you end up here, Mr. Lewis?"

"It's a long story." He turned and started walking again.

"I've got time," she said, falling into step beside him. "You told Mrs. Slater that your parents met when your father came across your mother washing clothes along the Tungabhadra River. It's a romantic story."

Lewis said nothing, but there was a shadow behind his carefully composed expression. "You disagree?" she pressed.

"I think romance is for poets and has little to do with reality." He came to a halt beside one of the rosebushes on the footpath. The sweet scent wafted around them. "My mother married my father against her family's wishes. My father was not a nabob. He was a lowly clerk in the British East India Company. My mother's family cast her out, and for as long as I lived in India, I was regarded by Indians as either English or the son of an Englishman."

"Where are your parents now?"

"Dead. My parents died seven years ago when their boat capsized while traveling to Bombay."

"I'm sorry."

He acknowledged that with a small nod.

"Do you have other family? Brothers, sisters?"

"Two sisters. Older. Both were able to arrange Indian marriages, and now have families of their own."

"When did you decide to come to England?"

"Shortly after my parents' death. Like my father, I worked as a clerk for the British East India Company. I thought I would find better opportunities in England. I traveled here to meet my father's family. I discovered that the attitudes in England are remarkably similar to the ones in India. Except now I am regarded as Indian, or 'that foreign wench's son.' My father's relations were not… receptive to finding me on their doorstep."

"That must have been difficult."

He contemplated her, as though trying to determine her sincerity. "I should not have been surprised," he said at last. "They live in a small hamlet in the northwestern part of the country. I returned to London and found work in a teashop. In the backroom. The proprietor thought that my—how did he explain it?—*unusual* heritage was an asset to his business." Amusement briefly lit his eyes. "The English assume everyone from India must know all about tea and spices. Especially if one worked for the British East India Company—even if one worked as a clerk."

Kendra cocked an eyebrow at him. "And were you familiar with tea and spices?"

"My employer, Mr. Robson, was far more knowledgeable. However, I learned quickly."

"So, how did you end up at Shay House?"

"Dr. Shay was one of Mr. Robson's customers. He was interested in calming tea blends for his patients, and approached me about creating proprietary blends for Shay House."

Kendra was vaguely surprised. It wasn't a bad marketing idea. "He hired you to make tea?"

He smiled slightly. "Among other things. At the time, Shay House was much busier, and Dr. Shay had grand plans."

She eyed him closely. "You knew Miss Osmond, then. Were you aware of what happened to her?"

He stiffened. "No, I was not aware. Nor was Dr. Shay. It was a shock when it became known that she was … she was increasing." He moistened his lips. "Dr. Shay immediately sent Mr. Dodd packing without references. But it was too late. The lady's father was very vindictive, spreading rumors. Shay House lost most of its patients, and staff. I was extremely fortunate to be kept on. Dr. Shay has been trying to repair the asylum's reputation ever since." He blew out a troubled breath. "It's been a dreadful time."

Some of the sympathy that she'd felt for him evaporated. "More dreadful for Miss Osmond, I think."

Their attention was caught by Booker's return, the man now steering a flatbed wagon pulled by a swaybacked horse. Bruce sat on the seat next to him. They rumbled past, the wagon tilting at a precarious angle as it rolled down the hill.

Kendra glanced back at Lewis. "Where were you last night? Around midnight."

"Why would I kill Mr. Willoughby? That's what you are implying."

"Not necessarily. It's a normal question in the course of an investigation. It's not personal."

"Odd, it seems very personal to be considered a murderer," he countered coldly. There was a slight pause, then he said, "I was home in bed. At midnight, I was asleep."

"Home? You mean your room here?"

He shook his head. "I don't live at Shay House, Miss Donovan. I have rooms over the haberdashery shop in Needlham."

"I thought only the women staff left Shay House at night."

"I stayed here when I first arrived, but there were… complaints, concerns." Now he smiled thinly. "The English accepted me when I blended calming teas and served restoratives to their mothers, sisters, daughters, and wives. But they objected to me sleeping under the same roof as their gently-bred womenfolk."

The specter of Miss Osmond rose up between them. These families had spent their time fretting about Mr. Lewis, but their worst fears had been confirmed by a fellow countryman. By the glint in Mr. Lewis' eyes, he recognized the irony as well.

"No one can verify that you were home in bed last night?" She knew that she'd shocked him, her implication being that he had been in bed, but not alone. Gently bred women did not ask men such questions.

"I was alone," he replied tersely.

"How about last Wednesday night—around nine?"

"I did not kill Lord Craymore."

"That's not what I asked."

He stared at her like she had grown two heads. She met his gaze directly and made no attempt to break the silence.

After a moment, he let out a breath. "I was home then as well. After that disastrous musical recital, Mr. McBride and I finally managed to get the ladies in their room. I made tea. Normally, I only brew a blend of herbs and leaves, but that evening Mr. McBride suggested that I add a mild sedative to the tea to calm down the ladies."

"Where was Dr. Shay?"

"He was in his office with Lord Craymore."

"Did you hear what was being said?"

Lewis shifted his position slightly, his expression uncomfortable. "No."

Kendra gave him a skeptical look. "No? Because from what I heard, they were arguing, and it was quite loud."

But Lewis refused to be drawn. "After we served the tea, I rode back to the village."

"What time was that?"

"Close to nine."

"Right after Lord Craymore left."

It wasn't a question, but Lewis nodded. "Yes."

"Did you see him on the road?"

"No."

"What about Mr. Booker? He drove the rest of the staff back to Needlham. When did they leave? Before or after you?"

"Before. I don't see what—"

"How long before?"

"I don't remember. Not long."

"Did you see them on the road?"

Lewis frowned. "No."

"You were on a horse, and they were in a wagon. Horses usually travel faster. You were traveling on the same road." Kendra shrugged. "I would think you would have caught up with them. It's odd that you did not."

"Mrs. Strong lives with her husband on a nearby farm. They had probably already turned down that lane, and we missed each other."

"What did you do after you got to Needlham?"

He gave her an impatient look. "I told you. I went home."

"What did you do with your horse?"

"My horse? I stabled him in the public livery. Miss Donovan—"

"Did anyone see you?"

"Not that I am aware. There are stable hands that work there but I didn't see them."

"And you didn't run into anyone else?"

"No."

"Have you heard of the Anahita Pink?" Kendra asked suddenly. She was watching him carefully, saw him twitch in surprise. But that could have been the sudden change of topic.

"No." The denial was automatic.

She kept her gaze on his. "No one mentioned that Lord Craymore may have been carrying it on him when he was killed? Lady Evelyn tried to bribe Mr. McBride with it; I would think she would have tried to bribe you as well."

He said nothing.

"You say you have never heard of the Anahita Pink, but you don't ask me what it is. Most people would, you know."

He sighed. "I have heard of the diamond. I don't know why I denied it, except I feared it would cast suspicion on me. Because of who I am, *what* I am, I am often viewed with suspicion." Lewis shook his head. "But I ask you, if I stole the diamond, why would I continue to work at Shay House?"

"It will take time to arrange a sale."

"Possibly, but I do not have it to sell. I would not kill because of greed, Miss Donovan."

"Maybe it's not greed. The Anahita Pink once belonged to Sayf al-Din Muhammad, the king of the Ghurid dynasty. You've heard of him?"

"Of course."

"The diamond was believed to have been mined in Mysore, possibly around the river where your parents first met."

He stared at her incredulously. "You think I have some sort of affinity for the diamond because I was born in India?"

"I think India would be appreciative if one of their native-born sons restored a national treasure. Think about it. You would no longer be an outsider. You'd be a national hero."

And because I understand what it's like to be an outsider, I know how tempting it would be to change that, she added silently.

"That is absurd! I am not a thief. I am not a murderer. You either believe me or you do not. Now, I must attend to the ladies. If you will excuse me." Abruptly, he strode away.

Kendra stayed where she was, watching him climb the steps to the verandah. He glanced back at her when he yanked open the French doors. Kendra thought she recognized the expression in his eyes before he disappeared: fear.

Are you afraid because you are a thief and a murderer? Or are you afraid because you know how easily you could be falsely accused of being a thief and a murderer?

Slowly, Kendra turned away and retraced her footsteps down the hillside.

You either believe me or you do not, Lewis had said. Unfortunately, that was the problem. She didn't know what to believe.

29

"Both Dr. Shay and Mr. McBride claim ter have been asleep last night at around midnight, and didn't hear the dogs barkin'," Sam told Kendra when she returned. The Bow Street Runner, Alec, and Rebecca were standing slightly away from the rest of the men, who were fully occupied with transferring Willoughby's body to the wagon.

"Not a good alibi, 'cause no one can verify it," he continued. "Mr. McBride shares a room with his wife, but he tells me that she doesn't have her wits about her ter confirm that he was with her."

"Unfortunately, he's telling the truth," Kendra said.

"If Mr. Willoughby was killed at midnight as everyone assumes, being asleep is reasonable," Rebecca said. She was watching the men haul the corpse to the flatbed. She shuddered slightly and averted her gaze. "The man was a rogue, but I would not wish for his death."

Sam scratched the side of his nose. "I knew the bloke was being sly about somethin' when I last spoke ter him. Thought it had somethin' ter do with his lordship's murder, but now…"

"It did," Kendra said. "He might not have witnessed the murder, but it looks as though he saw the murderer. He didn't realize it at the time, not until after—"

"Not until after I told him," Sam finished grimly.

"Not until after he learned of Lord Craymore's murder on Wednesday night," Kendra corrected.

Sam shook his head. "I didn't just tell him about the murder, lass. I told him about the Anahita Pink. I should have realized that was too tempting a morsel for someone like Mr. Willoughby ter resist."

"You cannot blame yourself, Mr. Kelly," Alec said. "If anything, it was Willoughby's own greed. He didn't share his suspicions, but rather contacted the villain himself." He glanced at Kendra. "That ought to narrow the suspects down to Shay House—"

"Not necessarily. I found out that Jonah Lansing was here yesterday, visiting Lady Evelyn. He could have arranged to meet Willoughby later that night." Kendra's gaze traveled to the flatbed wagon. They were now securing Willoughby's body by squeezing it between bags of grain. "The murderer could be someone at Shay House—or the murderer is pointing the finger here."

Rebecca pushed a wayward curl the breeze had loosened back into her bonnet. "Is Mr. Lansing really so clever?"

Kendra recalled her first impression of Jonah Lansing, that he had secrets and guarded them well. "I wouldn't underestimate him."

"Instead of asking whether the new Lord Craymore is clever, perhaps we ought to be asking is if the men at Shay House are so stupid?" Alec put in. "Why kill a man so close to home? They must have realized they would come under suspicion?"

"Except the villain was interrupted by Mr. Booker's hounds," Sam pointed out. "Mayhap Mr. Willoughby was supposed ter disappear. Plenty of places out in those woods ter bury a body."

Or perhaps Willoughby was meant for the bottom of the lake, Kendra thought.

The Bow Street Runner continued, "Speaking of Jonah Lansing, he wasn't exactly truthful about his whereabouts on the evenin' his cousin was murdered. Me lads quizzed his fellow shopkeepers on Paternoster Row. More than one remembered seeing him lock up and leave his shop around half past six."

Kendra said, "Another reason to interview him again."

"Aye." Sam hesitated. "I also spoke ter Phineas Muldoon." He darted a quick glance at Rebecca before firmly fixing his narrowed gaze on Kendra. "He doesn't seem ter think Mr. Lansing would've killed his cousin in cold-blood for the title or fortune, or even for the money that the Anahita Pink might bring. He did say that Lansing was known ter have a temper, which ain't surprising given his reputation as a firebrand. If Lansing killed his cousin, Mr. Muldoon has a curious reason as ter why."

He looked like he was going to say more, but his eyes shifted. Kendra turned. The crowd was dispersing. Booker, with the kid beside him, flicked the flanks of the horse with his reins, sending the wagon moving up the hillside. The wagon's flatbed jerked and swayed. If Willoughby hadn't been anchored between the sacks of grain, Kendra imagined he would have been catapulted to the ground.

Durst, McBride, Crump, and the two wet, shivering men began walking after the wagon like a funeral procession. Munroe, the constable, and Dr. Shay broke away to come towards them.

"Mr. Durst, Mr. Gulliver, and I shall be going to Mr. Dockery's butcher shop to conduct the postmortem," Dr. Munroe said as he joined them.

"Ah, well." Mr. Gulliver grimaced, placing a hand on his stomach. "I'll make the introductions, Dr. Munroe, but I ain't staying. Can't abide that gruesome business. Mr. Dockery won't appreciate it if I cast up my accounts in his shop."

"I'll come with you," Sam told them, then switched his focus to Kendra. "We can continue our discussion later, if you don't mind, lass. I was planning on stayin' in Aldridge Village for the inquest tomorrow."

Alec said, "Come to the castle at eight. We can speak further then."

Kendra looked at Dr. Shay. "We'll need to speak to Lady Evelyn."

The doctor pursed his lips, the expression in his eyes wary. "You'll be telling her that Mr. Willoughby is dead?"

Kendra shrugged. "She deserves to know."

There were only a handful of ladies in the library. Mrs. Maddox and Mr. Lewis were serving tea, and the assembled appeared to be calm. But beneath the apparent tranquility, Kendra sensed tension. And a ripple of fear.

Lillian Slater was sitting in the corner, her catlike eyes watchful. A cup of tea was cooling untouched on the table next to her. Kendra met her eyes briefly and tried to decipher the emotion she saw there, but Lillian was already looking away.

The back of Kendra's neck tingled. Glancing over, she found Lewis regarding her. She had no difficulty deciphering the distrust in his eyes.

"Lady Evelyn will be upset," Dr. Shay said as they moved through the room into the foyer. Their footsteps sounded loud against the tile. "I shall give her laudanum to ease her mind before we tell her about Mr. Willoughby."

Kendra shook her head. "I don't want Lady Evelyn drugged when I interview her."

Dr. Shay scowled at her. "Miss Donovan, you do not understand the female psyche, the hysteria that—"

A scream, followed by the sound of shattering glass, interrupted him. Everyone looked up, then Kendra picked up her skirts and sprinted up the stairs. A feeling of déjà vu assailed her, but the screams weren't coming from the treatment room. As soon as she hit the second landing, Kendra saw Meg standing in front of an open door, her hand clamped over her mouth, her eyes wide.

"Don't touch me!" Someone screeched from inside the room. "Don't touch me!"

"Please, Miss Dora, you must compose yourself. You are distraught," came the soothing rejoinder.

Meg fell back as Kendra and Alec ran to the doorway. Inside, McBride was standing in front of Miss Dora, his hands lifted toward her in a placating gesture. Jagged pieces of white porcelain littered the floor, most in a pool of tea. Miss Dora held a shard tightly in her hand. A thin trickle of blood was dripping down her wrist, adding to the mess. Her face twitched; her eyes bounced around in her eye sockets, shining with fear bordering on madness.

"Stay away!" she screamed. "Do not lay hands on me!"

"What is happening?" Dr. Shay demanded, having reached the door with Rebecca.

Meg looked at Dr. Shay. "Miss Dora refused to drink her soothing tonic, and then smashed the teapot and cup."

Miss Dora pivoted to fix them with her mad gaze. "The devil's apprentice walks the earth! I saw him in the moonlight with that wicked creature—"

"Enough!" Dr. Shay snapped. "You will go into the chair to come to your senses, Miss Dora, if you do not put down that piece of porcelain."

Tears sprang in the woman's eyes. "But I'm warning you! Why won't you *listen*? We will all suffer the torment of the damned!"

Kendra's eyes moved past the woman to scan the bedchamber. Unlike Lady Evelyn's room, Miss Dora's room was brutally sparse. A wooden crucifix hung on the white wall above a plain, single bed. There was a nightstand and narrow wardrobe, and a washstand in front of the window. Keeping one eye on Miss Dora, Kendra crossed to the window.

"What are you doing? *What are you doing?*" Miss Dora shouted, jerking sideways, her gaze cutting back and forth between Kendra and where the rest of her audience stood. "*Devil,*" she hissed when Dr. Shay took a step towards her. "Stay back!" She raised the shard and made a thrusting gesture.

Kendra wasn't sure who Miss Dora thought she was threatening but she ignored her, looking out the window. She confirmed her suspicions, and swung back to the agitated woman. "I'm listening to you, Miss Dora. What did you see in the moonlight?"

Dr. Shay sucked in a furious breath. "Miss Donovan, we cannot accommodate her delusion."

"It might not be a delusion," Kendra countered. *Not exactly.* She kept her gaze on the woman. If possible, she was becoming even more twitchy. "I'm listening, Miss Dora. Tell me what you saw."

"I *am* telling you. The devil's apprentice. He drinks the blood of virgins with a serpent." Miss Dora trembled, her eyes clinging desperately to Kendra's. She let her hand drop, the bloody shard momentarily forgotten. "I've seen the chalice of the underworld—"

She screamed when McBride lunged at her to snatch the jagged piece of porcelain out of her hand. Despite McBride outweighing Miss Dora by at least fifty pounds, she fought back with a high-pitched howl and adrenaline-fueled frenzy, arms flailing, fingers curved into talons. Dr. Shay jumped into the fray, grasping her arms and wrestling her towards her bed.

"Tell Mr. Lewis to bring another tonic." Dr. Shay was breathless as he fought to subdue the woman, pinning her down on the bed. She twisted and kicked. He glared at a wide-eyed Meg when she remained standing in the doorway, next to Rebecca. "*Now.*"

Meg spared Miss Dora a quick glance, then disappeared down the hall. Rebecca remained standing in the threshold, her hand clasped to her throat, her eyes glued to the thrashing woman on the bed.

"I shall not take one dram from that pagan!" Miss Dora cried tearfully.

"Mr. McBride, bring me a confining jacket!"

"Yes, sir."

Rebecca stepped aside as McBride barreled past her. Crump replaced him, coming into the bedchamber. He must have been out in the hall.

"Can I help, doctor?" Crump asked, his beady eyes fixed on Miss Dora.

"We must bring Miss Dora to the chair," Dr. Shay said. "Mr. Crump, your assistance, please!"

It took a moment to transfer the flailing woman to the attendant. Once that was accomplished, Dr. Shay hurried over to Kendra and Alec. "I must ask you to leave me to my duties. Miss Dora needs my full attention."

Kendra hesitated, but Alec put a hand on her arm and they moved into the hallway. Dr. Shay shut the door as soon as they crossed the threshold. Dora's muffled screams and sobs continued from the other side.

"Dear God," Rebecca said, looking aghast.

"That's nothing. You should see what happens in the treatment room," Kendra muttered sarcastically. But she had to take a moment to get her own rapid pulse under control.

"I see Miss Dora is having one of her episodes."

They turned to find Lady Evelyn regarding them from the doorway to her bedchamber.

She smiled thinly. "Good morning, Lord Sutcliffe, Miss Donovan."

Kendra studied the woman. Lady Evelyn appeared lucid. She wondered how quickly that would change when they delivered the news about Willoughby.

"I know you," Lady Evelyn said suddenly, her eyes narrowing on Rebecca.

Rebecca nodded. "We've never been formally introduced, but we've attended a few of the same functions in society. Lady Rebecca Blackburn."

"Of course! How wonderful for you to visit!" Lady Evelyn pounced on Rebecca, clasping her arm to practically drag her into her room. Rebecca threw a startled glance at Alec and Kendra. "Please come in, Lady Rebecca. And Lord Sutcliffe, Miss Donovan," Lady Evelyn called out gaily. "We shall have a tête-à-tête. You can tell me what is happening in London."

"I doubt if London is as exciting as what's happening here, Lady Evelyn," Kendra said drily, following them inside.

Lady Evelyn flicked a hand dismissively. "Dora's a lunatic. You must not pay her any heed."

Kendra watched the other woman closely. "I was referring to what's happening outside."

"Oh, *that.* They told us some fool slipped and fell into the water. No doubt a villager poaching. Come, let us sit."

Lady Evelyn guided them to the table. "Is there any more news on the Coburgs?" she asked, her gaze fixed on Rebecca. "I have heard that Princess Charlotte and Prince Leopold will be taking up residence at Claremont."

Rebecca hadn't been treated to Lady Evelyn's peculiar behavior, but after her first start, she managed to keep up a polite smile. "I have heard that news as well," she said calmly.

Lady Evelyn clapped. "Very good! I am a great admirer of our future queen. She refused to allow her father to come between her and the man that she loved."

Rebecca's smile became more genuine. "I agree with you, my lady. Princess Charlotte has her critics, but I believe she will make a wonderful monarch when the day comes."

Kendra couldn't stop herself from looking away. Princess Charlotte would never become queen of England. In little over a year, she would die after giving birth to a stillborn son.

She focused back on Rebecca and Lady Evelyn, who were still talking about the royal couple. She cleared her throat to draw their attention. "Lady Evelyn, we heard that your cousin came here yesterday."

Lady Evelyn tilted her chin. "He *is* the new Earl of Craymore."

"What did he want?"

"Want? Nothing. He came because I wrote to him, petitioning him to release me from this place. I do not belong here. Jonah knows that Reginald put me here because he didn't want me to be happy." The thin lips twisted into a pout. "I deserve to be happy."

Kendra exchanged a glance with Alec and Rebecca. She would be destroying the other woman's happiness soon enough. "You wrote to your cousin before, didn't you? You told him about the Anahita Pink."

Lady Evelyn jumped to her feet. "I ought to ring for tea."

"Dr. Shay has already ordered tea," Kendra lied. "Please sit down, my lady."

Lady Evelyn complied, eyeing Kendra warily, and huffed out an exasperated sigh. "The Anahita Pink, the Anahita Pink!" she mimicked, her pale face twisting. "Everyone cares about the diamond. 'Tis a chunk of stone! I'm flesh and blood! What about *me*? Yes, Jonah came yesterday to quiz me about it. He is like all the men in my family, obsessed with it!"

Kendra studied the other woman's flushed face. "What did your cousin want to know about the diamond?"

"Much of what you asked me. Whether Reginald had it on him that last evening."

"What did you tell him?"

"The truth. That Reginald was bringing it to Mr. Griggs that night." She thrust up her chin, her eyes glittering with defiance. "No matter what you say, Miss Donovan, Reginald was killed by a highwayman for that wretched diamond." Her fingers twisted the material of her skirt. "I do not wish to discuss this unpleasantness."

"Your cousin asked you specifically about the Anahita Pink? You were not the one to bring up the subject?"

Lady Evelyn flicked her an impatient look. "Why would I do that? I don't want to talk about this!" Abruptly, she turned to look at Rebecca. "Your carriage dress is lovely, Lady Rebecca. May I ask, who is your modiste?"

Rebecca blinked, not sure how to handle Lady Evelyn's mercurial temperament.

"When Jonah has me released, I shall request a new wardrobe," Lady Evelyn confided, seemingly unaware of Rebecca's uneasiness. The pale fingers plucked distastefully at the black bombazine skirt. "Basil does so adore seeing me in blue."

Kendra exchanged a glance with Alec and Rebecca. Alec gave a slight nod. She drew in a long breath, and fixed her gaze on Lady Evelyn. It was time.

"Lady Evelyn, I'm sorry to inform you that Mr. Willoughby is the man that they found in the lake."

Lady Evelyn stared at her. There was a beat of silence, then she let out a shrill laugh. "That is a tasteless joke, Miss Donovan!"

"I'm not joking." Kendra watched the fear and shock ripple across the plain face. "When was the last time you were in communication with Mr. Willoughby?"

"No. I don't believe you!" Lady Evelyn jerked to her feet, her eyes on Kendra. "You hate me. How can you be so cruel? You don't want me to be happy either."

Rebecca leapt up. She went around the table to lay a comforting hand on Lady Evelyn's narrow shoulder. "Miss Donovan speaks the truth. I am so very sorry, Lady Evelyn."

"No. *No!*" She twitched her shoulder to dislodge Rebecca's hand, and staggered back several steps. "It was a poacher. A poacher fell into the water and drowned!"

Kendra and Alec stood. She said, "It was Mr. Willoughby and it wasn't an accident. The same person who killed your brother killed him. If you want to help them, help me find their killer."

Lady Evelyn shook her head, denying Kendra's appeal. "You *lie!* No one would kill Basil." Lady Evelyn put a trembling hand to her mouth. But Kendra could see that she was beginning to believe. Tears filled Lady Evelyn's eyes and fell down her ashen cheeks. "He cannot be dead. I won't let him be dead." This time she didn't resist when Rebecca put an arm around her.

"Did you know that Mr. Willoughby was planning to come here last night?" Kendra asked. "Did you have plans to meet?"

"No. *No!*" Lady Evelyn was starting to weep.

"Oh, you poor dear." Rebecca urged Lady Evelyn over to the bed. "Sit down. You must sit down. Sutcliffe, fetch Lady Evelyn tea."

"I don't want any damn tea!" Lady Evelyn spat, sobbing in earnest. Dropping down on the mattress, she hugged herself, rocking back and forth. "I have no one now. I am alone."

"You are not alone," Rebecca insisted bracingly. She rubbed the distressed woman's shoulder. "Shall we send a message to your cousin? Or anyone else?"

"It doesn't matter," Lady Evelyn mumbled. "Nothing matters anymore."

"Finding the killer matters," Kendra said quietly. She waited. *You know something about your brother's murder*, she wanted to say. Maybe Lady Evelyn wasn't guilty, but she wasn't entirely innocent either. Of that, Kendra was sure.

But Lady Evelyn turned her face away, lost in her own tortured thoughts.

30

Lady Evelyn's misery wasn't an easy thing to push aside, and Rebecca spoke of it with the Duke later that evening. "It was dreadful, Your Grace," she said, lifting the glass of sherry to her lips to take a slow sip. "I confess my heart quite broke for Lady Evelyn."

They had gathered in the study. Kendra was leaning a hip against the desk, jiggling a piece of slate in one hand after updating the board, while Rebecca sat on the sofa opposite the Duke. Alec had taken up a familiar position against the fireplace mantle. A fire crackled merrily in the grate, the scent of applewood mingling with melting wax from the dozens of candles casting the room in a honey glow that reflected off the dark windowpanes.

The Duke expelled a horrified breath. "What will this do to the poor woman? Her grasp on reality seemed tenuous at best when I met her. Regardless of whether Mr. Willoughby's intentions were honorable, she believed that he cared for her."

"More than that, she believed he would be the one to rescue her from Shay House," Kendra said. "Maybe her cousin will step in. I find the timing of his visit interesting." She hesitated, then added, "She said that he asked her about the Anahita Pink."

The Duke understood the implication. "Ah. And he had no reason to ask such a question if he murdered his cousin and stole the diamond."

Alec straightened, sauntering over to the sideboard with the decanters. He glanced at her as he pulled out a stopper. "I'm not certain we can trust anything Lady Evelyn says." He refilled his glass with brandy. "The woman is quite unstable."

"I would have to agree with Sutcliffe," Rebecca said with a troubled frown.

"Maybe. But I think she knows more than she's telling us," Kendra said. "I also believe Miss Dora saw the murder."

The Duke eyed her. "Miss Dora?"

"Good heavens. The woman who was screaming about the devil's apprentice?" Rebecca stared at her. "She is clearly demented."

"The mentally ill can witness crimes, too. Her window overlooks the back garden and the lake."

"There is considerable distance between the two," Alec said. "And it was midnight."

"It was a clear night, the moon shining." Kendra's gaze traveled to the slate board, where she'd written Miss Dora's words. *The devil's apprentice walks the earth. He drinks the blood of virgins with a serpent. Chalice of the underworld.*

She said, "She witnessed the murder but it's filtered through her own madness. Just like when she saw Willoughby and Lady Evelyn meeting in the woods. She was right about that, but the truth was distorted by her delusion."

Rebecca's brow puckered. "How does one go about separating truth from her fantasy?"

"I don't know."

Kendra glanced over when the door opened and Harding stepped through. The butler's eyes went to the Duke. "Mr. Kelly and Mr. Muldoon have arrived, sir."

"Ah. Very good. Send them up."

A few minutes later, the Bow Street Runner and Phineas Muldoon came into the study. "Mr. Kelly, Mr. Muldoon, good evening." The Duke pushed himself to his feet. "Did Dr. Munroe not come with you?"

"Nay, sir. He had business in London. But we spoke after he conducted the postmortem," Sam said.

"Would either of you care for a whisky? Or brandy?" Alec asked, setting down his own glass to reach for the decanter.

Sam's golden eyes brightened. "Aye. A whisky would be excellent. Thank you, sir."

"Thank you, my lord." Muldoon slid a quick glance at Rebecca before casting a veiled look around the study. The Irishman had been in the Duke's luxurious London residence, but this was his first time at Aldridge Castle.

Kendra remembered her first impression of the castle in the twenty-first century. The stone walls radiated wealth and power, and an almost awesome sense of history. It was easy, by contrast, to feel small and insignificant. She wondered if that was what she was seeing in Muldoon's face now, the difference between his world and the Duke's.

His world and Rebecca's.

"I hope you don't mind me accompanying Mr. Kelly," Muldoon said now, accepting the glass that Alec handed him. "I'm staying in the village for tomorrow's inquest. Mr. Kelly was kind enough to invite me when we encountered each other at the King's Head."

Sam shot him a look that made Kendra think Muldoon was stretching the truth a bit about the invitation. Most likely Muldoon had invited himself.

The Irishman took a hasty swallow of his whisky. "I have heard tales about Aldridge Castle, Your Grace. Except for a few royal palaces, it is considered one of the grandest homes in the kingdom. I now see that is no exaggeration."

"Thank you, although the grand size is a bit of a problem these days. I've been looking to modernize the castle with gas lighting," the Duke said. "I'm finding the project to be much more complex than I initially realized."

"There are worse problems to have, Your Grace."

"I cannot disagree with you there, Mr. Muldoon."

Muldoon turned toward Rebecca. "Good evening, Lady Rebecca."

"Mr. Muldoon." A faint flush rose in Rebecca's cheeks. "Shall we be seated?"

"What did Dr. Munroe find out in the postmortem?" Kendra asked, positioning herself in front of the slate board. Rebecca, the Duke, Muldoon, and Sam settled into chairs and the sofa. Alec returned to the fireplace, propping an elbow against the mantle as he sipped his brandy.

"Willoughby didn't have any water in his lungs, so he was dead before he ended up in the lake," Sam told her. "Dr. Munroe says the fiend struck Willoughby on the back of the head with the barrel of a pistol. The first blow was hard enough ter knock Willoughby ter the ground. He had bruisin' on his knees. Dr. Munroe believes that the angle of the first injury indicates someone who is relatively the same height as Willoughby."

Kendra jiggled the piece of slate in her hand, thinking. "He's about five feet, ten inches tall. That doesn't eliminate anybody, except for maybe Mr. Booker. Booker is also one of the few who actually had a verifiable alibi during the time of Lord Craymore's murder."

"That blow was hard enough ter cause swelling and drop Willoughby ter his knees, but it was less severe than the other injuries," Sam went on. "Munroe believes Willoughby was wearing a hat that softened the attack, but it fell off when the villain bludgeoned him again. It's probably at the bottom of the lake. The other blows were violent enough to crack open his skull."

"The increased force from the other blows could also come from the different position," Kendra mused. "Willoughby below, the unsub above. It gives you more leverage."

"After he was dead, the fiend pushed the body into the water. Dr. Munroe can't give an exact time of death on account of the cold water."

Kendra nodded. "We can thank Booker and his dogs for a time of death."

"I don't understand why the villain bothered to push Mr. Willoughby into the water," said the Duke. "If the man was already dead, why waste time? He risked being caught by Mr. Booker and his hounds."

"Impulse." Kendra glanced at Sam. "I think you're right, Mr. Kelly. The original plan was to either to bury the body or weigh it down so it would sink to the bottom of the lake. If Willoughby was ever discovered in the lake, his death would probably be ruled an accident. Dr. Shay was pushing that angle. If we hadn't been there, who would have contradicted him? The village butcher?"

Sam spoke up. "By the by, a local farmer found a saddled horse roaming a few miles from Shay House. Mr. Gulliver didn't recognize the animal, so it's most likely Willoughby's."

Muldoon had been frowning into his whisky glass, but now he lifted his gaze. "Willoughby was a fool. An absolute fool. Me sainted mother would have whacked my backside good if I had met with a villain in the middle of the night alone, let alone a villain who'd already murdered a peer of the realm. Sweet Mary and Joseph, what did the man think would happen?"

"I doubt he expected ter be clubbed on the back of the head with a barking iron," Sam muttered.

Kendra shook her head. "It wasn't stupidity—it was arrogance. Willoughby's character indicates a man who was self-indulgent.

He'd gambled away his inheritance and then used his looks to go after an heiress to replenish that fortune."

"Not unlike many young bucks in society," Muldoon interjected, his lip curling.

"Yes, but he also targeted heiresses that he considered easy marks."

Rebecca sipped her sherry. "Like me."

Muldoon stiffened, shooting her a sharp look. "What do you mean?"

"A few years ago, Mr. Willoughby pursued me, thinking that I was desperate for attention."

Muldoon's eyes sparked. "As I said, the man was a fool."

Kendra watched her friend blush under the Irishman's regard. She said, "For someone like Willoughby, blackmail would be easy money." She looked at Sam. "You'll be searching Willoughby's place?"

"Aye. After the inquest tomorrow. Why?"

"Willoughby had to contact the killer somehow, and presumably the killer responded with his own note. Maybe Willoughby kept that message."

"Dear heaven." Rebecca's eyes widened. "Mr. Willoughby could have a message signed by his killer!"

"Even if the killer didn't sign his name, we'd have a sample of his handwriting. It's a paper trail." A *literal* paper trail. In the twenty-first century, most paper trails were digital—cell phone and computer records—but they were one of the most valuable tools law enforcement had.

Another possibility occurred to her. "What about associates, friends, colleagues that Willoughby might have confided in?"

Sam thought about it, but shook his head. "Willoughby wasn't exactly the trusting sort. I don't think he had mates ter confide in."

"What about women?"

Rebecca made a disparaging sound. "Mr. Willoughby was not the kind of man to regard women as anything other than useful tools or soiled doves. He would not confide in our sex, Miss Donovan."

"Okay, not confide. What about boast?"

"Yes," Rebecca said slowly. "Yes, I can see him doing such a thing. He enjoyed talking about himself. His version, of course, was more heroic than I found reality to be."

"I'll send some of me lads around the establishments that Mr. Willoughby was known ter frequent," said Sam.

Muldoon let his gaze travel to the names on the slate board. "I see you have Jonah Lansing as one of the suspects."

Kendra met his eyes. "And you don't agree."

"I think he could have killed for the Anahita Pink, but not because of greed," Muldoon replied. "Lansing is passionate in his views. He is part of a movement pushing universal suffrage, reform and repeal of the Corn Laws."

"Mr. Muldoon believes Lansing is interested in the Anahita Pink as a symbol," Sam put in with an impatient glance at the Irishman. "Seems a peculiar reason ter murder somebody, but I reckon there have been more peculiar reasons."

Muldoon rolled his shoulders in a defensive gesture. "I told you, symbols have always been important to revolutionaries."

"You're right." Kendra could see that her agreement surprised the reporter. She smiled. "Every cause—good and bad—makes use of symbols. It's basic psychology. Human beings are social animals. People want to belong, to identify with a group. How would Lansing use the Anahita Pink?"

"I'm not certain," he admitted. "'Tis part of English lore. It would be like finding Excalibur. A diamond with the Anahita Pink's history would have great appeal to someone like Jonah Lansing, I think." He paused a moment, then shook his head. "But I don't believe he would have plotted to murder his cousin for it. Or shot him in the back after he stole it."

"Lansing didn't steal the diamond—assuming we can trust Lady Evelyn's account," Alec said. "He visited his cousin yesterday and inquired about it."

Muldoon looked relieved. "Well, then, Jonah Lansing couldn't have committed the murder."

Sam frowned. "He lied about his whereabouts on the night of his cousin's murder. Maybe he's devious enough ter visit his cousin and quiz her about the diamond's whereabouts ter make it look like he doesn't have the sparkler."

Rebecca raised her eyebrows. "Do you really think Mr. Lansing so scheming?"

"He's in politics, ain't he?" Sam's golden eyes glinted with cynicism. "In my experience, those circling Whitehall are wily fellows."

"Mr. Kelly makes an excellent point," Alec murmured. "We ought not cross Lansing off the list."

"He may have an alibi for the night Craymore was murdered," Muldoon said.

The Bow Street Runner scowled at the journalist. "Then why not provide it? He lied to us instead."

"Yes, well, I have an idea about that."

They waited. When Muldoon didn't expand on his statement, Sam glowered at him. "God's teeth, are you goin' ter spit it out? Or are we just supposed ter guess at the stuff betwixt your ears?"

Muldoon grinned, unfazed by the Runner's irritation. "I want to speak to Mr. Lansing before I say anything. He ought to be at his cousin's inquest tomorrow."

"We're only theorizing here, Mr. Muldoon," Kendra reminded.

"I realize that, Miss Donovan. But I'd like to keep my own counsel until after I speak with Lansing."

Kendra studied the Irishman for a moment, then said, "Fine." She pivoted back to the slate board. "I'm ready to rule out Mr. Crump."

"Why?" Alec asked. "I would think he'd be as greedy for the diamond as anyone else."

"I agree." She turned back to look at him. "I also don't think he's very smart. If he stole the diamond, he'd have gone to London to try to sell it. Have you heard anything in that area, Mr. Kelly?"

"Nay." He shook his head. "Leastwise, Bear hasn't contacted me."

"Are we so certain that the criminal will inform you if the diamond comes up for sale?" the Duke inquired.

"Aye, I think so. Bear won't be handin' over the sparkler, mind you, but it won't trouble him ter hand over the thief."

Alec swirled the brandy in his glass as he met Kendra's eyes. "I agree with your assessment of Mr. Crump. He's not shrewd enough to wait to sell the diamond."

"With the exception of Lansing, all the suspects are associated with Shay House," Rebecca said in a small voice. "Do you really think Mrs. Devaney holds useful information?"

Kendra took a moment to seriously consider the question. Christina Devaney hadn't been a patient at Shay House for four years. What could she really contribute? Yes, she knew the men at the asylum. But was her insider knowledge really worth having her revisit a painful experience in her life?

Some things are not always what they may seem.

Kendra couldn't shake the feeling that there was something seriously wrong at Shay House. Maybe it was the horror of the treatment room. Maybe it was a young girl molested inside its walls. There were secrets... and Christina Devaney might know some of them. But did they have anything to do with the murders of Craymore and Willoughby?

Aware that the silence had stretched on for a beat too long, Kendra admitted honestly, "I don't know."

Muldoon flicked a look between Kendra and Rebecca. "Who is Mrs. Devaney? A possible witness?"

"No," said the Duke. "And I am of the mind that we leave the poor woman alone."

Muldoon seemed to sense that there was a story there and opened his mouth to follow up, but Alec cut him off by saying, "We do have a witness to Willoughby's murder."

That distracted the reporter, which, Kendra thought, was Alec's intention. "Who? What was seen? They couldn't have seen the murderer, otherwise we would not be having this discussion."

"Our witness saw the murder. I'm not certain she saw the murderer." Alec's lips quirked. "She's a patient at Shay House who says she saw the devil's apprentice kill Willoughby. Until her mind clears and she can provide us with a name—or at least a better descriptor—I think we need to look elsewhere for our answers."

31

At nine o'clock the next morning, Kendra, the Duke, and Alec swept through the door of the King's Arms. Despite having been to several inquests now, Kendra still felt a ripple of shock when her gaze landed on the mortal remains of Reginald Craymore.

The earl was on full display, laid out on a knotty pine table in the middle of the tavern. After five days in the icehouse, his body's natural gases now bloated it to nearly twice its size, splitting and blistering the discolored skin. The threads from Dr. Munroe's Y-incision were beginning to strain and tear apart. It was a ghastly sight. Worse, though, was the putrefaction process. Kendra clenched her teeth to stop herself from gagging as the sulfur-like stench from the decaying body hit her nostrils.

She lifted her hand to cover her nose, and scanned the considerable crowd that had gathered—all men, except for a middle-aged woman behind the bar. None of them seemed to have any difficulty drinking and talking next to the reeking corpse.

Someone had placed a linen cloth over the cadaver's swollen nether regions. She knew that this wasn't the norm; the attempt at modesty most likely was for her possible attendance.

"My God." The Duke pulled a handkerchief out of his pocket, holding it to his nose. "The man cannot be put in the grave quickly enough."

Kendra silently agreed, and retrieved her own handkerchief from her reticule. It was just a scrap of silk, but Molly had dabbed it with perfume, something for which Kendra was now grateful.

"After this is over, you might want to tell the tavern owner to burn the table," she commented. There wasn't enough disinfectant in the world—this world certainly, but maybe not even her own—to get her to sit down at that particular table post-inquest. She had to suppress a shudder as she imagined Craymore's bodily fluids absorbing into the knotty pine. And yet she was sure that Mr. Hawkings, the tavern's owner, would simply wipe off the surface after Craymore was disposed of, and customers would be having a meal there tonight.

The Duke's eyes brightened with interest as he studied the table in question. "I ought to buy the table and examine it under my microscope in the laboratory. A world of animalcules—or, as you call them, bacteria—could be revealed."

Kendra found herself smiling. Leave it to the Duke to think of the scientific value of a gross old table.

"I see Mr. Kelly and Mr. Muldoon are already here," Alec said, and placed a hand on the small of Kendra's back to guide her through the crowd to the two men.

"Good morning, Your Grace, my lord, Miss Donovan," Muldoon greeted, standing. "I suppose Lady Rebecca has left for London?"

"Yes, although her parents would hardly find it acceptable for her to attend an inquest if she'd stayed," Alec drawled. His mild tone belied the measured look he gave the Irishman.

Kendra expected Muldoon to offer one of his flippant responses, maybe pointing at her own presence at the inquest. But he remained silent, a shadow crossing his face.

"Good day! Good day!" Mr. Hawkings, bustled over as they settled into their chairs. He was a big man with an explosion of red hair and a luxurious mustache above a grin that might have been a little wider than usual because of the extra customers that the inquest had brought into his establishment. He bowed. "'Tis an honor 'avin' ye 'ere at the King's 'Ead, Yer Grace. W'ot can Oi get fer ye?"

"A round of ale—ah, plus one more tankard," the Duke replied, his gaze flicking to Dr. Munroe as he stepped through the tavern's door.

Munroe paused briefly to inspect the corpse before continuing across the room to their table. "Good morning," he offered once he reached them. "It appears the earthly remains of Lord Craymore have drawn a sizeable crowd."

"Nothing better than an inquest ter bring out folks," Sam agreed.

Dr. Munroe removed his hat, greatcoat, and gloves before sitting down. His dark brows drew together as he leaned forward, his eyes on Kendra. "I assume Mr. Kelly told you that Willoughby didn't drown. He was killed before he went into the water."

"Yes. Is there anything else you can tell us?"

"Nothing, except that it's my opinion that the second blow killed the man. The fiend pistol-whipped him twice more after that, quite viciously. Whether it was because he was enraged or wanted to be certain Willoughby was dead, I don't know."

Kendra's gaze traveled to Craymore's body for a moment before returning to her companions. "Do you see the difference in the two murders?"

Sam regarded her, puzzled. "Aye. One was shot, and one was brained. You're not suggesting that we're dealing with two different murderers, are you, lass?"

"No, I'm not suggesting that."

Hawkings delivered their tankards. When he left, Kendra added, "But the differences are interesting. And troubling."

"What are you thinking, Miss Donovan?" Muldoon asked curiously.

She kept her voice low, although she doubted anyone was paying them any attention. "Let's take the first murder. We already know that the killer didn't attempt to disguise himself when he approached Craymore. On some level, he knew he would have to kill the earl. So why didn't he do so immediately? Why not shoot Craymore in the chest, through the heart? Instead, the earl manages to ride off before the unsub shoots him? He couldn't even be sure Craymore was dead."

Alec frowned. "Obviously, the fiend demanded the diamond first. Once he handed it over, Craymore must have realized the villain could hardly let him live. Craymore took the fiend by surprise when he tried to gallop away."

"His lordship didn't get too far before the villain shot him, based on the evidence," Munroe commented.

"It's just as easy to go through the pockets of a dead man as it is to have someone hand over their valuables, and then shoot them. Easier, in fact," Kendra said. "And the unsub would have gotten Craymore's purse as well. Not everyone finds it easy to kill. So I'm thinking the unsub had to gather his nerve, which, in turn, gave the earl a chance to escape. The whole thing was messy… disorganized."

Her gaze fell to the tankard she clasped in both hands. Something shimmered on the edge of her consciousness, a pattern slowly taking shape. She became aware of her companions looking at her, waiting for her to continue.

She said, "Willoughby's murder was different. More organized. The killer brought a gun, but only to subdue Willoughby. He used his pistol as a cudgel."

"Well, aye," Sam said with a nod. "Makes sense, don't it? He didn't want ter fire the weapon, fearin' he'd wake those in the madhouse. He didn't expect the dogs ter catch his scent."

"The fiend was more prepared to kill the second time," Muldoon put in, "but he's still a coward."

The Duke eyed the reporter. "How so?"

"The injuries Willoughby sustained were on the back of the head. Seems to me that the villain either ordered Willoughby to turn around or waited for him to turn before striking. He didn't want to look into the other man's eyes when he killed him."

Jonah Lansing, the new Earl of Craymore, arrived ten minutes before the inquest was scheduled to begin. Kendra watched him push his way through a knot of men standing near the door. Was it her imagination or did Jonah carry himself differently? A swagger to his step? A more imperious tilt to his head?

His steps faltered and he paled when his gaze fell on his cousin. After a beat, he jerked his eyes away from the ghastly sight, moving to stand near the tap.

"Mr. Lansing—ah, Lord Craymore sent me a note informing me that he will be taking his cousin's body back to the family estate in Norfolk after the inquest," the Duke told them, his gaze on Lansing. "No doubt he will be laid to rest in the family crypt."

Kendra didn't bother asking about Lady Evelyn. She'd learned that ladies often didn't attend funerals, for fear their delicate sensibilities would shatter.

She fixed her eyes on Lansing. He'd ordered a pint and had his back pushed up against the wall. Unlike most of men in the pub, who were bantering, laughing, making wagers— Englishmen would bet on anything—Lansing's expression remained somber. A point in his favor, as far as she was concerned.

The door opened again. Kendra heard the mutterings, felt the hum of tension. Her own lips parted in surprise when she saw the colorful figure of Madam Patya. If the old woman was aware of the hostility rising up in the room, she gave no sign. She held herself like a queen. An expressionless Lensar loomed behind her, his dark eyes shuttered as he surveyed the crowd, his body language protective.

The Duke's chair scraped the floor as he hurriedly pushed himself to his feet. He cut through the throngs of men to meet the Romani. His greeting was warm and, Kendra could see, noticed by the assembled. Not that it lessened the distrust and outright antagonism she saw on their faces.

"Madam Patya." Alec stood as they approached the table. He smiled, taking her small, veined hand in both of his, much like how the Duke had greeted her the first time. "It is a pleasure to see you again."

The old woman's face creased in a smile as she looked up at him. "You are still a handsome devil, my lord. But, I think, no longer will you be breaking the hearts of ladies." She shot a shrewd glance at Kendra. "Miss Donovan," she greeted. "Perhaps one day we shall meet when there is no death to shadow our conversation."

Kendra once again felt the impact of those black eyes. "I would like that." She hesitated. "I didn't realize you would be coming to the inquest."

"Nor did I," said the Duke. "Your presence is not required, as I am testifying."

"I told her as much," Lensar replied, his gaze sweeping the room. "We are not wanted here."

"If we only went where we were wanted, we would have to leave England," Madam Patya replied.

"Sometimes it is better to travel than stay where trouble is simmering," Lensar muttered.

The Duke looked at him. "Your people will not be disturbed on my land."

Lensar's full lips thinned. "We have already been disturbed."

"Who is bothering you?" the Duke asked sharply.

Madam Patya's many gold bracelets jangled when she patted Lensar's arm. "You make too much of it." She shifted her gaze to the Duke. "Shandor has seen a man in the woods. He has come several days, but he has kept his distance and has not disturbed us."

Alec frowned. "What is he doing in the woods?"

The old woman shook her head. "I cannot say. He seems to have no purpose."

Lensar said, "I do not like it."

"I told you, you worry too much. As do you, boy," she said, smiling at the Duke. "Now, let us sit, and you may introduce us to your friends."

Kendra had to smile. It wasn't often someone had the temerity to order the Duke around. She'd only seen his sister issue commands, but even Lady Atwood had a line she would not cross. The Duke made the introductions while Alec hunted up two more chairs and then went to the tap to buy pints for the Romani.

The coroner arrived as Alec was returning to the table. The local constable, Roger Hilliard, a stocky middle-aged man with a florid face, escorted the man to a table and chair positioned near the unlit fireplace. The coroner—Mr. Longhorn, Kendra had been told—came from another village. He carried a ledger to the table and flipped it open, and the seven jurors—all men, of course— filed up to the table to scratch their names in it. Kendra recognized one of the faces: Simon Dalton. Even though he'd inherited the neighboring estate, Halston Hall, she'd rarely encountered him. Not for a year, when he'd been one of her primary suspects in a murder investigation.

One year... In three more days, there would be a full moon. Her pulse quickened. Would the vortex open again? Could she return to her own time? A time when she could walk outside without needing a chaperone. When she could drive anywhere she damned well pleased without fearing a thousand-pound ani- mal might have other ideas. Where she had the world—and databases—at her fingertips. She wouldn't have to monitor everything she said for fear that it might somehow twist the current timeline and change the future.

She wouldn't have Alec in her life.

Or Rebecca, the Duke, Sam. . . even Muldoon.

If the wormhole opened and she managed to leave, managed to make it back to her own time, it wouldn't be like moving to another country. She would be in another *time*, a time when everyone in this room, everyone she was now sharing a table with, would be long dead.

She was grateful when the inquest began, so she could focus on something else.

Madam Patya was the first witness called. She kept her shoulders back and her head high as she took the witness chair. The procedure allowed jurors to question witnesses directly. A plump middle-aged man who owned a local haberdashery shop was the first to speak.

"His lordship was alive when he came to be in your wagon?"

"I would hardly have spent so much time attempting to save him if he were already dead," Madam Patya remarked mildly.

The juror narrowed his eyes at her. "How do we know that his lordship didn't cock up his toes because of your potions and such?"

"The two holes in the earl's back would say otherwise."

Even though Madam Patya was careful to keep her expression neutral, the man stiffened.

It probably didn't help that her comment caused several guffaws around the room. The haberdasher jutted out his chin. "How do we know that it wasn't you or one of your ilk who put those bullets in the earl in the first place, eh?"

Lensar shot to his feet, glaring at the juror. "My people had nothing to do with that *gadjo*'s death. He was mortally injured when he was found."

"And we're just supposed to take *your* word on that?" sniffed the haberdasher.

Kendra's scalp prickled when a murmur of agreement swept through the room. There was no denying the hostility of the crowd.

"Oye!" Mr. Longhorn didn't have a gavel to pound the table, but he glowered at Lensar. "You cannot address the jury unless you are called as a witness, sir!"

"Enough!" The Duke pushed himself to his feet, putting a hand on Lensar's arm. His eyes were more steely-gray than blue as he scanned the crowd. Everyone seemed to hold their breath. "I will testify on behalf of Madam Patya's character—and all of the Romani who currently reside on my land, if I must. Not one of them shot Lord Craymore."

The juror wasn't a fool. When you ran a shop in Aldridge Village, it was wise not to argue with the man whose family had founded the town. In fact, the tavern was filled with merchants, mill workers, and tenant farmers who were either beholden to the Duke or hoped to continue to do business with him. With some amusement, Kendra felt the shift in the atmosphere.

Other jurors asked Madam Patya questions, but their tone was now careful, cautious. Was Lord Craymore conscious at all? Did she see anyone in the vicinity that could have been the villain? Perhaps she saw the murderer's identity when she was scrying or crystal gazing?

For her part, Madam Patya answered calmly enough. No, Lord Craymore hadn't regained consciousness, she had not seen anyone else, and she had no knowledge of the murderer's identity, in this world or by supernatural means.

Technically, she was telling the truth. Craymore had regained consciousness with Shandor, not Madam Patya. *No, thief, no!*

Dr. Munroe was called next. Neither the Duke nor Kendra was asked to testify. Not that they would have been able to add any new information.

In the end, the Honorable Mr. Longhorn declared that Lord Craymore had died by foul means. Given that his lordship was shot in the back, it was determined to be murder, not manslaughter, by person or persons unknown.

Verdict issued, chairs scraped back and feet thundered across the wood floor as men headed for the tap for one more pint, or for the exit to resume their workday.

The Duke leaned forward to touch Madam Patya's hand. "Thank you, Madam Patya. I know that you do not seek trouble."

The old woman laid her hand on his. "It is true that we would prefer not to be drawn into your people's grievances, but the Romani do not run from our responsibilities. Our caution can sometimes be mistaken for cowardice." She patted his hand to stop the Duke's angry objection. "Do not fly up into the boughs, boy. I've lived long enough to know that people will always make assumptions, right or wrong." Her mouth curved into a slow smile, black eyes glinting. "Like most things in life, it's all a matter of perspective, is it not?"

32

J onah Lansing was in a conversation with a muscular man wearing an ill-fitting coat over a homespun wool smock and breeches when Kendra accompanied Muldoon across the room. The scent of manure clung to the other man, which helped Kendra place him as the owner of the village's public stables. Lansing gave the stable owner a couple of coins, which the man quickly pocketed. He spotted Kendra and tipped his tricorn cap before hurrying out the door.

"I shall be bringing my cousin with me to Pelsley Hall," Lansing said in a clipped voice, his eyes meeting Kendra's. "I am leaving immediately."

Kendra nodded. "We just need a moment of your time."

Muldoon gave a brief bow when Lansing looked at him in silent inquiry. "I am Phineas Muldoon—*The Morning Chronicle*."

Lansing stiffened. "What is a London scribbler doing here?"

"The murder of a peer of the realm is always of interest," Muldoon replied. "Especially when the next in line to inherit the earldom is someone like yourself, sir. I've attended a few speeches where you have addressed the plight of war veterans."

Lansing held himself still for a moment. "I see," he said slowly. "And what was your opinion, Mr. Muldoon?"

"I hoped I wasn't hearing a politician's rhetoric to win over the populace. Of course, your status has changed with your cousin's death."

"Yes, but my sentiments have not." He shifted his gaze back to Kendra. "What do you need to speak to me about, Miss Donovan?"

"Basil Willoughby." She studied him carefully, but his only reaction was a slight crinkling of his brow.

"I fail to see—"

"He was murdered last night."

That got a response. Lansing's eyes widened. "Basil Willoughby—the man that Evelyn has formed an uncommon attachment to?"

"One and the same. He was pulled out of the lake at Shay House yesterday morning."

"Shay House? What the devil was he doing there?" His mouth flattened, and he answered his own question. "Lady Evelyn, I suppose. My God, what happened? He drowned?"

"No—blunt force trauma. He was struck several times in the back of the head before his body was thrown into the water on Saturday night. I was told that you visited Lady Evelyn on Saturday."

He stared at her. "In the afternoon—half past one! Surely, you are not accusing me of Mr. Willoughby's murder? I didn't even know the man!"

"Mr. Willoughby was at Shay House on the day your cousin was murdered," she said. "We think he might have seen something—or, rather, someone. Your cousin's murderer. Where were you this Saturday evening, around midnight?"

"I returned to London after I met with Evelyn. I had no reason to stay, and no—"

"Can anyone verify that?"

His nostril's flared as he sucked in a quick breath. "No. My visit with Evelyn left me… disturbed. She is not well." His eyes narrowed. "You've spent time with her, Miss Donovan. You know how she is."

Kendra ignored that. "What did you do after you returned to London?"

"I had correspondence and needed to review Reginald's account books, which I'd received from his man-of-affairs. There is much to be done as the Earl of Craymore." He pursed his lips, frowning. "I went out around eight, and had a meal and a pint at a nearby tavern. I wasn't there long before returning to my rooms."

"What's the name of the tavern?"

"The Red Fiddle. It's on the Old Bailey Road," he answered promptly. "It was busy. I'm not certain if anyone will remember me."

"What about your horse?" Muldoon spoke up for the first time. "You must stable it somewhere in London. There are grooms, stable boys to confirm when you stabled the animal."

"I do not own my own livestock," he said stiffly. "I have spent most of my life in London, and never could justify such the expense. I rented a horse. A stable boy might remember me from when I returned the mare."

Kendra regarded him. "You don't sound sure about that."

"I'm not. It's a busy stable on Dryden Street—not far from the Red Fiddle—and the stable boys are just that—boys. *Children.* They are run ragged for a shilling. I doubt they paid me any mind."

"You didn't give these boys, these *children*, an extra shilling?" Kendra asked. "You didn't talk to them at all?"

Lansing jerked as though stung. "I… no."

"Too bad. If you had, maybe you would have stood out to them." She watched him flush. "You lied about being in your printing shop on the night your cousin was murdered. We've got witnesses saying that you locked up shortly after six."

For the first time, Kendra saw real fear flash in Lansing's eyes, followed by anger.

"I did not kill Reginald," he snapped. "I am of the mind that there should be no titles—much like your own countrymen, Miss Donovan."

"Are you giving yours up?"

His jaw tightened, and he glanced away. "It is not that easy."

"What about the Anahita Pink?" Kendra asked. "You argued with Lord Craymore about the diamond a week before he was killed. Do you deny it?"

Lansing hesitated, obviously thinking about doing exactly that. But something—maybe fear of being found out—had him shaking his head. "No, I won't deny it. Lady Evelyn wrote to me. She... hinted that Reginald had the diamond in his possession."

"Why?"

"She offered to help me get the diamond, thinking I would return the favor and get her out of Shay House." He waved a hand. "It was ludicrous, of course. I had no say in the matter."

"You contacted Craymore instead," Kendra guessed.

"I wrote to him. I expected him to reply in a letter. I was surprised when he came into Polaris." He sighed. "Reginald and I rarely saw eye to eye. We couldn't be in the same room without quarreling about the inequalities in government, where half of Englishmen do not have a voice."

"And all Englishwomen," Kendra couldn't resist saying.

He gave her a blank look.

Kendra pressed on. "The Anahita Pink came up during your discussion, though."

"Yes," Lansing admitted reluctantly. "I told Reginald that if he truly had the Anahita Pink, it should be given to the people. It belongs to the English people."

Muldoon shook his head. "You must realize that if you managed to get a hold of the diamond and used it at one of your rallies, it would have been immediately confiscated by the government."

A crafty glint came into Lansing's eyes. "You are correct, Mr. Muldoon. But our point would have been made. And Whitehall is not known for having a light and loving touch when dealing with the common folk."

The reporter rocked back on his heels as he regarded the other man. "Are you saying you *wanted* to incite a riot? You are aware that people—*common folk*—could get hurt? Possibly killed?"

"I am aware of the risk," Lansing said coldly. "But no great cause has ever succeeded without sacrifice. Miss Donovan can attest to that with her own country's bid for independence."

"I'm not going to get into a philosophical debate with you, Mr. Lansing," Kendra said. "Right now, I'm more interested in where you were on the evening your cousin was murdered."

She waited. When he remained silent, she said softly, "You just admitted that every cause requires sacrifice. Maybe Lord Craymore was the first to be sacrificed to get the Anahita Pink."

Lansing drew in a quick breath. "I would not commit cold-blooded murder for it."

"Then let's eliminate you from the list of suspects. Where did you go after you left your shop on Wednesday night? And where were you on Saturday night when Willoughby was murdered?"

Kendra tried to decipher the emotions that played across his face. Frustration, she thought. Anger. Maybe even fear. But in the end, he simply shook his head.

"I went home. Alone." He slammed his tricorn hat on his head in a jerky gesture. "You will have to look elsewhere for your villain, Miss Donovan."

She watched Lansing's rigid back as he stormed out of the tavern. "You know how Mr. Kelly thought Mr. Lansing asking Lady Evelyn about the Anahita Pink might be a clever deception to throw us off?" she murmured, sliding a glance at Muldoon. "He might be right."

The Irishman let out a breath. "Mr. Lansing is not the man I thought he was, but I still don't think he killed his cousin. I think he was at a meeting on that particular evening. The Spenceans held one. They are organizing a public meeting at Spa Fields for November."

"The Spenceans?"

"'Tis a philanthropic movement started by Thomas Spence. There are those who believe he spearheaded the bread riots in London at the beginning of this century. Mr. Spence died two years ago, but his ideas of a more fair-minded society continue. Of course, his followers are viewed as radical—a few even wish to overthrow the government."

"And Lansing is a member of the Spenceans?"

"Not necessarily, no. But I am aware that Mr. Lansing—ah, the earl—is closely connected to Henry Hunt. The Spenceans have been attempting to recruit that orator to speak on their behalf at the rally. I was informed that they had a meeting about it on Wednesday evening."

Kendra lifted her eyebrows. "He'd rather be considered a murderer than admit to attending this meeting?"

"The government takes a dim view of radicals, Miss Donovan. They are beginning to view their rhetoric as an act of sedition. That means prison or being transported. Why do you think they hold their meetings in secret?"

"But you knew about it."

He grinned, tapping a finger against his bold nose. "I have my ways, Mis Donovan."

"Then you can use your ways to find others who attended the meeting that night. If Lansing won't talk, someone else might."

33

Kendra spent the rest of the day in the study, updating and reviewing her notes. She suspected that Muldoon was right, and Lansing had been at the Spenceans meeting on the night his cousin was murdered. Still, she wouldn't cross his name off the list until she heard from the Irishman.

Jiggling the piece of slate in her hand, she paced and considered the new information.

The horseback rider that Shandor had seen around the Romani camp was new. But was it connected? Madam Patya said the stranger kept his distance, neither causing trouble nor approaching them. But Kendra didn't like the timing. Why would someone be circling around that particular area—the same area where Craymore was found—*now*?

Something brushed at the edges of her consciousness. She stood very still, trying to capture it.

Then it was gone.

Damn, damn, damn. She pinched the bridge of her nose. What was she missing?

Dropping her hand, Kendra resumed pacing. Willoughby's murder was straightforward. He'd figured out who had murdered Craymore. Instead of contacting authorities, he'd tried his hand at blackmail. Muldoon was right—Willoughby had been stupid to meet with the killer, stupid not to think he'd become a victim as well. For whatever reason—overconfidence, arrogance, or stupidity—he had underestimated his killer.

Craymore's murder bothered her. It should have been as straightforward as Willoughby's. The motive was clear: a priceless diamond—especially one steeped in history—was enough to tempt a saint into committing the ultimate sin.

Except why hadn't the killer tried to disguise himself? The answer: he intended to kill Craymore from the outset.

She imagined Craymore on that dark and lonely road. He'd most likely still been furious after the musical recital had descended into chaos and he'd discovered Lady Evelyn had been meeting with Willoughby. Lost in his anger, maybe he hadn't become aware of the other rider until he was close. And then?

Then he'd recognized the other rider and reined in his horse, waited for the unsub to catch up. And recognized his mistake when the other man pulled a gun on him, and demanded the Anahita Pink?

"Penny for your thoughts?"

Startled, Kendra swung around to find Alec watching her from the doorway. "You are in a brown study," he remarked with a faint smile. Walking over, he took her in his arms and kissed her. "What are you thinking?"

"I was trying to put myself in Craymore's shoes on the night he was murdered." Because Alec was there, solid and warm, she slid her arms around his waist. "What he did when he realized the other rider was going to kill him."

Alec lifted a hand to brush a tendril off her cheek. "Craymore obviously tried to flee when he realized he was in peril. That's why he was shot in the back."

"I think he did something else before that. He probably had a gun pointed at him, remember? The unsub had no intention of letting Craymore live. So, why didn't he shoot him in the chest? I think Craymore did something to distract his killer, and that allowed him to spur his horse into a gallop, to give him a chance to escape."

Alec released her, and turned to look at her notes on the slate board. "Something with the Anahita Pink."

"I think he threw the diamond towards his killer."

"So the fiend was forced to catch it… or Craymore deliberately threw it wide, and the killer took his eyes off Craymore. The villain shot Craymore anyway, but maybe that's why he never caught up with the earl. He was forced to stop and retrieve the diamond."

"It's a theory."

"It's a good theory.

"It helps me understand the what and the why—not the *who*."

"Let's walk."

"What?"

"Walk." He gave her a slow smile. "'Tis a simple pastime, but a cherished one. A walk in the garden before dinner with my beautiful betrothed. The weather was remarkably mild today. Didn't you notice?"

"I was a little busy."

She thought of her life before she'd come here. Alone. Driven to prove herself.

"My career was always the most important thing in my life," she said slowly. Leaning into Alec, she lifted her chin and met his eyes. "It always came first. Always. It's who I am."

"I understand that. I accept that."

"It's a part of me," she said again, "but I'm realizing it's not the whole of me." She paused. "Life is a lot slower here than in my time. It drives me nuts."

He huffed out a soft laugh. "You say the damnedest things. However, I believe I comprehend the sentiment."

"A slower pace isn't a bad thing. Life is so fragile. I should know that more than most," she said. "I deal in humanity's darker impulses. In death. When Craymore rode away from Shay House, he didn't know his life was over. None of us can know."

Not just death—if the vortex opened again in a few days. That would be an end, too.

But she didn't want to think about that now.

Alec was gazing at her intently. "Kendra—"

"No. I need to say this." She drew in an unsteady breath, more emotional than the situation warranted. "You've made me a better person, Alec. Being here, in this time…it drives me crazy, but it has made me a better person. I need to remember that."

His eyes narrowed. Because he probably saw more than she wanted him to, she pulled back to take his hand, lacing her fingers through his. She smiled at him. "Let's go. I want to walk in the garden with my gorgeous fiancé."

Later that evening, Kendra sat in front of the mirror, having changed out of her afternoon dress into a gown of ice-blue silk with an ivory organza overskirt. Molly's nimble fingers flew over her hair, brushing, braiding, and using the curling tongs for an elaborate updo.

"And Monsieur Anton accused John of stealin' a bag of turnips," the maid was saying. Part of a lady's maid's role was keeping her lady informed of everything that was happening in a household. "The froggy boxed John's ears but good. 'E as a terrible temper, 'e does. Always mutterin' in that foreign tongue of 'is."

"Well, he *is* French."

"Aye, 'e is." Molly made that sound dire.

"And he is an exceptional cook."

Molly pouted. She didn't like hearing anything positive about the French chef. When Kendra had worked in the kitchens, she'd observed firsthand the animosity that existed between Monsieur Anton and the English staff.

"'Ave ye 'eard from that London cutthroat?" Molly asked suddenly.

"Bear?"

"'Ow many London cutthroats do ye know, miss?"

Kendra grinned. "I feel like I've met quite a few, now that you mention it, but I'm on speaking terms with only one. And, no, he hasn't contacted me or Mr. Kelly yet."

Molly pursed her lips as she carefully pinned a curl. "Seems peculiar that the thief is takin' so long ter sell the bauble."

"It won't be an easy bauble to sell."

"Aye, ye've said that. But 'e 'asn't even tried ter sell it, 'as 'e? Or made inquiries? W'ot's 'e waiting for?"

Kendra frowned. There were valid reasons to hold onto the diamond. It was too hot; attention needed to die down. But Molly was right, and she too was beginning to wonder if there might be another reason for the delay. What it was, though, she had no idea.

34

Kendra jerked awake with a gasp.

Alec's arms came around her, gently stroking her back. "Hush, sweetheart. Nightmare?"

Heart pounding, she squeezed her eyes shut, trying to recapture the dream. An elusive, shadowy figure was riding through a forest shrouded in fog. In the distance, she could see the Anahita Pink on the ground, glowing like a beacon through leaves and brambles. Even awake, she could still feel the almost unbearable zing of excitement as she raced towards the gem in the dream. She recalled how her fingertips brushed its hard, silky surface...

Then Shandor appeared, screaming, *No thief, no thief, no thief!* As his shouts faded, she watched, horrified, as the diamond melted into a crimson pool of blood. Somewhere in the endless fog, there was the echo of mocking laughter, and then—

"Kendra?"

"Sh-sh." But the dream was already dissolving, retreating to the back of her mind. She opened her eyes, looking into Alec's shadowy face above her. "Damn. It's gone."

"The nightmare?"

"Dream. Dreams can be a way of working out problems. My subconscious is sending me a message."

"Hmm. What's a subconscious?"

She smiled. "That's a discussion for another time."

"Then tell me your dream."

Her smile faded, and she let her gaze drift to the canopy overhead as she described the shadowy rider, the dark forest, the way the Anahita Pink turned into blood.

"Grisly, but understandable. God knows how many lives have been sacrificed for the Anahita Pink."

"Yeah. Then Shandor appeared."

"Shandor?" His fingers brushed her hair. "I don't believe I need to be jealous of him appearing in your dreams for another decade or so."

"He said, 'No thief, no thief.'" She closed her eyes again, frowning as bits and pieces of the dream came back to her. "Madam Patya appeared out of the mist and told me that it was a matter of perspective. Miss Dora was there, too. She was screaming that it was the devil's apprentice, that the pagan boy was right, but I wasn't listening."

"Those are memories, not your imagination," Alec murmured. "Those were Craymore's last words, and Miss Dora did scream about the devil's apprentice."

Kendra didn't say anything. She was remembering something else. The moon had risen behind Miss Dora, swelling to five times its original size. Fear had speared through Kendra as it came closer, its silvery glow washing over her, the light burning and blistering her skin. Then the moon swallowed her whole. She didn't need to be Freud to figure that one out.

Two days… two days until the full moon.

"Kendra? What else do you remember?"

She swallowed hard, opening her eyes. "Nothing."

He cupped her chin, forcing her to look at him. "Are you certain?"

"I think so. What time is it?"

"Nearly four. I should go."

"No. Stay." She wound her arms around his neck. "I'm awake now."

"You should sleep."

"I can think of something better."

Alec's teeth flashed white in the darkness. "What is that?"

She laughed softly. "Something else to dream about."

If Kendra did dream again, she didn't remember. When she woke to the feathery gray light of dawn, Alec had already left. For a long moment, she stared up at the bed's canopy, once more trying to recapture the strands from last night's dream and weave them into something substantial, something that made sense. But whatever her subconscious had been trying to tell her remained elusive.

An hour later, dressed in a plain, dark-blue paisley round gown and with her hair pulled back with a ribbon, Kendra walked into the morning room. The Duke and Alec were already seated at the table, halfway through their breakfast. The Duke was perusing a newspaper, freshly ironed to prevent the ink from staining his fingertips, and muttering, "Rubbish. Absolute rubbish!"

Kendra raised a brow. "What happened?"

Alec smiled. "Uncle is annoyed by a report about sunspots."

"A completely *nonsensical* report on sunspots." The Duke shook the paper, then tossed it to the side. "It's irresponsible for a newspaper to continue to give credence to that astronomer Bologna! For God's sake, that idiot said that the sun would cease to be on July 18. The fact that the sun shone the very next day should have put an end to such drivel. But no! They continue to harp on the spots, even suggesting that they are lakes of water on the sun that are growing ever larger and will soon douse its flame."

Kendra brought her plate and coffee cup to the table. "They actually think there are lakes on the sun?"

"'Tis absurd, I know. Good heavens, we've been aware of these spots since the telescope was invented!"

Alec reached over and picked up the newspaper, scanning it. "Hmm. Well, the populace's fear has been exaggerated because of the unusual cold spell we've been in." He looked over at his uncle. "Your friend bears some responsibility for the paranoia taking hold."

"Friend?" The Duke looked baffled. "What friend?"

"Hershel. Didn't he theorize recently that the sunspot activity could be linked to the weather, and might even be used to predict harvests?"

Kendra managed to swallow the piece of toast before she choked. She'd discovered several months ago that one of the Duke's scientifically-minded correspondents was none other than William Hershel, who'd discovered the planet Uranus thirty-five years ago. She was almost used to hearing the noted astronomer's name thrown about in casual conversation. Almost.

"Well, yes," the Duke admitted grudgingly. "And William was soundly ridiculed by fellow members of the Royal Society." He glanced at Kendra. "Perhaps this debate has been resolved in the... in your America?"

"It's not exactly my field of expertise." What to say? What not to say? "I think there's consensus that sunspots can disrupt the earth's magnetic field. That can sometimes create havoc with the power grids, radio signals, and satellites... which"—she smiled at the Duke—"doesn't affect anything here."

The Duke looked like he wanted to discuss that further, but he stopped himself. He pointed a finger at Alec. "'Tis Lord Byron's fault. His *Darkness* has caused the paranoia."

Alec shook his head. "I don't think he's responsible for the paranoia taking hold as much as he is capitalizing on the fear that we are in the end of times."

"The poem foretells the end of the world when the sun is extinguished!"

"It's a poem, not a scientific treatise," Alec pointed out mildly.

"It's poppycock!" the Duke huffed, exasperated. He pinned Kendra with a look. "I sincerely hope that people in the future are more pragmatic and not prone to such outlandish fantasies."

Kendra laughed. "People have been predicting the end of the world for a variety of reasons since the beginning of time. And newspapers have been writing about it for about as long for the oldest reason."

Alec arched a brow at her as he slathered jam on his toast. "Which is?"

She smiled. "To sell newspapers."

"You make an excellent point, my dear," the Duke sipped his tea. "To be fair, the *Morning Post* dismissed the apocalyptic predictions at the time, and pointed out how brightly the sun was shining the day after its flame was supposed to be extinguished. Unfortunately, it was too late for some. A cook here in Kent even hung herself in a moment of hysteria."

Kendra shook her head, bewildered. "Committing suicide because you're afraid to die in an apocalypse?"

"Perhaps it is not death itself but the manner in which one dies that people are most afraid of," the Duke murmured quietly.

He was right, of course. People in burning buildings often jumped to their deaths rather than face the flames.

The door opened, and Harding materialized. "Pardon me, sir, but we've received word that the boat with the French buhrstone has left London. It should be in the village in an hour."

"Ah. Excellent. I must confess that I'm as excited as the villagers to see the stone installed in the mill," the Duke said as Harding took his leave. "I suspect there will be quite a crowd. Alec and I shall be supervising. You are welcome to join us, my dear."

"Thanks. I'll think about it."

Alec pushed himself to his feet, looking at Kendra. "I have something for you. Stay here, please."

Surprised, Kendra watched him leave the room. She glanced at the Duke, but he shrugged. "I have no idea what this is about."

She was pouring herself a second cup of coffee when Alec returned. He fixed his gaze on her in such a way that made her slowly set down the coffeepot, a flutter deep in her belly.

"I realize our betrothal will be announced publicly at the house party's ball," he said, coming to stand in front of her. "However, I have been remiss in not presenting you with an engagement gift. It is custom for prospective grooms to give his lady a token to show their troth."

Out of the corner of her eye, Kendra saw the Duke smile. She remembered her time at Princeton, when a few co-eds had gotten engaged. They'd squealed in excitement as they showed off their engagement rings to their friends. She'd always thought their reaction excessive. Now she was shocked to find her own heart racing, her palms dampening even as her mouth went dry.

"We have the same tradition," she managed to say.

Alec smiled at her, and he reached into his pocket. She eyed the flat, rectangular box he presented to her. Not a ring. The dimensions were all wrong.

Aware that she was under scrutiny by both men, she took the box and untied the velvet ribbon. Lifting the lid, she found herself staring blankly at the ruched white satin gloves edged with delicate French lace and decorated with seed pearls.

"I thought you could wear the gloves for the wedding ceremony," Alec said.

"Ah…" She touched the delicate fabric, then glanced up to meet Alec's eyes. Pushing aside her preconceived ideas, she summoned a smile. "They're beautiful. Thank you."

Alec wasn't fooled. "You said that you had the same tradition."

Kendra laughed. "Maybe things had changed a bit."

"What is the tradition in your America?"

She hesitated. "The custom is engagement rings, not… ah, engagement gloves."

The Duke's eyes brightened. "This is fascinating. The custom here is a betrothal gift, not a specific item. I gave Arabella a diamond jasmine flower broach as my token."

Alec said, "If you prefer, I can get you a ring."

"No." She clutched the box and gloves to her chest, meeting Alec's intense gaze. "They're perfect. I will cherish them."

"Uncle, you might want to leave the room." Alec settled his hands on Kendra's shoulders without breaking eye contact. "I don't want to offend your sensibilities, but I'm going to kiss my fiancée now."

The Duke grinned as he headed toward the door. "I shall meet you in the stables."

After Alec and the Duke left for the village to supervise the installment of the French buhrstone, Kendra requested a fresh pot of coffee for the study. There, she poured herself another cup and contemplated the information on the slate board. Something niggled at her. Something—

"I heard that my nephew gave you a betrothal gift," Lady Atwood said as she swept into the room.

Kendra glanced at the countess's set face. "Yes."

"Well, then, as it appears that neither one of you will change your mind about this marriage…" The countess seemed to hold her breath, as though hoping Kendra would contradict her.

Kendra said nothing, but couldn't stop herself from glancing at the tapestry that concealed the hidden passageway. *Two more days.* What would she do? What *should* she do?

Lady Atwood sighed. "Then I shall make arrangements for us to go to London."

Kendra's gaze snapped back to the older woman. "What? Why?"

"You can hardly use the modiste here in Aldridge Village for your bridal dress, Miss Donovan," she sniffed. "I shall make an appointment with Madam Gaudet. You need a new gown for the ball. We shall leave tomorrow morning."

Kendra stared at the countess, aghast. "I can't go to London tomorrow. I'm in the middle of an investigation!"

Lady Atwood arched her perfectly plucked eyebrows. "You are not listening, Miss Donovan. I did not ask a question. I was making a statement of fact. I am *telling* you that we will be traveling to London tomorrow."

The countess didn't allow Kendra to respond. With a grim little smile curving her lips and her shoulders squared into a steely purpose, she swung around and sailed out of the study.

Kendra had to resist throwing her coffee cup at the door. "No, *you* are the one not listening," she muttered, temper spiking. "I was making a statement of—"

Kendra froze, the breath whooshing from her lungs as a thought came to her. "Oh, my God."

A statement of fact.

A statement…

Her dream rushed back. Her subconscious *had* been trying to tell her something. Shandor insisting that he wasn't a thief, and Madam Patya saying, *It's a matter of perspective, isn't it?*

A chill of awareness and excitement danced over her skin. Carefully, she set down her coffee cup before snatching up a piece of slate. In three quick strides, she was in front of the board, her gaze fixed on the words she'd written almost a week ago. *Could it really be so simple?*

Her subconscious had put the pieces together for her. She erased the punctuation in Craymore's last words, then she circled the sentence twice. She stepped back to look at it again. *Holy shit, it really is a matter of perspective.*

Everyone had assumed that Craymore had been calling Shandor a thief when he'd regained consciousness. A natural assumption, given the hostility and prejudice directed at the Romani. Hell, Shandor himself had believed that was what Craymore had said.

But what if the earl had said something else in his delirium?

Not *No, thief!* But instead: *No thief.*

It was such a minor difference. And it could change everything.

35

Kendra needed to take a moment to allow the puzzle pieces to shift and realign in her mind. The horseback rider that Shandor saw near the Romani camp took on a new meaning now.

An idea, a suspect, began to emerge from the shadows, taking shape and solidifying the more she considered him. It worked, she thought. *He* worked. Even Miss Dora's ramblings about the devil's apprentice fit, if one looked at the world through her mad eyes.

She wanted to talk to Shandor again—*now*. Kendra tossed the piece of slate on the table and hurried to her bedchamber. She kicked off the delicate shoes she wore, and searched the wardrobe for the sturdy half-boots that she always donned when she walked the countryside. Briefly, she sorted through her coats and cloaks, settling on a dove-gray wool redingote for its warmth. The sun might have been shining, but English weather was unpredictable.

Snatching up her reticule, she checked to make sure the muff pistol was inside. Like the weather, this was another area where it was best to be prepared.

Upstairs maids and tweenies were dusting and polishing in the hallways, and only gave her a cursory glance as she passed by. The Romani camp had taken her and the Duke twenty minutes by gig. Kendra calculated that it would take her at least an hour, at a healthy pace, to get there by foot. She should arrive around twelve-thirty.

The sun was warm on her face, but the temperature and the breeze made her grateful that she'd selected the wool coat as she struck out in the direction of the campsite. She realized belatedly that the Romani could be gone. They'd stayed for the inquest yesterday, but might have felt compelled to move on afterward.

If nothing else, the long walk would give her time to think again about her suspicions. To put herself in the mind of the killer.

Craymore's murder had been an impulse, to a certain extent. Maybe the unsub had hoped to talk the earl out of his temper. *But you brought the gun, didn't you? You were prepared to kill.* Still, she now understood his hesitancy, why Craymore had been shot in the back, not pointblank in the chest. The unsub wasn't a cold-blooded killer. At least, not then…

Willoughby changed everything. As soon as he contacted the killer, foolish, arrogant Willoughby was as good as dead. He just didn't know it. The lure of the Anahita Pink had been too strong.

Kendra shivered a little as she moved into the forest, where the towering trees blocked the sun's rays. The rich scent of pine and loam teased her nostrils. Nature's concerto played around her—trilling birds, droning insects, and the sly rustling of grass and shrubs, caused by either the breeze or woodland creatures.

Mentally, she circled back to Miss Dora, testing for holes in her theory. *The devil's apprentice. He drinks the blood of virgins with a serpent. I've seen the chalice of the underworld.* On the surface, that might all seem like the ravings of a lunatic. But there was a thread of sanity—or, at least, an awareness—in the gibberish.

The sound of voices, children's laughter, and the clang of metal and vague commotion drifted through the trees. Kendra angled herself in that direction, and a few minutes later, she broke free of the woods into the clearing where the Romani were still camped, though not for long.

The youngest children were chasing each other around the camp, shrieking and giggling, while the rest of the Romani were in the process of packing up. The women were washing dishes in a cauldron over the fire, drying and packing them in crates. The men were harnessing the horses to the colorful wagons. The scent of something savory lingered in the air, making Kendra's stomach rumble.

Madam Patya emerge from her wagon, looking much as she had the other day in her swirl of skirts and gold. She called out to a young man in their tongue. Maybe a joke, because he tilted his head back and laughed. Then the old woman turned her head, and her dark eyes locked on Kendra.

"Miss Donovan," she greeted, and gestured to the young man, who hurried to assist her to the ground.

"Madam Patya." Kendra was aware of the scrutiny of the Romani, but this time no one stopped their chores to openly stare at her. "You're leaving?"

"It is time." That came from Lensar. He strode over to them. "Why are you here, Miss Donovan?"

Not exactly hostile, she decided. But not friendly either. "I need to speak to Shandor." She glanced over to where the boy was helping with the horses.

Lensar's gaze was penetrating. "Why?"

"I'd like to talk to him again about when he found Lord Craymore. And the man that he's seen in the forest."

"He doesn't know anything more," said Lensar.

Rather than argue, Kendra said, "I promise not to take up too much of his time."

Lensar's jaw tightened. "This is *gadjo* business, not ours."

Madam Patya placed a hand on Lensar's arm, but kept her gaze fixed on Kendra. "Will this assist you in finding the man who killed the earl?"

"Yes, I think it will. I hope it will."

The old woman studied her for a moment longer, then glanced at Lensar's stony face. "If Shandor can help Miss Donovan, we cannot stand in the way." She added something in their tongue. The mutinous expression remained on Lensar's handsome face, but he slowly nodded.

Madam Patya raised her hand, the gold bracelets colliding in its familiar musical discord. "Shandor!"

The boy looked over.

"*Av akai!* Come here. Miss Donovan needs to speak with you again."

Putting down the feedbag, he sprinted over. He regarded Kendra with wary, dark eyes.

"If you don't mind, I'd like to speak to Shandor privately," Kendra said to Madam Patya and Lensar. She shifted her gaze to the boy. "Could we take a walk, Shandor?"

Lensar scowled. "Shandor has nothing to hide from his people."

"I'm sure that's true," Kendra agreed easily. "But sometimes it's easier to talk when a person of authority… or when a person one respects isn't listening so closely."

Surprisingly, Madam Patya laughed, shooting a sly glance at Lensar. "I seem to recall you not wishing for your father to overhear a mishap or two in your misspent youth, Lensar."

A reluctant smile ghosted around Lensar's mouth. "Your memory is too sharp, *Baba*."

"My memory is just how it should be." Madam Patya cut her gaze to Kendra. Dark and intense. "You are His Grace's daughter—"

"I'm not."

Madam Petya waved that off with an impatient gesture. "You are the daughter of his heart. And because he holds you in high esteem, I shall do the same. I will trust you, Miss Donovan, just as I would trust him. Shandor." She turned to cup the boy's chin, tilting his head back so she could peer directly into his eyes. "You shall walk with Miss Donovan and answer her questions."

Shandor nodded, and glanced at Kendra when Madam Patya released him.

Kendra pivoted, and began walking away from the campsite. She kept her pace unhurried, allowing the boy to catch up to her. She stopped next to an ancient oak. They were still within sight of the camp, but far enough not to be overheard. Or interrupted.

"I need you to remember the night you came upon Lord Craymore, Shandor," she finally said.

Shandor's forehead crinkled. "I told you everything."

"I know you did. I need to hear it again." The next bit was tricky. It was too easy to influence or manipulate memories, especially of children. "I want you to close your eyes and visualize the scene. Right before you saw the earl. Can you do that for me?"

Shandor hesitated, then closed his eyes. "I was picking wood for the fire. That's why I was there. To collect firewood."

"Okay. Good. Keep your eyes closed, Shandor. What did you smell?"

"Smell?"

"Yes, I want you to bring me back to that night, so I can imagine it with you."

Another slight hesitation, then he gave a jerky shrug. "Smoke from the fire at the camp. Roasting meat. It made me hungry. The leaves of the forest around me." He inhaled deeply, remembering. "The scent of pine and cold air."

"That's good, Shandor. How dark was it?"

"Dark, but I have very good eyes. And the moon was out. Not yet full, but almost. The sky was full of stars."

"And you were picking wood for the fire..." Kendra prodded gently.

"Yes. I heard a noise. I thought maybe it was an animal. Maybe a boar, like we were roasting on the fire. I'd picked up a branch, a large one, and thought I could use it to defend myself."

This is good, Kendra thought. *New information. More details.*

Shandor went on softly, "I looked at the trees and raised the branch. Then Kezia came out of the woods." Eyes closed, he huffed out an annoyed breath. "She's such a pest. Always following me about. We had words, and I chased her off. She deserved it, but… I felt bad. When I heard another noise in the forest, I thought Kezia was returning. She's a stubborn brat." That was said with a faint smile, though it faded quickly. "It was the earl. He was slumped over the saddle. I thought he was foxed. I-I thought I should return to the camp before he woke and saw me, but we have every right to be here. It's the Duke's land. I thought maybe the *gadjo* was a friend of the Duke's, so I decided to help him."

Kendra made a murmuring sound of encouragement when the boy paused, not wanting to break his concentration.

"I saw that the horse had been ridden hard," he continued. "It was lathered. I started calming her when he… when the earl woke. He grabbed my arm and looked at me. He said, 'No thief… No thief.' Then he started to fall off his horse. I grabbed his coat. It was wet. I thought he must have fallen into a lake or a river. But then I… then I realized it was blood."

Shandor opened his eyes. "I brought him to the camp, and *Baba* Patya told the men to put him in her *vardo* so she could tend to him."

"Why did you think he called you a thief?"

The dark eyes flashed. "Because he is a *gadjo*, and they are always calling us thieves."

She thought she now knew the truth, but she still had to ask, "Shandor, did you see the pink diamond that the earl had on him? Did you take the diamond?"

Shandor's chin jerked up, his nostrils flaring. "No! I told you— I'm not a thief!"

"I don't care about the theft, Shandor. I don't even care about the diamond. I only care about catching a murderer."

Shandor's eyes went wide. "I didn't kill him!"

"I know. Calm down, Shandor." She put her hand on his thin shoulder, felt it quiver. "I only want the truth. You can help me, Shandor; you can stop a murderer. But only if you tell the truth." She waited a moment, watching the boy closely. "Did you steal the diamond? Do you know anyone who might have taken it?"

"I'm not a *choro*! The Duke is our *kotaresko*—our host. To do such a terrible thing on his land would be an insult to him."

Kendra studied the boy. Pride kept his head held high and his gaze unwavering on hers. "I believe you, Shandor."

Shandor said nothing.

"That leads me to the next question. Can you describe the man that you've seen in the woods?"

"I see that Shandor has helped you," Madam Patya said when Kendra and Shandor emerged from the woods.

Kendra didn't bother to ask her how she knew that. The old woman seemed to have a unique ability to read people. "Yes, he was very helpful."

They watched Shandor sprint back to where Lensar and several men were hauling bags into a wagon, then Kendra glanced at Madam Patya again. "You know that you don't have to leave."

"Because you know who killed Lord Craymore."

It was not a question, but Kendra answered, "I think I know who the killer is, yes. The investigation should be wrapped up in a day or two. No one should bother you or blame you for what happened to his lordship."

"Perhaps. But it is time. There is a time for everything, Miss Donovan. For everyone. To stay and to go."

Kendra gave the old woman a sideways look, wondering if she was reading too much in that statement. Madam Patya's expression remained enigmatic.

"Where are you going to go?" she finally asked.

"North, for now. Then west to Ceredigion. Wales."

Kendra went still. "You'll be traveling through Needlham?"

"Near there, yes." Madam Patya regarded Kendra. "Shall I send word to the castle that you will be traveling with us?"

Briefly Kendra had a vision of Lady Atwood receiving word that she was traveling alone with the Romani to a madhouse. *Hell, no.* "The Duke and Alec… ah, Sutcliffe are in the village, putting in the mill's French buhrstone."

"We can send a messenger there."

"I can send a message when I get to Needlham. Or I'll hire someone to drive me back." She felt the comforting weight of the muff pistol inside the reticule dangling from her wrist. "I don't anticipate any problems."

The old woman smiled thinly. "Ah, but it is always the problems that one doesn't anticipate that are the most dangerous."

36

Kendra wasn't worried about Shay House, but she did have a twinge about not sending word to Alec. He wouldn't be happy, she knew. Still, what she planned to do was hardly risky. It wasn't like she was venturing alone in the middle of the night to meet with the killer. She was going to a house teeming with people in broad daylight.

She pushed aside her misgivings, climbing up to sit next to Madam Patya, who drove her own wagon. As they traveled, Kendra began to see the world through Romani eyes. The convoy avoided the macadam roads and more populated areas. Instead, they moved across open fields and through forests. The times the Romani journeyed through villages, the townsfolk stared at the caravan—some out of curiosity, many with distrust. A few gawkers spat as they rolled by. A few brazen children threw apples and tomatoes.

Kendra knew that her own presence, a *gadjo* sitting next to Madam Patya, caused more than a little consternation. She made sure that she smiled and talked to Madam Patya during those times, not wanting anyone to think that she was not part of the caravan of her own free will.

They were back on the main road when she began to recognize the scenery. "You can drop me off at the gate of Shay House," she told Madam Patya. There was no point in the whole caravan going up to the madhouse. Kendra could only imagine how that would set Miss Dora off. "I'll walk the rest of the way."

Madam Patya glanced at her. "If you are certain…"

"I am."

The old woman said nothing, but slowed the wagon when they approached the rundown gateposts that led to the old monastery.

"Thank you," Kendra said, gathering her skirts as the wagon came to a stop.

Before she could jump down, Madam Patya's hand clamped down on her wrist.

"You know the identity of the villain who killed his lordship, Miss Donovan. Why don't you go to the authorities?"

"I *think* I know who killed his lordship. I don't have any proof."

"You believe you will be able to get proof?"

"I'm hoping to get a confession." She smiled, but Madam Patya didn't return it.

"Be careful, Miss Donovan. Humans are very much like animals. When you try to trap them, they become vicious."

"You don't need to warn me about humans." Kendra leapt down. "There's no species more vicious."

Rebecca stepped down from the carriage, her gaze going to the spectacle taking place in the open space of Green Park. Crowds had already gathered around the enormous balloon that was currently being inflated, its flamboyant colors an eye-searing splash against the velvety green grass. A few constables were standing around the perimeter to keep the throngs from getting too close to the handful of men racing around the balloon to make adjustments to the basket and lines and monitor the hydrogen being pumped into the balloon.

Excitement thrummed through Rebecca's veins. James Sadler was once a pastry chef, and he'd become the first Englishman to ascend in a hot air balloon thirty-two years ago. He'd been involved in aeronautics ever since.

"Ain't natural, milady," her maid, Mary, muttered from behind her. "If God wanted folks ter be up in the 'eavens, 'e would 'ave given us wings."

"Oh, wouldn't that be lovely? Can you imagine the freedom to soar into the clouds?"

"I 'ave enough freedom with me shoes planted on the ground, thank ye kindly."

"Don't be a spoil-sport, Mary." This was not Rebecca's first encounter with ballooning.

She'd attended a balloon event two years ago, which had opened the country's Jubilee celebrations, and had found it quite thrilling.

But watching Mr. Sadler ascend to the heavens was not her purpose today.

She started across the field, her maid scurrying to keep up. The sizable crowd gave her some pause, but it was, as Kendra would say, a process of elimination. She didn't have to bother with the men, or the women who were with a male companion. She focused only on the women who either had children with them or were keeping a watchful eye on the groups of children racing across the soft field.

It took her about five minutes to spy her quarry, who was standing by herself, her gaze on the two children sprinting around each other a short distance away.

"Mrs. Devaney?" she said, approaching the woman.

Christina Devaney née Osmond took her eyes off the playing children to glance at Rebecca. She was an attractive blonde with big brown eyes, which widened when she recognized Rebecca.

"My lady." She gave a quick curtsy. "How do you do?"

"Very well, thank you." Rebecca smiled, hoping to ease the nerves that she saw in the other woman's tightly clasped gloved hands. "I didn't realize you had an interest in aeronautics."

"Oh. I cannot say that it is a particular interest of mine. I find it all rather terrifying, to be honest. I can't imagine floating up to the heavens in that tiny basket." She shivered and smiled at the same time. "But I thought it would be diverting for the children."

"I always find these spectacles diverting. I regret that I never saw Mrs. Sage take to the skies, but I read her account of her flight."

Christina gave her an uncertain look. "She is an actress, is she not?"

"She is. I believe she's currently treading the boards on Drury Lane." Rebecca hesitated, and found herself fidgeting. "I… ah. Could I have a word, Mrs. Devaney?"

Christina offered a puzzled smile. "Are we not already having a word, my lady?"

Rebecca drew in a breath, realizing for the first time that broaching such a sensitive topic was not going to be easy. She wondered how Kendra did it. The American never shrank away from such confrontations or unpleasantness. It wasn't that she was indifferent to the discomfort she might cause, Rebecca knew. But Kendra refused to let it stop her. She wasn't being rude, as Lady Atwood no doubt thought; she was simply being single-minded in her approach.

"I would wish for more privacy," she said now. "We can still keep an eye on the children," she added when she saw Christina's eyes flick in their direction.

"Very well, my lady," she agreed slowly.

They walked away from the spectators, up the hill a bit. Rebecca gave the other woman a sideways glance. "Have you heard that Lord Craymore was killed last week?"

Christina's eyebrows bounced up in surprise. "Yes. I was not acquainted with the man, of course, but I had heard he was shot by a highwayman."

"That part is debatable. He was shot when he left his sister. Lady Evelyn is in Shay House." Rebecca was studying the other woman closely, and so saw the shock cross her face before she was able to control it.

"W-why are you telling me this? I have..." Christina swallowed hard, her gaze fixed on her children. "I have never been introduced to Lady Evelyn."

"You are familiar with Shay House, though." Rebecca felt a pang of remorse when the other woman shot her a look of fear. "I apologize for causing you distress, Mrs. Devaney. That is not my intent."

"What is your intent, then, Lady Rebecca?" Christina's voice was low and harsh. "Shay House..." She licked her lips, her gaze returning to her children. "Shay House is not something I wish to think about."

"I understand. Truly. I... I am aware of what happened to you, and... and I'm sorry," she said lamely. Yes, this was far more difficult than she'd imagined. "My godfather is the Duke of Aldridge. His ward is Miss Donovan."

"I have heard of Miss Donovan," Christina said. "She is American."

Rebecca heard the note of caution in the other woman's voice. "She is looking into Lord Craymore's murder. She believes that the person who killed him may be from Shay House."

That brought Christina's stunned gaze back to Rebecca. "She thinks Dr. Shay shot Lord Craymore? Why would he do such a thing?"

"Dr. Shay—or anyone who works at Shay House, really. Lord Craymore had a valuable diamond on his person when he left his sister. Are you aware that Shay House's fortunes have been in decline since your… since you left?"

Christina bit her lip. "No, I didn't know. It's because of my father, isn't it? He was enraged."

"Understandable," Rebecca said, and was surprised when Christina flinched.

"You have to know that I was… I was not myself at that time, Lady Rebecca. My mother had died the previous summer, and my spirits were low. My father… he was at loss on how to control the situation, to control me." Her lips twisted in a humorless smile. "He is used to being in control."

Rebecca said nothing, but thought of the financier. Pierce Osmond was successful, and one did not become successful in that industry without being in control—and ruthless.

"Dr. Shay promised my father that he would cure me of my melancholy," Christina continued quietly, her eyes darkening with memories. "I was so lonely. It was a terrible time for me. That is no excuse, of course, for my mistake."

Rebecca stared at her, noting the blush rising in her pale cheeks. Even though she knew it was unforgivably forward, she took Christina's hands in hers. "Mrs. Devaney. You are not responsible for what happened. The assistant who… who molested you is to blame. Listen to me." She squeezed Christina's hands when she felt the other woman jolt. "*Listen* to me. It's not your fault."

Rebecca wasn't surprised when Christina shook her head in denial. Society tended to condemn the women who'd been violated rather than their molester. And the law was on the molester's side, especially if the woman found herself pregnant. It was the belief of the medical establishment that females could only get pregnant if they had enjoyed the sexual congress.

Rebecca's throat burned with the unfairness of it all, and she had to take a moment to clear it. "At least you do not have to worry about the man who violated you," she assured the other woman, giving her hands a final pump before letting go.

Christina frowned. "What do you mean?"

Rebecca hesitated, eyeing the other woman. It made sense, she supposed, that Christina didn't know what had happened. Mr. Osmond had whisked his daughter out of the madhouse and married her off as a way to protect her. If the financier had heard about what had happened to the Shay House assistant, he would never have shared it with Christina.

But she had a right to know, Rebecca thought. It might actually give her some comfort.

She said, "I was told that he killed himself."

"*What?*" Christina pressed a gloved hand to her mouth, her eyes widening in horror. "No. Oh, no… this is all my fault." Tears sprung to her eyes. "No, no, no…"

"No, it's not!" Rebecca insisted.

"It *is.*"

Rebecca inhaled sharply as she studied Christina's stricken face. *I've made a terrible mistake*, she thought suddenly. "You weren't molested, were you?"

Christina wiped away the tears tumbling down her cheeks, and shook her head. "No. I told you. I was so very lonely. And he was so kind to me. I think he was as lonely as I was. We… it shouldn't have happened, of course. I know it was sinful," she whispered, fresh tears spilling over. "Now I have an even greater sin to bear, if what we did caused him to take his life. I never imagined he would do such a thing."

"Mrs. Devaney," Rebecca began, struggling to find the words to console the distraught woman as she absorbed this new information.

"What will happen to—" Christina broke off when her daughter sprinted toward them with her brother in tow. The woman patted away the tears from her face as her children came to a laughing halt. A girl and boy, four and three. Rebecca knew that from Mrs. Pullman's literary salon. Now she knew more.

"When is the balloon going up into the clouds, Mama?" the girl asked.

"Darling, you mustn't be rude. Curtsy to Lady Rebecca. Lady Rebecca, this is my daughter, Henrietta. And my son, Ernest." Her smile trembled slightly as she laid a hand on their shoulders, turning them to face Rebecca.

Because she saw worry in the other woman's eyes—a mother's protective instinct, hoping to spare her child from scorn—Rebecca widened her smile as she leaned down to look at the children. The girl tilted back her head, grinning up at Rebecca as she dutifully bent her knee in a curtsy.

Rebecca's smile froze when she saw the small winsome face beneath the bonnet, and realized she'd made another mistake.

37

The maid, Meg, opened the door to Kendra's knock. Her expression was harried. "Oh, Miss Donovan. Is Dr. Shay aware that ye were comin' today?" Her eyes flicked over Kendra's shoulder, no doubt expecting to see the Duke or, at least, Kendra's maid.

"No." Before she could elaborate, a shriek and crash sent Kendra's eyes to the ceiling. "What's happening?"

"There is no need for you to fret, Miss Donovan," said a voice—Lillian Slater's. The woman glided down the stairs. "Lady Evelyn is simply expressing her displeasure."

Another crash reverberated through the house, causing Lillian's mouth to curve in amusement. "I think Mrs. Maddox has just lost another tea service to her ladyship's temper."

"Ooh!" Meg lifted her skirts and flew across the foyer.

Lillian laughed, stepping aside as the maid sailed past her up the stairs, and then leaned forward, planting her arms on the banister. Her pendant glinted in the afternoon light streaming in through the hall's fan window. "Lady Evelyn has been in a state ever since she learned that Mr. Willoughby won't be rescuing her from Shay House. Will you?"

Kendra moved forward, her eyes on the woman. "Will I what?"

"Will you attempt to rescue her?" Lillian studied Kendra like she was an unknown species. "You appear to be driven by a peculiar quixotic impulse, Miss Donovan."

Kendra knew Lillian was trying to provoke her, but said anyway, "It's not idealistic to want to stop abuse."

Lillian's lips twisted. "You would have to shut Shay House down to stop the abuse."

"Maybe that's exactly what needs to happen."

"Miss Donovan!"

Kendra glanced over to see a white-faced Dr. Shay striding towards her.

"I will not tolerate your slander," he snapped, obviously having overheard her comments. "You have no right to disparage this institution! I've tried to explain to you that the practices at Shay House are recognized by the medical establishment."

"That doesn't mean they aren't barbaric," she shot back.

"They are *not* barbaric! How dare you!" His eyes were jittery with temper, his face flushing a dangerous red as he came toward her. "I know about you!"

Kendra had to resist the urge to dip her hand into her reticule for her pistol.

"You don't think that I have my own connections in Town?" He was invading her space now, his chin jutting forward aggressively. "You are an unnatural female, always involving yourself with the criminal element. You appear to have delusions of being a Bow Street Runner."

"I think you need to calm down, doctor." She managed to keep her voice steady, even though her heart had begun to race. Adrenalin prickled her skin with the classic fight or flight response.

"*Do not speak to me as though I were an imbecile!* I am a respected doctor!"

Kendra shifted, flexing her gloved hands. She glanced at the staircase, but Lillian had disappeared. From upstairs, the commotion continued, another shout and crash.

But Dr. Shay didn't look away. His eyes were locked on Kendra, his angry, sweating face pushing forward to fill her entire vision.

"His Grace is an eccentric, otherwise he would have had you committed to a madhouse as soon as you landed on his doorstep!" he spat.

She sucked in a breath and considered the methods that she could employ to subdue him without resorting to the muff pistol. She didn't want this to devolve into a physical confrontation, but the man was spiraling out of control.

"I am still held in esteem by London society!" he yelled.

"You need to back off, doctor—*now!*"

"Don't issue orders!" He reached out and clamped his hands on her shoulders, as though to shake her.

"*Dr. Shay!*"

Kendra glanced at McBride as he hurried down the steps. Lillian was hovering near the top of the staircase, for once no longer looking amused.

"I will not let you destroy everything I have built!" Dr. Shay bellowed at Kendra, squeezing her shoulders hard.

"Dr. Shay, release Miss Donovan at once." McBride grasped the doctor's arm to pull him away.

"She said that she's going to shut down Shay House!" Dr. Shay shouted, keeping his gaze locked on Kendra.

"I'm certain you misheard," McBride said. "Let her go. You must let Miss Donovan go."

There was a beat of silence, the air crackling with tension. Kendra knew the instant the situation changed. Awareness came into Dr. Shay's eyes. The aggression was replaced with horror.

He released Kendra, his hands dropping to his sides as he took a quick step back.

"Oh, my God," he whispered.

"Let us go to your office, doctor," McBride said quietly.

"We cannot afford another scandal," Dr. Shay muttered. His eyes darted from side to side. The flush in his face ebbed, leaving him ashen. He wiped a trembling hand across his forehead.

"Mrs. Slater, perhaps you can go to the kitchens and tell Cook to send up a tea tray to Dr. Shay's office," McBride said, easing the doctor backwards a few steps before guiding him toward the stairs.

"I didn't mean… I didn't mean…" Dr. Shay mumbled. "Forgive me, Miss Donovan."

Kendra said nothing, but she followed them up the stairs.

Mr. Lewis was coming out of Lady Evelyn's room when they reached the second story landing. "I gave Lady Evelyn something to sleep," he began, then frowned. "What is wrong?"

"Miss Donovan is threatening to close Shay House," Dr. Shay muttered.

Lewis glanced sharply at her. "Is this true?"

"This is not the time to discuss it," McBride interjected. "I'm having Cook brew us a pot of tea. Perhaps you can help her with your special blend, Mr. Lewis?"

Dr. Shay stirred, and looked at the closed door to Lady Evelyn's room. "I should see to her ladyship."

"You shall, but first you must have a cup of tea yourself, doctor," McBride said kindly. "We don't want to overset Lady Evelyn anymore, do we?"

Dr. Shay nodded distractedly. "No. No, of course not."

"I shall help Cook with the tea," Lewis said, and disappeared down the stairs.

McBride led Dr. Shay down the hall to his office. Outside the door, he glanced at Kendra for the first time. "Perhaps it would be best if you wait in my office, Miss Donovan. Dr. Shay, please excuse me while I escort Miss Donovan."

Kendra had to admire how adroitly McBride separated her from Dr. Shay, gently pushing the doctor inside his office and closing the door before turning to usher her the short walk down the hall.

"I apologize, Miss Donovan," McBride said as he opened the door to his office. "Dr. Shay has been… not right since Mr. Willoughby's body was found."

"I can imagine how that would shake up a person."

"Please be seated." McBride waved at one of the two wooden chairs that faced the oak desk. "I shall return as soon as I see to Dr. Shay."

Too restless to sit, Kendra wandered around McBride's office. It was smaller than Dr. Shay's. One window on the other side of the room, behind the desk, let in the afternoon light. A credenza was next to the window, littered with medicinal-looking dark amber bottles. Shelves lined the wall opposite the desk, filled mostly with books, but there were other items that drew the eye.

Kendra glided her fingers over a pestle and mortar and another object that was no doubt a remembrance of McBride's previous apothecary work. She then found herself studying the small gilt-framed portrait of his wife in happier times.

Minutes ticked by on the gold and marble Ormolu clock on one of the shelves. Kendra eventually moved to the window behind the desk, and was watching the shadows stretch across the lawn when the door opened and McBride returned.

"I apologize, Miss Donovan. I didn't intend to be gone so long, but I have tea." He smiled at her as he raised the tea tray that he was carrying. "And biscuits. Please be seated."

She moved to the other side of the desk and sat in one of the chairs while he set the tray down on the credenza.

"So, this is where you listen to the ladies' complaints."

He flicked a glance at her over his shoulder. "I would say concerns. How do you take your tea, Miss Donovan?" He turned back to the tray, and she heard the clink of porcelain as he fiddled with the teapot and cups.

"Black. One sugar. You listen to all the ladies concerns?"

"Everyone has come here at one point or another. And this… well, it's better than the treatment room." His mouth curved slightly. He handed her a teacup and plate with several shortbread cookies, before pouring his own cup of tea. Settling behind the desk, he lifted his cup and studied her over the rim. "Not to sound immodest, but I have found that a sympathetic ear can be soothing. You must try the biscuits. Cook made them less than an hour ago."

Because they were there and she was hungry—she'd never had lunch—she picked up a biscuit and bit into it. Not bad, but dry. She chased the crumbs down with a swallow of tea. "I imagine Miss Dora gave you a litany of complaints."

He smiled. "Miss Dora is one of our more challenging patients."

"She seems to have a religious obsession. Does she always call Mr. Lewis a pagan?"

McBride sighed. "I'm afraid so."

"Such prejudice has to be difficult for him," Kendra murmured, taking another sip of tea.

"I suppose."

"Mr. Lewis told me of his time before he came to Shay House. One forgets that everyone has a history, a life story. For instance, I forgot that you were an apothecary."

He raised his eyebrows. "No. I was training to be one, before the war."

She nodded. "Still, you've kept a few things from those days. The mortar and pestle. And that. That looks familiar."

McBride followed her gaze to the shelf. "The bowl of Hygeia—a common symbol in apothecary. A gift from my wife." His smile turned sad. "Like many young ladies, she was interested in Greek mythology."

"It's a distinctive design," she said. "Similar to the caduceus."

"No, not the caduceus," he said, shaking his head. "The caduceus is the staff of Hermes. You are thinking of the staff of Asclepius. That, along with the bowl of Hygeia, are apothecary symbols. Aesculapius was the Greek god of medicine and healing. It was said that Zeus feared Aesculapius would be able to heal mortals, thereby making them immortal, so he killed him with a thunderbolt."

"Rather petty of him," Kendra murmured as she sipped her tea.

"The ancient gods were often petty," he said with a smile. "The Greeks didn't let that stop them, though, from building their temples to honor Aesculapius. It is said that serpents slithered inside. The reptiles appeared dead to the temple's patrons. Yet when they tried to remove them, the snakes came to life. Naturally, they credited Aesculapius with the serpents' resurrection. Aesculapius' daughter Hygeia was the goddess of health, and was tasked with caring for the temples."

Kendra nodded, remembering the long-buried information. Probably from her mythology class at Princeton.

"Artisans created statues of Hygeia with a serpent wrapped around her arm. She always held a bowl in her hand. The two merged and became the Bowl of Hygeia."

"Interesting."

"I wish I could claim this knowledge, but I only know because my wife told me."

"You love her very much."

"She's the love of my life. She *is* my life."

Kendra contemplated him. "You would do anything for her." She paused, watching him closely. "Even kill for her."

McBride jolted, the teacup and saucer rattling in his hand. He set them down quickly. "What an absurd thing to say, Miss Donovan."

"It actually makes perfect sense," she said slowly. "Miss Dora saw you kill Willoughby."

"You can't possibly believe anything she says. She thinks the devil killed Mr. Willoughby!"

"She said the devil's *apprentice*." Kendra's skin tingled. The puzzle pieces were finally falling into place—except for one major piece. "If she'd seen Dr. Shay that night, she would have called *him* the devil. And as you just admitted, she always called Mr. Lewis the pagan. But you… you were an apprentice before you became a surgeon."

McBride stared at her.

Kendra could feel her heart thunder in her chest, and had to take a breath before continuing, "What did she say? *I've seen the chalice of the underworld.* I'd say that the Bowl of Hygeia would look a lot like a chalice of the underworld to someone with Miss Dora's psychosis. She's been in your office. You've lent a sympathetic ear, haven't you?"

"No one would believe Miss Dora," he said softly.

"They'll believe me."

She watched the change come over his face, the violet eyes darken with emotion.

"What happened, Mr. McBride?" she pressed. "You heard Lord Craymore argue with Dr. Shay. You heard him threaten to shut down Shay House. Where would that leave you? Leave your wife?"

"You don't understand, Miss Donovan," he said softly, so softly that Kendra had to strain to hear him. "I only went after Lord Craymore to reason with him, to make him realize how many people would be hurt if he followed through on his threat."

"You brought a gun when you went after him." Kendra's throat felt so tight, she had to push the words through. "You knew what you were doing."

McBride suddenly surged to his feet; his eyes locked on hers. "No! I just wanted him to listen to me. He's a peer of the realm. Do you think he would have listened to me otherwise? But he was livid. He told me that he should have heeded the warnings and not put his sister in Shay House. My God, it was Christina all over again."

Kendra blinked. "Christina?"

McBride's lips tightened. "Christina Osmond and the babe… Her father's vile campaign against Shay House nearly destroyed us." He scraped his palms over his face. "Don't you see? I couldn't let Lord Craymore go. He had even more power than Mr. Osmond. He's an earl. You understand that I couldn't let that happen, don't you?"

Kendra felt a little sick. *He really believes that he's the victim.*

"I begged him. *Begged*! But it mattered naught," McBride went on. "All I could think was how my wife and I would be put out on the street. Or I would be forced to commit her to Bedlam as a pauper. I cannot afford better care." He raised his hands, stared at them like he'd never seen them before. "I swear I don't even remember firing the gun. I thought I might have hit him, but I was not certain. I chased after him, but my horse was no match for his mare. I lost him in the forest. It wasn't until the next day when you arrived that I knew that my aim was true."

"It was never about the Anahita Pink."

"No, fiend seize it! I had no idea he was carrying such a valuable gem that night."

"Did you think you could find the diamond in the forest?" She peered at him. "You've been searching for it, haven't you?"

McBride's eyebrows shot up in surprise. "How did you know?"

"A witness saw you."

He huffed out a breath. "I only went out a few evenings. I tried to follow the route that the earl must have taken to the gypsy camp." He gave a jerky shrug, looking oddly embarrassed. "Foolish, I know. But, my God, if I would have found it, it would have changed everything."

"The odds…" She shook her head, and was assailed by a wave of vertigo. McBride's face seemed to waver in front of her eyes.

She blinked and managed to pull him back into focus. "Willough-by thought you had the diamond."

"He saw me that night, after Craymore— Willoughby should have been *gone*, damn him. But he saw me. He contacted me, demanding the diamond. Or a monetary reward." McBride's lips twisted. "I had neither. He gave me no choice."

"He didn't realize…" She frowned, the thought drifting away from her.

"He was an arrogant bastard. Thought he was clever. He was shocked when I met him with my weapon already in hand. But he still thought he could convince me that we could be partners. *Partners*." He let out a quick, bitter laugh. "As if I were a flat or some feather-brained chit who could be charmed.

"I planned to fill his pockets and boots with rocks and throw him in the lake so he'd never be found. The lake is ornamental, but there are fish in it. He would have sunk to the bottom. Maybe it would have taken a month or two, but there would have eventually been nothing left of him. But then Mr. Booker's damned dogs started barking."

Kendra shook her head, not in denial but to clear the fuzziness in her head. *Damn, damn, damn.*

"I only had time to throw him in the lake, no weights. Still, Willoughby underestimated me."

As Kendra watched, McBride moved forward, gently lifting the teacup and saucer from her lap and setting it aside. "And you, Miss Donovan… you underestimated me."

38

"Good afternoon, Princess."

Even though she'd been expecting him—waiting for him, really—Rebecca's heart fluttered at the slightly mocking voice. Snapping shut the book that she'd been perusing, she turned slowly to regard Phineas Muldoon. He doffed his battered tricorn hat, which, as far as she was concerned, was his only indication of good manners.

"You continue to elevate my status, Mr. Muldoon," she said, deliberately keeping her own tone cool. "You are far too bold."

He grinned, unabashed. "Baltasar Gracián once said, 'Put a grain of boldness into everything you do.' I was always fond of that quote." His bright cerulean blue eyes traveled over her face.

For a moment, Rebecca's breath evaporated from her lungs. She'd been stared at most of her life, ever since the bout with smallpox had left her disfigured, but she'd never been regarded like this. It was strangely intimate, though they were standing in one of the aisles of Hookham's circulating library. There were

plenty of people only yards away, scanning books or talking quietly in small groups. There was no reason for her to feel so unnerved, her cheeks flaming under the Irishman's scrutiny.

"Do I have horns? Cloven hoofs?" Muldoon wondered.

"Pardon me?"

"There is a woman over there who is looking at me as though
I were the devil himself. I don't recognize her, but from her sour
expression, I must have slighted her in some way."

Rebecca followed his gaze to one of the tables in the atrium.
"Oh. That is my maid."

Muldoon lifted his eyebrows. "I don't remember provoking
her. Unless you have been maligning my character in such a way
that she feels the need to measure me for a shroud."

"Mary is protective— What in heaven's name are you doing?"
she gasped when Muldoon snatched the book out of her hand.

"Finding out your interests," he said easily, scanning the title. "*The Italian*. I didn't realize you are an admirer of Mrs.
Radcliffe's romances."

Rebecca tilted her chin defensively. "Who isn't? She's an excellent writer, and her characters—especially her women—are so
real. You are impudent, Mr. Muldoon." She lifted her hand in silent demand for the novel's return.

"She's become a recluse since this novel was published." Muldoon returned the book. "They say that she was driven mad by
her writing."

"The same individuals spreading that rumor also believe that
the female sex is so simpleminded that we ought not to read too
many books for fear we, too, shall be driven mad," she sniffed. "I
do hope you are not one of those fools, Mr. Muldoon."

"Me sainted mother would box my ears for believing such an
idiotic notion, my lady."

"I would like to meet your mother someday," Rebecca said,
then wished she had bitten her tongue. Before the Irishman could
say anything, she hurried on to cover her embarrassment. "I did

not request your presence for idle conversation, Mr. Muldoon. I asked you here to speak about Mrs. Devaney."

"Mrs. Devaney?"

Rebecca lowered her voice to explain, "She was committed to Shay House four years ago by her father." She paused. This was not an easy topic to discuss. "She was discovered to be with child. The father, it was believed, was an assistant, who was dismissed without references. He later killed himself."

He eyed her quizzically. "Is there some doubt?"

"What we knew was a fabrication," she said. "I spoke with Mrs. Devaney. She claims that her relationship with the father of her child was consensual."

"I don't understand. Why didn't her father force a marriage? I would think the assistant would choose to marry her rather than commit suicide."

"Because the assistant in question was *not* the father of the babe. Unfortunately, the father is already married—Mr. McBride, the surgeon at Shay House, is the father."

"She told you this?"

"Some of it. But I met the child. Mr. McBride has very distinctive eyes, a shade of violet. The girl has her father's eyes. In fact, she is the very image of her father." Rebecca let out a sigh. "It is all very sad."

"It's worthy of a Shakespearean tragedy, but I'm not certain why..." He broke off, not sure how to go on.

Rebecca understood. "Why I summoned you? I'm not certain either. Except that Miss Donovan is a stickler for details. I thought to write her a letter about what I had learned, or send a note to Mr. Kelly..." Now she was the one who trailed off, not sure how to go on. She felt her cheeks burning. She'd rarely blushed in her entire four-and-twenty years. Why she should be suddenly afflicted with the malady, she didn't dare contemplate.

"I am honored that you thought to summon me, my lady," he said, for once with none of his usual levity.

"Yes, well." She wished that she had thought to bring a fan. She could have used it to cool her face. "This is not the kind of information I wished to put on paper. And it would be difficult to explain if someone should see me meeting with a Bow Street Runner." She couldn't quite meet his eyes as she told the falsehood. It was true that she didn't want a letter recording Mrs. Devaney's humiliation, on the off-chance that it fell into the wrong hands. But it would have been easy enough to meet with Sam Kelly in the park or some other innocuous part of town.

"I thought if I told you this new information, you could pass it on to Mr. Kelly and Miss Donovan."

Muldoon frowned. "Miss Donovan already has this information, only it's the wrong man. Do not fret, Princess. I shall call upon Mr. Kelly before riding to Aldridge Castle to deliver the news myself."

Rebecca sighed. "I wish I could go as well, but I have appointments that I cannot avoid. And Mama and I are committed to dining with Lord Grant this evening."

Muldoon's mobile face went still. "Lord Grant?"

"My mother's uncle." She studied his grim expression. "Pray, do you have something against him?"

"Nothing. Why would I have anything against one of my betters?" But his tone was brooding. "I will take my leave, my lady." He gave a brief bow, turned, then swung back. "This new information does change things, you know, and may help Miss Donovan."

"How so, Mr. Muldoon?"

"It reveals Mr. McBride is not an honorable fellow. Another man was accused of a misdeed that he himself had committed. But he kept quiet and let an innocent man be considered a debaucher of women, his reputation destroyed before being dismissed without reference…" Muldoon shook his head. "Mr. McBride may have just as well killed the poor bastard himself."

39

Awareness came to Kendra by degrees. She wasn't dead, but the icepick-stabbing sensation right between her eyes made her almost wish that she was. Her mouth was dry, her skin clammy. The tight knot in her stomach made her feel as though she'd downed a gallon of curdled milk.

Slowly, she became aware of other things. She was lying on a hard surface. Something was sticking into her lower back. Her arms and chest were bound tight. It was like a boa constrictor had wrapped itself around her torso in preparation of having her for lunch.

She forced her eyes open. Not an easy task; her eyelids felt glued shut. When she finally managed to open them, her vision was blurry. She blinked—once, twice, three times, before her eyesight focused and she realized she was staring up at a ceiling at least twenty feet above her. High arched mullion-paned windows were set in all four walls. Several windows were broken, the grime-smeared glass panes chattering like jagged teeth as the cold breeze swirled inside.

Four walls? It took a moment—her brain was stuck on slow-motion—for her to figure out that she must be inside Shay House's tower. From the outside, it had looked dangerously off-kilter and derelict. From inside, she couldn't see the hazards of the structure, but it was definitely derelict. Birds were nesting in the corners near the ceiling. Spider webs and lichen draped the stone walls.

She blinked a few more times to clear the gray fuzziness from her vision, then realized that it wasn't her eyesight that was the problem. Daylight had waned, draping the tower in a soft gloom.

Christ, how long have I been out?

She drew in a deep breath, and was instantly reminded of the constriction holding her immobile. Her legs were free, but her arms were bound across her torso. No, not bound. She was wearing something…

With dawning horror, she saw that she'd been bundled into a leather straitjacket, the abnormally long sleeves twisted around her body, binding her hands as effectively as shackles. *Worse than shackles.* At least she had a chance of getting out of shackles.

The leather was thick and stiff, pressing tight against her breasts. The buckles beneath her were digging into her back, along with a jagged chip that had come loose from the stone floor. A moan escaped her as she struggled to sit up. It took her four attempts, with the world spinning each time. When she finally managed to pull herself into a sitting position, she had to wait until the wooziness subsided. Sweat slithered down her face, irritating because she couldn't wipe it off.

Breathe in; Breathe out.

She fought back the dizziness, the nausea, and slowly scanned her prison. The room was perfectly square, and spacious, probably twenty-five feet on all sides. The soaring ceiling made it appear even larger. Windows frosted with grime and dust were set into three of the four walls, two windows per wall. The fourth wall was an interior wall, with a medieval-looking, arched door connecting the tower to the rest of the monastery.

The chamber might have been used for storage at one time, or studying. Kendra could imagine monks silently working at long tables, creating beautifully calligraphed copies of the bible before the printing press was invented. She could almost hear the scratching of quill against paper…

She wasn't imagining the sound. It was in the walls. Mice—or something bigger.

She wiggled her hands and arms, testing the restraints. *Damn, damn, damn.* She couldn't move more than a centimeter. Panic bubbled inside of her, but she shoved it down. Her legs were free, much good that did her. She'd be able to get to her feet, but what then? Even if the door was unlocked, she wouldn't be able to open it, not when she was trussed up like a Thanksgiving turkey. She would still be trapped.

But she'd rather be trapped standing up.

She rolled onto her knees, and after several sweaty moments, managed to hoist herself to her feet. It felt marginally better. She was still helpless, strapped into the old-fashioned straitjacket, but didn't feel so vulnerable now that she was standing. Which was stupid, of course. She would be as much at McBride's mercy standing up as she was lying down.

Unless she could somehow get out of the damned straitjacket.

She twisted her torso, trying to move her arms inside the leather sleeves. Slow and deliberate.

Nothing.

Her breath hitched and her composure suddenly snapped. Frustration and fear surged through her. Gasping, she began contorting her body in a frenzy, jerking her arms as though she could tear apart the constraints.

Impossible.

Panting, stomach roiling, she fell back against the wall. The straitjacket's metal buckles clanked against the stone. Her pulse jumped as another thought occurred to her. She arched her back against the stone, seesawing back and forth. If she could create enough friction to fray the leather tabs holding the buckles locked in place…

Time vanished. She didn't know how long she worked at it, sawing the leather straps against the stone, but the room was filled with shadows when she paused for what seemed like the millionth time, testing, pulling. A sob of frustration rose up in her throat when she finally admitted to herself that the leather cocoon remained as tight as ever.

"Goddamn it!" she shouted, slumping against the wall. Her voice rang in the empty room, disturbing a couple of pigeons high up in the nests. She froze, then yanked herself upright. She still had one more option. The hope that had died out a moment ago came roaring back.

She strode to the door, drew in a deep breath, and began screaming.

40

By the time Alec and the Duke galloped into the castle's stable yard, night had fully fallen. Lamps spilled light across the graveled yard and limned the faces of grooms and stable hands working the area.

Alec tossed his reins to one of the boys that raced over, and swung down from his stallion. The French buhrstone had taken them much longer to install than they had anticipated, but frustration had eventually given way to satisfaction. He and the Duke had been surrounded by cheering villagers, and the celebratory mood had carried them into the King's Head. Alec had almost forgotten that Lord Craymore's decomposing body had been laying inside the pub just yesterday as he shared a pint—well, several pints—and a warm meal with many of the village's menfolk.

Someday, these people will be my people, my responsibility. He'd always been acutely aware of his legacy, and there had been times when he'd resented that duty to his family, to the estates, to the people who relied on those estates for their livelihood. His future had been written for him before he was born.

Of course, part of that responsibility required him to marry, to bear a son. In his station, marriage was often a business arrangement. When done correctly, it could offer both parties a certain contentment. He'd never expected love. He certainly hadn't expected to find his entire life turned upside down by a beautiful, stubborn American from the future.

"Something amuses you?"

Alec was brought out of his reverie by his uncle's voice. He gave the Duke a sideways look as they walked out of the stable yard to the footpath that looped around the gardens to the front of the castle. It would have been much easier to simply go through the servant's entrance that would lead them past the kitchens. That, however, would send the staff into a flurry. He'd learned when he was a boy that it simply was not appropriate to invade the servants' domain.

Kendra often ignored the rule. Indeed, she found most of the rules that differentiated the classes to be silly. Life would never be dull with Kendra as his marchioness. He could feel his smile widening. "I was thinking that Kendra will not make a typical wife."

The Duke regarded him. "Apparently, that does not concern you."

"The only thing that concerns me is that she will bolt before the wedding."

"Ah. She told you about her theory that the vortex may open again during the next full moon?"

Alec felt like he had slammed into an invisible wall. He stopped and turned to stare at his uncle. "*What?*"

The Duke halted as well. "She never told you," he said slowly. "I apologize. I thought you—"

"What did she say?"

"It was nothing more than speculation, Alec."

"Tell me what she said."

The Duke sighed. "She mentioned the possibility that the vortex could open again during the next full moon. It will be almost one year since she came here. I reminded her that the next full moon—"

"Thursday evening."

"Yes, but it is not the same *night* as last year. It's not a true anniversary. Do not fret, my boy. Bridal nerves are typical."

"There is nothing typical about Kendra Donovan," Alec muttered, frowning.

They started walking again. Alec tried to control the spiraling sense of panic inside him. He'd sensed Kendra's distraction, and growing distance.

"Why is she thinking about this?" he asked aloud.

"I told you—nerves. You must admit that she has more to deal with than most brides."

"I have to speak to her." A sense of urgency quickened his pace. He heard his uncle call his name, but ignored him, sprinting up the front steps and yanking open the door with such force that he startled the footman who was lighting the wall sconces in the entrance hall. He jogged to the staircase, taking the steps two at a time.

She'd be in the study, he knew. Pacing in front of that bloody slate board, her mind focused on murder. Or maybe she was contemplating returning to her own time…

Hell and damnation. By the time he reached the study, his temper was running hot, a direct contrast to the ice that had settled in his gut. Primed for an argument—just how long, how *bloody* long had she been thinking about leaving him?—he shoved open the door, and was immediately thrown off-stride when he was confronted with a dark, empty room.

He spun around just as the Duke came to the door. "Where is she?"

The Duke walked to the bellpull. "You must calm down before you speak with her."

"I think I am justified in my anger. She never confided her theory to me. *Not once.* I am her betrothed. Or, at least, I thought I was."

"You are taking this too personally, Alec. Look at the situation from her perspective." Guided by the light spilling in from the hall, the Duke strolled to the side table. "She is not of this time, Alec," he said, using a tinderbox to light two stout candles. He glanced at his nephew over the dancing flames. "It is natural for her to wonder if there is a possibility of returning to her own timeline. I am not suggesting that she will act on it—I don't believe she will—but I can understand her mulling over the possibility, especially as the anniversary to the phenomenon approaches."

Alec rubbed a hand over his face. Was he being unreasonable? He recognized that the nasty twist in his gut wasn't only anger—it was hurt.

He drew in a breath, let it out. "I can't lose her. I love her."

"And she loves you. You both ought to have more faith in each other, on the life that you will build together."

"I thought I was doing that," Alec replied.

Harding came through the door. "Your Grace, my lord." His gaze traveled around the dark study. "I shall send a footman to light the fires and wall sconces immediately."

"Where is Miss Donovan?" asked the Duke, pulling out a stopper on a decanter and splashing three fingers of brandy each into two glasses.

Harding considered the question in his usually grave manner. "I am not certain, sir. She did not join Lady Atwood for nuncheon, but… well, that is not unusual. Shall I make inquiries, sir? I believe her maid is in the kitchens."

"Yes, do that."

The butler began to retreat, then paused. "If I might be so bold to inquire, but was your venture at the mill successful?"

The Duke smiled. "Yes, it was. The village has a working mill again."

"Very good, sir." Harding nodded, and withdrew.

The Duke walked over to Alec, offering him the glass. "You look like you could use some fortification."

Alec smiled ruefully. "I suspect that I will need to keep my cellars well-stocked after my marriage." He took the glass. "I should never have allowed myself to be talked into keeping quiet about our betrothal until the house party."

"It matters naught. Do you think a public engagement would keep Kendra tethered to your side if she doesn't wish it?"

"No." He sighed, and sipped his brandy.

A footman arrived with kindling, and was lighting the fire when Harding returned, with Kendra's maid in tow. There was something on the girl's face that made Alec stand straight, a lick of fear curling in his gut.

Harding said, "Miss Donovan is not in her bedchamber."

"Then where is she?"

Molly swallowed visibly. "Oi… ah, thought she was in 'ere, but when Mr. 'Arding came ter me… well, now Oi think she's outside. 'Er coat and boots are gone. And—"

"It's dark," the Duke interrupted. "She cannot be outside."

"Aye, but there's somethin' else, Yer Grace."

Alec couldn't explain why he suddenly felt cold. "What?"

"She took 'er reticule."

The coldness became ice.

The Duke said, "She didn't walk to the village. We would have seen her there. And that's the only reason she would need her reticule."

"It's not about the reticule," Alec said. "It's about what's inside it."

The muff pistol.

Kendra screamed for what felt like hours, trotting back and forth between the door and the windows, hoping that she'd manage to attract someone's attention. But the only attention she'd attracted thus far was from the birds, who flew off at the commotion. Maybe the noise would keep the rats and mice away, at the very least.

Eventually, her screams dwindled, her vocal cords too raw to continue. She was either too far away from anyone else in Shay House or the inmates and staff were too used to hearing screams. Panic rose up again, choking her.

She leaned against a wall, trying to regulate her breathing. She needed to stay in control, to stay… sane? A laugh escaped her. Then another. She doubled over as she gave into the hilarity assailing her, aware that it was edged with something darker. She gulped and shuddered as tears wet her face.

Get a grip, Donovan.

The laughter vanished and she became instantly alert when the door opened with a hideous groan of rusted hinges. McBride, holding a lantern, stepped inside. She narrowed her eyes against the sudden glare, seeking the shadowy figure behind the light. For a long moment, he said nothing, simply stared at her. Then he pivoted. The bubble of light shifted as he shut the door, and shifted again when he turned back to face her. There was genuine regret in his voice when he spoke.

"I am sorry, Miss Donovan."

Kendra had to bite back a stinging retort. "You don't have to do this," she said instead, her voice little more than a rough whisper.

He contemplated her. "You've been screaming. It will do you no good. No one comes to this part of Shay House. For all its disrepair, the walls are quite thick."

"I figured that out," she rasped, taking a moment to swallow. "Think about what you're doing, Mr. McBride. How many deaths do you want on your conscience?"

"It's too late," he said sadly. "My soul is damned, but I must protect my family."

"Do you think your wife would approve of what you're doing?" She watched him flinch. "To know that you've killed because of her. From what you've told me about her, she was a good woman—"

"*Is.* She *is* a good woman!" he flared up suddenly. "She is still there. I need to care for her and she will come back to me. She need never know about… about what I've done. We will leave here. We can still be happy."

"She will hate you if she ever finds out."

"She will never find out. You won't tell her."

"What do you plan to do? Leave me here until I starve to death?" She had to suppress a shudder, because she could imagine that too easily. "You think that no one will be looking for me? The Duke and Alec know that I was coming to Shay House," she lied. "They'll soon be here."

McBride frowned, considering the possibility. Then he shook his head. "I don't believe you, Miss Donovan. You've been here all afternoon and evening, and no one has come to inquire about you. You came on foot." He tilted his head to the side as he regarded her. "You could not have walked all the way from Aldridge Village. Did you take a public coach? But why would you, with your resources, do such a thing? You didn't even bring your maid."

"Meg knows I'm here," Kendra whispered, chilled.

"Meg knows that you *were* here," he corrected. "She has been busy with her duties. I told her that you were satisfied with your inquiries and left. Meg is a simple girl. She has no reason to doubt me. Besides, she and the rest of the staff have left for the evening."

"Dr. Shay." Her breath hitched; she had to lick her dry lips. "Dr. Shay knows I'm here."

"You really ought to curb that tongue of yours, Miss Donovan." McBride's tone was gently chiding. "You upset him, you know. He's been in his office for most of the day, drinking. When

I last saw him, he was quite foxed. I suspect that he's fallen into a stupor by now. He won't wake until morning. And by then, it will be too late for you."

Kendra realized she was breathing too fast. But God, oh, God, he was right. She'd been in this room the entire day. No one would think twice if he told them that she'd left hours ago.

McBride gave her a somber look. "I can promise you that your death will be painless."

"You expect me to be grateful?"

"No, but I hope it will give you comfort."

Kendra stared at him incredulously. "The wrong person is in the straitjacket."

McBride blinked, surprised. "You are an odd creature, Miss Donovan. Mr. Lewis is expecting me to supervise the ladies' bedtime, but I shall return later," he said quietly, and retreated to the door.

"What then?" she demanded hoarsely. "What are you going to do then?"

He paused with his hand on the doorknob, glancing back at her. "I will bring you something to drink. You will go to sleep."

"Poison?"

"You will feel nothing," he insisted.

"And if I don't drink it?"

He contemplated her for a long moment. "I think you will."

Kendra drew in a steadying breath. "Okay. What then? You're going to leave my body here?" She refused to think about it. Refused to think about the rats in the walls. "Alec will come. He will come and won't leave until he searches every square inch of Shay House." Of that she was absolutely certain.

"He'll find my body," she forced herself to continue. "And Shay House will be finished. Killing me won't protect this place. You will have no choice but to commit your wife to another insane asylum, one where she will be in the care of other attendants. Attendants like Mr. Crump."

That got a reaction. "No! I'll kill her myself before I give her to such miscreants."

"You will never get away with this, Mr. McBride. You know it. Killing me won't save you. It will destroy you."

He shook his head. "I don't intend to leave you here, Miss Donovan. There is plenty of space in the forest. You will disappear. No one will find you."

"There are too many variables. Think about it! Someone will see you carrying a dead body out to the forest. The staff may have left, but there's still Booker and Crump. And Dr. Shay. You can't be certain he will be drunk enough to remain in a stupor. And there's the women."

"I don't plan to do it this moment. I shall wait until everyone is asleep."

"Like Willoughby. Look at how well that worked out."

"I hadn't completely thought it through with Mr. Willoughby. This time I have." He paused, his violet eyes filling with compassion. "I have no choice."

He turned around and left, taking the light with him.

41

"W*here the bloody hell is she?"* Alec demanded, pacing the length of the study. He couldn't sit down, couldn't stand still. They'd spent the last hour and a half quizzing all the servants inside and outside the castle. One of the undergardeners reported seeing Kendra walk toward the woods on the north end of the property. He hadn't considered it unusual; the American often walked alone.

He hadn't seen her return, though.

"There is no reason to think Kendra has come to harm," the Duke cautioned. Despite his words, worry dug a line between his eyebrows. He leaned on his desk, fiddling with his pipe as a way to occupy his hands.

"Something is wrong," Alec snapped, and thrust a finger toward the windows as he moved. "She wouldn't be walking through the blasted forest in the dark. She's been gone hours. *Hours.* Where did she go?" His gaze traveled to the hidden passageway, and he stopped cold.

"No, Alec," the Duke said, interpreting his look. "Kendra's hypothesis connects the full moon to the vortex. She wouldn't leave without telling us. Without saying goodbye. Think, Alec. Her coat and reticule are gone."

Alec scrubbed his palms over his face. "You're right." He took a deep breath, looking at the slate board. "This has to do with Craymore's and Willoughby's deaths. But where would she go? Kendra could hardly walk all the way to Shay House. She doesn't ride, nor did she order a carriage."

The Duke moved to stand in front of the slate board, also studying it. He frowned as he noticed the circled *no thief*. "Look. This has changed, has it not?"

Alec joined him to stare at the slate board. "She had a strange dream last night. Shandor was in it," he said slowly. "She *could* walk to the Romani campsite."

"They're camped in the north woods." The Duke strode toward the door. "I know where the campsite is. Come on. I'll take you there."

The night was cloudless. The moon was in its waxing gibbous phase, its light strong enough to illuminate the countryside. Stars pulsed across the heavens—a perfect evening to observe the celestial bodies through his telescope. As it was, the Duke was grateful that they had the light to push their horses into a gallop, only slowing after they entered the woods and were forced to proceed with more care.

The Duke knew before they came into the clearing that the Romani were gone. The forest only carried nocturnal noises, no human voices or laughter, no scent of roasting meat. He glanced at Alec. He'd never seen his nephew look so grim.

Alec swung off his horse, crossing to the fire pit. Squatting, Alec tugged off one glove and dug his fingers into the dry ash.

"Cold," he said, thrusting himself to his feet. "They've been gone a while. Where did they go?"

"You think Kendra is with them?"

"Where else would she be?" Tight-lipped, he mounted his horse, and yanked the reins, wheeling the stallion around. "We need to find the Romani."

"First, we will go back to the castle. We need to gather more men, Alec." The Duke brought his mare forward, so he was next to his nephew, and met Alec's eyes. "Alec, we will find her. Remember who Kendra Donovan is. What she is capable of. She has her reticule with her weapon inside. She is not a helpless female."

Kendra had never felt so helpless. Despite all her efforts, her arms and hands remained tightly secured in the straitjacket. Her throat burned from having screamed her head off, a pointless exercise. She'd broken down twice, sucked into a mental abyss where there was no light, no hope.

She prayed that she would live to be ashamed of her hysterics. *Breathe in; breathe out.*

What time was it? She couldn't see the moon through the grimy windows, but its silvery light filled the tower room. The only sound she heard was the blustery wind, the birds cooing after their return to their nests, and the damned scratching inside the walls. She wasn't surprised when a plump brown rat emerged from one of the cracks. An involuntary scream tore out of her throat then, and she kicked some of the loose stone chips on the floor at the rodent, sending it darting back into its lair, its long skinny tail whipping behind it.

Soon McBride would return. And when he did, what would she do? What *could* she do? She couldn't imagine herself passively drinking whatever concoction he planned to give her. She wouldn't make it easy for him to haul her body out of the asylum, to bury her in a shallow grave in the forest.

She still had use of her legs. Maybe she could aim at least one well-placed kick. And then… and then…

She was under no illusions. Without her hands and arms, McBride would be able to subdue her. Hell, she didn't even have the option to run away from him.

Maybe she needed to accept that. To make peace with her death, like a condemned prisoner. But that submissive response was alien to her personality. There had to be some way.

There had to be—

The scratching again. She thought of the giant rat she'd chased away. Maybe the rodent had pushed aside its natural timidity to venture out of its nest again.

But the noise was from the door, not the wall. The doorknob was turning. *I've run out of time…* She braced herself to face McBride and her inevitable death.

She let out a disbelieving gasp as she stared at the person who slipped inside, wondering if she'd plunged off the emotional precipice into insanity after all.

"Sh-sh," Lillian Slater whispered as she shut the door and moved forward. "Not that anyone can hear. Ewan is currently in Dr. Shay's office, but we must be quick."

Ewan? She must have said the name out loud, because Lillian gave her a long look. "Mr. McBride."

Kendra stared at her.

Lillian's lips curved. "You appear quite shocked, Miss Donovan. I'm used to shocking people, of course… never like this, though. I dare say you weren't expecting me."

"No." Kendra had to clear her throat. "No, I can't say I was. But I've never been so happy to see anyone in my life." Yet in the next instant, she wondered if she should be happy. Maybe McBride hadn't worked alone. Maybe Lillian was McBride's—*Ewan's*—accomplice. Was she here to administer the poison? Or convince her to take it when McBride returned?

Lillian let out a soft chuckle, stepping around her. Kendra could feel the leather straps and buckles tug as the other woman worked to undo them. "You rescued me once, Miss Donovan. I am returning the favor."

"How… how did you know that I was here?" Kendra asked a bit breathlessly, her voice still rusty from screaming. "What time is it?"

"I knew you hadn't left, even though Ewan has been telling everyone that tale. Quite pointedly. I had to wonder why. It's approaching ten." She went quiet for a moment. "He killed Lord Craymore, didn't he?"

"Yes."

Another pause. "He has the diamond?"

"No. The diamond seems to have disappeared."

Kendra felt the straitjacket suddenly loosen, the buckles undone. The relief that rushed through her made her dizzy. She peeled off the garment as though it were on fire, and threw it with more force than necessary to the floor. McBride had removed her coat, hat, and gloves— they were probably with her reticule—but she welcomed the cold. She slapped her hands, shook her arms for the simple joy the freedom of movement gave her.

She realized Lillian was watching her. "He killed Craymore because the earl threatened to destroy Shay House."

"It's because of his wife," Lillian said quietly. "She can no longer be a wife, but he will not let her go."

There was something in Lillian's tone—a note of sympathy— that made Kendra regard her more closely. "We're talking murder, Lillian. McBride is a murderer. He planned to kill me tonight."

Lillian said nothing. She turned and went to the door, pulling it open an inch to peer out into the hall. "You must go, Miss Donovan. The village is four miles southeast."

"I know where the village is. I need my reticule. It's probably in McBride's office."

Lillian's eyebrows rose. "You don't need your reticule. The villagers know you are the Duke's ward. They'll give you whatever you need on credit."

"It's not… I have a pistol inside my reticule. I don't intend to escape, Lillian. I intend to bring a murderer to justice. That will be easier with my gun."

Lillian's mouth parted in astonishment. "You brought a weapon?" Then she shook her head. "Never mind—it matters naught. I don't know where your pistol or reticule are, Miss Donovan, but we are running out of time. I am trying to help you escape. Are you seriously turning me down?"

Kendra hesitated. She was confident that she'd be able to subdue McBride, with or without the gun. But she remembered what Madam Patya had said, that humans were like animals—and when trapped, they could be vicious. McBride had even threatened to kill his own wife if he thought she'd end up in an institution outside of his control.

She became aware that Lillian was waiting, watching her. She nodded. "Okay. Let's get the hell out of here."

42

Fear turned Alec's belly to ice by the time he and the Duke returned to Aldridge Castle. "She *has* to be with the Romani," he snapped as he and the Duke strode down the footpath. "But you know very well that she didn't join them to appreciate their culture. She has a purpose. She went to talk to Shandor about Craymore's dying words, but something must have happened, something that made her go with the Romani."

The Duke nodded. "An impulse. Yes, I agree."

"Your Grace, my lord…" Harding materialized out of the shadows as soon as they walked into the castle. "Mr. Kelly and Mr. Muldoon arrived ten minutes ago. I thought you would want me to put them in your study, sir."

The Duke gave Alec a look. "They must have news."

They found Sam standing in front of the study's hearth, his gaze on the dancing flames as he sipped his whisky. Muldoon also had a glass in his hand, and was studying the slate board. Both men turned when Alec and the Duke walked in.

"Your Grace, milord." Sam's gold eyes were dark with concern. "Forgive us for intruding so late. Your majordomo told us that Miss Donovan is not here."

"No, she's not. We believe she's traveling with the Romani."

Muldoon's eyebrows shot up in surprise. "But why?"

The Duke shook his head. "We're not certain, but she must have a purpose. Do you have news?"

"Aye. We came to deliver a message ter Miss Donovan from Lady Rebecca," Sam said, continuing to frown. "She met with the lass who was involved in the scandal at Shay House."

Alec let out a frustrated breath. "What the hell can that scandal have to do with what is happening *now*?"

The Duke laid a hand on Alec's shoulder, then glanced at Sam. "What did you find out?"

Muldoon was the one who answered. "Lady Rebecca said that Mrs. Devaney wasn't molested by the assistant who was let go. She had engaged in a consensual relationship with Mr. McBride."

"*Mr. McBride?*" The Duke was shocked.

Muldoon nodded. "Lady Rebecca saw the child. She bears an uncanny resemblance to her father, especially her eyes. Lady Rebecca thought Miss Donovan ought to know."

Alec dragged a hand over his face. "I ask again, what does it matter? Why does any of this matter? Lord Craymore was killed for the Anahita Pink, not because of some bloody disgrace that is ancient history."

"What was the lass working on before she sought out the gypsies?" Sam asked.

The Duke shook his head. "Alec and I were at the mill most of the day, but she highlighted the last words that Lord Craymore spoke to Shandor." He indicated the slate board. "I think she went to talk to the boy again. I do not know why she left with them, but something must have occurred to her."

"We're wasting time." Alec started for the door.

"Where are you going, Alec?" the Duke demanded.

Alec paused, his hand on the door. "I'm riding to Shay House. We know that the Romani always go north to Wales after they leave your lands. That route takes them near the asylum. If Kendra went anywhere, she went with them there. I will not sit here and do *nothing*."

"Why wouldn't she have sent word when she reached Needlham?"

Dread speared through Alec when he met his uncle's eyes. "Because something went wrong—terribly wrong."

Kendra followed Lillian down the corridor. Stretches of the space had no windows and so were pitch black, making those sections feel abnormally long. The only sound was their ragged breathing, the whisper of their skirts, and the soles of their shoes sliding across the floor. The servant stairs were the worst, with no light penetrating the stairwell, making each step treacherous.

"I didn't have time to bring a candle," Lillian whispered in the darkness.

Kendra didn't reply, but let out a relieved breath when Lillian pushed open the door to another hallway that was marginally less dark.

"This way," Lillian whispered, and led the way past the kitchens and stillroom.

The eerie quiet scraped against Kendra's nerves and made her heart pound. Sweat dampened her forehead and palms, trickled down her spine. *Damn it.* It was too quiet. Where was McBride?

Lillian opened the servants' door, and stepped outside. Kendra went through, shivering as the cold night air hit her. She lifted her skirts and started forward at a jog, but stopped when she realized she was alone. She wheeled around to look at Lillian, who remained by the door, her beautiful face glazed by moonlight.

"What the hell are you doing?" Kendra whispered furiously. "Come on!"

"I'm not going with you."

Kendra stared at her, dumbfounded. "What? You don't belong here!"

The catlike eyes gleamed with sudden amusement. "Are you trying to rescue me again, Miss Donovan?"

Even though every impulse urged her to run—run, run, *RUN!*—Kendra forced herself to stand still. "I'm trying to help you."

"I have a husband, Miss Donovan. Even if I escape Shay House, he'll only put me in another institution."

"We can fight it. The Duke is a powerful man."

Lillian regarded her with a strange expression. "It must be because you are an American," she murmured softly, and shook her head. "Your duke may be powerful, but he is not above the law—or the Church. Mr. Slater has the right to do whatever he wishes to me. As his wife, I am essentially his property. You would do well to remember that, Miss Donovan. If you have any resources, better to remain a spinster."

"It depends on the husband," Kendra said.

"Possibly. But some of us aren't so fortunate in being able to choose."

"Come with me and we'll figure it out."

Lillian contemplated her as she toyed with the cross pendant she wore, the ruby garnet glinting colorless in the moonlight. She looked, Kendra thought, like she had all the time in the world. Then she shook her head. "You are the oddest creature, Miss Donovan. The score is settled between us. Now, go!"

"Fine," Kendra hissed. "I'll be back tomorrow."

But Lillian Slater was already gone.

Kendra picked up her skirts and bolted down the path that would lead to the back gardens. Needlham was four miles away. If she cut through the woods and over the fields, she might be able to shave off some time. Her half boots weren't exactly made for running—she could feel the unforgiving hard soles and heels slamming against the ground—but they were better than the delicate slippers she often wore.

She sprinted along the footpath with its heavy scent of flowers. She couldn't resist tossing a quick look behind her. The former monastery had a few windows glowing with light. *Where was McBride?* she wondered again.

Don't think about him, she ordered silently, and jerked her gaze forward. Adrenalin sang through her bloodstream, thundered in her ears. She veered off the path and down the sloping hill, nearly wiping out when her hard leather soles hit the slick grass. She recovered and made it past the lake, with its oily black waters lapping against the shore. Toward the trees.

Toward freedom.

Fifty yards.

Twenty-five.

Fifteen.

Ten yards.

She plunged into the woods, wheezing, as icy sweat dripped down her face and spine. The trees and uneven terrain forced her to slow down. Grass and shrubs clawed at her skirts. Stones and vines rose up to trip her. The smell of vegetation and putrefaction was overwhelming. *That could've been me, slowly decomposing in an unmarked grave.*

She darted around oak and maple trees. Ahead, the woods began to thin. She could see the fields, now limned by the rays of the moon.

A bubble of giddy laughter suddenly rose up in her chest. *Holy shit.* An hour ago, she had been helpless, hopeless. Now she was alive.

She had to pause, to regain her breath. Once the cold air had filled her lungs, she started to jog again, her spirits lifting.

Freedom.

Then she heard the dogs.

43

ngry barks tore through the night air. Distant, but—*oh, God*—coming closer. Visions of Booker's two rottweilers flashed through Kendra's mind, all teeth and terror.

She broke into a flat-out run. She'd gained about fifty yards when her toe caught on something and she was sent flying. She hit the ground with enough force to knock the breath from her lungs and scrape a layer of skin off her palms and chin. Blood oozed, dripping off her face, wetting her palms. The ominous baying from Freddie and Adolphus was louder now.

Gritting her teeth and ignoring the sting of her injuries, Kendra got up and took off again. She could see the moonlit fields through the trees. There was, she remembered, a farmer's cottage just over the hill. If she could reach it...

"Halt!"

The dogs howled.

Too close.

Lungs burning, heart galloping in her chest, Kendra dodged the last line of trees, charging towards the open field. But her strength was already ebbing. The farmer's cottage could be a million miles away.

The next instant, she felt the heat of muscular bodies rush past her.

She half-expected to feel their teeth sink into some part of her anatomy. Instead, the hounds ran ahead, then wheeled around, blocking her flight. Their eyes fixed on her, glinting malevolently in the moonlight. The rottweilers' had identical poses, bodies quivering with excitement, lips pulled back in ferocious snarls.

Kendra skidded to a stop. She struggled to draw in a ragged breath, but fear made it difficult to fill her lungs. She'd seen a mauling victim once. She knew what those teeth, those jaws, could do to human flesh.

"Adolphus, Freddie—sit!"

The dogs instantly obeyed, but kept their eyes locked on Kendra. Ready to pounce at the least provocation.

She started to shake. It took every ounce of her willpower to drag her eyes away from the rottweilers, to glance at the two men jogging towards her: McBride and Booker. They were both out of breath by the time they got to her.

"Oy! W'ot's this?" Booker croaked, clearly surprised, as he drew in a deep breath. "She ain't an inmate!"

Hope flickered to life again. "No, I'm not," Kendra said hurriedly. "McBride killed Craymore and Willoughby, and he is going—"

"Shut up!" McBride snapped, and drew a pistol from the pocket of his coat.

Booker gaped at the other man. "Are ye mad?"

Gone was the soft compassion and sad aura from McBride's person. His face was hard, his eyes shining in the moonlight as he aimed the weapon at her. He did look mad—and capable of anything.

"She knows too much," McBride bit out. "She'll destroy us, destroy Shay House, if she's allowed to go to the authorities. We can't let that happen, Mr. Booker."

"Oi ain't no murderer!"

"Do you want to be sent to the workhouse?" McBride countered furiously. "Do you really think you'll be able to find employment with so many people already begging for scraps from our betters! Look at what's happening around us! The sun is changing. The earth is getting colder. Crops are dying. If Shay House closes, how do you think you'll fare out there? What do you think will happen to your dogs? They'll be put down when you're sent to the workhouse!"

Booker looked uneasy. "Better the workhouse than the gallows. She's the ward of a duke! *A duke, for Chrissake!*"

"We'll plant her in the ground. No one will ever know."

"Ye're stark raving mad, ye are." Booker took a step back, eyes widening when McBride swung the gun around to point at his chest.

Kendra seized the opportunity, lunging at McBride. She caught his arm and twisted before he could pull the trigger. He cursed loudly as the pistol thudded to the ground. Before she could dive for the weapon, McBride let out a howl and punched her in the head, with enough force to make her release him. Ears ringing, she fell back. But only for an instant. She yanked up her skirts to issue a counterattack, kicking toward his groin. If it had connected, McBride would have been puking up a kidney. But McBride turned at the last minute, and the kick glanced off his hip. *Shit.*

She danced back a few steps, her gaze locked on McBride. He shuffled to the side and she followed, as they circled one another. They were both breathing heavily. Kendra swiped the blood dripping off her chin. She saw his eyes flicker just before he threw a wild punch. She dodged to the side, avoiding his fist, and felt a zing of triumph.

Until she realized he hadn't been coming at her.

She watched him drop to the ground, his hand closing over the pistol. She tried to recalibrate, scrambling forward, but it was already too late. He pointed the gun at her and pulled the trigger.

44

Alec crushed his fear as he leaned forward in his saddle, flicking his reins left and right to propel Chance forward. It was a dangerous, full-speed gallop across the countryside. He was vaguely aware that the Duke, Muldoon, and Sam were somewhere behind him. Their steeds were no match for his Arabian. He only eased up the punishing pace when he swung into the long drive to Shay House. The moon, an almost fully formed orb, hung above the former monastery, which was dark except for light in two windows.

Alec yanked on his reins so abruptly that Chance reared up, front hooves slashing the air. Mentally apologizing to Chance for the harsh treatment, Alec leapt to the ground and sprinted up the steps to the door. He turned the knob, ready to burst through, but was stymied when the door refused to budge. *Damnation.*

"Open up!" he shouted, pounding on the door. "Open this door!" Nothing.

The panic he'd been keeping under control began to slip loose. He banged the door with his fist again, then kicked it twice, feeling the wooden panel vibrate beneath his boot. Where the bloody hell was everybody? Where was Dr. Shay? The place was eerily silent.

"Alec!" the Duke called out as he rode up.

Alec kicked the door again in frustration, before spinning to jump down the steps. He spared his uncle only a quick glance. "I'm going around to the back. If I have to break a window to get in, I will."

He took two steps when he heard the crack of gunfire.

As Kendra fell, she heard Booker shout something, and she pushed herself upright just in time to see the two rottweilers spring at McBride. He cartwheeled back, squeezed the trigger again, but the shot went wide as the jaw of one of the rottweilers clamped on his forearm, sending the now spent weapon tumbling to the ground. McBride's scream rent the night air. Then he disappeared beneath nearly three hundred pounds of muscle and fur and snarling fury.

Horror washed through Kendra. She thrust herself to her feet, swaying as she witnessed the carnage. Booker seemed dazed as well.

"Stop them!" She finally managed to find her voice, although it was hoarse. "For Christ's sake, stop them!"

A movement in the woods drew her attention. For a moment, she had a vision of a mystical, mythical beast flying out of the trees. Then reality clicked in, and she realized that what she was seeing was Alec on Chance. The black stallion stretched in a graceful arc as it leapt over some tangled vegetation, and then Alec was swinging off the saddle before Chance had even come to a full stop. He raced toward her, the barrel of the flintlock he held gleaming in the silvery light of the moon.

His stride faltered for a beat when he caught sight of McBride, sprawled and bloody on the ground. Booker had finally called off the dogs.

Kendra started forward—McBride's fingers and arms were moving in odd jerking motions—but Alec blocked her path. "He's gone," he said quietly. "He's in the death throes. There's nothing you can do." Even as he said it, McBride released a harsh, gurgling breath, then went still.

The Duke, followed by Sam and Muldoon, galloped out of the forest toward them. "God's teeth," uttered Sam, his gaze on the corpse. "Is that… ?"

"McBride," Alec replied, but his gaze was fixed on Kendra. He lifted a hand to her face. "You're bleeding."

"I fell. It's nothing." She became aware of an ache in her upper arm. She glanced down, studying the tear in her sleeve. "Shit," she murmured, lifting her gaze to Alec's. "And I might have been shot."

45

The group finally made it inside Shay House through the servants' entrance, and Kendra and Alec settled in the library. The Duke had gone in search of Dr. Shay and Sam was still with McBride, while Booker traveled to Needlham for the constable. And probably the butcher. Kendra wasn't sure where Muldoon had disappeared to.

"Might have been shot. *Might have been shot.* And you said it like you might have torn the hem of your dress." Alec glared at Kendra.

Looking into Alec's furious green eyes, Kendra wished she'd disappeared with the reporter.

"It's just a graze," she assured, and started to rise from the tufted chair, only to have Alec push her firmly back down.

He kept his hands on her shoulders, leaning down to look her directly in her eyes. "Sit. And stay sitting."

Before she could object to the order, Muldoon came into the room carrying a linen sheet and a bottle of whisky, the amber liquid glinting from the candles that had been lit around the room. "Found these in the cupboards," he said, setting the bottle down on a nearby table. He grinned at her as he began to rip the sheet into strips. "We'll have you fixed in a trice, Miss Donovan. It's been years since I played nursemaid, but as the eldest of four brothers, I often took care of their scrapes and bruises. This ought to help until we can fetch a doctor."

"I don't need a doctor."

"That hole in your arm says otherwise," Alec said coolly. He poured whisky on one of the linen strips.

"It's not a hole. It's a scrape. The bullet barely touched me—"

She hissed out a breath, glaring at Alec when he slapped the whisky-soaked cotton on her arm. "I hope Muldoon has better doctoring skills than you do."

Alec smiled nastily. "I could cauterize the wound with the fire poker instead."

"No, thanks."

Muldoon chuckled as he took Alec's place, and with quick efficiency he cleaned and bound Kendra's upper arm. He studied her face, then dabbed the raw skin on her chin with another whisky soaked strip. Kendra cursed.

The Irishman grinned. "I don't know how to bandage your face, but it's stopped bleeding and will soon scab over."

Kendra stood up, earning a scowl from Alec. "I told you to sit," he said firmly.

"It's not like I need my arm to walk." Her gaze went to the French doors. "I need to get back to the crime scene."

"No, you don't," Alec said. "Mr. Kelly is quite capable of handling it. Mr. Booker has no doubt fetched the constable and whoever is needed to take care of Mr. McBride's remains."

"Don't know what else you could do out there anyway," Muldoon put in cheerfully. "It's not like—" He broke off when the Duke brought a befuddled-looking Dr. Shay into the room.

"He was sleeping in his office," the Duke explained. "I had a devil of a time waking him."

Dr. Shay gave them a bleary look. His hair was standing up in tufts, his cravat askew. "I don't understand any of this," he complained, rubbing his forehead. "It makes no sense."

Kendra said, "He's been drugged. Someone should make coffee."

"I'll do it," Muldoon offered. "On the condition that no one speaks until I return. This is a tale I want to hear from start to finish."

By the time Muldoon returned, carrying a tray with a coffee-pot and several earthenware mugs, Sam Kelly had finished with the gruesome business outside. "Constable Gulliver and the village lads have taken McBride ter Needlham," he told them. "It wouldn't be wise ter leave the body *in situ* for the inquest. Booker's beasts caused enough damage; we don't need ter give a feast ter the wild animals.

"Mr. Booker said that his dogs saved Miss Donovan's life," the Bow Street Runner added, looking at Kendra.

For a brief moment, Kendra remembered looking into the deadly muzzle of the flintlock before the two canines took down McBride. "Mr. Booker is right—Adolphus and Freddie saved my life," she said.

Sam eyed her bandaged arm. "McBride still managed ter wing you, though."

"A flesh wound." The scrape on her chin actually hurt worse than her arm. And her vocal cords, which were raw from having screamed her lungs out. "The second shot went wide."

"I cannot believe this," Dr. Shay mumbled from his chair.

Muldoon handed him a coffee mug. Instead of drinking, Dr. Shay stared morosely into the cup.

Sam said, "Mr. Booker claims that he had no idea that they were after Miss Donovan. Thought it was one of the lunatics who escaped. He was right shocked when he saw that it was you, lass."

Kendra thought of the groundskeeper's horrified expression when he recognized her. "I believe him."

The Duke shook his head. "How could Mr. McBride think that Mr. Booker would become his accomplice in murdering my ward?"

"Queer in the attic, he was," said Sam.

"No. Desperate. Thank you." Kendra reached for the mug that Muldoon offered, and took a grateful sip. The hot liquid felt like a balm against her abused throat. She sighed, lowering the cup. "After Craymore threatened to take away his sister, McBride went after him, to plead with him to reconsider. At least that's what he said."

Muldoon looked at her. "You don't believe him?"

"I think he told himself that. But he brought a gun for the 'discussion.'"

Muldoon shook his head. "The irony is that Mr. McBride is the one responsible for putting the madhouse in such a precarious financial position."

That roused Dr. Shay. "What are you talking about?"

"Mr. McBride was not true to his wife," Muldoon replied. "He's the father of Mrs. Devaney's child."

Kendra eyed the reporter in surprise. "What? How do you know?"

"Lady Rebecca spoke to the woman and realized the truth. Her daughter bears an uncanny resemblance to her father."

Some things are not always what they seem. Lillian's words drifted back to Kendra. She'd known the truth.

"Mrs. Devaney said they were both lonely," Muldoon added. "She did not blame him."

Kendra sipped her coffee as she considered that. Mrs. Devaney wasn't the only one. She remembered Lillian's expression of longing as she looked at McBride when he was with his wife. The way she'd taunted him about a wife who couldn't be a wife.

McBride was attractive and relatively young. Lillian Slater was locked in an abusive marriage, and in Shay House. Beneath her brittle exterior, Kendra imagined that she was as lonely as Mrs. Devaney had been. McBride had taken advantage of both women.

"But that's impossible," Dr. Shay whispered now. "Why didn't she say? I dismissed Mr. Dodd. She never said a word!"

"Was she given the opportunity?" Muldoon wondered, his gaze narrowing on the doctor. "Or did her father take her away before the truth—the real truth—could come out?"

Dr. Shay said nothing, but Kendra thought Muldoon was right.

"Didn't Mr. Dodd tell you that he was innocent?" Sam asked.

The doctor glared at him. "Well, yes, but he would say that, wouldn't he?"

"Mr. McBride told you that the other man was responsible," Kendra guessed. "And you believed him."

"There was no reason to think Mr. McBride was lying."

Muldoon's mouth tightened. "You dismissed the poor wretch without a hearing, without a character reference. As far as I'm concerned, you hold a certain responsibility for the man committing suicide."

Dr. Shay's lips parted in shock. "What are you talking about? I never heard from Mr. Dodd after he left Shay House."

"The dead are poor communicators," Muldoon said dryly.

"Well, how could I know that he was dead? And if he wasn't guilty, why would he kill himself? Only someone suffering from a guilty conscience would commit such a sin!"

Being fired without references, under a cloud of suspicion for molesting a patient, could drive someone to commit suicide, Kendra thought. But there was also another possibility: Mr. Dodd *could* have been McBride's first victim. That was no more than a hunch, impossible to prove or disprove. She decided to let it go.

Dr. Shay's mouth puckered. "I am hardly to blame if Mr. McBride lied about Mr. Dodd. The man hid his treachery well. I am as much a victim of Mr. McBride as Lord Craymore!"

Sam flicked him a look of contempt, before shifting his gaze to Kendra. "What made you realize Mr. McBride was the fiend who murdered Lord Craymore, lass?"

"I didn't. Not exactly. But I didn't like it when Madam Patya told us that the Romani had seen a stranger around their campsite. It seemed too coincidental not to have some connection to what happened to Lord Craymore. I can't explain it other than to say it occurred to me that we might have leapt to an assumption over Lord Craymore's last words. Maybe he wasn't calling Shandor a thief. Maybe he was telling him that there'd been no thief—no robbery."

The Bow Street Runner frowned. "Aye, but the earl didn't have the diamond on his person either."

"Yes. But the earl likely wasn't thinking clearly after he was shot. At the time, I thought that he threw the diamond at his attacker to distract him. But maybe, in his confusion, he tossed the diamond, thinking he was keeping it safe. He could have planned to retrieve it later."

The Duke gave her a dubious look. "In the forest? How would he ever find it?"

"Maybe there was a marker of some sort. I don't know. As I said, we can't apply rational thought to the earl in those last moments. All that matters is that killer knew that *he* didn't have the diamond. That left the possibility of Craymore throwing it somewhere between where he met his killer on the road and the Romani encampment."

Muldoon shook his head in amazement. "You're saying that Mr. McBride was actually searching the area for the diamond? The man was mad to think he'd find the gem."

Kendra regarded him. "If I told you that I know for a fact that the Anahita Pink is out there in that general vicinity, what would you do?"

The Irishman stared at her for a moment, then broke into a grin. "Well, when you put it like that, Miss Donovan, me palms are sweating just thinking about it."

"Do you really think the Anahita Pink might be out there?" the Duke asked.

Kendra smiled. "Mr. Kelly was right. Diamonds and gold give people a fever."

"Forget about the diamond," Alec snapped, leveling a look at her. "You went to talk to Shandor. Alone. Without leaving word."

Kendra felt her chin go up a defensive notch. "I wanted to interview Shandor again, to see if he could give me a description of the rider he'd seen in the forest. The Romani were getting ready to leave. When I found out they were traveling in the direction of Needlham, it seemed expedient to go with them."

Sam eyed her. "You knew then it was Mr. McBride?"

"The description fit. But there was no proof. Just speculation. I wanted a confession."

"You put yourself in harm's way for a confession," Alec said softly.

"I didn't think there would be any harm. It was in the middle of a day; I'd be surrounded by people." She glanced at Alec, and had to swallow. "Obviously, I miscalculated."

"Obviously."

She pressed her lips together. She refused to feel guilty for following her instincts. Well, maybe she felt a *little* guilty. "McBride was more desperate than I realized. He drugged my tea." Her breath hitched as she recalled how helpless she'd been when she woke up; she couldn't find the words to explain. Aware that everyone's eyes were on her, she cleared her throat. "He put me in a straitjacket and kept me in the tower. Which sounds like a bad gothic novel." She smiled, although it might have been more of a grimace.

No one returned the smile.

"Good God," the Duke breathed. "He would have murdered you."

"That was the plan."

"How did you escape, Miss Donovan?" Muldoon asked.

Kendra took a long swallow of coffee to give herself a moment to think. It should have been easy to give credit to Lillian Slater, but she wasn't entirely sure that the woman's initiative would be viewed as positive—at least not by Dr. Shay.

"I got lucky," she finally said.

Alec narrowed his eyes, staring at her in such that way that made her feel like he could see right into her brain.

"Well, thank God for your resourcefulness," the Duke said. He set down his coffee mug. "The hour grows late. I shall need to hire a carriage from the village stables to take Miss Donovan home."

"I'll be staying in Needlham," said Sam. "I shall make arrangements for a carriage to be sent to you, Your Grace."

Muldoon grinned, blue eyes brightening. "I shall accompany you, Mr. Kelly. I want to see the ostler's surprise when you wake him to hire a carriage for a duke."

As they waited for the carriage, Dr. Shay's sense of duty finally kicked in and he made the rounds to check on his patients. He returned, frazzled, with news that one patient was not in her room.

Lillian Slater had disappeared.

46

They didn't make it back to Shay House until the following afternoon. Rain pelted the carriage as Benjamin steered the carriage down the long drive. *Even the weather has turned against the madhouse,* Kendra thought, gazing at the rambling structure through the streaked windows.

Her stomach clenched as her eyes traveled to the tower before she quickly averted her gaze. She'd had a couple of bad moments during the night, when she'd woken with her bedcovers twisted around her. Too much like the straitjacket. She'd been grateful that Alec had already left her bedchamber. She didn't need for him to see her sweaty and shaking. She didn't need another lecture.

Alec took her hand in his own, lacing his fingers through hers. The expression in his eyes warmed her. Maybe lectures weren't so bad when you knew they were driven by love.

"That looks like the Craymore crest," the Duke said, looking out at another carriage already parked outside the front steps.

"So it does," Alec murmured, as they came to a stop next to the vehicle. "Jonah Lansing appears to be settling quite comfortably into his new position in society."

"It's only a carriage, Alec. That doesn't mean the man has abandoned all of his previous ideals," the Duke said lightly. "I wonder why he's here? Surely it's too soon for word to have reached him about Mr. McBride's villainy."

"There's only one way to find out." Kendra took it upon herself to open the carriage door, which elicited an offended grunt from Benjamin, who was unfolding the steps with one hand and holding an umbrella with the other.

Alec took the proffered umbrella, and they dashed up the front steps and into Shay House, not bothering to knock. Only a few wall sconces had been lit around the foyer, leaving it cold and gray.

And empty.

The faint notes of a pianoforte drew their attention. Alec shook out the umbrella and placed it against the wall before they walked down the hall to the library. They paused in the doorway, scanning the occupants. All the women appeared to be there, minus Lillian Slater and Lady Evelyn. Kendra's gaze lingered on McBride's wife, who was sitting in her wheelchair, staring vacantly out the window. A sleepy-eyed Crump stood against one wall. Meg, grimmer than Kendra had ever seen her, was making the rounds, filling teacups. Mr. Lewis was talking in low tones to Mrs. Tilly, who was huddled and crying in the corner of the room. When he saw them, he murmured something, then rose to come toward them.

"Your Grace, my lord, Miss Donovan." He gave a brief bow. "I cannot believe…" He shook his head and had to take a deep breath. "I was shocked to learn what had transpired here last evening," he said in a low voice. He flicked a look at Mrs. McBride, his mouth tightening. "There can be no excuse, of course, but…"

"But he loved his wife," Kendra finished for him. It wasn't an excuse, but it was some sort of explanation. Love and money. Two of the most common motivators that drove homicides.

She asked, "Where is Dr. Shay?"

"He is upstairs with Lady Evelyn and her cousin."

"Is Lord Craymore taking Lady Evelyn away?" the Duke inquired.

A shadow passed over Lewis's face. "Now that he has learned about what happened last night? Yes, I imagine so. Dr. Shay will be writing letters to all the families. I suspect Shay House will not survive another fortnight."

Kendra contemplated him. "What will you do?"

"I don't know."

"You have a lot of valuable skills, you know. Your idea to incorporate music as a cognitive therapy is excellent. The Quakers who are running private institutions might be receptive to it."

Why was she involving herself in this? Lewis's future was his own to deal with.

He gave her a surprised look, obviously thinking the same thing. His lips twisted. "Thank you, Miss Donovan. However, I'm not certain those qualities will overcome the scandal here. I shall inform Dr. Shay of your arrival."

They followed him back to the foyer, where Dr. Shay, Jonah Lansing, and Lady Evelyn were already descending the stairs. Mrs. Maddox thumped along behind, carrying two large portmanteaus. Lady Evelyn and her cousin were dressed in coats, hats, and gloves.

"Your Grace! My lord!" Lady Evelyn gave a delighted shout, and pushed past Dr. Shay to dart over to them, dropping into a deep curtsy. "Did you hear? I am leaving! My dear cousin is taking me home!"

"I am pleased for you, my lady," the Duke said, smiling, but there was reservation in his eyes.

Lady Evelyn's normally pale face was flushed. "Jonah is bringing me back to Norfolk, but that is only temporary. I am most anxious to return to London, to the balls and soirees. And to my dressmaker. I shall require a whole new wardrobe."

"You are in mourning, cousin Evelyn," reminded Lansing.

She waved a hand. "You make too much of it, Jonah. Will I see you in London, my lord?" She fluttered her pale eyelashes at Alec. "Will you save me a dance?"

Lansing's expression was uneasy, as though he were getting a glimpse into the future as Lady Evelyn's guardian and did not think himself prepared. Dr. Shay's face was creased from lack of sleep and worry, but his lips began to curve into the faintest of smiles. Kendra didn't think it was her imagination that she saw spite in that smile.

"I would be delighted," Alec replied smoothly. Lady Evelyn giggled.

"Dr. Shay, would you be so good to escort my cousin outside to the carriage?" Lansing asked. "I shall be along shortly."

Dr. Shay glanced at Kendra, the Duke and Alec, but nodded. They stepped aside as the doctor guided Lady Evelyn outside, with Mrs. Maddox trotting along behind.

"This was only supposed to be a quick visit on my way to Norfolk," Lansing told them. "But when I learned what had happened…" He spread his gloved hands, palms up. "I could hardly leave her here, could I?"

No one said anything.

Lansing released a troubled sigh, and started toward the door. He'd only taken a few steps when he paused and turned back around. "There's something I don't understand. If Mr. McBride didn't steal the Anahita Pink, where is it?"

Kendra held her breath as she imagined hordes of treasure hunters descending upon the Duke's land if it became known that the late earl had tossed the diamond somewhere in the forest. The Duke must have thought the same thing, because he said,

"Unfortunately, 'tis a mystery that we may never solve. Alas, the Anahita Pink is lost again."

Lansing shook his head, puzzled. "Good day."

A wet Dr. Shay and Mrs. Maddox came through the door as he reached it. They quickly moved to the side, allowing the new Earl of Craymore to pass.

"I need a strong cup of tea," Mrs. Maddox announced after Lansing left. She shook out her damp apron, looking at them. "Should I have Cook fix a tray?"

"We're meeting Mr. Kelly in Needlham," said Kendra. "We only came to see if you found my coat and reticule." They had looked for her things in McBride's office the night before, but had come away empty-handed. Kendra was mostly concerned about the muff pistol inside her pouch.

Dr. Shay huffed out a breath. "I had Meg search, but she found nothing. If you want my opinion, Mrs. Slater stole them just as she stole the horse from the stables. I have sent a message to Mr. Slater. He is responsible for his wife's actions and must make reparations."

"What will happen to Mrs. Slater if she's found?" Kendra asked.

"It will be entirely up to Mr. Slater. He could turn her over to authorities or put her in another madhouse." Dr. Shay screwed up his lips, no doubt thinking that Shay House wouldn't be around to keep Lillian Slater. "If it were up to me, I'd wash my hands of the woman. She's been nothing but trouble since the day she came here."

47

The inquest for McBride was held on Thursday morning at the Red Pigeon. Like most inquests, a crowd had gathered. Unlike most inquests, they had decided to keep McBride's body in the butcher shop, rather than displayed on one of the tables. The selected jurors trotted down the street to the butcher shop to peer obligingly at the body, before returning to declare that McBride's death had been caused by misadventure of his own making, given that he was the fiend behind Lord Craymore and Mr. Willoughby's murders.

In the twenty-first century, Kendra would have had paperwork, analysis, and evaluations to occupy her time. She had never enjoyed it, but the drudge work had always given her a sense of closure. She assumed the lack of action was contributing to her strange restlessness when she returned to Aldridge Castle and wiped down the slate board.

Or maybe it was Lillian Slater's disappearance. Mr. Slater had hired a Bow Street Runner to find his runaway wife. In Sam's opinion, the Runner in question was barely competent.

Kendra hoped that was true; Lillian Slater deserved her freedom.

Or maybe her tension had nothing to do with the investigation and everything to do with the full moon that would rise later that evening.

Should she ignore the possibility that the vortex could open again? The possibility that she could return to her own timeline?

A person's life was marked with crossroads—those unique moments when you made a decision to go left or go right. Going after Sir Jeremy Greene a year ago had been her choice. Being transported to the early nineteenth century through some sort of wormhole as a result had *not* been her choice. Would she now be given the choice to go home? Didn't she owe it to herself to find out? Didn't she owe it to herself to be happy?

Maybe that was the heart of the matter. Where exactly *would* she be happy?

She would never truly belong in this era with its tightly regulated class system and subjugation of women. Where butchers performed autopsies and husbands could put their wives in madhouses without cause. Where everything was so bloody *slow*. How could she take it, a lifetime at this pace, with these *rules*?

A painful knot formed in her stomach that seemed to grow larger throughout the day. She was aware of the scrutiny of the Duke and Alec, but managed to brush aside their questions or attempts at conversation.

Lady Atwood proved to be more formidable. When they gathered for dinner, the countess snapped, "What in heaven's name is wrong with you, Miss Donovan? You've been blue-deviled all day! As abhorrent as I find these criminal investigations of yours, you have found your justice for Lord Craymore, yet you look absolutely dreadful."

"Caro!" the Duke reprimanded.

His sister waved a dismissive hand. "The creature must know that she looks simply *awful*. She has a looking glass! Even a blind person couldn't miss those scabs across her chin. Thankfully, they ought to be gone by the house party." She gave Kendra a pointed look. "Really, Miss Donovan, the next time you brawl, please have some consideration for your face."

"I'll keep that in mind," Kendra murmured dryly, lifting her glass of wine for a mock toast before sipping. She wondered if it meant anything that the countess seemed to think there would be a next time.

Lady Atwood's eyes narrowed. "I'm quite aware that you care naught for your appearance. So what *is* the matter with you? Why are you upset?"

"I'm not upset," Kendra said. "I'm thinking."

"Well, stop it."

"Stop thinking?"

"Yes," snapped Lady Atwood. "Or if you must think, then you ought to turn your mind to more pleasant considerations. I have made an appointment with Madam Gaudet. Because of your little adventure, she won't have as much time to fashion a ballgown for the announcement at the house party." She paused, letting the silence hang for a moment. "There will be an announcement?"

"Yes," Alec said emphatically.

Kendra thought Lady Atwood covered her disappointment well. "Very well. Then Miss Donovan will need to look presentable."

"Maybe you can start calling Kendra by her Christian name, Caro," the Duke said, and smiled at Kendra across the table. "She is, after all, going to be family."

Lady Atwood lifted her glass of wine and drained the entire contents in one unladylike gulp before answering, "I suppose you are right, Bertie. Welcome to the family… Kendra."

✦

"Did you notice that Lady Atwood retired for the evening with a bottle of wine?" Kendra commented later that night when Alec stepped into her bedchamber. She had been standing at the window, contemplating the brilliance of the full moon as it rose over the treetops, but now swung around to smile at Alec. "Do you think she's privately toasting our engagement?"

He laughed. "Mayhap you should also start calling her Caro. Or Carolyn. Or aunt. She will be your aunt, too." His green eyes danced with amusement. "I don't think I've ever seen you looking so appalled—not even that time when you were gifted with a severed tongue."

"Maybe I need a bottle of wine."

Alec's arms came around her. "I love you."

Kendra's throat tightened. "I love you, too."

But would love be enough? Or would the differences between their worlds be turned into stones—stones they could toss at each other, or use to build walls to separate them?

"My aunt was right about one thing. You have been distracted today." Alec framed her face with his palms. "Talk to me, sweet. What are you thinking?"

Kendra met his eyes. "Just for now, I don't want to think about the past or the future," she said huskily. "I don't want to think at all. I want to be in the present. With you." She lifted her arms to wind them around his neck, raising herself up on her toes to arch against his hard body. Their breath mingled as they kissed.

"If I don't look too hideous," she murmured as they broke apart, "maybe we can go to bed."

"That's all right. I can always blow out the candles—ow!" He laughed when she pinched him. Then she let out a gasp when he swung her up into his arms, carrying her over to the bed.

✤

Kendra didn't remember falling asleep, but when she opened her eyes again, the fire in the hearth had dwindled to a few pulsing embers. Moonbeams pierced the window, slanting across the floor. For a long moment, Kendra contemplated the shadows and light, savoring Alec's warmth against her, the sound of his slow and steady breathing. Then she forced herself to move away.

Careful not to disturb him, she slipped out of the bed. She hastily donned the nightdress and robe she'd discarded on the floor and found the slippers under the bed, shivering in the cold.

Instead of moving toward the door, though, she lingered by the bed, her gaze tracing the familiar contours of Alec's face, the sweep of dark lashes against his cheekbones. Her heart twisted painfully in her chest. She resisted the urge to brush a kiss across his lips. It took every ounce of her willpower to turn away from him and walk across the darkened bedchamber to the door.

She couldn't explain her actions other than she felt compelled. She couldn't—*wouldn't*—think about it too closely.

The hall was dark, the silence broken only by the pounding of her heart and her accelerated breathing. By the time she walked into the study, her legs felt like they were made of Jell-O. She had to take a moment to lean against the door as dizziness washed over her.

Breathe in; breathe out.

Even as the dizziness subsided, she remained where she was. The fire in the hearth had gone out hours ago, and a servant had shuttered the windows for the evening, leaving only a skinny line of moonlight penetrating between the frame and slats. But she didn't need any light to guide her to the tapestry that hid the stairwell.

Slowly, she straightened, and began walking towards the hidden panel.

Memories assailed her. The plunging temperatures, the vertigo, the sensation of being torn apart and stitched back together.

She was sweating. Her pulse beat erratically. She felt lightheaded, like she was going to pass out. *Keep going, keep going…* Then she was at the tapestry. Her hands shook violently as she pushed aside the material to reveal the dark panel. She swallowed. Instead of reaching for the mechanism that released the panel, she placed her palms against the smooth wood.

She sucked in her breath. Beneath her fingertips, the wood was hot and vibrating, like a powerful engine was running on the other side of the door.

Or was it her imagination?

There was only one way to find out.

Alec came awake in a rush, and knew instantly that he was alone in the bedchamber. Shoving aside the bedclothes, he snatched up his banyan from the floor, thrusting his arms through the sleeves and tying the belt as he raced across the room. Because he knew—*he knew*—where Kendra had gone. Fear, like icy talons, tore through him as he ran down the hall. *What if I'm too late? What if she's gone?*

The corridor seemed to stretch on forever, the air as thick as molasses, making it difficult to breathe. Then the door to the study was suddenly before him. He yanked it open, barreling through.

He stopped abruptly. The air left his lungs as his gaze locked on the tapestry that had been thrust aside, exposing the hidden panel. *She's gone.*

For one horrible moment, he couldn't move. Couldn't *think*. A strange buzzing invaded his ears. His body felt numb, like his soul had left its mortal coil. Then he was sprinting forward toward the panel, his hand automatically reaching for the mechanism to unlatch it.

"Don't!"

He froze, then spun around. His gaze traveled the darkened room to look at Kendra, curled in one of the chairs. Her face was as white as her robe and nightgown, her onyx eyes impossibly huge. The relief that rushed through him left him feeling lightheaded.

"You're here. You didn't leave."

"I'm staying."

The silence beat between them, then suddenly they were both moving, flying into each other's arms.

"I'm staying," she whispered again, pulling away slightly from his embrace to look into his eyes. The certainty he saw in them made his head spin all over again and the last of his doubts and fear slip away.

"Would you really have gone through the door?" Kendra asked, wrapped in Alec's arms.

They'd finally made it back to her bedchamber. She was feeling blissfully languid, her ear pressed against Alec's chest. She could hear the beat of his heart, much slower now than it had been a moment ago.

He smiled. "Yes."

She lifted her head to regard him. "You know as well as I do that there's no guarantee that we'd end up in the same period of time."

"It was a chance that I was willing to take," he said simply, brushing a tendril away from her face. "Do you think the vortex opened again?"

Kendra thought of the surge of power and heat humming beneath her fingertips when she laid her palms on the door. "I don't know," she admitted softly. "But I didn't want to take the chance." She raised her hands to frame his face, looking directly into his eyes. "I choose you, Alec. I choose you."

Emotion flickered across his handsome face, then he captured her hand. "Thank God." He kissed her, then drew back to capture her gaze with his own. "I can't live without you, Kendra. You've stolen my heart—and how do you live without a heart?"

She started to smile, but them jerked back before he could kiss her again.

"Oh, my God." She stared at him, stunned. "I think I know where the Anahita Pink is."

48

Eight AM was an unpardonably early hour to visit any establishment, even a madhouse. Mrs. Maddox certainly regarded Kendra, Alec, and the Duke with wide eyes when she answered their knock. While the housekeeper wanted to summon Dr. Shay, who was still abed, the Duke wielded his authority, and they were soon following Mrs. Maddox up the stairs.

"Mr. Crump handed in his notice," she told them. "He's off ter search for work in London."

God help anyone who hires him, Kendra thought.

They paused in front of a door, so Mrs. Maddox could withdraw a heavy loop of keys from her pocket and sort through them until she found the right one. "She ain't gonna be up yet," she said, inserting the key. "If you could wait out here while I get her dressed."

Alec said, "My uncle and I shall wait, and you can bring Miss Donovan inside."

"Aye. She'll be less anxious if it's me and Miss Donovan," Mrs. Maddox said with a nod. "She can be right skittish around menfolk."

Kendra walked into the room after the housekeeper. It was simply furnished, with a single bed, a nightstand, a rocking chair, a small armoire, and a washstand. The girl was in bed, but awake. At their entrance, she jackknifed into a sitting position, hugging her knees to her chest as she regarded them through long strands of red hair.

"Good morning, Miss Sybil," Mrs. Maddox said cheerfully. "Lookee here, ye have a visitor. Ain't that lovely?"

"I don't know her." The girl blinked at Kendra. "I don't know you."

"We've met, but we haven't been formally introduced," Kendra said, and smiled at her. "My name is Kendra Donovan."

"That's Irish. Are you Irish? You don't sound like a bogtrotter."

"Now, Miss Sybil, ye shouldn't be calling the Irish such things," Mrs. Maddox admonished gently.

"Why not? My papa does." She pushed back a few tangles. "But you don't sound Irish."

"I'm from America, but I'm living here now." *For better or worse.*

"Did someone scratch you?" Sybil stared at Kendra's chin.

"No, it was an accident, but I'm fine. Well, I'm *almost* fine. I was hoping you might help me." She paused, searching for the right words. "I'm going to marry the Marquis of Sutcliffe, you know."

Sybil looked intrigued. "You are?"

"Yes. Our engagement is going to be announced at a ball in a castle. I am going to wear an evening gown made just for the event."

"Oh," Sybil breathed, leaning forward eagerly. "Like a princess?"

"I'm sure I will feel like a princess. Except it's missing something. I was hoping to find a very special jewel to wear with it. I thought I had found it. Lord Craymore was keeping it for me, but it's disappeared."

Sybil scuttled back against the headboard, hunching her shoulders so that her hair fell forward to cover her face.

"I'm not upset with you, Miss Sybil," Kendra continued, careful to keep her voice low and easy. "In fact, I'm happy. You found the diamond, didn't you? The big pink diamond. Did you see it when Lord Craymore came to visit his sister?"

One eye peeked out, but was quickly covered again.

"Did you see the diamond?"

"So pretty," Sybil whispered.

"Yes, it is. Something that pretty is difficult to resist." Kendra wondered if the girl had lifted the diamond off the earl during the altercation in the library, before he'd stormed off to confront Dr. Shay, or if it had been earlier. "I was hoping you'd do me a great favor, Miss Sybil, and loan me that pink diamond so I can wear it on the night of the ball."

Sybil locked her arms around her legs as she drew her knees up to her chest. She rocked slightly, shaking her head.

"The diamond would make me feel like a princess," Kendra pressed, watching her. "You want to help me, don't you?"

"I can't," she muttered.

"Please, Miss Sybil. I need something sparkly and pretty just like that to wear to the ball."

Sybil stopped rocking to regard her. "To make you feel like a princess?"

"Yes. Can you help me?"

Emotions flitted across the girl's freckled face. After a moment, she glanced at Kendra, then unfolded herself and slid out of bed. Her simple ivory nightgown swirled around her bare ankles and feet as she padded over to the wardrobe.

Kendra's pulse accelerated with a strange excitement as she watched the girl open the wardrobe. She'd never been particularly entranced by diamonds—they were just chunks of natural carbon subjected to great heat and pressure—but now she had to admit that she was feeling slightly feverish at the prospect of holding the pink diamond in the palm of her hand.

Sybil bent over to retrieve the jewel, then straightened, turning toward Kendra with her hands cupped around her prize. She gave Kendra a tentative smile as she walked toward her.

Kendra's hand trembled slightly as she lifted it to receive the diamond—and she stared in astonishment as Sybil dropped the jewel into her palm.

The early morning light danced across the gemstone, glinting off the fine gold filigree and turning the garnet cross a fiery red.

"The girl stole the Anahita Pink from Lord Craymore, and Mrs. Slater stole the diamond from the girl," the Duke said once they'd returned to the carriage and were traveling down the road again. He gazed at the garnet cross pendant that was swinging from the chain wrapped around Kendra's finger. "And Mrs. Slater has now disappeared with the Anahita Pink."

Kendra couldn't stop herself; she laughed. "Lillian didn't steal it—she traded this pendant for the diamond. Sybil thought this was just as pretty, so she willingly agreed."

"I could point out that the Anahita Pink was not for the girl to trade," said Alec.

Kendra shrugged. "Maybe the Anahita Pink does not belong to anyone specifically. I hope that Lillian trades it for a chance at happiness."

The Duke huffed out a breath. "Well, I would have liked to have seen the diamond. But I believe that happiness is more valuable than any diamond." He paused, casting a keen eye between Kendra and Alec. "The full moon has come and gone."

Kendra smiled. "Yes, it has."

"Do you think that your wormhole reopened?"

Kendra once again remembered the heat and power beneath her fingertips. Or had her brain conjured up the sensation because she'd wanted to be given a choice? She didn't know, but she had made her choice. Even if she'd imagined the sensation, her choice was real. Wasn't that all that mattered?

"I guess we'll never know," she murmured, and reached for Alec's hand. She still had a lot to learn about living in this era. She had no doubt that it's norms and mores would continue to provoke her, but for the first time in her life, she wasn't alone.

She smiled. "It doesn't matter. Not anymore."

Two weeks later, the ballroom in Aldridge Castle glowed with a thousand candles, the scent of melting wax mingling with the perfume that emanated from the many guests crowding into the chamber. The orchestra that Lady Atwood had hired from London was currently playing a traditional English dance, the notes from the musicians' harps, lutes, flutes, and spinets floating in the air. It almost obscured the pounding of Kendra's heart. Almost.

Drawing in a deep breath, Kendra crossed the threshold into the ballroom, and caught a glimpse of herself in one of the gilt-framed mirrors. Lady Atwood would have no complaints about her appearance this evening. The bruises had healed nicely, and Molly had outdone herself with the elaborate updo that she'd spent the last two hours working on, weaving ribbons sewn with seed pearls through Kendra's dark curls. The style was nothing short of regal, and complemented the ballgown that Madam Gaudet had designed for her—an ivory chiffon that frothed over gold silk. The low-cut, square neckline forced her to put aside the arrowhead pendant that the Duke had given her, but, on impulse,

Kendra had slipped on Lillian Slater's red garnet cross. Lady Atwood probably wouldn't approve, but it felt right.

Across the room, Kendra saw Alec standing beside the Duke. Warmth surged through her as she let her gaze rove over the man who would be her husband.

This feels right, too.

The delicate silk and chiffon swished as she moved forward. She found herself smiling when Alec glanced over at her. Something flashed in the green eyes that made Kendra feel like she was walking on air.

"My God. You are beautiful," Alec breathed when she reached his side. Eyes locked on hers, he lifted her gloved hand, bringing it to his lips. "I am the luckiest of fellows."

"You are indeed, nephew," the Duke put in, his blue eyes twinkling at her. "My dear, you are a diamond of the first water." He signaled a passing footman carrying a tray filled with champagne flutes. He handed her one, then another to Lady Atwood as she joined them. "Doesn't Kendra look lovely, Caro?"

Kendra endured a critical once-over before the countess said gruffly, "She'll do."

High praise indeed, Kendra thought wryly.

The dance was winding down, and as Kendra scanned the dispersing crowd, she was a little surprised to see so many people that she recognized. Rebecca was talking to her parents, while Lady St. James looked like she could take flight with all the ruffles on her evening gown.

Alec offered her his arm, leaning down to whisper, "Are you ready?"

Kendra smiled. "It's time, I think."

The Duke raised his flute in a silent toast, then stepped forward as the orchestra ended the set. "If I may have everyone's attention?" He waited until the murmurs died down. "I have an announcement to make…"

AUTHOR'S NOTE

Every book comes with its own set of unique challenges, whether it's the journey of writing or the business of publishing. *Ripples in Time* has been more challenging than most. Consequently, it has made me extremely appreciative to be surrounded by my wonderful circle of friends, family, and professionals. Once again, I want to thank Katie McGuire, whose deft editing skill made this book shine; Derek Thornton/Notch Design, who continues to make the most stunning covers I've ever seen; and the talented Jessica Kleinman, who is responsible for the interior design. Last but by no means least is my agent, Jill Grosjean, who has been with me from the beginning and remains part of my team. I am also incredibly fortunate to be able to call upon the services of Karre Jacobs. We met in a past life, when I was a newbie journalist and she was my editor, and I am incredibly thankful that all these years later I can still lean on her for moral support, not to mention her editing prowess. A big shout-out goes to my very first Beta Reader, Shantana LeFevre Dodge. Shan's sharp observations were invaluable in creating a polished manuscript. And I would like to thank Leslie McCormick, a marketing genius responsible for creating the campaign to let readers know about signing up for my newsletter.

The decision to take charge and continue Kendra and the gang's adventures was surprisingly difficult, and without the support of Bonnie McCarthy and Lori McAllister, I don't know if I could have made the first step. My biggest thanks, though, is reserved for you—the reader. I can't begin to tell you how touched

I have been in receiving all your messages telling me how much the books have meant to you and asking when *Ripples* would be released. In the mysterious way the universe seems to work, the very days when I was truly at my lowest, ready to give up, I would receive the most wonderful email, text, and message from you, and that, in turn, gave me the courage to continue this journey. So thank you with all of my heart. No one can tell me that prayers and positive vibes don't work.

On a different note, one of the biggest challenges in writing historical mysteries is...well, the history. Or, rather, trying to be accurate in that history. As with all of my *In Time* books, *Ripples* required a lot of research, poring over books and looking through blogs. The process became much easier when I joined Regency Fiction Writers, which allows me access to the knowledge of its remarkable members, as well as its online classes. Louisa Cornell's class, *Insanity in the Age of Madness,* was particularly helpful, guiding me through mental health and mental institutions in the Regency era. Sadly, the treatments I described were not a figment of my overactive imagination but, rather, horrifyingly real. And women did not fare well, with very little being required to commit them to a mental institution. Once committed, women needed a male relative's permission to obtain their release.

The Anahita Pink described in the story is a work of fiction. However, the other famous diamonds are real, as are the treasure hoards that have been discovered throughout England. The story of King John losing England's treasure in the Wash seems too fantastical to be believed, but it is part of English history. How accurate that history is, or whether the tale was fabricated by anti-royalists at the time—or maybe the truth is somewhere in the middle—I do not know. I do think that, whether a prince or a pauper, we are all human, so King John making such a blunder doesn't strike me as all that outlandish. Again, any historical errors are mine and mine alone.